EMPIRE OF THE DRAGON

AN EVENT GROUP THRILLER

DAVID L. GOLEMON

EMPIRE OF THE DRAGON

AN EVENT GROUP THRILLER

DAVID L GOLEMON

QUOTH PUBLICATIONS

Empire of the Dragon (An Event Group Thriller)
ISBN: 978-0-692-13221-0

Copyright © 2018 by David L Golemon
Cover Design by J. Kent Holloway
Published by Quoth Publications

PROLOGUE

A BROTHER'S EMBRACE

"I have not told half of what I saw..."

~ Marco Polo
Upon his return from China

700,000,000 Years Ago...

SIX THOUSAND LIGHT-YEARS FROM THE NEWLY FORMED PLANET CALLED Earth, the Black Hole today is designated Cygnus X-1. Seven-hundred million years ago, this Black Hole spewed forth debris from a dying world at the edge of the universe whose distance from the Earth is still unmeasurable. Since then, the giant silver imbued rock made an annual tour of the outskirts of the Milky Way Galaxy. The asteroid made its fly-by of its five-million-year trip near the planet Jupiter as it had for eons. The sixteen-mile-long rock had never been close to a trajectory that threatened the small blue planet that was placed third in orbit around the yellow star many millions of miles away. The journey of this asteroid through the eons of time had come and gone

1

without incident. Without incident until the day a small rock from the solar system's outer asteroid belt, named 'The Trojan Asteroid Field', nicked the speeding body at only seven hundred kilometers a second, a relatively easy bump in celestial terms.

The newcomer to the young solar system spun off in a dizzying roll that sent the sixteen-mile-long rock blazing past the older, outer planets of Jupiter and Saturn. In its direct path was a world that would be unrecognizable to the universe today. The continents had yet to separate into the land masses that is known in today's geography.

The asteroid would have slammed directly into the relatively new world, and smashed out the young life that had spread throughout the jungles and forests of the baby planet. This did not happen. The asteroid came into contact with the blue planet's small moon on its dark side. Although only a glancing blow, the brush with the moon changed the attitude of the giant rock and made a glancing blow off Earth's atmosphere, flattening out its orbit and sending the asteroid into a crazily spinning bullet. Instead of coming straight down onto the surface of the Earth, the glancing blow leveled the asteroid out. The friction of entering the world's airspace diminished the weight and size of the object by half, sending shards burning off into the sky of the new world. The rest was sent sliding into a lush, green jungle. The silver-green ore material that made up the visitor stayed intact as it hit mountains and evaporated inland seas until it came to rest, sliding deep into the Earth and creating a new mountain range on the surface of the young planet.

The lush jungle terrain gave the elements of the newcomer the fertilization of nutrition the rock had not had in over six billion years. There, the newcomer settled in and lived alongside the growing world and its varying new species of animal life.

That place today would become known as the Rift, or, outer Mongolia.

Hunan Province,
China, 221 BC

THE FORTY-SIX-YEAR-OLD RULER OF HUNAN WAS BROUGHT FORWARD and forced to kneel before the line of men standing rigid in front of his flaming palace. The dead and dying were strewn about just as the bodies of countless thousands in other provinces had before this night of nights—the destruction of the last army standing in the way of a dynasty.

King Tao Che cast his eyes about as the flat side of a sword struck his armored chest, forcing his eyes away from the carnage that had once been his glorious and peaceful capital. He was kneeling in a large puddle of blood that had once flowed through the strong, vital bodies of his palace guard. A thousand men killed and beheaded in less than the time it took to eat a meal. The hundred men standing before him were dressed in the red and black colored armor of the usurper who was walking across all of China in his quest to unify the giant nation. The horse-hair plumes on the apex of their helmets told the king that these were the personal guard of that man, and the scene also explained to him that, no matter what happened in the next few minutes, his nation of Hunan would shortly cease to exist.

As he was forced to kneel, he heard the cries of his subjects as they were torn asunder by lance, arrow and sword echoing in his head. The screams of the children as they were rounded up tore at his very soul. As his attention was forced back to the front by sword tip, he saw the men before him come to stiff and disciplined attention. The center-most ten men separated as a large black roan eased forward. The King raised his eyes and caught a fleeting glimpse of the man he had fought against for three months in the flickering fires of his home. The false deity himself eased the horse to a stop and then one of his men went to all fours as the rider used him as a stage to dismount. Tao Che lowered his eyes, not out of respect, but self-preservation as he wanted nothing more than to spring forth and kill the man that had butchered hundreds of thousands in his quest to subdue all of China.

The man that used to be known in his younger years as Ying Zheng, who was once thought of as a mild-mannered boy who did nothing but read scrolls of bamboo and dream about other-worldly places, glanced around the capital of Hunan and its flaming structures. He used the boot of his right foot to kick out at a severed arm, sending it across the mud, and then stood before the kneeling King of Hunan. The small man, who was now called Qin Shi Huang, finally lowered his gaze to take in the last king to defy his promised rule of the nation now known as China. His eyes studied the unbroken man kneeling before him, a gentle king who was once known across all the land as a proud and just ruler. Qin Shi once thought King Tao Che could be persuaded to add his province to those already conquered and destroyed without the persuasiveness of battle and the coercion of death. But after months of defiance, he had instead brought his kingdom to this sad end. This, in Qin Shi's opinion, could never be forgiven. His eyes darted to his men, and two of them took the king by the arms and hoisted him, one going so far as to mercilessly twist the man's arm until he complied.

The sword came free of the scabbard so fast that his imperial guard didn't see the flash of steel in the firelight's reflection. The head of the guard that had hurt the sovereign king came free of the body while his torso remained standing. The headless body finally slid to the muddy ground and spewed blood, forcing Qin Shi to step aside. He sheathed his sword and then remained looking at the man before him. He then turned to his men who had not reacted to the sudden and brutal beheading.

"This man is a King and will be treated as such." He reached up to the taller man and placed an armored glove on his shoulder. "You have my profound apologies for the actions of this fool. He failed to heed his instructions about the respect he was to afford my one-time teacher."

Hunan King Tao Che finally looked into the eyes of the man he despised above all others. He then turned his head and the black eyes fell on the fallen defenders of his capital. Women and children, the last survivors of his kingdom, were even now being rounded up by

4

the usurper's soldiers to be herded to camps to begin their adjustment and reeducation to a different life and a new leader—that of servitude in the continuing construction of the conqueror's new wall far to the north.

"I see the same treatment you profess in regard to myself, does not extend to my subjects."

The smaller man smiled as he looked around the burning capital, the black beard and hair shining brightly in the fire's light. "They are no longer your subjects. They are mine. There will be a certain amount of persuasion that has to be made to make my new province more," he again looked around as children and their mothers were roped together for transport out of the province, "educated in the new world I will create for them."

"A world in flames—one that is awash in blood and sorrow."

"To build anew, you sometimes must destroy the old." His dark eyes, reflecting the burning buildings, turned back to Tao Che. "A man of wisdom once taught me that." He took Tao Che by the chin and made the older man face him. His left brow rose to the apex of his helmet. I believe that man was you, my old teacher." His face went blank of all expression. "Now, who am I?"

The meaning of the question failed to register. The king looked at the heavily armored man from the south. His eyes went from his helmeted head to his handmade boots that had not escaped the blood flow from his beheaded man.

Qin Shi took a menacing step forward, quickly releasing Tao Che's chin and moved his right hand to the hilt of his sword. "I will ask once again, *who...am...I?*"

"You were once a boy that had my admiration. A smart child, a kind child, and besides one other, my best student. You were a boy that was once a dreamer that I once called 'son'. In my tired old eyes, I still see the boy named Ying Zheng, who once played in the bamboo forest with his little brother."

The mention of his half-brother caused Qin Shi to falter. Then his eyes became fury and wrath. "What is my name and title?" This time the sword came free and its tip went to the throat of Tao Che.

The king started to refuse, then his eyes went to the taskmaster's whip as it popped and cracked, bleeding the backs of the small children and their mothers. His eyes lowered and then he went to his knees.

"You are Qin Shi Huang, King of all the lands that are China." His hands went to the booted feet of the new ruler of all, as he bowed even deeper.

"Not King, I am the Emperor of China. Do you know what this word means? You should, it was you who instructed me on its definition." He lightly kicked at the chin of Tao Che as he groveled upon the soaked ground. The head nodded, and the fingers clawed at the blood-soaked mud.

"You are, huángdì, the 'First'. You are Emperor Qin Shi Huang."

The sword eased away from the man's neck. Qin Shi then nodded at his commanding general. The man gestured toward the flaming wooden palace that used to be the home of Tao Che. The man kneeling before the new Emperor heard the cries of his two small sons as they were led from where they and their mother had been captured. Tao Che could not help himself, he raised his head and saw what he feared most. The two boys, thirteen and eight years of age, and their mother, Yao Lin, his wife of fifteen years, were being forced to their knees. General Li Kang looked at his Emperor and saw the man smile. The general remained still, his sullen face not showing the disgust he had for what was about to happen.

Once more the sword appeared at the throat of the king. The blade dug into his neck until it found what the steel searched for. The blade was lifted free of the armored chest plate of the king. There, gleaming in the firelight, was a chain. The blade twisted until the object that dangled from the small, gold links was shown to the new Emperor. The nugget of ore was bright and silverish in color. The blade twisted again, and the chain snapped. Once more the twist of the sword's edge forced the necklace and the nugget into the air where the Emperor caught it with a gloved left hand. He held it up to the dying moon and examined it.

"Where is he?"

Tao Che's head dipped as he heard the cries of his two boys behind him.

"You were close to my father and his bitch concubine. You were with him when he brought her back from her home where he had captured her far to the North. Where is that home? Did he and his people flee to this mysterious land?"

The king looked up and with trembling lips answered.

"You seek the great secret of his power. All of this," he gestured around him at the carnage that once held the populace of a proud nation, "is for that? You will kill millions to get at the thing your father said would always be protected. To dampen your cause, to make all of this even more senseless is the fact that your father never told me where he found the source, nor his concubine."

The new Emperor pursed his lips in anger and then closed his gloved fist over the chain and the silverish green tinted nugget it held. He angrily nodded his head just once and the General gave the order.

Suddenly, Tao Che threw himself to the feet of his conqueror, embracing the man's embroidered boots and begged for the lives of his family. He pawed at the emperor's bloody boots and cried until he heard the swish of blades through the air and the sudden cessation of crying coming from his two boys and his wife.

General Kang turned to his emperor and nodded that the deed was done. The general then turned away and gave the order to remove the headless bodies of the king's family.

Qin Shi kicked away the grasping hands and then brought the curved sword down.

"I must not have ghosts threatening my rule. I can combat any force upon this earth, but I find no defense against the souls of the dead. If one descendant is left alive from the loins of my father's whore concubine, their brethren will come for revenge." He once more held the strange silver nugget, that was etched in a green vein, into the air, so the forlorn king could see it in the fire's light. "This is only a part, I want the whole, and the man who knows how to wield its power. I want my half-brother!"

Tao Che suddenly stood. The blinding speed of the action made the Emperor's guard move forward, but with a simple hand gesture they were stopped by Qin Shi himself.

"Ghosts?" Tao Che laughed as his tears still flowed. "All the ghosts of all those you have butchered will not be comparable to the foe you still have to face if you attempt to run him and his people down. This man will not be as obliging to your rule as the rest. This was something I taught him, a thing your father taught you both, and it is a thing you have forgotten and will be your undoing."

Tao Che saw the sword falter somewhat as it came up. The doomed King smiled, this time the gesture made it to his eyes as he saw the effect his words had on the new emperor.

"Yes, the one man that you fear. The one soul in all the world who can stop you. The man who has the power of that," he nodded at the silver nugget in the emperor's hand, "flowing through his heart and blood stream. The last true magic upon this Earth" He laughed as Qin Shi's eyes blazed with hate. "The one man—"

The sword came down and silenced the hate-filled warning. The cutting edge sliced deeply through the leather armor of the king from the man's right shoulder to his left hip, cutting him into two halves. Qin Shi watched the body falling in two differing directions, and then viciously kicked out with his boot at the still moving parts. Qin Shi threw his sword into the burning embers of the palace and then turned to his general.

"You told me he was dead! Now this fool says he is alive!"

"My Emperor, it was reported that your brother," he saw the anger once more flare into the eyes of his emperor at the mention of the relationship, and he quickly continued as he lowered his eyes, "...it was said that he died many years ago. I have not been able to confirm this from any of the conquered provinces. I have eyes and ears out all over China, and there has been no word on his being seen alive anywhere."

The emperor held the chain and nugget up so the general could see it clearly. "I thought I only had to be concerned with his fanatical followers who would know where the source of the ore is, now I am told its not only them that have to be found and destroyed, but the bastard child himself, my one-time half-brother is still alive!"

"If he is alive, I swear to you, my master, he and his people will be found. The war is over, they have no place to hide. But he must be dead. He must be."

"That is not good enough!" he stormed to his horse and kicked out at its tender. He turned back to General Kang. "I must know. If he is truly dead, I want his rotting corpse dug from his burial mound and brought before me!"

"Perhaps great one, if you had not killed Tao Che before questioning him, we may know where it was Li Zheng went to ground...if he is truly alive. Without any information and absent any witness accounts of his still being alive, we need not worry, unless you intend to carry out another search of all China?"

The emperor mounted his horse and cruelly steadied the animal with a slap to the side of its head, making the large roan rear and then finally settle. He pointed his finger at his general, the iron nugget hanging from his shaking fingers, and then moved the accusing digit to his personal guard. Shaking with anger, he once more reared his horse to its hind legs.

"Find him! I do not care how many villages you sack, kill as many as need calls for, but find Li Zheng, find him or your heads will join those of the fallen!" He wadded up the chain and the nugget and threw it angrily into a pile of burning rubble. The resulting explosion flared bright blue and green, killing five of his own personal guard from the debris thrown up by the nugget striking the flame. "My bastard brother knows how to control *that!* It is in his very blood. If he turns this against me, I cannot stop him. If he is alive, find him and bring him before me. Then execute all who ever followed him."

General Kang watched the Emperor as he turned his horse and sped from the burning Hunan capital, followed by his personal guard of fifty cavalrymen. Kang started giving orders as Hunan's capital buildings fell in embers and flames.

"Use ten thousand men, all of our scouts, assassins, scoundrels, but find him!"

THE ORDERS HAD GONE OUT ALL OVER CHINA—FIND THE MAN KNOWN as Li Zheng, the long-lost half-brother of the new sovereign Emperor of China, and the last of the mythical *Elementals*.

Huang He River (Yellow River) Region, Thirteen miles south of the Great Wall, five years later

THE LARGE VILLAGE OF LANZHOU WAS ONE POPULATED BY TEACHERS, artisans and engineers, and the men and women they supported, the laborers. They all had equal voice in village affairs. These were men who had fled with their families to escape the genocide in the south. With their women and children by their sides, they sold their skills to the new emperor's task masters in the construction of the massive wall that would separate the new nation from their far-off enemies of the north, the Mongol hordes. This was the place they had chosen to hide—right beneath the very nose of the man they feared most— Emperor Qin Shi Huang. They lived in relative obscurity, due to the valuable work the engineers and scholars offered the new empire. They were left to their own devices after trading their knowledge for food and other bartered items from the large army of the emperor's soldiers that guarded the Great Wall's construction.

After the day's work was completed, the villagers moved back into the relative safety of the small city they called home. Traveling outside of the area was forbidden by the elders as that was deemed too risky. Any chance discovery or loose talk would cause them all to lose their heads. The emperor had been searching for them for the past five years, never realizing they were right here in the north, actually assisting him to build his great barrier. This was a joke told many times around village camp fires and caused the horde of followers many a laugh at the man they deemed a devil.

The cries and shouts of children met the smiling faces of the men as they moved into the village after their labors at the wall. They were greeted with hugs and offers of water from the river. The men laughed and scooped the smaller of these children into their arms as they were more formally greeted by their spouses. Life was a constant fear of discovery by the Emperor, but at this moment, life was also good.

It was after the moon had risen high when the men of the village met in the great hall made of tall logs and covered in a heavy cotton tent. The fire in the middle of the enclave offered warmth and gave the men a sense of camaraderie. The laughter and goodwill were prevalent and much food was had. Men told stories about the failed attempts of their taskmasters to rope them in. The soldiers and the emperor's engineers knew the wall could not be built without their knowledge, and they used that to great advantage over the entities of the man that wished them found and beheaded.

The men sat upon bundles of soft woven pillows. Women appeared every few minutes with even more food—food that was bartered for through their skills as artisans and engineers and chief laborers, as they all considered each other a valuable asset to their survival. The emperor's construction specialists and soldiers were so dependent on these strange people that they were able to hide in plain sight among the Emperor's spies and informants.

Qui Li, the eldest member of the village council, stood and smiled at his friends. The old man had to be helped to his feet. Qui Li was the man responsible for keeping the secret that was Lanzhou. The old man raised his right hand and the large enclosure quieted.

"I wish to offer my condolences to Wei Chi and his wife. The loss of your eldest son at the wall last week was a blow to our family of man, beyond which we will not soon recover."

All faces turned toward the center of the crowded hall and a middle-aged man sitting with a wooden cup of water. He nodded his head in deference to the man standing before him. The father slowly poured the water from his cup and stood. He bowed to the east, the west, the north and the south. He straightened and then looked around him at the men in the meeting. He faced the front once more.

"I thank our elders for their consideration and condolence." The man grew somber as he reflected on his son and all in attendance felt the mood change from jovial to serious. "My son was a proud boy, but also a curious one. We have yet to learn just what it was that our son died for. He and many others. We help the Emperor build his wall, a man that would kill every man, woman and child here if he knew where it was we were hiding. We have yet to hear the grand plan." A man reached up and tried his best to still the words of hurt feelings of the father, but the hand was eased away by the sorrowful man. "Why isn't this plan shared with those who follow? For many years we have lived and died without explanation as to what it is we are truly doing." The father of the dead boy looked around at his brethren. "We assist the beast we should be meeting in battle. We build a wall that will eventually be used to corral us like animals, ready for slaughter. This Great Wall is not for the defense of this new, evil empire. It is to be used to cage us like the animals the Emperor thinks we are. The time has come for this grand plan to be told to the people. The Great Wall is nearing completion. It is time our Master shares with us the escape plan he has promised for so many years."

Slowly, there were nods of agreement from the two hundred men of the council. The elder remained standing and his eyes told the men he was in complete understanding of their fears. Again, he nodded to the father of the dead boy and the man reluctantly sat down. Many a hand reached out to convey to him the village's sorrow over his loss and agreement with his thoughts.

"Our hearts are with you, brother Sum. To have a boy crushed between blocks of stone is disheartening to all. Even our Master. He has heard all of the people's anger and extreme blackness of loss. The mistake you make in your harsh judgement of our Master is the fact that this wall we assist in building is not to keep the Emperor's subjects caged like beasts, it's to keep our Master and ourselves out if we escape his evil grasp. It is our Master he fears, thus this Great Wall."

"Then, where is he, why can we not hear this from the Master himself?" shouted one man from the darkness at the back of the wooden building. This same question was echoed by a few others as the old man tried to bring back order.

"You receive messages from him, but we have not seen the Master since he went North of the construction. Has he been killed by the barbarian hordes of the North? Has he abandoned us to the murderous rampage of the Emperor?"

The elder looked at the man who had spoken. It was General Jai Li Chang. The once proud soldier who had served the Master since the beginning. His words stung only because of the weight it carried for the other ears listening. The shouts of agreement were louder. The old man could see the conflict in the eyes of the General. If the Master lost his closest military leader, all could be lost.

"If this is so, we must come up with a plan of our own. For too long have we awaited the Master's views on what happens when our skills are no longer needed. As a man trained in the art of war, it is my feeling that the long arms of the Emperor are reaching for us, growing ever closer. A feeling of gut? Yes, that has always been a general's strength—my strength. He is coming, make no mistake. Strangers have been seen in and around the wall and villages, asking questions. Men and soldiers that we have never seen before scour the land, asking questions about our Master. The emperor has never believed the false rumors perpetrated by us of the Master's demise. Our time is short," the general said as he looked around, his eyes finally settling on the row of elders at the head of the gathering and the old man standing before them. "My old friend and mentor, General Kang, is rumored to be near. A rumor that includes an army of ten thousand men traveling with him. This force is not here to celebrate the final blocks of stone as they are placed in the wall. They are here for us. I cannot train artisans and engineers for battle against such a force. If we cannot fight, then we must either flee or disband forever, to melt into the heart of China. Only the Master can give us guidance about this deadly quandary."

The old man again raised his hand as the last of the goodwill escaped the meeting. He shook his head as he had no answer. It would be a knife straight to the heart of every man present if it were known that he had not spoken words with the Master for over three years. He looked at his fellows who sat in silence as they too saw the former general's point. Time was indeed running out.

"Is the Master dead?" came an ominous question from the dark. Men stood and faced the elders and shouted their agreement of the query.

"I am afraid the question you ask is somewhat without merit, as I sit here among you."

The council chamber quieted as if by magic as the voice carried to every corner. The fire blazed and erupted as a man in a torn and battered robe stood and then lowered the hood of his cloak. The figure moved easily through the stunned men as he took up station in front of the grieving father who had started the small revolt. He touched the man on his shoulder and bade him to rise. The father stood, tears coming to his eyes as he recognized the man who had sat with them unnoticed.

"My heart breaks for you, my friend," the man said as the father lowered his eyes in shame for speaking out against him. "But soon there may be many more sons and daughters that will join him in the darkness that is death." The man nodded and then removed his robe. As it fell to the floor, he turned and faced the men in the room, each getting a good look at the man they had not seen in three long years. "The General is right. The time has finally come, my brothers of the earth. Many of you think that we may have clung too long to the hope of blending into this new world, but it was an unavoidable evil. The Emperor would have become aware of us if we had suddenly packed everything and left before the wall's completion. This, my brothers, would not have given us the time and cover needed to go to our new home. It is time—now *is* that time."

Every man in the council chamber went to their knees as his face looked about them. Even the elders kneeled and lowered their eyes.

Li Zheng, the half-brother of the Emperor, raised both hands to the air and bade the men to rise.

"No brothers, no. Rise and face the world and you will never bow to a man again. I have been away too long. You are not to bow to me. I am a brother of every man in this council, not your ruler." He turned so all could see. "Rise, you are men!"

General Jai Li Chang took the six steps toward Li Zheng and went to his knee, taking the older man's right hand, and kissing it. "You will forgive my harsh words, Master?"

"Stand, old friend, there is nothing to forgive. I cannot fault a man when he is right," he looked about at the faces that were now raised to see the great one. "I cannot lay blame for men fearing for their families and loved ones, if I did, I would be far worse than my brother. The General is right." He looked over the men as they rose to their feet. "By the next full moon, we will be well on our journey to our new home, my birth place. The land of my mother. For every man, woman, and child who choose to follow me, we will vanish into a new life far beyond the borders of the Emperor's new China."

"My Master, where is this new home?" asked the father who had led the revolt.

The silence made those watching Li Zheng afraid. He looked around those faces and settled on the General.

"You will prepare our people to travel far North of the Great Wall."

The men were shocked as they saw the words spill from the Master's mouth. They looked from him to each other.

"Yes, my brothers, we will escape into the great desert to the north. Our new home, where we can live out our lives in peace for generations to come."

"Into the hands of enemies that are worse than the Emperor?" came many voices at once, only in differing forms.

Li Zheng tried in vain to silence the men around him. Even the village elders stood in disbelief of the final plan for escaping the wrath of the Emperor. The shouts of doubt and anger filled the ears of Master Li Zheng, and for the first time in years he felt his anger boil to the surface.

Both arms flew into the air, and the graying beard of Li Zheng rose and fell in a wash of wind that sprang from nowhere.

"Silence!" came his strong voice. The wood of the structure shook, and many planks popped free of their notched anchors. The fire pit erupted, and the flames shot straight into the air. The force was so powerful, the cotton fabric of the roof burned away into nothingness as it rose with the flame toward the stars. The water in the rain barrels also erupted into the air, washing the men free of their sudden anger and fear. Debris, along with wooden and porcelain cups went flying, some striking men that shouted the loudest.

They had gained the unwanted attention of the Master—the last Elemental.

He lowered his arms and the fire retreated back into the pit. The water, not as controllable, was still soaking most of the stunned villagers. One by one they sat. One by one they lowered their gaze from the eyes of the small man standing amongst them. The few burning remnants of the roof flitted away into the night as if fireflies, and all was silent.

"Those of you who choose to stay, may stay. I make no demand. I give no orders. I have told you the plan I have for some, but not all. Many of you will be able to blend in with the new world order. I cannot. Many of you will choose to follow me into the wilderness, and many of you may die. I make no promise as to life, only the freedom for you to choose where and when that life may end, or flourish. Sometimes that is the only true freedom one has in life."

"But how will we—"

The man asking the question was silenced by a young boy, dressed in ill-fitting ancient leather armor handed down to him by his father and his father before him. The boy stood at the doorway trying to catch his fleeing breath.

Li Zheng nodded for the boy to enter. He went straight to General Chang.

"We have received word from our outer pickets, the soldiers at the Wall are gathering. One of our men at the construction site has heard word that they are to be the advance element coming here. General Kang is nearing the wall from the south. It looks as if they seek to catch the village in-between. Many of our spies' voices were silenced before they could get word to us."

"Get the boy some water," Li Zheng called out as he took the runner by the shoulders and pulled him from the general. "Where is General Kang now?"

"Still across the Huang He River, thirty miles distant," the boy said, breathing heavily. He gratefully accepted a cup of water and drank greedily. He was patted on the back as the Master turned to the men who stood nervously.

"Those of you fleeing northward across the wall, prepare. Those of you who have chosen to stay, take your families to the river and hide amongst the forest and the rocks, you will know when it is safe to flee south."

"When will we know that?" shouted the voice of a frightened man.

"When the sounds of battle and the cries of many soldiers as they die have subsided," Li Zheng said loudly as he turned to the General. "You, my old friend, we will face General Kang. You and I."

"How many men shall I muster to assist?" Jai Li Chang asked with an appeased nod and bow, as he was finally going to face his old friend in combat, even if doing so meant his own death. He was tired of hiding.

The man with the deep brown eyes smiled softly as he squeezed the general's shoulder. "No soldiers other than your personal guard, General. You and I. Together we will face General Kang at the river." He again smiled and for a reason the general would never be able to explain, he understood what it was that was being asked.

"It will be my life's honor to die at your side, Master Zheng."

Li Zheng accepted the robes that he had discarded earlier from one of the elders as other men prepared to do as ordered, while the rest ran for their families in preparation to flee the coming battle and imminent slaughter.

"Many men will die this night, General, but our deaths will not be counted among them."

The general nodded his head. He still didn't understand but knew the plan he had so worried over was about to be explained to him in deadly detail. He would bow to the power of the last Master of the natural elements of the very planet. They were to rely on the magic of the far North.

"Elders, take those that are coming north of the wall for a new life, to the low plane of wall at the village of Hinn Shu Wei, the wall is still incomplete there. Wait until I arrive to cross over. Now please, go."

Men scrambled from the council chamber. Many ran for families to flee with Li Zheng, many more others to flee with wives, children and as many belongings as they could carry for their flight to the south and the protection of the river.

"Shall we go and admire the rays of the moon by the river's edge, General?"

In minutes, the village of Lanzhou, a home which had stood for fifteen years hiding the fugitives of the Emperor, would vanish into history and myth.

THE GENERAL SAW THAT LI ZHENG ALTERED HIS COURSE TO THE RIVER. He held his hand in the air and his personal guard turned with the Master. The General slid his horse in beside that of Li Zheng.

"The only reasonable crossing point for General Kang and his army is three miles further on, Master. We are heading for the village of Ti Zuay."

"You and your men will not join me at the river, General. I have another task for you and your guard that I could not explain adequately in front of the elders and the council."

The General watched as Li Zheng eased his horse into the creek that fronted the small village of Ti Zuay. The wooden huts were dark. That was when the General noted that there was absolutely no sign of life. Even at this early morning hour, farmers and their wives were usually up and preparing for their day. As their horses exited the slow-moving water, Li Zheng eased his horse to a stop. His eyes scanned the darkened living spaces that once held the populace of Ti Zuay.

"General Jai Li Chang, you have been a loyal friend."

The general looked from the darkened and abandoned village and placed his right fist to his chest armor and bowed his head. He suspected something was coming and knew he would not like it.

"It is time for you to take charge of the people until their new Master comes of age."

"New Master? You are the only Master our people have ever known. I do not understand."

"Your duty to me ends here, this night. You will not accompany me to the river. Your mission is here, and then it lies beyond the Great Wall, in the ancient lands that will be the people's new home."

The general sat upon his horse as his men held fast in the shallow creek to their rear. He removed his plumed helmet from his head and then lowered it.

"If I have done something to offend you, Master—"

He was taken aback when Li Zheng laughed heartily. He removed the hood from his cloak so he could see his old friend better, and in return the general could see the deep brown pools of his eyes. Finally, with the general looking on, Li Zheng stopped laughing as he placed his free hand on the man's shoulder.

"Offense? My friend, you have done nothing to have ever given offense. You and your men have laid blood and bone upon this earth to protect me. No, no offense—just a new task, one which I could only give to one I trust above all others. Do you remember when you were but a boy and we spoke of things, events, people, that could destroy the world? What were my two points that I pointed out again, and again?"

Jai Li Chang closed his eyes as he thought. He remembered, but what did that memory have to do with what they now faced and the Master's mysterious request? He did remember the lesson.

"That it is not the horrid acts of men that will kill the world but lies and deception. Every time a man lies it is like a sword point to the heart of the world."

The Master smiled. "Yes, and here you sit upon your magnificent mount facing a man that is guilty of both."

"I do not understand."

"I regret that I could not foster the trust in you that I should have. But many years ago, I foresaw this night of nights when my people would be forced to leave their homeland for the burnt soil of another world. A barren place that witnessed my birth. A place where my father and that of the Emperor found and fell in love with a woman of that far off land. You believe that I am a hermit. A strange being who holds power that is unimaginable." Again, the Master smiled as another confused look came to the general's features. "I am all but the most human man. My weakness in my beliefs will be your new mission. To safeguard my legacy to the people."

"Master, we are short of time. I can even now hear the thunder of many horses across the far river bank."

"My vision many years ago told me I would not further venture with our people after tonight. I took it upon myself to safeguard their future."

"Master—"

"Come, my love," he called out as he turned to a darkened home at the center of the old village.

The general peered into the inky darkness but could see nothing. He gestured to one of his men and he was handed a torch. He held it high to see. There, in the deep shadows, a figure stepped into the weak light.

General Jai Li Chang felt his heart skip a beat in his chest. The woman was dressed in modest clothing. He handed the torch back to the soldier when his Master dismounted and went to the woman. He took her into his arms and kissed her cheek and then held her close. The general was shocked. He watched as Master Zheng turned with the woman and nodded at him as he dismounted. He approached and then the general bowed his head.

"This is my wife, Mai Li. We have been married for seventeen years."

The general almost lost his balance as his continued bow threw him off. He straightened and took in his Master and the woman at his side. Before he could say anything, the joyful scream of a small child erupted from the dark night. Li Zheng broke the embrace of his wife and then took up the weight of a small boy who had burst from the darkened house where he had been sleeping. He watched as his Master picked the child up and hugged him. He swung him around and then approached the general.

"My son, Tao Mei. It means, 'big brain'. At four he can already read and write better than most."

The general felt his mouth open as his jaw dropped.

"You see, I am most human, my old friend. *If* love of family is a human condition, which I suspect it is."

General Chang bowed again, and the small boy grabbed for the red feather plumage and missed. The general raised his head and then smiled at the grinning boy-child. He turned and tried to speak but found no words. The woman smiled as she relieved her husband of their son.

"Wife, are you ready?"

The woman just nodded her head once. The general could see that she was not happy in the least. The smile and love shown seconds before vanished just as quickly.

Three women emerged from the same house with large bundles. The general gestured for four of his men to take their burdens. As he watched, Master Zheng assisted his wife and child as they mounted his horse. He nodded at the women and then bade them farewell as they bowed deeply. One even ran to the wife and child and threw herself onto the wet ground at their horse's prancing hooves. Zheng assisted the woman back to her feet and gently eased her over to the other two.

"Go now. You have served my family well."

In tears the women departed, crying heavily and consoling themselves as they vanished into the night.

"You must now leave this world," he said as he squeezed his wife's leg as she sat upon the horse. He turned to face the general. "Protect them as best as you can. My son is the people's future. They will eventually come to call him Master. Then they will call his son the same. There will always be a part of me with the people. Through the centuries I will be there, watching, protecting." He smiled at his grinning son.

"But—"

The general's words were cut short by the sound of horns. The morning sun was only minutes away. General Kang's army would soon follow the rising of that sun.

"Go, get the people to safety beyond the wall."

"My husband—" the woman started to protest once again for the millionth time in their married life.

"I will be with you, wife. Just look into my son's eyes as he grows to manhood. I will be there. Now," he turned again to Cheng, "go, flee to the wall with all haste."

"Kang's entire army has arrived, they will overtake not only us, but the people. We have waited too long."

"The General is more fearful of my one-time half-brother than he is of military defeat, old friend. He has made a mistake in his choice of offensive operation and lacks the knowledge of a land he has yet to see. You will never see the army of General Kang after this dawn. Now, goodbye my faithful General." He turned and looked at his hidden family for the last time. "This is for the people, my love. For the people." He slapped at her horse and with one last look at his old Master, the general bade his men to follow as they headed back north.

Li Zheng felt the hot roll of tears as they came from his dark, brown eyes. He placed the hood on his head as he raised a hand to the dark air around him in a final goodbye that only he could see.

Master Li Zheng turned back and strode across the small creek and started for the river. It was now a time of war for the last of the air benders, the elemental wizard of the great desert.

THE FLAGS OF GENERAL LI KANG CRESTED THE SMALL HILL THAT fronted the large river. His scouts had found a place to ford the large force of cavalry, and that mass of humanity soon joined the flags of the army.

The last to arrive was the general himself with his personal guard. As the sun crested the Earth to the east, the general saw the shiny river and the far bank beyond. He steadied his restless mount as his general's eyes took in all. He saw the distant deserted village. He also noticed there was no enemy activity on the opposite bank. Then something caught his eye. The lone figure came into view as a small fire flared to life. One of his captains pointed to the lone figure that was stooped to the flame he had just started.

"A monk perhaps?" the captain asked.

General Kang watched as the figure, barely discernible in the weak morning light, turned slowly away from the small campfire and then sat easily on the soft, sandy bank. His legs were crossed and his hooded head lowered in prayer. The general looked up at the sky and saw only a few wispy clouds as the rising sun gave them a luminous sheen. His attention then went back to the man across the way. As his ten thousand men formed along the opposite ridge and the tone of assembly horns wafted across the river, the monk they faced seemed not to notice. The small fire was just large enough to cast flickering patterns on the man's brown robes.

"That is no monk," the general said just as his hackles rose as high as his new-found concern.

Kang had been expecting at least a rear-guard action to give the rogue people the time they needed to disband, or whatever their plan was. Instead his greatest fear may be sitting two hundred yards away. His spies had finally brought the news the Emperor had waited upon for many years. His half-brother and his wayward clan had been found. Upon learning that he had been so close and hiding right beneath their noses, the Emperor had flown into a rage and killed the bringers of the news. After Kang dispatched the people following his brother, his orders were to bring Li Zheng to the emperor in chains. Now the general faced the hard truth—Zheng was alive and ready to face him.

"Bring me your best archer. We will soon discover the truth of who this lone man is. I fear I already know who it is we face."

The captain to his right turned his horse and, in a few minutes, returned with a solitary soldier. The general nodded his head. The soldier looked from the general to the captain awaiting his orders.

"Get this man's attention," the general ordered without taking his eyes from the man with his head bowed and the small fire by his side. The man's hands were held out and the index fingers and thumbs touched, as his palms were turned toward the brightening morning sunrise.

The archer nocked his arrow and the longbow came up. The shiny arrowhead caught the rays of the rising sun and it flashed brightly. The arrow was loosed. It traveled high into the sky and then came down and speared the sandy earth only a foot from the praying man. He didn't react. He didn't even look up at the sound of the arrow's impact.

General Kang watched all of this silently as his men were confused as to their delay in crossing the Huang He River.

"Kill him."

The archer nocked another arrow. The red feathers at its end shone bright in the morning sun until a small wisp of a cloud passed overhead. This time the arrow was loosed with power. It didn't climb as high as the first shot. It flew straight and without wind, true to the target.

General Kang saw the man move his right hand in a swirling motion. Suddenly, a small breeze sprang from nowhere. Kang felt the softness of the cool wind just as his heart froze. The arrow was on target, and then it suddenly veered off to the man's right side. It was if an invisible hand had simply moved it from its track. The long projectile thudded into the sand and buried itself deep. The man's hand went back to its original position. He had never even looked up from his silent prayers.

Without a verbal order being given, the captain brought up three more archers. Before he gave the killing command, he noticed that the man across the now brightly illuminated river slowly rose. He placed both of his hands into the sleeves of his robes and that was when General Kang felt his heart skip a beat in his chest. The hood and head of the stranger was still bowed in either prayer or arrogance.

"Nock!" came the command.

The four archers drew their arrows taught. They raised their aim and then waited.

"Loose!"

All four arrows flew straight and true. They arched into the blue morning sky as the robed man remained still across the waters of the river.

Again, the breeze sprang from nothingness. This time it was a swirling mass that picked up sand and dirt as it swirled toward the flying arrows in a funnel of moving material. In shock, the cavalrymen watched as the arrows were suddenly upended as they reversed their course just as if they had hit a stone wall. Then the wind picked up even more as General Kang lowered his head as sharp grains of sand pelted him just as the four arrows turned and shot back across the river. One of the killing sticks fell to the water's surface as it traveled away from the altering current of air. The other three gained speed as they crossed the river in a blinding race to the far shore. They impacted three of the archers and they fell to the ground, as the long shafts pierced their armor and nearly shot through the other side. The three men fell to the ground as the remaining archer lost his grip on the longbow and it fell to his feet.

It all had happened so fast that Kang's horse reared up. His eyes were still on the stranger as his men behind him tried to steady their horses as once more the strange wind died down and then ceased altogether.

"So, we truly face the great one, that is most assuredly Li Zheng."

The captain swallowed the lump in his throat as he heard the name. He stiffened his resolve even as he watched his general lose his.

"Prepare to ford the river!" came the order.

Before the general could calm his men, the captain gave the order as Kang sat upon his horse in helpless silence. He had grown up on the emperor's stories about the man they faced and the strange power he wielded.

The captain drew his sword as he turned to face his cavalry. "Death to the traitor, Li Zheng! First division, prepare to charge!"

Kang tried to stop his onrushing cavalry, but the charge command drowned his voice out.

"Charge!" the captain screamed as the first line of men and horses bounded down the slope toward the river.

As the first three thousand rode forth, the action scared Kang's horse and it spun in a circle. Finally, the general saw the man across the river slowly lower his hood. The eyes were staring straight ahead as the first of his cavalry struck the river's edge.

Li Zheng's head turned toward the sky as the shouts of the cavalry reached his ears. Their bloodlust was up. Then he lowered his head after calling forth the God of Air. He looked at the water at his feet, then his hands, palms up, shot out and again they raised toward the bright sky. The waters of the calm river rose straight into the air. The wall climbed high, higher, and then it crested. The wall of river water came down on the first three thousand men, crushing man and horse beneath its tonnage, as the river splashed down after reaching a height of a thousand feet. Men, horses, and weapons, were washed away by a sudden rush of river flow. Li Zheng than repeated the move of his hands stretching out across the river. The water rose once more as he twirled both hands in rapidly expanding circles. The wall of river water again shot high, and then even higher. This time, with his face turned toward the heavens and the Gods that powered his magic, Li Zheng held the water. The wall of frothing river now separated the far shore from the near.

A thousand arrows were loosed at the wall and they all shot straight up and vanished among the violent and writhing wall. Again, and again men and horses tried to charge through, and they too were lifted high into the air and thrown a half a mile away as if swiped aside by the hand of God. Still, Li Zheng twirled his hands. The wisps of clouds over their heads expanded into a dark mass of swirling death as it shot down and joined the impenetrable wall of river.

Arrows rose into the sky and were brushed aside by the tornado-like barrier as the wind met the river. General Kang tried in vain to steady his horse. Even the stories he had heard could not compare to the power they now faced. He had never thought to see such a sight. Li Zheng was gathering the very forces of nature against them.

Master of Earth, fire, air and water, Li Zheng felt the power draining as quickly as it had come on. Sections of the wall of water were falling, splashing down into the river bed, and then slowly, haltingly rising again. He knew if General Kang just waited it out, his power to control the elements would soon fail him. He had never gathered all of his strength before this day. Men were even now starting to get their horses through the weakening wall of river. Arrows and lances shot forward, only missing the Master by inches. Finally, he used his left hand and then it too swirled in a rapid and ever-increasing circle. He was using the last of his strength. His hand motions stopped as he reached into his robe and pulled free something that looked like small stones. These stones of silver were flecked through with greenish streaks, the same as the ore that once was necklaced around the great King of Hunan. Li Zheng tossed them into the small fire. The bonfire he had started earlier puffed, enlarged, and then a long line of burning air rose and spread out in line with the raging wall of water as a brightly flamed tornado. Of this, small balls of flame broke away from the tornado and shot across the river. The first cavalry to breach the wall were met by fireballs from Li Zheng. The flames struck man and horse and they burst into flame as they fell into the starved river bed.

Li Zheng felt his legs give out as he collapsed to the sandy shore. The river collapsed as it smashed four thousand men in its haste to return to its natural state. The tornado of flame diminished and almost flamed out. The water suddenly rebounded, sending a forced tide-like surge across the way, washing up on the remaining two thousand men who sat in silent shock at what had just killed their fellows. The tornado again burst into the morning skies and then steadied. Then Li Zheng collapsed to the sandy shore of the river's edge.

As his enemy collapsed to the sand, General Kang saw his moment. He withdrew his sword and this time he would lead the final charge. The clouds overhead dissipated as if they had never been, and the river once more flowed as if it had been as normal as the day before. The fire storm of tornado dwindled to nothingness.

Li Zheng looked up as the last of the general's army started their charge to kill the Elemental. Again, his hands turned up to the sky, then they both came down. He once more reached into his robes and brought out the last nugget of his strange powers. This one was larger. This was the last of the ore he had brought from his travels back to his birth place. Once more he prayed to the heavens as his fingers, with the large silverish nugget in his right hand, dug deeply into the soil. He never felt the sand and rock as it scraped his finger-nails to nothing, as he clasped the earth into his now balled fists. Sand and rock flowed from his fingers over and around the silver rock-like ore.

"Forgive me, my people. Your life will now start amidst your enemy's deaths." His hands left the earth and shot skyward. The sand of the riverbank and the ore flew high into the sky just as the stone and river sands left the fingers of the Master.

General Kang and his last two thousand men were only fifty feet from the far shore as arrows flew. Five of them struck Li Zheng, but still he held his hands even higher than before as the fists emptied of the damp earth.

Before the charging cavalry knew what was happening, it was as if the earth exploded. The water from the river shot once more into the skies. This time however the riverbed came with it. Earth and water joined the remaining flame from the firepit as it too rose. The cavalry was lifted with the natural elements of the world, and once more men, horses and equipment flew into the air. The first of the rising waters caught General Kang and threw him and his mount into the air. Kang felt his body swirling through the air and water, and then jarringly falling, crashing back onto the river bed that had once been the base for that water. He came to his senses in time to see his last two thousand men and their animals tossed a thousand feet into the sky with the exploding earth battering them to pieces. Then, as the earth and water were lifted totally free, he sat and watched as Li Zheng, who had finally become visible, slowly lower his hands, and with the arrows buried deeply into his chest and stomach, collapsed onto his face.

"We have met the Devil, and he has sent us all to the hell we deserve," Kang moaned aloud, just as the river and earth, followed by the remaining flames of the fire, crashed back down, covering Kang and his dead ten thousand.

THE SKIES CLEARED AS IF NOTHING HAD HAPPENED. THE SUN ROSE higher into the sky and the river was once more calmed. It flowed to the far shore and its waters slowly lifted the lifeless body of Li Zheng. The body swirled gently in the current for the briefest of moments and then it joined that of ten thousand of the emperor's best soldiers, along with their General, as they started their long journey southward.

THE LAST AIR BENDER, THE GREAT ELEMENTAL WIZARD OF THE GREAT desert, bereft of the power of life, was now relegated to the annals of myth and legend.

FIFTY MILES TO THE NORTH, GENERAL CHANG WATCHED AS THE LAST OF the men and women of Li Zheng's tribe crossed over the bottom row of giant stone blocks. There had been a brief battle with the soldiers guarding the unfinished portion of wall, but his men dispatched the Emperor's killers with little effort or loss of life. The soldiers were buried in hidden places inside the wall for their witnessing of the great exodus of people. They would be buried in the wall for all of eternity.

The last two people he assisted up and over the low wall were the wife and child of Li Zheng. He felt the woman's sorrow as he too knew they would never see the Master again. As he watched Zheng's wife and infant man-child join those who now started North into the unknown lands, he looked in that direction. He knew what kinds of danger awaited them, but he knew that the Master had given them this once chance at life and freedom. He swore he would take these people to safety into the lands of the Master's birth—the desert and rugged mountains of Mongolia.

THE PEOPLE OF MASTER LI ZHENG CROSSED THE GREAT WALL AND would vanish from history for over two thousand years.

Altai Mountains,
Mongolia, 1182 A.D.

THE LINE OF HORSES WAS PACKED FULL OF THE TRADE GOODS THAT WERE bartered for, near the Great Wall. The trip had been a long and arduous one for the thirty-six volunteers from the village of Hanshu, near the Gobi Altai Mountains. They had traded the spices drawn from the plants found only in that region for the seeds and poultry they now carried. They had also traded small ingots of gold and the silverish mineral they sourced from the mountains for the more expensive livestock. The silverish ore was found to be an excellent source for producing harder than normal steel and they used this to barter for the trade goods that were hard to come by in the forbidding mountains that protected the village of Hanshu. These long trips were made once every five years so as to avoid any observant eyes of the Empire of China.

The campsite they had chosen this night was a protected canyon where a small trickle of water was to be had from a creek that coursed its way down the rugged and rocky mountain. The camp was jovial as each man knew they would not have to set up another camp as they were only ten hours away from the borders of their hidden village. The horses had been unpacked and were now standing and feeding on the last of their grain supply. All in all, it had been a good trip to the enemy's homeland, and the joviality came from the fact they had come and gone without spies from the empire catching on that their greatest threat had been amongst them.

The cooked chicken and rice was passed from eager hand to eager hand as the men talked and joked of their successful trade expedition.

Wei Mei, the oldest of the travelers, was sitting cross-legged by the fire as his men laughed. He felt the tension of the last four months of dangerous travel slipping from the men as if it were an important bodily discharge. He could not help but allow his own guard to lag as they neared their hidden home of over a thousand years.

"Wei Mei, this is the first time in the months that we have been traveling that I have seen your sour face smile," said one of the men, who was removing one of the small chickens from a spit over the fire. The man reached out and slapped the leg of the man next to him, "I told you he was human."

The men laughed, and Wei Mei finally nodded and also smiled. Suddenly he lost that smile as he held up a hand for silence. The men automatically lost their joviality, and each cocked an ear to the dark night. Wei Mei placed a hand on the sandy soil and felt the earth.

"Horses, five of them."

The men, as experienced as they were of the dangers of their travels, automatically reacted. Each stood and retrieved their choice of weapons. Fifteen gathered bow and arrow, the other twenty-one, swords. Archers to the rear, swordsmen to the front. They circled the campfire, each wishing for the darkness that fire magnified.

Wei Mei slowly withdrew the sword that had been handed down to him by his great-great-great-grandfather. He heard their own mounts as they nervously pawed the ground as the five horses and the sound of hoof falls came closer. Suddenly, the noise stopped, ceasing just out of sight cast by the cooking fire.

"Greetings the camp," came a voice from the darkness. "We are travelers in need of assistance. We mean you no harm."

Wei Mei stepped forward, parting the swordsmen to their front. "How many are you?" he asked, knowing full well the visitors were outnumbered by his own men.

"We are five. We have two wounded men. May we approach the camp?"

"The speaker alone, come with hands outstretched into the light. There are many arrows ready to judge your actions."

As the men watched, a single man came into the flickering firelight. His hands, complete with the battle gloves of a soldier, were held straight out in front. The clothes he wore were rough animal skin, his armor thickened leather. He was helmetless, and he looked to be himself one of the wounded he spoke of.

"We mean you no harm, brothers. My companion has taken many an arrow, all we need is clean water and the light and warmth of your fire. Perhaps food if you can spare it."

Wei Mei gestured for ten men to leave the camp and gather at the base of the mountain trail, hidden from view. They would assure the newcomers would remain well-behaved.

"Bring your men forward, we will do what we can."

They watched as the grateful man turned and vanished into the darkness. Wei Mei and his men tensed. They relaxed when the five men reappeared entering the circle of firelight as if ghostly specters from the desert beyond. Two men were holding another up and the last two had their loosed equipment. Wei Mei could see the group was heavily armed.

"Bring the injured man closer to the fire." He stepped closer to the visitors from the Gobi. "I feel you will find no complaint if my men hold your weapons for you?"

The five men stopped short of entering the camp. "You are not men of the Gobi?" the man who had initially spoken asked.

"If a people who have called the Gobi home for over twelve hundred years are considered not of the desert, then yes, we are strangers in a strange land."

Wei Mei saw the broken shaft of an arrow as it protruded from the speaker's thigh. He handed off his burden to another and then stepped forward, heavily limping.

"We have heard the rumors of an ancient tribe that hides in the Altai Mountains. We thought the tales only myth, as no one can live in such desolation."

Wei Mei remained silent. He watched as the man nearly collapsed from his thigh wound. Wei Mei sprang forward and caught the boy before he struck the earth. "Come, assist this man to the fire," he ordered.

As seven men came forward and helped the wounded men and their three companions, they all saw who it was who came in from the dark night. One of Wei Mei's men turned and looked at the older man. "They are Mongols, General."

The visitors, even the man with three arrows in his leather covered breast, reacted to the word 'general'. They looked up in fear, or was it killing anger.

"They are but men. Bring them in."

With trepidation attacking the normal kind hearts of the traders, the visitors were allowed in. The severely wounded man was brought to the fire and the speaker of the group knelt beside him. The broken arrow was causing him much pain as he leaned in close to the man who looked to be dying.

"We are safe for now, my old friend. These men will help…"

Wei Mei watched as the man collapsed onto his dying friend. He moved to take the weight from the silent man lying near the fire. He gestured to his men. "Get these men food and drink." He helped the wounded man to sit up. "We need to get that arrow out of your leg, my son."

"No, I am not important, please help my friend."

Wei Mei looked back at the boy by the fire. He shook his head as he placed a hand on the wounded man's shoulder and forced him to lay down. "I fear your friend is beyond our help. You, we can assist, but this man will soon join his ancestors."

The man fought to sit back up.

"Here," Wei Mei said as the men of both tribes gathered around the fire. The newcomers were drinking from bronze cups greedily, "bite upon this. It will not be pleasant." He took hold of the broken shaft of arrow. The piece of rolled leather was placed into the man's mouth and he bit down with his angry eyes still fixed on his dying friend near the fire. In a moment of pride, the Mongol spat the leather from his mouth. His concentration was only upon the boy. Suddenly he closed his eyes and swallowed as the pain engulfed his sun scorched features as the arrow and its barbed tip was yanked from his thigh. Wei Mei immediately placed a folded cloth on the spurting wound. "You did not cry out. Either it is because you suffer wounds like this often, or you are just too stubborn to allow strangers to see your pain. Yes, you are truly Mongol."

The man tried to sit up. "My friend."

"I have seen many battle wounds," Wei Mei slapped the cloth holding the man's blood flow at bay, and then took the man's left hand and made him compress his bleeding wound. "Two of the arrows can be pulled free of his body without killing him. The third however is lodged too close to his heart. As I said, your friend will join his ancestors before the breaking of the dawn."

The man reached out with his free hand and grasped the cold one of the dying man. "I have failed you. Before the dawn I will guide you to those ancestors. I will join my brother in death."

"Mongols are so very dramatic. Foolish, but dramatic."

The voice came from the darkness. "And as well trained as my General is at battle tactics, he does not fare as well as a physician."

The men moved to their weapons for the second time that night. Soon they heard the ten men that had been sent into hiding run into the camp.

"Apologies, General, we heard no one approach the camp," said one of the breathless bowmen as he stumbled into the fire lit encampment.

"Calm yourselves," Mei Wei said as he tried to ease the minds of his scared men and their Mongolian guests. He knew the voice well. He stepped toward the darkness and the voice beyond. The Mongols wanted their weapons and Wei Mei's men held them at bay. "How many times have I warned you not to venture from the village alone?"

"You fret as much as my wife, General," said the voice in the dark. "Now, may I enter the camp without receiving a welcoming arrow from your frightened men?"

"Stand down," Wei Mei said to his men. He turned to the wounded man he had just assisted. "Fear not, he is our Master."

The Mongols did not relax as the other men did. They watched as the lone figure in the long robes of a monk entered the circle of light. Wei Mei stepped forward and then went down on one knee. The newcomer placed a hand on the man's dark hair and then assisted him to his feet.

"Why are you so far from home?"

The newcomer lowered his hood and looked at the more relaxed faces of Wei Mei's men, and then turned and looked at the apprehensive faces of their visitors. Then his attention went to the man lying nearest the fire.

"Not only do I like greeting the supply trains when they return from their long journey, I am here for him," he said as he gestured at the boy. The small man slowly approached the fire. The three Mongols dropped their cups of water and surrounded the dying man. Even the man with the leg wound tried to stand.

"He will not live to see the dawn, Master."

The man stopped and smiled at the men surrounding the wounded boy. Then he turned and faced Wei Mei. "You left these many months ago as a General, now I learn you have returned not only a commander of the home watch, but that of a healer as well?"

"Master, I have seen many wounds in my lifetime—battle wounds, and even those received in stupidity. This is a dead man."

"Don't say that again," the man who had just had the arrow removed from his leg said as he struggled to sit up.

"Calm, my Mongolian brothers. No one is dying here tonight." The newcomer smiled and then turned in a circle to face every man present, Chinese and Mongolian.

"Who is this purveyor of riddles?" the barbarian asked as he was assisted to his feet by his brother Mongolians.

"He is fire, air, earth, wind and water. He is Master Zheng."

"This is a lie. The wizard you speak of died a thousand years ago." The man struggled in the arms of his men as he became angered at such a brazen falsity.

"Yes, he did die over a thousand years ago, but his bloodline lives on," Wei Mei said as he turned to face the startled Mongolians.

"We all live, we all die. Our destiny has always been to rejoin the earth from which we all spring," Zheng said as he lowered to his knees with the palms of his hands touching as he bowed his head in prayer. When he was done, he kept his eyes closed and, with his right hand, he reached for the boy. He placed the hand between the three arrows that protruded from the leather chest armor of the Mongolian.

"What is he doing?" the Mongol asked, favoring his wounded leg as his companions held him up.

"This boy, he fevers from far more than his wounds." Zheng looked up at the men surrounding the scene. "I see the arrows' feathers are of the same tribal colors as your own."

The Mongols remained silent.

"Familial squabbles are usually the harshest of all." Zheng placed his right hand on the boy's fevered brow. He tilted his head to the left as he once more closed his deep brown eyes. "Do you wish to speak to the boy?" Zheng asked as he finally looked up again. He faced the man with the wound to his leg.

"I find it difficult to speak to the dying. He will not hear my words."

Zheng smiled as he took the hand of the wounded man and placed his other upon the chest of the boy. Suddenly the doubtful man felt the electricity flow through Zheng as the feeling hit him as a lightning bolt. His eyes fluttered as Zheng closed his own. The memory was as clear as the man had ever remembered it being. Two boys playing on a plain of grass. It was himself and his dying friend. He was ten and the boy seven. They were stalking five wild horses that had wandered down from the great rift. That had been a good day as they had both caught two of their horses. They had made their small village proud that day. The man pulled his hand free and looked upon a smiling Master Zheng.

"Witchcraft," he mumbled.

"Possibly. But as you see, the boy's brain is still functioning quite nicely." Zheng once more lowered both hands to the feverish boy. "His mind is even now seeking a safe place for his wounded body. He is with whom he wishes to be with in his final moments. We will now try to change his mind about leaving us."

As the men watched, the campfire flared as Zheng closed his eyes. Without looking, he grasped the first of the three arrows. The one lodged just below the left of his ribcage. He eased the arrow out, making the boy cry out in his unconscious way. Zheng laid the arrow aside. He then took hold of the second shaft. It was lodged about four inches beneath his heart. He pulled. The arrow still remained lodged and the boy cried out again.

"You're killing him with even more haste than his wounds!"

"Still yourself if you wish your friend to live," General Wei Mei said as he placed a hand on the wounded man's shoulder to steady him.

Zheng closed his eyes as he placed more pressure into his pulling of the arrow. This time the arrowhead came free of the leather armor and once more he placed the bloody projectile near the first.

Zheng relaxed and then sat upon his haunches. He again prayed to the sky with eyes closed. He rubbed his two hands together and the fire flared again, startling those watching. He clapped three times in slow succession. He opened his eyes and everyone one of the men took a step back. His eyes had gone from dark brown to a flaming green. It was if the eyes were illuminated from some inner fire. Those eyes looked into the clear, starry skies above the lee of the canyon. Again, three claps of his hands. He then twirled his fingers as he gestured to the sky. Before anyone knew what was happening, rain drops came from a clear night and inundated the camp. The Mongols gasped as they could not believe what it was they were seeing. Water rushed over the slow rising of the boy's chest under his hand-me-down armor. Suddenly, Master Zheng reached for the shaft that was embedded just an eighth of an inch from the wounded man's heart and pulled. The arrow was struck so deep that the leather armor tented upward as Zheng pulled. He doubled the effort and the shaft came free. The boy screamed in pain as Zheng laid the arrow down beside the two others.

The man with the leg wound slid from the grasp of his fellows as he knew his friend, the boy he had been sworn to protect, was dying before his eyes. The blood spurted, becoming a lesser flow as he watched the seconds tick by.

"The boy's life blood mingles with the earth he sprang from. The rain he was born into," Zheng said as he dug his fingers into the earth and came up with two handfuls of mud as the rain came down at a greater rate. He then reached into a leather pouch and produced several small nuggets of the mountain's wares. He held the ore out to Wei Mei. "General, crush these as best as you can with the hilt of your knife."

The general did as he was told. He placed five of the nuggets into a wooden bowl, and then using the hilt of his blade, slowly started to crush them. Not as fine as he would have liked, he handed the bowl over to Zheng.

"Now General, the three offending shafts."

Wei Mei reached for the three arrows, which had been removed from the dying man, as the blood coming from the third wound near the heart ceased to flow. He held the arrows out to Zheng. The master, without opening his eyes, took both hands full of the crushed ore and grasped the arrows sharp points, covering each of the deadly warheads with the ore that was now damp with the rain. His eyes were still closed, and his lips moved. The arrow heads were dripping with the silverish material.

"To die and be reborn is the rarest of gifts bestowed upon the lowest of man. You will arise with a new name, a new tact for a life that has yet to be revealed." His eyes opened, and he looked down on the boy and then, when the last rise of his chest came, he placed the first arrow, dripping silverish looking mud from its barbed point, into the first wound. The body didn't react. The second arrow was jammed harshly into the second of the wounds, just beneath the heart. The arrow dug deep into the wound that had been created when the arrow first struck the boy down. Still no movement from a body and heart that had stopped working.

"Stop, stop!" cried the boy's friend. He moved with the rest of his companions to stop Master Zheng from driving the third arrow back into the dead man's chest.

With the last ore-covered arrow in his hand, Zheng's free hand shot out with the palm facing toward the men that were trying to stop him. A hurricane force wind rose from nothingness, throwing stinging rain into the charging men. The force threw the Mongols from their feet as they flew backward, landing them in the fierce flood that was now inundating the campsite. The fire burst free from the pit and rose high into the sky. In that light they saw the arrow, the silver ore still clinging to the sharpened point, rise and then come down into the boy's still chest with a force that drove the head deeper than it had been the first time. This time the dead man's body arched, and the boy's eyes sprang open with a scream into the storm that had sprung from nothingness. As the boy screamed, Zheng reached for the arrows and pulled them free once more. The motion was so fast the astounded men weren't really sure it had been made at all. Tossing the arrows aside, the wind and the rain ceased as suddenly as they had started.

"General, remove the boy's armor—quickly!" Zheng called as Wei Mei stepped forward and did as he was ordered. He slashed at the leather straps and the animal sinew that held the breast plate in place. The other Mongols were just now starting to pick themselves up from the ground and stared wide-eyed at the unbelievable scene before them.

Master Zheng tore away the shirt made from homespun sheepskin. He then started slamming the remaining crushed ore from the bowl into the once more flowing wounds. The boy screamed again. Then Zheng lowered his entire body onto the boy and covered it with his own. The night became still. The fire died down to almost nothing as the wet wood finally realized it was wet. The flame was just enough to show the scene. Zheng eased himself up with the aid of a shocked General Wei Mei. The general could feel the weakness coming from his master. He eased Zheng over to a blanket and allowed his tired body to sit.

"Cover your friend from the cold night air, for I have no power to stop the common cold as well as I do wounds."

The wounded man limped up to the boy and, in the dying light of the fire, he saw the mud-covered chest rising, and then lowering with every beat of his once still heart. His eyes went from him to Zheng, who only nodded as a blanket was placed over his shoulders by the general. The wounded man did the same. He put a rough woven cover over his body and then stepped back as the boy's eyes fluttered open. His jaw dropped as he rose slowly onto an elbow. Instead of looking at his shocked and stunned companions, he turned his head, his long hair dripping water, and stared at Master Zheng.

"I know...you," the boy said as his friends rushed to his side. He gently shoved them away when they blocked the view of the man that had just saved his life. He continued to look at the tired old man before him covered in a blanket. Then his eyes went to the wounded man who was now kneeling at his side. "He was with us that day many years ago when we caught the wild horses by the Krall."

"I have been watching you for many, many years, boy."

All eyes went to Zheng. Even the General was taken aback.

"I have even seen this night many, many times." Zheng looked up at a stunned General Wei Mei. "As you know, I never venture out this far to greet a trade mission. I knew this boy would be here."

The Mongol boy gently pushed grateful hands from his body and, with soreness and difficulty, rose to his unsteady feet. He looked at the silverish and roughly crushed mud covering the wounds on his chest. He brushed away the layers and what everyone saw made them go to their knees. There was not even a mark where the arrows had been. The long braids of the once dead man shone brightly in the sitting moon, whose surrounding skies were now clear of any weather. His eyes went to Master Zheng and he slowly moved toward him as he pulled the blanket closer around his body. As he approached, Master Zheng lowered his head and his body slumped. General Wei Mei helped him once more sit up straight as the master's patient approached. The boy stepped up and, with a shaking hand, reached out and placed his fingers under the old man's chin and slowly raised it so he could see into his eyes.

"I am looking at myth. I am looking at legend. I have seen you many times in my life, have I not?"

"Yes, you were always a serious boy. You will become even more of a serious man."

"Why have you been an unseen savior of one who is worthless to the world?"

"Do you have children, my son?" Zheng asked, his voice growing weak. His eyes were once more brown and deep seated, as if his eyes were retreating into his head.

"I have not the time," the man said as he lowered himself to sit beside the Master.

"I have. I have a boy child not much younger than yourself. I have an entire tribe of children. We dwell in these lands. This is our home and one day men such as yourself will come to claim them. This is why I have been a protectorate of your young life."

"You are he whom my father's father, and his fathers before him, have spoken of, are you not?"

"I am but a man of the earth, as you are now."

The boy looked up at his four Mongol brethren. He spoke strange words to his guard and they all went wide-eyed and then suddenly went to their knees and bowed.

"You are an Air Bender, the Elemental kin to the natural world. Not myth, not legend, but as real as I." He spoke again to his brethren. "Elemental. Wizard of earth, air, wind and fire."

Master Zheng lowered his head and took the boy's roughened and scarred hand.

"I am nothing more than a man lost in the world. This we have in common. You will be a great man, as I am not, nor ever will be. My choices here tonight have sprung from my greed. My greed of wanting my people to remain hidden within a world you will create. A world where you will eventually conquer enemies of many years. Your enemy, and my people's historical enemy. A longtime foe that would see my people wiped from the face of this, our earth."

"I do not understand," the young boy said as he squeezed his savior's gentle hand.

"You will know the day when it comes. Hide my people of the mountains. Chase away all those who threaten us. I have traded a life for one who will become great, whereas we are not a great people. A simple trade. Honor among those lost in this wilderness. In exchange for the life I have given back to you, protect and hide my people from those who would destroy us. End this tragic game of life and death over offenses long forgotten by the people who play this shameful game."

There was a gasp when Master Zheng slid forward into the boy's arms. General Wei Mei sprang forward and assisted Zheng back to a sitting position. He removed the blanket and raised the robe's front. The blood flowed freely from three wounds, the most serious at Zheng's heart. The evidence was clear. The wounds of the dying boy had been somehow transferred to the body of their Master. He was even now breathing his last.

"Master!" Wei Mei cried as he took the weak man into his arms. The general cried when the realization struck that he would lose the most important man in the world that night.

"I will always be with the people. Only I will see them through the eyes of my child, and his children after. This man will save us from a world that wishes to hide the truths of our land, a world they will never understand." His hand reached, not for the general's, but for the man he had just given his life for. It was grasped in the now strong fingers of their guest. "Do what you will to the world but join me in keeping the people safe. Do I have your word?"

The boy looked around at his men. Then he went to one knee and bowed his head as Zheng placed his dying hand on his long hair.

"I will keep the secret of your people if I have that power within me to do so."

"The boy I found so many years ago has now become a man. Some will hate you, others worship you, but greatness is yours on both sides of that life telling story."

"General, we have spied many torches in the valley below," one of the pickets reported as he took in the scene he had just joined.

Wei Mei looked up and fixed the man with the wounded leg with his own darkened eyes. "Your foes have tracked you."

"Yes, I am afraid we have led them straight to you."

The boy's hand was squeezed tighter by Master Zheng. Then the grip lessened, and the hand fell away as fast as the flow of blood from his self-imposed wounds. The boy bowed his head and then placed the Master's hand over his chest as he gently laid him upon the ground. He stood and faced the General of the man who had saved his life.

"Armor!" he said loudly as his eyes remained fixed on the Chinese General. "We will now lead them away from your camp. You have my solemn oath; no army of men will ever breach these mountains if I can stop them. This is my only promise as I have nothing. Nothing in this life as valuable as the man you just lost. But if I am able, I will give you the only thing worth any value—my word. No matter what ills or disaster befall me and mine, you will live hidden from the eyes of men. This I owe to him," he once more knelt as his leather armor was brought forth. He stood as the armor was slipped on. "We will ride to the south, drawing our enemies from this mountain. Go, take the Elemental back to your people. He will always be remembered, as this place will never be spoken of in our lifetimes. On that you may depend," he said as his leather armor was tied off and his horse brought forward. He touched the three holes in the thick leather and the blood stains surrounding them. His four men and himself mounted. "May the Elemental's force push us like the wind away from this place."

As he turned his horse away toward the direction of the soon to rise sun, General Wei Mei stepped forward with his men. He was lost as to what had happened this night.

"Boy, who are you? I must know that our people will learn the value of a debt paid."

The boy didn't answer; he kicked his horse in the side and it sprung forth, away from the dying campfire. His friend remained for the briefest of moments.

"He is the divine one, he is Temüjin, horse lord of the plains." The man's horse was spurred forward and then five men vanished into the night with war yelps that would frighten any man on earth as they would do for the next twenty-five years.

As the body of Master Zheng was prepared for his journey home to the hidden mountain, the general saw the torchlights far down in the valley below suddenly turn as their pursuit changed course. The boy named Temüjin had kept his word. He was leading his pursuers away from their mountain.

In the many years that followed that long-ago night, the man who would eventually be known as the greatest conqueror in world history, would indeed keep his word and the secrets of the Elemental Air Bender and his hidden kingdom in the wastelands of the Gobi.

Genghis Khan would forever be a protectorate of the hidden Empire of the Dragon.

Gobi Desert, July 1945

The B-29 lost three hundred feet of altitude before the pilot and co-pilot could fight the controls hard enough for the wings to catch more air. The bomber known as 'Slick Willy', with her painted nose-art of cartoon character 'Boxcar Willie' on a locomotive dropping bombs onto the head of the Japanese minister of war, Hideki Tojo, fought her way back up to altitude. Both men at the controls felt their arms cramp with the effort. The damage they had taken over

Manchuria by a high altitude 'Zero' fighter, while on the most heavily guarded secret bomb run in United States military history, had damaged the bomb bay doors, jamming the 'device' just feet above the twin doors under her belly.

The B-29, 'Mama's L'il Helper', the camera plane, and the third B-29, 'Summer Solstice', the weather platform, went down not long after the failed experimental drop over Manchuria, which covered the exact same miles and course adjustments that another B-29 would make the very next day. The name of that aircraft was—the 'Enola Gay'. The bomb itself was one you will never find mentioned in the history books. Instead of taking the chance that the atomic bombs, Fat Man or Little Boy, would fail to detonate over a target on mainland Japan, making the American threat to Japan a moot point, 'Slick Willy' carried 'The Thin Man' apparatus over territory that was uninhabited in the barren wastes of the Gobi Desert. If this test failed, the Americans would be the only ones to witness it. When the nightfighters attacked, they caught 'Slick Willy' in the middle of its bomb release over its target. Now, that bomb hung precariously in her bomb bay.

Their chance to bail out was passed over through unanimous vote to ride the aircraft until their fuel was exhausted, rather than the inevitable prisoner of war camp and the torture they would receive over their top-secret mission. They all agreed that falling from a height of twenty-five thousand feet, with a weapon that they still had no idea the power of, was their clear choice. With their compass shot away and their escorts blown from the skies, and with their radio blown to a thousand smoldering pieces, no one would ever know what became of the 'Slick Willy' and the top-secret payload she carried. The best they could hope for after crashing was rescue and the recovery of the bomb that no one outside of Washington even knew existed. To cover their mission parameters, they had launched from India for secrecy.

"Damn, that was close," Major Douglas Pierce said as he flexed his right arm, trying to relieve the cramp that had developed in his effort to regain control of the ship.

"Hydraulics are completely shot, and there is no way to get the doors closed, Skipper."

"Goddamn S-2 said there was not a night-fighting Zero anywhere near the Gobi, and we run into a whole squadron!" Pierce said as he angrily slapped at the broken glass of not only their hydraulic pressure gauge, but also the compass.

"S-2 intelligence my ass, those bastards have been wrong more times than right," the co-pilot, Captain Everson Krensky, said as he released the control yoke and flexed his gloved fingers.

"We're going to have to sit this thing down into that sandstorm while we still have enough control to hop over a few of those sand dunes."

"Damn, I hate doing that," Krensky said as he peered out of his window at the raging mass below them. "With those bomb bay doors jammed open, that thing just may detonate. Armed or un-armed."

"Better than getting our skin peeled off by that sand if we bailout. I'll take my chances with '*Slick Willy*'."

Both men were silent as they listened to the drone of their remaining three engines. Number four was starting to backfire and the co-pilot adjusted the mix to that engine. It sputtered and then suddenly fell into sync with the other two. Krensky placed a thumb on his throat mic.

"How you fellas doing back there?"

"Still breathing in the forward spaces," came the reply from the pressurized compartment behind the cabin.

"We lost Jimmy about five minutes ago. Bled out on us."

Krensky lowered his head and then glanced at the Major. His eyes told the story after hearing the latest bad news from the rear pressurized compartments. Sergeant Jimmy Blackwell, a baseball player from Muncie, Indiana, had just recently joined the crew after his transfer from B-17's. When the war in Europe had ended, instead of going home like he should have, he retrained in the remotely operated fifty caliber machine guns of the B-29 Superfortress, and then was transferred to the Army Air Corps Pacific command.

Pierce shook his head and swallowed. That was crewman number four. The other three had died when a twenty-millimeter exploding round shattered the bombardier and radio stations, also taking out the forward operator's radar powered station for the turret mounted upper fifty. Four of his men were now dead. His crew, the boys he had promised to get home at war's end, were now gone.

"Roger, hang tough men, we are about to sit '*Slick Willy*' down, we may not have that long to dwell on what's happened." He knew they would have had a better chance jumping over Manchuria, and the Major gave the ten-man crew every opportunity to do so. They had chosen, to a man, to escape the Japanese occupied area of Manchuria, to take a chance over what they hoped was a sparsely populated area of Mongolia. Only after they had arrived did they find the desert area socked in by one of the worst sand storms in recorded history. Now they had no choice, they would ride '*Slick Willy*' down to the desert's floor. "Okay you bunch of cowpokes, keep your external oxygen supply ready, we could lose all pressure at any time. We're starting our descent. It should be fun. Out." He smiled at his copilot. "How's that for putting a brave face on our rather dire situation?" Pierce asked with a wink at Krensky.

The co-pilot cleared his throat as he placed the memory of the young baseball player from Muncie out of his thoughts for now. "Just like they taught in command school." He then examined the remaining and still functioning gauges of the shaking and damaged B-29. "Try as I might, I cannot see a break in the weather anywhere down there, Skipper."

"The damn storm is reaching up for us!"

The giant aircraft buffeted and rose to an altitude of thirty thousand feet before it seemingly hit the ceiling. The impact was like hitting a brick wall, straining the harnesses of all onboard. Before anyone could realize what was happening, all hell broke loose. The rivets between frame sixteen and seventeen separated from the bomber's ribs and that was that. The air was immediately evacuated from the aircraft. The B-29 Superfortress started to shake violently.

"All crew, go to external O-2!" Krensky tried to shout over his throat mic. He managed to secure his mask and then take the control yoke, so the major could squeeze his over his mouth and nose. The temperature inside the bomber went from a bearable thirty-two degrees to minus six in a split second.

Behind the main cabin's bulkhead, they heard a screeching, ripping sound and then all went dark as the last of the pressurized air escaped the aluminum aircraft. The control yoke was yanked out of both the pilot and co-pilot's hands.

"...gone, they're...just ripped out of the plane...they're just...,"

The call came over their headphones, but whatever was meant by the frantic message went unheard as the B-29 started a death roll toward the storm below. Pierce knew that they had lost internal integrity of the giant Boeing plane. They had a hole ripped into her somewhere and the major had a sickening feeling it was the frame where the remainder of his crew had taken station for safety reasons. How many more of his young crew had he just lost?

"We're losing the starboard wing!" Krensky screamed as the vibration coursed through their entire beings.

Before Pierce could respond, the starboard wing folded completely in on itself. The massive wing twisted and the force of their downward spiral sent the five-ton aluminum reinforced wing crashing into the side of the aircraft. The 'Slick Willy' started burning in its death plunge.

The centrifugal forces made the control yoke spin and sent it back and forth enough that the motion became blinding. Then Pierce could feel the entirety of the large fuselage twist as it was corkscrewing downward. The major closed his eyes as the cabin started filling with debris and sand from the raging storm. This was how he and his crew would meet their end. No goodbyes, no job well done, no homecoming to family and friends. Their war ended here, and it ended now.

Blood was rushing to parts of the remaining crew's bodies, where blood was never meant to go. Pierce felt his brain grow fuzzy as the B-29 spun out of control. He felt his stomach as it was sent back into his spine. His vision grew dim and he was grateful for that one mercy as the right wing of the giant, and once lethal, bomber separated and flew off into the sand storm. He knew through his fading consciousness that he and his men would never feel the impact of the 'Slick Willy' hitting the sands of the Gobi traveling faster than the speed of sound.

His wife and son's faces came unbidden to his dying brain as his eyes started to close. Then, in the briefest of moments before his brain shut down, Pierce saw the silvery haze, and that was when he knew his time was at hand. The spinning view and the forces working against him dulled his mind and he thought he was seeing the image and color of what death looked like. It was beautiful, it was terrifying. The silverish hue took over everything as his mind shut down.

THE B-29 BOMBER KNOWN AS 'SLICK WILLY', WITH THE FIRST ATOMIC weapon, 'The Thin Man', vanished into the largest sandstorm in recorded history that night in 1945.

PART I
THE GATHERING STORM

"War may sometimes be a necessary evil. But no matter how necessary, it is always an evil, never a good. We will not learn how to live together in peace by killing each other's children."

~ *JIMMY CARTER,*
December 10, 2002

CHAPTER ONE

The Mekong River,
Udon Thani, Thailand

The Vietnamese fishing village had survived along the banks of the Mekong River for centuries, as they fished for their living while watching for Thai drug lords from across the river, as they shipped their wares to nations that sought such destructive products. The small village had survived the wars of the ancient peoples of the land, and also the French colonialism incursion of the eighteenth century. Not until the war with America had they been affected much. Now their only concern was the political war with neighboring Thailand, and a concern for the growing power of their one-time ally, China, that worried them most. The war was over fishing rights and the way Thailand ignored the United Nations decree about over fishing the giant Mekong River far north of the small village and the drug trade that made many in Thailand very rich. Their daily catches dwindled more and more each year. The small village near the large city of Udon Thani was dying a slow death as their fortunes dwindled each day.

Dai Mihn and his family had fished these waters through war and peace for the past fifty of his sixty-five years, and he felt the pinch Thailand presented each and every day to the village's livelihood.

Dai scolded his grandson for being careless with their only fishing net, claiming a slow and steady pull would allow the net to be brought aboard their small boat far more efficiently than tugging. The grandson was always in a hurry, especially since the small village had gotten electrical power for the first time in its long history. Even when the war with the French and then the Americans raged along the Mekong in the fifties and sixties, they had been one of those backward villages that lived their lives without the electricity found even during the roughest of the war years by most towns and cities. Now the boy was in a hurry to play his video games that had so absorbed the youth in the village as to cause trouble with the elders. The old man shook his head in exasperation as the grandson continued to try and hurry the day's catch aboard.

"I said stop tugging at it. It will come easy with a steady pull," the old man admonished.

"Why don't you try it!" the kid retorted. "It's like I'm pulling in a whale here!"

Dai did notice the net looked to be dragging heavier than normal. He knew his luck couldn't be that good to have a haul of fish that big. With consternation etching his wrinkled features, Dai slid toward the front of the small boat to assist his grandson. Before he could grasp a side of the net, the boy yelped and then flew backward, nearly knocking him and his grandfather off the boat. The old man caught the boy and angrily pushed him back to a standing position.

"What in the hell is wrong with you?" he asked as he took in the young, frightened features of the youth.

The boy took another step back from the net as he pointed again and again at the many times repaired fish catching tool. The old man again shook his head and then pulled on the net once more, as his grandson cowered against the gunwale of the old boat. One tug, two tugs, and then his own eyes widened as the body popped free of the net. He instinctively let go just as the boy had done. It wasn't the first time in Dai's life that he had netted a body. During the war years with the French and the Americans, it was almost a daily occurrence for someone from the village to pull a dead soldier from the brown waters of the Mekong. The arm was large as was the torso. Dai slapped his grandson along the side of his head.

"Help me!'

The boy moved and assisted the older man. Soon they had the body and net aboard. There, amongst the pile of small catfish, was a large body. It was a white man. Both fishermen untangled the net. The boy jumped back when one of the dead man's arms swung out and touched his bare leg. He screamed and again fell back to the worn and weathered side of the boat.

"With all of the violent video games you play, this shocks you?" Dai continued to unravel the dead man from his one and only net. "You act as an old woman, boy." Dai finally had the task done and he examined the large man in his boat. He jumped back after he rolled the body over. He was white and had short cropped blonde hair.

"Look at that," the boy said as he noticed something on the upper arm of the shirtless body.

As the grandfather leaned in for a closer look, he saw the small tattoo. He reached out and rubbed his thumb over the colorful marking. He had seen this tattoo once before, many years ago. They had recovered a crew of Americans from a downed helicopter that had crashed into the river during the war. They had rescued three United States navy men from the waters. One wore a small tattoo like the one he was looking at.

"What is it?" the boy asked, regaining his courage to get a closer look.

"A seal. We don't have many of them here," the old man joked. "He's juggling a beachball."

"What does it mean?" the grandson asked as he had never even seen a picture of a real seal.

"It used to mean that this was a very special soldier."

"We have them in our video games. I think they're called Special Forces. It's confusing sometimes, the Americans have so many different soldiers in those games, it's hard to keep them straight."

"In the old days I think it was a navy soldier, I don't know if it means that now."

"Look, he's been shot three times," the boy ventured.

"Yes, the Americans seem to always be getting into trouble over here. I don't know why they don't just stay home."

"What do we do, throw him back?"

The old man straightened and looked around. "We have enough fouling the river. No, we have to get the body to the police at Dienmei. They'll know what to do."

The boy was happy to wash his hands of the body. He made his way to the back of the boat to start the small Yamaha motor when the hand took hold of his ankle. He screamed. This time it was a manly expression of pure terror. He fell back as the Grandfather saw the body move as the hand released the boy's ankle.

"He's still alive," he said as he kneeled down and checked the large man for a pulse. "Not by much, but he's still breathing."

Suddenly the same hand grasped the old man by his worn shirt front. Dai leaned in close as the blonde giant was mumbling something. The grandfather peeled the man's strong fingers from his shirt and then gestured for the boy to start the motor. Dai went forward after removing his shirt and placing it under the unconscious man's head.

"What did he say?" the boy shouted over the noise of the motor.

"My English is bad these days."

"Well, what did it sound like?" the grandson persisted.

"Something about someone named Jack. And Colonel. I don't know."

As the boat sped toward the local constabulary, the man awoke several times. The same word was said time and time again in his fevered state.

"Jack!"

Gobi Desert, Mongolia,
Present Day

THE DAY HAD DAWNED BRIGHT AND THE WEATHER WAS MILD FOR EARLY March. The sky was the bluest any member of the American team had ever witnessed. The Gobi was turning out to be a far more hospitable place than they had been warned about.

The mood inside the camp was not very jovial as the American, Australian, and Chinese teams of geologists spoke around the morning breakfast table inside the main tent. The joint expedition, sanctioned by both the Mongolian internal government and the powers-that-be in Beijing, had had nothing but failure since arriving in the Gobi two weeks before. The iron ore found in the region wasn't as abundant as the American claim had placed it. Coupled with the fact that the deep bed of copper wasn't as plentiful as first thought, meant the expedition to find the resources was not going to go a long way in assisting the Chinese government in regaining their feet after the devastating alien attack on their capital of Beijing during the short but costly confrontations of a year past. The spoils of both finds would have been split between the Mongolian government and the Chinese superpower to their south. The Americans, who had forwarded the satellite information about the possibility of a large ore strike in Mongolia, were there with the Australians, who were there as a goodwill gesture for Anglo-Asian cooperation after the short-lived war with the Grays.

The American team was led by fifteen professors and students from the University of Wisconsin and Temple University out of Philadelphia. With their meager samples in secured cases, the group was preparing to leave the Gobi in the good hands of their colleagues from China and Australia. After the larger American and Chinese teams left, there would only be six geologists left in camp as they checked the last of the survey grids. The small group had said goodbye to the bulk of the field mission team at dawn that morning. The remainder, five Americans, one Australian and one Chinese rep sat despondent inside one of the last tents to be struck.

"Looks like our compatriot from Beijing isn't too fond of the breakfast you made them, Louie," said an American professor as he stood up to shovel more scrambled eggs onto his plastic plate.

"I think it's the sausage, mate," the Australian said as he brutally chomped down on the link he had in his mouth.

"Hey, we like sausage, it's just that the many times you Americans and Aussies eat the stuff, every breakfast as I remember, your arteries will clog up long before us rice-eating Asians."

"You Chinese are always so serious, Lee," said Professor James Anderson, from Temple University. "I mean, after the war with those little Gray bastards it seems like you folks would have started living for today, rather than tomorrow."

The professor could see that the subject of the devastating Gray attack on the Chinese nation still affected the young professor of Geology, James Lee Hong, of Beijing University, very deeply.

"Sorry Lee, old man, still a sore subject. Didn't mean anything by it," the Australian said as he knew the joke would have gone over better if they had come up with better results on the mineral dig.

Professor Lee smiled, and then handed his half-empty plate of rice and chicken over to the Aussie cook and nodded that he would take a link of sausage.

"You are right to a point, Professor, we do have to start living. After all, we never know what's right around the corner." He smiled and nodded as three sausage links were plopped over his chicken and rice.

"Next time I'll bring some Kangaroo sausage, that will really prove your manhood!" the large Aussie professor snorted.

As the group laughed and ate, a lone figure stood up and placed her empty plate on her stool and made her way outside.

"Where are you heading, Tiny?" the professor from Temple University asked the small woman whom it took all of thirty seconds to nickname after meeting the rest three weeks before.

She turned and held out a plastic bag. "Time to find a secluded sand dune somewhere," she said as the other faces turned away. One of the dimmest aspects of expeditionary work was where and when to go to a private place for comfort while doing the business of the human body. "You'll excuse me, the Kangaroo sausage remark has bidden me to take my leave."

A second American, a man almost as small in stature, stood. The woman just looked at him and, in the smallest of moves, shook her head that she didn't need her private security watchdog following her outside to guard her while she relieved herself. The man, grizzly with a seven-day old growth of beard, winked and then sat back down to finish his breakfast. He exchanged looks with the dark-haired woman sitting next to him and she just shook her head, indicating she needed alone time for personal reasons.

The group of remaining professors relaxed and started to eat again as the woman exited the large tent. She nodded her head at the expedition's Mongolian escorts as they sat around an open campfire eating their own breakfast. They nodded to her as the eye-pleasing American meandered by them smiling. She spied a dune that would cover her well enough and made her way out of sight.

Sarah McIntire, a captain in the United States Army, and a hidden asset that had been a good reason to attach herself as a guest geologist from the United States Geological Survey, vanished behind one of the larger sand dunes in the area, turning the makeshift sign stuck in the sand around to where it read 'occupied'. From there she was careful not to step in any areas of previous use by the large team.

She looked around at the endless sand surrounding her and then took a deep breath as she looked at her watch and then toward the blue azure sky above. One minute. She reached into her belly-pack and brought out a small device no larger than her palm. She opened the front and then selected the coded number. This was the fifth and final check-in she had to make before getting on a military fight from Beijing for her trip home to Nevada. Sarah was not a part of the group, but wholly separate. She worked clandestinely for the darkest organization in the American government—Department 5656 of the National Archives. A division known to a select few in officialdom as, the Event Group. The task afforded to their agency was to make sure incidents from the world's past never reared their ugly heads again.

Their job was simple, track, identify and, if possible, remove any obstruction that could cause a cataclysmic repeat of an Event that could become world or history altering. That meant that ninety-five percent of their investigations turned up nothing. However, the remaining five percent could cause the deaths of millions for their failure to recognize an historical trend to such an Event. Her credentials were expertly forged. Even though she was actually a U.S. Army geologist, she was also a spy by trade for Department 5656 of the National Archives or, the Event Group.

The Event Group had attached itself to the survey because of an anomaly that their own KH-11 satellite, *Boris* and *Natasha* had detected on a routine survey of the land north of China. At first it was decided that the reading was a false positive of uranium, but soon after arriving, Sarah had come to the conclusion that the old KH-11 was wrong in its information. Sarah was convinced that the readings they received revealed that something was under the mountain range, she just didn't know what. Without more time on site, she could not justify extending the Group's interest in the area. Now it was only Crazy Charlie Ellenshaw who had any reason to be here at all. She smiled as she thought about the ridiculous reason he gave the Director for being attached to the assignment. Since his presence was considered a harmless bow to his cryptozoology department, he was allowed to tag along, as long as he never voiced his strange claims as to why he was there. Thus far his theory, along with Sarah's that something strange was hidden in the desolate mountain range in the Gobi, had both proven laughable.

Sarah looked once more at her wristwatch. She pushed the call button for the only number listed in the satellite phone designed by the communications specialists at Group. A one of a kind device that scrambled any message and then sent it through over a million varying cell towers all over the planet after it left the American made communications satellite operated by the United States Air Force, and then the message would bleed off to nothing—a truly untraceable phone call.

"Good Morning, Captain McIntire," came the automated response

from the Supercomputer, Europa. Her Marilyn Monroe synthesized voice came through clear, and for Sarah it was a comforting sound. For her simple way of thinking about it, it was if the computer was watching her, and that made her feel that much closer to home.

"Good morning Europa," Sarah said as she glanced around to make sure no prying eyes were on her.

"Communication logged in at 0100 and thirty-two seconds. Signal is secure at this time."

"Thank you. Please connect me with the Comp Center duty officer."

"Transferring now, have a safe and pleasant flight home, Captain."

There came a series of beeps and then an extension was picked up.

"Comp Center," came a familiar voice.

"Xavier, that you? What are you doing up at this ungodly hour?"

"Captain, great to hear your voice. You know I never sleep, next silly question."

Sarah and the rest of the Event Group complex had become very close to the wheelchair-bound computer genius since he took over for a very dear friend who had lost his life in the latter days of the war with the Grays. Doctor Pete Golding would have also liked his young replacement. Xavier was just that good at running the most complex computing and artificial intelligence system in the world. The boy was instinctive and had reprogrammed several of Europa's protocols in order to achieve a better understanding of how to research more with her help. She ran investigations on her own now thanks to the paralyzed Mexican American youth from Central Los Angeles. It was Europa that had alerted the Group as to something strange in the Gobi. With help from the U.S. Geological survey, they had talked the Chinese and Mongolian officials into allowing a team of geologists inside the barren country. She just never believed Europa could be wrong about anything.

"Last check in before the helicopters remove us from the Gobi."

"Roger, it will be good to see you home again. Sorry about the false run. I would have bet my mother's pension that you would have found some-

thing there to get the Chinese economy back in the black. By the way, I booked you and your team on a United flight instead of the C-130 Hercules out of Beijing. First class."

"Oh, shit, if the director finds out he'll kill you."

"The director made the change, not me."

The call went silent as Sarah tried to quickly figure out why Department 5656 Director Niles Compton unclasped the purse strings for her return flight. Where a travel budget was concerned, Niles was as cheap as the day was long. Then she realized what it must be. Compton was trying to get on her good side. In other words, he had bad news coming her way. Sarah knew instinctively from which direction that bad news was coming.

"What's happened, Xavier?" she asked, closing her eyes as she waited.

"Nothing...well, something I guess, but really nothing."

"Damn it Xavier, I'm going to lose signal here in a minute, now what is it?"

"Okay, okay. I think, and it's only a guess, that the Director is feeling somewhat responsible for the situation between you and the Colonel. He thinks because he gave authorization for the Colonel and Captain Everett to chase down leads on this Russian shadow government, you're mad at him."

"The director knows for a fact this thing is in the bailiwick of the C.I.A. and F.B.I. Not the Group. Those assholes didn't hesitate in eliminating an entire crew of Russian sailors, so what makes Jack and Niles believe they won't slice his throat in a split second if they think he's snooping around?"

"I can tell you're still a little hot about the colonel's decision making. Anyway, you're not the only one angry as hell around here. Captain Mendenhall is furious."

"Yeah, I hear it every day from his butt-buddy, Ryan. But their anger stems from being left out of this macho hunt Jack and Carl are on. They're both pissed because they're not in on it."

"How is Major Korvesky taking Carl's end of this?"

"She's as mad about it as me. But she comes from the same game as they do. She understands the drill far better than myself. Now, I can tell by your questions that something else is going on. What is it, Xavier?"

"Nothing, just trying to keep everyone here from being at each other's throats."

"Liar. Now, what are they up to?"

"Okay. They have uncovered a lead. But you didn't hear that from me. That's all I know." Xavier didn't like leaving Sarah out of the loop, but he feared the Colonel far more than the diminutive geologist. *"By the way, since your failure to secure new minerals for the Chinese didn't pan out, I hope Charlie was able to prove his ridiculous theory. Imagine, Shangri—"*

The satellite phone beeped once and she looked at the phone. *Signal loss at 0110.*

Sarah angrily looked at the loss of transmission display on the phone and was tempted to throw the thing as far as she could. Instead she closed her eyes and placed the phone back into her belly pack.

"Damn you, Jack!" she said aloud, not caring who heard her. She was tempted to go and tell the dark-haired woman inside the tent eating breakfast what Jack and Carl were up to, but knew Anya understood their actions far better than she ever could. Anya Korvesky had too much Israeli intelligence still wracking her brain to totally side with her.

Sarah McIntire didn't want to return to camp the same way she got to the dunes. She would take the long way around as she tried to think this thing through. Jack and Carl, along with the leadership of the Event Group, were now obsessed with finding the Russian entity designed after their own group for the murders of close to three hundred Russian sailors. This mysterious Russian group was a part of a whole—a whole that included a shadow government that had secretly taken over after the fall of communism inside Russia. This group was the puppet master running things, and now the idiot heroes, from the President on down to the higher chain of command of Department 5656, was hotly chasing the truth down with little or no help from the disbelieving C.I.A. and F.B.I.. Sarah was angry that she was now a secondary concern to Jack and she was hating it. She knew the difference between love and hate were so close they resembled each other. She also knew Jack Collins loved her, but with equal ferocity he hated the mysterious Russian entity even more for their murder of innocent Russian sailors and their officers.

As she entered a deep depression between two very large sand dunes, Sarah's boot struck something in the sand. She fell face first into the warming earth and that was when she couldn't help but scream. The eyeless skull was looking right at her. She tried her best to scramble up and away from the skeletal remains, but something had wrapped itself around her foot and she was held in place.

Sarah pulled her leg back, and finally whatever had her by the ankle relented its hold. Her eyes widened when she saw what it was that had grabbed her. She again yelped in shock when she saw that the skeletal hand, and most of the arm, was still holding her boot. She scrambled backward until two strong arms hastily picked her up. She thrashed her leg forward and back and finally the arm and hand came free to fly away into the dune next to the grinning skull.

"Whoa, looks like the restroom facilities were already spoken for," Commander Jason Ryan said as he saw the horror of what was buried in the sand.

"God, I feel like such an idiot," Sarah said as she reached down and felt her ankle just above her boot.

They were soon joined by Anya Korvesky and the others after they, along with Ryan, heard Sarah's scream. The remaining six-member field team, minus Charlie Ellenshaw, gathered around the partially buried remains. All stood staring at the find, with the exception of the five Mongolian guides. They were gathered in a group at the top of the dune just looking on silently at the scene below. They stared down upon the circle of geologists, not moving. Sarah noticed this, and was curious as they spoke quietly amongst themselves high above them. She turned her attention back to her unsavory discovery.

Ryan and Anya exchanged looks of wonder as Professor Anderson and Doctor Lee Hong knelt by the sleeve that used to cover the skeleton's arm. Sarah watched as Professor Anderson started brushing away some of the sand, careful not to disturb the find directly.

"Is it Mongolian?" Professor Birnbaum, the large Australian, asked from the circle of curious scientists.

"If it is, it's larger than a normal native." Doctor Lee moved away about five and half feet and started brushing away more sand. "Here's the feet. And unless the Mongols wear American made boots, this is not a local indigenous person."

They all saw the dark brown boot that was attached to the right foot.

"I'll get the guides to bring down some marker flags to make a perimeter around the remains. We'll treat this as an archaeological site for the time being," the Australian said.

"Good idea," Anderson agreed as he winked at Sarah, who was at the moment feeling silly for acting like a frightened school girl.

Professor Louis Birnbaum, the large Australian Professor of geology, turned and looked up at the dune where the Mongolian guides had been, but the dune was empty. "I'll be buggered. Where did our guides go?" he asked as everyone looked up at the empty space where the native guides had been. Ryan and Anya again exchanged looks. This time it was one of warning they both felt at the sudden disappearance of the Mongol guides.

"I'll get the marker flags," Anya said. She wanted to get to the tent and retrieve the firearms she and Ryan had hidden inside a large spectrometer. The major left the circle of onlookers and went to the tents to retrieve the flags and a little insurance.

At that moment, they all heard the sound of one of their Range Rover trucks speeding away. They watched on as their guides hurriedly left the strange scene.

"Hey!" Anderson screamed, waving his arms as the Range Rover sped away across the sand.

"What in the hell was that all about? Bloody wankers!" the Australian chimed in.

Anya returned from the campsite out of breath. "They took all of the communications gear!"

"For our last day on-site, this has decidedly turned a different color of weird," Professor Anderson said.

The morning had grown chilly as the sun rose near to mid-morning. The group of six geologists looked around, but no one was smiling.

"Well, shall we see what spooked our native contingent so bad they felt they had to steal one of our Rovers?" Anderson said as he and Sarah both went to a knee to examine the makeshift burial site.

Sarah reached for the forearm and hand that had attached itself to her ankle. She gingerly picked it up and looked it over. She gently pulled a shiny item from the wrist of the arm.

"Timex," she said as she reached up and handed the wristwatch to Jason Ryan, who examined it.

"Professor," Ryan said as he lowered the Timex wristwatch, "check the sleeve of that jumpsuit, would ya?"

"I'll be buggered," Louis Birnbaum said as he easily brushed away a good portion of golden sand. "Look at this," he said as he straightened from his kneeling position.

The material was sun damaged and worn through in places but still attached. It was the patch that stood out on the right shoulder of the gray coveralls. The cartoonish chicken had boxing gloves on and a cigar in its beak. The patch was round and embroidered. The only indication of its designation was the 'Fighting 40th' stitched at the bottom of the round patch beneath the image of the chicken.

Sarah, looking momentarily at Jason, moved to the skeletal remains. As militarily trained as they, Anya suddenly knew what it was they suspected. Sarah leaned over and approximated where the other shoulder would be and brushed the sand away. She looked from the second patch to gaze up at the others standing around her. Her eyes found Ryan.

"Now how in the hell did he get all the way out here in the damn Gobi Desert?" Jason asked no one in particular.

The group of scientists took in the patch and they were confused as to its significance. The golden star with the large capital 'A' with green colored wings was the famous patch worn by all U.S. Army Air

Corps aviators during World War II. Sarah brushed away more sand and saw the silver captain's bars on the collar of the overall near the remains of the spine and neck bones.

Sarah stood up and glanced around the emptiness of the Gobi. She felt eyes on them but for the life of her she didn't know from where.

"A captain from the 40th Bomb Group. That unit hasn't existed since the end of World War II," Sarah said as she continued to look around their surroundings with a bad feeling creeping into her bones.

"And how would you know that, Tiny?" Anderson asked with a serious look as he continued to gently wipe sand away from the remains.

"Uh, I have a boyfriend, or used to have one, that's kind of a history buff, mostly military." Sarah looked at Anderson and saw that he wasn't concerned if her explanation was a lie or not.

It was Professor Lee that gently reached into the collar and pulled out the round objects that were still attached to the chain. He pulled the 'dog tags' free and looked them over.

"Krensky, Everson, Captain," Lee said as he handed the dog tags over to Sarah.

"Well, I guess the least we can do is take the Captain home with us," Anderson said as he finally stood. "Let's get a blanket down here and get him out of this godforsaken sand. Whoever he was, he deserves better than this. We'll leave it to the Air Force to come up with an answer as to how he got here."

"Jason, we need to find Charlie. He's been gone since before dawn. He said he wanted to do some digging around the base of the mountain before we abandon this place."

Ryan looked at Anya and shook his head. "That damn lost city of his again. How can Crazy Charlie bring himself to argue with every geological survey satellite in the world and still think there is some ancient city buried out here. Jesus, sometimes he pushes things a little too hard. I'll find him."

As the uneasy geologists bent to the task of assisting Anderson in removing the long lost American aviator, Ryan moved off to search the area for the missing Ellenshaw. Sarah placed the dog tags around her own neck and then helped with the recovery.

The three members of the Department 5656 personnel knew in their gut, from their many experiences with the Event Group, that something strange was awaiting them, and as usual it wouldn't be good.

With the exception of Ryan calling out the name of Charlie in his search for the crazy cryptozoologist, the desert around the group had become preternaturally quiet.

Event Group Complex,
Nellis Air Force Base, Nevada

THE MOST AMAZING FACT ABOUT THE COMPLEX, WHICH WAS constructed during the years of 1941-45, were the vaults that housed the world's greatest archeological finds. Each were one-foot thick solid stainless-steel and were protected by the most complex A.I. computer system ever created—Europa. Her number one priority at the complex was to protect the secrets hidden there. The complex itself was secondary and was relegated to the human staff that worked security. This daunting task had since fallen to the second generation of security personnel that had been trained by the most influential duo in the history of special operations—Colonel Jack Collins and Captain Carl Everett, army and navy respectively. The man chosen to replace them in their absence, Major William Mendenhall, was not too happy about his recent promotion, nor the duties that promotion entailed.

Mendenhall felt alone in a complex that housed the most influential minds in the nation. With Collins and Everett on assignment, and Jason Ryan off galivanting through Mongolia with Sarah, Anya and Crazy Charlie, Will was left to ponder if this was his future—a future that required him to stay stateside while the rest of the security department went out on field assignments. He had a horrid feeling that would be the case.

He sat at the same desk that Jack Collins had occupied for the past twelve years, and it was that act alone that made him uncomfortable in his new settings. He had noticed the way in which men and women he had served with for the past many years didn't joke with him as they had before. They confided in Ryan far more now than himself. He was now higher management and that just wasn't sitting well with the newly promoted Major. After going from enlisted man to officer, and after endless hours in the officers training courses set up by the Colonel, Mendenhall had earned the respect from everyone in the Event Group Complex. Now he sensed that respect was born out more of fear than friendship over his new duties.

Will shook his head and started the endless paperwork his new job called for. He glanced at the roster and saw that a good portion of the security department was out on field assignments. The need for more security was a result of learning about the Russian black operations group in Siberia, who had a deep cover department attached to the hidden section that mirrored their own Event Group charter. He read the personnel reports of previous weeks and had concluded that enough of his personnel were on assignment that they had kept on the security department retirees to replace those at Gates one and two. The new policy was handed down by Director Compton. Every field excursion was now under very close scrutiny by the military element inside Department 5656 due to the bad guys knowing that the Event Group existed, something that had never officially occurred before the *Simbirsk* mission the prior month.

He checked off the names that were unavailable to the complex. The last name was that of Jason Ryan, who was in Mongolia serving with Sarah McIntire's field operation in assisting the Chinese government's bid to gain the mineral riches of the barren landscape of the northern region—Mongolia, after the devastating attack by the Grays in Beijing that destroyed most of the city and three quarters of their economy. He was well aware that the mission was not what was advertised. Sarah and the others were there to see what the strange readings were about that was uncovered by *Boris* and *Natasha*.

"Damn you Ryan, leave me here while you have fun in the field? Well, just wait until you get back, asshole, you're going on vault detail for a month, see if you like sitting on your ass."

"Talking to yourself is not a good habit to get into, Major. Group psychiatrists would have a field day with that."

Will looked up from the printed roster and saw Department 5656 Director Doctor Niles Compton leaning against the door frame watching him. Mendenhall started to stand but Niles waved him back down. Compton removed his hands from his pockets and the balding man entered and smiled at the startled Mendenhall.

"Have a minute?"

"How many minutes in a day?"

Niles smirked as he sat down in a chair facing the new commander of the Group's security arm. "Well, there are eighty-six thousand four-hundred seconds, and fourteen hundred and forty minutes."

"Is everyone out to make me feel stupid today?" Will shook his head. "I knew that. So, you asked if I had a minute, yes. I have four-teen hundred and forty minutes I can spare."

"That bad, huh?" Compton asked while he pushed his horned-rimmed glasses back up his nose as his smile grew. "When you've been cooped up in an office for as long as I have, you'll learn those numbers by heart."

"What can I help you with, Sir?" Mendenhall asked as he stood with a wary eye on the director and went to a filing cabinet and placed the daily roster inside. He turned back and then sat and waited for another terrible and boring part of his new duties to be announced.

Before Compton could answer, Virginia Pollock, assistant director for Department 5656, stepped into the outer security office and made her way to the private office of the security director. She tapped on the door and Niles waved her inside.

"What's up?" she asked as she went toward the pot of old coffee, smelled it, wrinkled her nose and then faced Niles. "We're having a hell of a time installing that damn electron microscope down in nuclear sciences, and that bull of a man's engineering department is no help. The Master Chief is really chafing my ass. So, again, what's up?"

"Your guess is as good as mine," Niles said. "Doctor Morales called my office and asked if he could meet privately with you, Will and myself. Said it had to do with something he didn't want to bring up in the morning's daily brief."

"Mysterious," Mendenhall quipped.

"Come to think of it, Xavier looked a little morose this morning. His comp center report was a little boring to say the least," Virginia offered.

"Yeah, when he doesn't brag about some new feature of Europa, or how he and that box of circuits and diodes may have saved the world, something just may be wrong."

Niles sat down as he listened to the endless possibilities of Xavier's circumstance from Virginia and Mendenhall.

They sat silently when the speculation dwindled. Will was feeling a little uncomfortable with the total amount of brainpower sitting in his office. Finally, he saw motion in the security bullpen. It was Morales. He slowly wheeled his non-electric wheelchair into the security office, not even looking up as two of the security men nodded and said good morning to him. He came to the door and after a few hesitant seconds, knocked on the frame. He wheeled in and looked from face to face and then slowly closed the door.

"Thank you for meeting me here. I figure no one voluntarily likes coming in here, so we should be undisturbed." The small man lowered his head and placed his hand over his face. After a moment, he looked up with tears in his eyes. He reached under one of his thin legs and pulled out a sheet of paper. He handed it to Niles who scanned it. His brows rose over his thick, horned-rimmed glasses, and then folded the note and fixed Xavier with a stern look.

"Resignation?"

Both Virginia and Will looked at Niles as he made no further comment.

"Did you and Europa have a lover's spat?" Will joked, and then quickly saw his humor was somewhat out of place.

"Yes, I don't deserve my post," Morales said without looking up.

Niles had seen this reaction before from men and women inside the group that had done something they weren't too proud of. He gave Xavier space. He had learned in his past experiences to allow the guilt of that person to tell the story.

"I may have assisted in getting two of our people into some deep trouble."

Niles reached into his shirt's front pocket, and behind his ever-present six pens there, pulled out a folded sheet of paper. "Does it have something to do with three communications packages from Jack and Carl that were not listed on Europa's field team communications log?"

Mendenhall looked at Morales and saw a barely perceptible nod of his dark hair.

"Colonel Collins contacted me five days ago and requested two Canadian passports for he and Captain Everett, and I was instructed to list them as farm equipment reps. So, Europa fixed them up with John Deere product catalogues and sales rep paperwork and the Canadian I.Ds." He stopped and wiped his eyes. Mendenhall stood and got a bottle of water from the small refrigerator and uncapped it, handing it to Xavier. Morales nodded his thanks and then took a long pull. He sat the bottle on the front of Will's desk and then fixed Niles with his wet and reddened eyes. "He said they had a lead on that Russian, the arrogant man we met on the *Nimitz* after the *Simbirsk* mission."

Will remembered. "You mean that strange old man, that Doctor Leoniv Vassick, the head of the organization that mirrors our own Group?"

"Yes. They said while they were in the Ukraine on their authorized part of their mission to gather intel on this Group, they received a hot lead that Vassick was in Thailand on business. What sort of business the Russian was there for, the Colonel didn't know. They said the Director would only worry and that the request was theirs and theirs alone. I sent them the two Canadian passports and other forged material to the Marriott in D.C."

"Jack and Carl pulled the old, *'Pete Golding did it for us all the time maneuver'*, I suppose?" Virginia asked with a knowing look toward Niles who was sitting silent.

Xavier could only nod his head.

"What went wrong?' was all Compton asked, with his face a growing mask of concern.

"Excuse me, Major, is your terminal on?" Will nodded that the Europa link was indeed on. "Europa, display Colonel Collins and Captain Everett's transponder coordinates on the main viewer in security, please."

All sets of eyes went to the large fifty-two-inch screen on the wall of the office.

"Current location for Colonel Collins is near Phnom Penh, Cambodia. The location for Captain Everett is currently 10°49'22.87"N, 106°37'46.74"E."

"These map coordinates are not in Thailand," Mendenhall said. "It's somewhere in southern Vietnam."

"*Correct, Major Mendenhall. Exactly twenty-two miles east of Ho Chi Minh City to be precise,'"* Europa corrected.

All eyes want to Morales once more. "Captain Everett and Colonel Collins have been separated." Morales again lowered his head, and this brought Niles Compton to life.

"Stop feeling sorry for yourself and start explaining what happened, or you're going to see a side of me that you wish you hadn't, Doctor."

Morales straightened in his wheelchair and then nodded determinedly. "Europa, display the last medical update on Captain Everett's transponder, please."

Europa didn't verbally respond. Instead she placed the last information available on Carl's location and medical transponder on the screen.

"My God," Virginia said as the data started scrolling across the monitor. For Mendenhall it was easier...his heart froze.

Virginia stood and approached the large screen and started running down the list. "Sudden drops in blood pressure, heart rate and respiration, and look at this, his brain activity output is barely perceptible. Is this all the data?" she asked, turning to face Xavier.

"He's hurt bad," Mendenhall said as his anger flared momentarily toward Morales.

"Europa, exact location for Captain Everett's transponder?" Morales continued.

"Coordinates are—"

"Just the name of location," Morales snapped.

It was the first time they had ever heard Morales lose his temper with Europa.

"Location...the town of Bin Hua, three hundred miles north of Ho Chi Minh City."

"I checked earlier," Morales stated. "Bin Hua is a small fishing village on the Mekong River. Nothing but a bunch of clapboard houses and poor fishermen, at least as far as Europa can tell. Nothing extraordinary."

"Doctor, I have further classified information on Bin Hua from U.S. Army records in St. Louis."

"Continue," Niles said to Europa, not waiting for Xavier.

"The town of Bin Hua was a cooperative entity in the battle of Ang Nah. The villagers assisted United States Army Special Forces in eliminating drug trafficking along the Ho Chi Minh Trail in 1972, a month before the withdrawal of American forces from South East Asia. It is still considered by the present-day Vietnamese anti-drug forces as a current trade route of heroin smuggling coming in from Cambodia, Laos and Thailand."

"Thank you," Niles said. He stood and placed his thick arms behind his back and paced as he thought. "In the presidential brief delivered by the FBI fifteen days ago, they stated Russian money and influence from illicit drug trafficking could be a financial resource for organized crime figures in Russia. The C.I.A. claimed it was possibly a drug cartel in the old Soviet Republic. But now I see it may turn out to be a possible way in which an illegal regime could launder money and smuggle it back into Russia without much notice. The shadow regime could be using drugs as a money scheme they can hide adequately."

"You think that Jack and Carl figured this was the lead, or was it just for this Doctor Leoniv Vassick?" Mendenhall asked, a bit ahead of Virginia's thinking.

"Perhaps both," Niles said. He suddenly stood rigid and then wadded up the resignation letter from Morales and tossed it back to the wheelchair bound doctor. "Resignation not accepted...at this time. I'm afraid you have a lot of work to do and a short time to do it in."

Morales took the balled-up scrap of paper and then nodded his head sadly at the director.

"Will, get as much information as you can on this small village. Europa may be able to fill you in a lot more with precise questioning. Get all the human intelligence that you can on the area. There's only one person here with the experience and knowledge of the area in question as far as I know."

"Don't tell me—" Will started to say as he froze after standing.

"Get with Master Chief Jenks. He's the only man who had actual duty near there during the war, he was just a kid SEAL, but he may have some thought as to the situation. He can get into detail about the people and who we may be able to trust."

"Good luck getting him to reminisce," Virginia added.

"If he gives you a problem, come and get me. I guarantee you he will be cooperative," Niles said with the most severe look on his features that any of them had ever seen. "Xavier, I want Captain Everett's condition and exact location immediately. If his transponder moves, track it. I don't care if you have to break into the Communist national assembly computer files in Hanoi to do it. Get me that info."

"Yes, sir," he said, grateful to be doing something.

"Virginia, you have the toughest job. Do whatever it takes, find me Colonel Farbeaux as fast as you can."

"Henri? What in the hell for?" she asked, stunned. "He won't assist us. We called his marker to the Group as closed after he helped us in the Atlantic last month."

"Find him, he's the only man we know with connections in Vietnam. The relations between our two countries are getting friendlier, but I don't think the government there would take too kindly if they found out an entity of the United States has reinvaded their country. We need Henri to get Mendenhall and the Master Chief in there to get our people out. Check out Monte Carlo, Henri likes to hide there."

"Okay, I'll look, but don't expect Colonel Farbeaux to come running," Virginia concluded.

"Also, Xavier, get me an exact location of Colonel Collins and most importantly, and I hate to drag him in on this, but contact Sergeant Van Tram. He's in Vietnam's 2nd Special Forces Element. He assisted us during the war with the Grays, both in South America and in the Antarctic. He knows and loves Jack. Find him and covertly, and I mean covertly, explain what's happening. If you're not cloaked in black on this, you could very well get Van Tram killed by his own people."

Xavier did not wait, he wheeled out of the office, anxious to do something, anything.

Compton went silent as he pursed his lips. "I'll fill in the President, we may need his help." He turned and faced Mendenhall and Virginia. "You two, find my people!"

They both watched as the Director left the security office.

"I haven't seen him this angry in years," Will said watching Compton's retreating form.

"That's not anger," Virginia corrected.

"Then what is it?"

"For the first time ever, you're seeing Niles Compton scared."

CHAPTER TWO

Gobi Altai Mountains, Mongolia

As the echo of Jason Ryan's calls dwindled to almost nothing in his search for Charlie Ellenshaw, Sarah, Anya, Professor James Anderson, James Lee Hong, and the Australian Professor Louis Birnbaum, eased the skeletal remains of the Army Air Corps flier onto the stainless-steel table. After the skeleton was found, their anxiousness to leave the barren desert flared brightly in all remaining members. Most didn't want to be around the body of the American flier any more than they had to.

"Poor bastard," Anya said as she bit her lower lip and studied the remains. "So far from home for so long."

"My World War Two history may be a little lax, but I do believe the Americans did have a campaign to bomb the Japanese and their Chinese partners in Manchukuo, or Mongolia. Manchukuo was a puppet state of the Empire of Japan in Northeast China and Inner Mongolia from 1932 until 1945 with the deposed emperor on the throne. That's as far as my history goes, I'm afraid," Professor James Anderson offered.

"Okay, that still doesn't help us to understand why this poor bastard is all the way out here in the east. The only valuable resource to bomb out here is sand and rock," Sarah said as she reached down and lightly touched a small leather bag still strapped to the torso of the remains.

"Well, I'm sure this man's family back in the States will be grateful for you bringing him back home," said Professor Lee. "Our most prioritized mystery at the moment is, what happened to our Mongolian guides. Even with them in our company this is still a very dangerous place. The locals," he looked out of the open tent flap, "although we haven't seen any, are still very hostile to outsiders."

"Maybe he has more information in here," Sarah said as she lightly fingered the tie-down strap to the leather satchel. She eased it open and then reached inside. Her fingers felt the loose sand inside and then they touched something solid. She withdrew her petite hand and saw that she was holding a small nugget of stone, which had silverish and green streaks of color. She held the small rock up to the light and then handed it over to Professor Lee. "Have you ever seen anything like this? What is the green material, mold?"

The smallish Lee took the sample and examined it. "It looks like silver ore. This," he said rubbing his fingers together after touching the green section of rock, "I have no clue. It's solid and definitely not mold. The flier must have thought it valuable enough to take from this place, but I see nothing valuable in its current state." He handed the ore over to the Australian. He just shook his head negatively and handed the stone back to Sarah.

"He has about a pound of it in here," she said as she pulled out four more small samples.

Anya was sorting through the ragged coveralls of the old flier. She pulled out three two-dollar bills, which elicited smiles from the small group. Next came a Swiss Army knife that was folded up and placed in a front pocket. She easily removed the shoulder holster and the rusted-out Colt .45 from the fraying leather. Then she suddenly stepped back. She swallowed, and pointed at the broken shaft sticking out from the skeletal remains of the pilot. The Australian pulled the shaft free of the fourth rib bone on the pilot's right side. He held it up. It was an arrow. The large man looked around at the others and then placed the iron arrowhead on the table next to the body.

"Well, I guess we now know the cause of death," he said.

"Professor Lee, as far as you know, did the locals still use bows and arrows in the forties?" Anya asked.

"Not that I am aware of. I do know the Japanese had a hard time in this region. But from my understanding, they faced just bullets, not this," he said as he waved his hand over the arrowhead.

Professor Birnbaum took a small piece of the ore from the table and tried to break a sliver off. It came free easily. "Well, it's not particularly a strong material. It breaks off like obsidian." He moved the small sliver over to a gas lamp and held it just outside of the chimney for a closer look. The others watched the geologist as he examined it. As he did so, the flame surged through the glass chimney and the fire licked at the small sample of ore, actually bending the flame toward the nugget.

Before anyone realized what had happened, the interior of the large tent came alive with a bright flash. The small sliver of ore became extremely hot as the Australian held it up to the gas light. Then it flared and shot from his fingers, tearing into his flesh. Before he could even yelp at the suddenness of the reaction, the sliver shot forth, slammed into the steel table, and then shot right through it and into the tent's nylon floor. From there it burned its way through and into the sand. The ground erupted as the initial contact had not slowed down the exploding sliver at all. Finally, all was silent with the exception of Birnbaum hissing out his pain.

The four scientists and an astonished Anya stood around the table in wide-eyed amazement. Sarah broke the spell when she reached out and slapped the remaining ore samples from the table as they lay next to the gas lamp.

"I think we better examine the rest under a battery powered light next time," Sarah said as she hurriedly placed a handkerchief around the middle and index fingers of Professor Birnbaum.

"I have never seen anything like that in my life," Birnbaum said as he nodded his thanks to Sarah.

"Jesus, look at this bloody thing," Professor Anderson said. He had his finger in the hole made by the sliver when it had shot from the large Australian's fingers and into the steel table. The hole it made was ten times the size of the sliver itself. "If I didn't know any better, I would have said that hole had been made by a .357 Magnum."

"We need to find out where this ore came from," Sarah said as she carefully picked up the five samples from the tent's flooring. "There is nothing like this reaction ascribed to any ore in the world."

"Maybe its properties have been enhanced by some form of refining," Anya offered.

Sarah held a piece up and looked closer. "No, this is unrefined ore. Whatever caused that reaction is fundamental to its raw state."

"Whatever this is, our Air Corps Captain thought it important enough to take. According to his satchel, it looks like he possibly chose those samples over food and water," Sarah said as she had a hard time coming to grips with men and their take on what was important.

"Or maybe he exhausted his supply of water and food. That would mean he had traveled quite a way from where he found this remarkable material," Lee inserted.

"Maybe," Sarah agreed. "I'd like to try something," she said as she picked up another small piece of ore. "Professor, hand me that coffee cup, please." Birnbaum handed over the tin cup. Sarah placed the cup upside down on the steel table next to the worn leather boots of the old flier. "Professor, get another cup and put a small amount of lamp kerosene inside."

"You're not going to do what I think you are...are you?" Anya asked as she stepped away from the table until her backside was touching the far wall of the tent.

Sarah didn't answer, but she did warn everyone to join Anya against the far wall of the tent. She dribbled a line of kerosene from the cup leading to the one she had placed upside down on the table adding one final drop of flammable fluid to the underside of the cup.

She handed the fuel off to the Australian and then she scraped a few shards of the ore off with her fingernail. The amount was virtually infinitesimal and hard to see at all. She then placed the shards under the overturned cup. She removed the glass chimney from the lamp and then with a warning and worried look at the others, she lowered the flame to the line of kerosene and struck the fuel. In a flash, the kerosene ignited and ran toward the cup. Nothing. Sarah was just about to give up on her small-scale experiment when the cup suddenly exploded upward in a blinding light of exhaust. The cup moved so fast and with such velocity that it shot through the top of the nylon tent and vanished into the blue sky high above the Gobi.

Anya saw Sarah and yelped out her concern. Sarah was on her ass and her hair was singed. Her face had smooth gray ash covering it and her eyes were as wide as saucers. Anya, along with Lee and Birnbaum assisted Sarah to her unsteady feet. Once they were all around the table again, they saw the large hole in the table's top, the missing lower leg of the skeleton and the totally bent frame of the steel examination table. As one, their eyes traveled up to the top of the tent and saw the hole there. It was Sarah who laid voice to the word they were all thinking.

"Wow!"

JASON RYAN TOPPED THE SMALL RIDGE AS HIS LAST CALL FOR CRAZY Charlie Ellenshaw was still echoing off the base of the mountains. Of all the places in the world for Ellenshaw to go wandering off, he had chosen one of the most dangerous terrains on the planet. The Gobi Desert, and the mountains that hemmed the great plains in, was different than any desert in the world. Compasses at times refused to work due to the magnetism of the surrounding rock. Mountains that seemed to move in the darkness of night, and the sands that covered massive holes in the desert that could swallow an entire division of soldiers without a trace. And the main fact has always been and will remain so for a thousand years—most Mongolians picked this particular area of the Gobi to avoid. The Mongol people, as they were throughout recorded time, feared little, but this part of their desert frightened them far more than any area of their desolate country.

Jason stood with hands on hips and saw the barren landscape and all the areas where Ellenshaw could be hurt or injured. His only thought was that he was going to strangle to death the man with the crazed white hair and wire-rimmed glasses. He removed his sunglasses and scanned the area directly beneath the drop off when a sudden noise caught his attention. As he turned back to examine the way he had just come, Jason was shocked to see a small fireball rise into the sky and vanish high into the cumulus clouds that had gathered in the valley. He was still watching the trail of heat and smoke as it vanished. The epicenter, of whatever it had been, seemed to come from the area of the geological campsite. As curious as he was at the sight, Sarah hadn't called him on his walkie-talkie, so he assumed they were alright. Besides, if he returned without Ellenshaw, Sarah and Anya would be the ones doing the strangling.

He replaced the sunglasses to cut down on the glare of the moving air. "Charlie!" he called out and then waited for the echo of his voice to die down.

"With the echo effect, I had a hard time pin-pointing where you were at," came a voice immediately behind Ryan.

Ryan jumped almost out of skin. "Damn it, Doc, you scared the crap out of me!"

"Sorry, Commander. This place *is* a little eerie, isn't it?" Charlie stated as he looked around the barrenness of the land.

Jason shook his head at the garb Ellenshaw insisted on wearing. Ryan could handle the short khaki pants and the black socks sticking out from his brown boots, but the Pith helmet he wore was ridiculous. Crazy Charlie had obviously watched one too many Tarzan movies in his youth.

"Doc, where in the hell did you get that funky-ass helmet?"

Ellenshaw removed the Pith helmet and then looked it over. "It was issued to me by Logistics at the Group," he said, confused as to the comment on his headgear.

"Doc, next time you go and get equipment issued, come to me or

Mendenhall before accepting. I think those pencil pushers down in the Logistics Department are having a little fun at your expense."

"Really?" Charlie said as he continued to look at the helmet. "I was wondering why I was the only one wearing one." He shrugged his shoulders and then returned the helmet to his crazed looking hair and head.

"Come on, we've got to get back to camp. We're packing up and finally getting out of this Garden of Eden. Three quarters of the group has already left."

"I take it that you find the Gobi to be less than exhilarating, Commander."

"Doc, I've seen more excitement in an intensive care unit."

Charlie looked at Ryan with a curious look, as he didn't seem to grasp that Ryan wasn't enthused at all about being here.

"Anyway, it seems you've drawn a blank on your theory, Doc, just like Europa's on some mineral buried up here. We all make our mistakes." Ryan looked around and then his eyes went to the large mountain in front of them. "Doesn't look like there has ever been anything here, much less a lost city...what did you call it in your pitch to the Director? Oh, Shangri-La." Ryan smiled and shook his head, trying his best not to laugh at the cryptozoologist.

"It's been my theory that the legend of Shangri-La did not originate in Tibet, or even China as most believe, but right here in Mongolia. The director saw some merit in the theory...I believe."

"It couldn't have been that Doc Compton wasn't just humoring you some?"

Ellenshaw actually looked confused at the question. More to the point he looked hurt that Ryan would even suggest such a scenario. Jason saw this and slapped Crazy Charlie on the shoulder.

"Nah, the director wouldn't do that."

This seemed to give Charlie his faith in the world back. He perked up considerably. "Do you think we could talk Sarah into giving us a few more days in the area? I mean, it is a rare chance to examine the landscape inside a basically closed nation."

Ryan almost turned white at the suggestion of staying longer than was absolutely necessary. "Forget it, Doc. The eggheads down there didn't find their copper and zinc, nickel and other exciting ores, so they're done," he half turned away, "and frankly Doc, so am I."

Charlie slowly nodded his head.

"It's not like you to give up on a crazy theory that easy, what's up?"

"Well, I guess I had better show you. I was hoping to stay longer to investigate, but since you and Sarah are anxious to get back home, I have no choice." Ellenshaw reached into his front pants pocket and pulled out a small object. He held it out to Ryan.

The item looked like a brooch. Ryan accepted the object and ran a thumb over the center piece. "Jade?"

"Yes. Jade and gold. I believe it was a cloak bob."

"A what?" Jason asked.

"A brooch that held the collar edges for a cloak...okay, a cape. They were very popular when capes were all the rage."

"Okay, its nice, Doc, but a cloak bob isn't exactly the lost city of Shangri-La, is it?"

"See the writing along the leading edges and just above the Jade?" Ellenshaw asked as he leaned over Ryan's shoulder and pointed it out.

"I see, but don't understand it."

"Chinese, Commander. It's Chinese. From the first dynasty." Charlie saw the confusion in the small navy man's face. "Does the name Qin Shi Huang mean anything to you?"

"Maybe Huang's Chinese take-out in San Diego?" Ryan joked.

"Commander, he was the first sovereign ruler of China. The very first man named as Emperor, not king, but Emperor."

Ryan handed the brooch back to Ellenshaw. "That's great Doc, you found something some weary traveler lost ages ago. That will surely make Sarah see the light as far as extending the mission. She's already pissed Europa was wrong about something buried under the Gobi, so that means that Doctor Morales is bound to get a piece of her mind when she gets back along with you if you even suggest we stay longer. She wants to get back to check on the Colonel and Mr. Everett."

He could see that Ellenshaw took it personally that he would request something that would anger Sarah. Jason saw that he had done it again. The hurt in the Doc's eyes was palpable.

"Look, you can't honestly have the opinion that there has ever been anything in this desert and mountain range larger than a hut used by Mongols. If there had been any city here at any time, *Boris* and *Natasha*, and a thousand other satellites would have found it by now. In recent years, the Chinese and the Russians have been pouring over this area looking for minerals. Your mythical city just isn't here, Doc."

"There we go again. The same areas in Tibet and deep China are also examined by the finest scientific minds in the world, and no lost city has ever been found there either."

"Doc, come on, listen to yourself. They failed because a mythical city that has never been proven to exist has yet to be discovered? The reason is the mere fact that Shangri-La has never existed in Tibet or here. Come on. It's a fanciful tale, Doc, but as far as I can see, that's all it is."

"I...I...," he stammered.

"Okay, let's go show Sarah your find and we'll let her tell you no. If it were up to me, Doc, we could vacation here all spring, but alas it's not up to—"

The rocks they stood upon vanished beneath their feet. The next feeling both men had was the sensation of falling.

To set up the experiment they had to use the heaviest piece of equipment they had—an anvil used to break apart ore samples. It was close to two hundred pounds of weight. Next, Sarah had arranged the experiment to be conducted outside the tent for obvious reasons. With the reluctant help of Professors Lee Hong and, a far more enthusiastic, James Anderson, they had cut a hole in the direct center of the stainless-steel table, and then Sarah had the Australian Professor Birnbaum use a small arc-welder to place two small steel cables, they had cannibalized from their weather balloon restraint system, from the anvil to a tin cup. Sarah then placed another sliver of the strange ore under the cup and then placed that over the small exhaust hole they had cut. It was Professor Anderson who insisted on recording the event. He joked that it was for legal purposes for their manslaughter trial over Sarah's untimely death. With that comment there were a few nervous chuckles from the group.

"What is the goal here?" asked a Chinese professor from Shanghai as he glanced around the empty campsite as if looking for someone.

"Hand me those night flares please," Sarah asked the Australian. She accepted the flares and then duct-taped them to the edges of the steel table. "We're going to see just how much power this ore has, and its potential speed. We have nothing here to measure velocity, so for now we just have to eyeball it. The flares will allow us to at least see the smoke trail and give us a ballpark figure on that velocity."

"This is why I don't like Carl hanging out with you people too much, you scare me with your knowledge, and scientific blind bravery," Anya said only half-jokingly.

Sarah smiled. "Yeah, Jack hates me too," Sarah answered, only she wasn't just half-joking and Anya saw that in the sadness of her eyes. "Okay, I would suggest we all get as far away as possible. It's my idea so I'll take the risk of blowing myself up."

On that point, the group of geologists decided that Sarah was absolutely right. They moved away a hundred feet.

"Well, if it works, at least it will act like a signal flare to anyone who sees it. Maybe the damn Mongolian guides will come back and guide us out of here," Birnbaum joked.

Sarah once more poured the line of kerosene from one end of the table to the anchored cup. She then pulled the plastic caps from the large flares and struck them to life. They gave off so much smoke that the table and experiment vanished momentarily. Then Sarah swallowed and looked back at Anya who nodded her head for encouragement as she confidently hid herself behind a large boulder. Sarah ignited the line of kerosene and then dove away and covered her head.

Again, it seemed as if the flame didn't do what was intended, and McIntire was just about to look up to find the problem, when the air became alive with power. The steel cables held. They tightened to piano string tightness and then the cup exploded from the steel table and into the air. The anvil went with it. It had gone so far out of sight that the observers were left wondering if the thing had just exploded into a million pieces of steel. It was Professor Birnbaum who saw the flares high in the sky and the barely perceptible line of smoke.

"Jesus Christ!" he exclaimed as he shielded his eyes.

"Its gone, just gone," Professor Anderson said as he watched and tried to keep his recording cell phone on the diminishing trail high above.

Sarah stood and brushed herself off. "Anya, you know speed somewhat, what would you guess the accelerated rate of climb might be?"

"Are you kidding? It took less time than the tick of a second hand for that damn thing to get higher than eighty thousand feet." She shook her head. "And that's just a guess."

"We have something here that could change the world," Sarah said as she turned to face the others. Her eyes held firmly on one man. The one holding the pistol in her direction.

"Is that standard issue at Temple University, Professor?" Anya asked when she also noticed the gun.

James Anderson was smirking. "No, but it is a must have item in my line of work."

"May we take it the real Professor Anderson is laying in a Beijing alley somewhere with a bullet in his head?" Sarah asked as the other scientists moved away from the gun toting imposter.

"Shot, stabbed, drowned, I don't go into instructive murder instruction with the enemies of my nation."

Sarah and Anya almost said too much simultaneously. They had a deep suspicion that this man worked for the same people and organization Jack and Carl were searching the world over for.

"Right at this moment, I don't care for any harshness with you people." With a weary eye on his captives, the man they knew as

Anderson looked at his watch and then pulled the smallest satellite phone they had ever seen from his back pocket and then pushed several buttons. There was static and then they heard the voice in the clear.

"You have reached the Captain, 04582. You have broken your field cover. This is unacceptable."

"The mission parameters have changed. A rather fortuitous event has taken place." Anderson saw Sarah move a hand toward her fanny-pack and the imposter impersonating Professor Anderson pointed the small .32 caliber pistol in her direction. He frowned and then moved toward her and reached into the pack and then his brows rose as he found Sarah's hidden Glock nine-millimeter pistol. He angrily placed the satellite phone between his shoulder and chin as he shoved her away. "I will download my visual report and await instruction. Sending video feed now." Anderson connected his cell phone to the larger satellite phone and then pushed a few buttons. "Transmission sent. I will await your orders." He lowered both phones and then pointed his pistol at Anya. "May I take it for granted that you are also armed, Major Korvesky?"

The other geologists with their hands in the air looked around in confusion. "Who in the bloody hell is Major Korvesky, mate?" Birnbaum asked.

The man posing as Anderson smiled as his eyes were still on Anya. "I'm afraid that I am not the only one posing as someone they are not. Would you care to explain that fact to these learned scholars, Major?"

Anya remained silent as all of the geologists save Sarah looked her way.

Anderson looked at the Australian. "She's former Mossad. I'm sure you have heard of their murderous exploits in defense of the Israeli nation?"

"Is anyone here actually who they say they are?" Birnbaum asked, looking from professor to professor.

Sarah lowered her eyes.

"Oh, come on?" Birnbaum said as he saw the guilt cross McIntire's face.

"Actually, Captain McIntire here is an actual geologist. But the Major, well, she's more in the framework of a professional killer."

"Captain McIntire?" Professor Lee Hong asked, shocked.

"Don't read too much into it," Sarah said as she kept her hands high in the air. "My government is here to assist in finding the resources the Chinese government needs to rebuild, nothing more."

"Maybe being straight forward in the beginning would be a good start," Lee said.

"Now, Comrade, what were your orders?" Anya asked as she eyed the chance at getting to her packed case and her own Glock.

"Simple. Keep an eye on you four," Anderson said as he made sure Anya knew he suspected her thoughts and moved the gun to point at her head. Anya deflated.

"Four?" Lee again asked. "There are four of you?"

"Yes, Professor Ellenshaw and our Commander Ryan. All here under a false flag of friendship," Anderson said with a smirk. "Now, speak of the devil, where are your two associates?"

Neither Sarah nor Anya said a word. Instead they were watching the sand dune just to the rear of the camp.

"I don't think our associates are your immediate concern, my Russian friend," Anya said as her eyes started counting.

The man impersonating Professor Anderson turned slightly and his heart froze. At least a hundred Mongolian tribesmen, none of them looking too friendly were there. They were all pointing what looked like AK-47's down into the camp. The Range Rovers stood behind them. Empty. There were no sign of the twelve scientists that had left camp earlier and their equipment had already been stripped from the vehicles.

"I think we just found out why our Mongol guides stole one of our Range Rovers, bloody thieves," Birnbaum said, as his attention went from being held at gunpoint by a Russian posing as one of them, to a hundred angry tribesmen who had obviously ambushed their colleagues somewhere in the desert on their return trip east.

"I should have known by the way they knew how to get here. These are Rangoli tribesmen. They are outlaws of the worst sort. Hated by all and loved only by their own murderous kind," Professor Lee said. "May I suggest you lower that weapon before these unimaginative people take offense."

Anderson did lower and then drop the small pistol as the one hundred brutal looking Mongolians advanced down into the camp of the invaders to their world.

Before Sarah knew what was happening, the satellite phone she had was ripped from her hand and smashed. When she was pushed to the ground and searched, her last thoughts were ones of hope that the signal she just sent made it out of the valley and that Jason and Charlie were high in the rocks watching them.

There *were* eyes watching. They just weren't the eyes of Ryan or Ellenshaw.

District Four, thirty miles Northwest of Ho Chi Minh City

THE BOY STRUGGLED WITH THE TWO-WHEELED FISH CART AS HIS sandaled feet fought with the uneven and cracked pavement that had turned into more or less a dirt road version of itself in very large spots. The grandfather assisted as much as he could by adding his meager weight to pushing the overflowing cart with his back to the wooden frame.

The cart maneuvered down the alley from a street where vendors sold everything from pork and chicken to fine examples of local jewelry making. The small town had been the service providers for the region since long before the war with the French and the Americans.

"This is good," the grandfather said as the cart was now far enough away from the other vendors that lined the street far to the front. The grandson eased the long handles of the cart to the filthy alley floor and then wiped his brow.

"I can't believe you, grandfather, throwing two days' worth of catch away for this American."

"If you cannot believe it, why dwell upon it?" the old man said as his eyes gazed upward at the row of apartments that seemed to be hidden away from the street by a dozen or more clothes lines stretched between the two buildings lining the alley. "I just hope the old fool is in."

"What old fool? Why did we not take this man to the village doctor instead of traveling for eight hours to this..." he looked around at the filth of the alley, "stinky hell hole?"

"As I said, this does not concern you. It is enough to say that I am paying back an old debt, and once that is done, so is my long obligation. Now, hand me that stone at your feet."

The boy did as his grandfather asked and tossed him the small rock. He watched as his grandfather looked around as if in great conspiracy and then raised the small stone up and tossed it up in the air. The boy heard the ping as it struck the window four flights up. The old man waited and nervously watched the street that was fifty yards away, and then looked at the passersby. He saw that no one granted the alley any special notice.

"I have heard many bad things about District Four, Grandfather. Is it true this is the place where all the war traitors are watched? That most of its citizens had to undergo reeducation training after the war?"

The old man ignored his grandson's questioning nature and then reached down for another, larger stone. Before he could raise the rock to throw once more at the window, the clothes that were hung out to dry parted with an angry swipe. The flow of Vietnamese curses came before the face was even visible through the parting wash.

"It has always amazed me, old friend, how fast and in inventive ways you come up with your foul language."

"Who is that, and why are trying your best to break my window? Do you know how hard glass is to come by around here?" The face in the dirty open window frame finally spied the two people below in the alley. "Oh, I thought you were that evil property owner of mine who I owe three months' rent to." The old face in the window finally changed expression as old memories flooded into his mind. "Is that you, Dai Mihn?" came the shrill voice. "Wait, I will come down."

The grandson finally joined the old man at the front of the cart, stopping momentarily to rearrange the fish in the cart so as to completely cover their strange cargo.

"Who is this man, Grandfather?" The boy nudged him and joked. "He's almost as old as you."

Dai Mihn only looked at the boy with no humor on his wrinkled features.

"I cannot believe it, are you still alive, my old friend?" came the voice from their left.

The grandfather lost the stern countenance on his face as he was greeted. "No, I am the ghost of better days here to escort you to your ancestors." He smiled broadly. "Thuyền trưởng, it is good to see you once more."

The two old men embraced, with the stranger hugging the boy's grandfather tight while patting him on the back. "No one has called me Thuyền trưởng in over forty years." The two men finally parted as they both had tears in their eyes.

"You will always be my Captain," Dai Mihn said as he held the man by his shoulders as they hugged once more. "I am glad to see that your reeducation did not kill you." They finally parted as the newcomer wiped the tears away.

The Nationalist reeducation program started after the downfall of Saigon in 1975. Many of the South Vietnamese army veterans were either executed for their wartime failure of vision or were sent to reeducation camps to learn how to be good communists once again. Many in the current government had learned the failure of that program and had since concluded that if you left people alone they would eventually follow of their own accord without 'reeducation' programs.

"I would not have survived it if my vital skills were not needed after the war."

"Yes, good doctors were hard to find. It does my heart and soul good to see you."

The man was named Hùng Quốc Vương. A former Captain and physician from the old South Vietnamese army. Dai Mihn had been his special protector on many operations around the old Ho Chi Minh Trail where north and south forces met in combat on many occasions.

"The funny thing is, the profession that saved me from many months of torture was not needed as badly as first thought. I am ashamed to say I have not practiced my arts since those darkest of days."

"Then my friend, I give you that opportunity this day. I need your help."

Hùng Quốc Vương looked from his old friend to the boy who stood silent as he learned about a mysterious life that had never been told to him by his parents, nor his grandfather.

"And who is this?" Hùng asked as he eyed the boy suspiciously.

"This is my grandson, he assisted me in finding you."

"To assist this old fool in this," the boy said, as he shoved a few of the large catfish and blue gill out of the way to expose the face of the American.

Hùng lost the color in his features. He looked from the face of the American to his oldest friend. He backed away from the cart.

"Why have you brought him here?"

"He needs your help. I could not have taken him to the local doctor, he is a true believer and would have turned him over to the authorities, and you know what they would do to him. He would have turned him over to the pigs that run our province. Children that don't understand the intricacies of our shared past. They would have imprisoned him. Until we learn why he was shot and thrown into the Mekong, he deserved a chance to at least tell us his story." Dai watched as the old doctor took in his excuse for possibly getting him shot for the charge of conspiring with a foreign element.

"Well, you have made a great error, my friend. Take him from here and put him back into the river. I need no part in this."

The old man lost his patience and then started to throw fish from the cart. He dug until he found the muscled arm of the American. He turned the wrist over to expose the forearm. The SEAL tattoo was easily visible even with the fish blood and foulness that covered it. Hùng looked from the tattoo to his old protector.

"Yes, you recognize the symbol, don't you?"

"Get that boy of yours and assist me in getting him into the apartment before someone sees us." He stopped as he reached for the body in the cart and looked at Dai. "This is not for you brother Dai, but for him," he said as he held up the filthy arm.

It took thirty long minutes to maneuver the large American up the rickety stairs of the apartment complex. There had been a few curious looks from neighbors, but Hùng's reputation as a surly old fool kept most seekers of curiosity at bay.

Dai and his grandson left the apartment and the grandfather instructed his grandson to set up on the street and to sell as much of the fish as possible to cut down on their losses. He returned just as Hùng finished wrapping the American's head with a semi-filthy gauze.

"Will he live?" Dai asked as he stood at the foot of the splintering cot.

"He is a big man. He has many old and deep scars upon him. Yes, he will survive. Two gunshots. One to the right side, just missing his liver. A graze to his right temple that would have slammed into his central lobe if it had been half an inch closer. And a knife wound to his abdomen. All grave, but survivable. Here," he handed Dai a small object, "you may find this of interest. This is the bullet I pulled from near his liver. You see something familiar?"

"It seems this is the same strange caliber bullet we came across a few times after battle with our Northern brothers. Russian?"

"Yes, a few of our officers had captured pistols such as this during the war. Believe me I took out many a bullet from soldiers on both sides, and I will never forget what pistol was used to deliver them."

A dawning of understanding crossed the old soldier's face. "A Russian made RSh-12."

"Yes, the most powerful handgun the Russian pigs make. And if this American had been shot by any other weapon, it would have lodged in his liver instead of just nicking it. But being as powerful as the bullet is, it just passed right through and lodged against his back bone, barely missing the spine. Luckily for this man, I was able to just cut to the skin and the bullet popped free."

Dai placed the bullet next to the head of the wounded man.

"I have given him all the antibiotics I had on hand, but infection could still kill him. As much as we both owe this group of soldiers, you may have to get him to the hospital. The American SEALs saved our lives many times, but I'm afraid I am out of practice in saving theirs."

Dai looked sad as he thought about turning over his charge to people that may or may not help him to survive. The two governments, both American and Vietnamese, may be getting closer in international relations, but they still had a way to go to quell old memories of a war long dead.

"If his fever grows worse, I will have no choice but to take him to the hospital," Dai finally admitted.

"No...hospital...no...hospital."

Both men looked at the prone American who was moving his bandaged head from side to side. Hùng went to the man's side and raised his wrist. His pulse was stronger than before, but still worrisome.

"You are near Ho Chi Minh City. Do you know who shot you? Was it government forces?" he asked as his eyes flicked over to Dai.

The man lay still for the longest time. Then one blue eye fluttered open. The left eye, still visible under the makeshift bandage, looked and then focused on Hùng.

"How long...how long..."

Dai Mihn stepped forward and looked down at the large man. "We found you in the river a day ago. We thought you dead," he said in broken English, a language he hadn't used since the war's end forty years before. "What is your name and your purpose being in a country you have no right to be in?"

The man moved his uncovered eye and it fixed on the old men, moving from one to the other. "I am...not...an enemy...of your people. My name is Captain Carl Everett. We...were here...tracking...tracking...a murderous Russian..." The words trailed off and then the eye opened once more and the American tried to keep it open. "Who...are...you?" he asked with great effort of will.

It was the old doctor who answered. "We are old friends of your country. From many, many years ago. We were a part of the ARVN during the war. We were of the 258th Marine Brigade, Special Operations Group attached to the 9th American Infantry Division. We worked very closely with your own organization." The doctor raised Everett's arm and rubbed a thumb over the fading tattoo. "Now, who was it that placed you in a very precarious position in a country that is slow on forgiveness?" He looked from Carl to Dai. "A Russian?"

They watched as the very large American swallowed. He tried to speak but held back as the memory came flooding back to him.

"No...no Russian. An...American." He closed his one eye as he tried to think a problem through.

"One of your own?" Dai Mihn asked, incredulous.

Both old soldiers exchanged looks of amazement. Evidently the Americans had not changed all that much since the war years. They were still as confusing as ever.

They watched the man named Everett slowly close his one eye as a single tear flowed down his grizzled cheek.

He whispered just one name as he lost consciousness—"Jack."

Event Group Complex,
Nellis Air Force Base, Nevada

VIRGINIA POLLOCK SAW NILES COMPTON AS HE ENTERED THE AIR-powered pneumatic elevator. She called out 'hold' as the director stopped the doors from closing. She stepped in and then waved two group paleontologists away who tried to join them. Both men saw the looks of angst on the two heads of Department 5656 and were more than happy to catch the next ride. The doors closed and the soft flow of air entering the system was near silent as the car shot downward into the complex.

"How did your conversation with the President go?" she asked.

Niles removed his horned rimmed glasses and rubbed the bridge of his nose.

"That bad, huh?"

"Yes, it was that bad. Not only won't the entirety of the intel community back the shoddy evidence we have on this Siberian group in Russia, most think the President has lost a nut. We just can't forward anything substantial about them for anyone to work out. Not even the navy, who witnessed these guys at sea, can convince anyone to listen to reason."

"That's not all that's worrying him, is it?" Virginia asked as she reached out and pushed the 'hold' button on the indicator panel. The elevator came to a silent stop. It never occurred to anyone in the complex that the one-ton elevator car was sitting in a tube with absolutely nothing securing it but pressurized air.

"He's near a breakdown. Both the senate and congress are on him about the expenditures for the war against the Grays. Now they're onto our plan to help the Chinese dig out of the hole they are in because of their war costs. We've got Senators digging into the war's intelligence and who came up with the *Overlord* plan, which of course—"

"Would lead to us," Virginia finished for him.

Niles replaced his glasses and then hit the button for level 'ten'. "We may be in for some tough times ahead in the election. Instead of the good man we have in office, we may be dealing with a budget hawk in Senator Lyle Lange." Niles looked at Virginia. "How do you think he'll feel about our little money absorbing agency?"

"You'll convince whoever is elected how important our work is."

Niles shrugged as the elevator came to a silent stop. "I need the President to guide me on this." He stepped out of the car with his head down. "Come with me so I can get an update on Doctor Morales' progress without me biting the boy's head off."

They walked down the curving, plastic lined hallway and stopped outside of the cleanroom doors. The Marine guard came to attention and Compton waved him to 'at ease'. He paused before placing his thumb on the glass fingerprint reader.

"Look, you do the talking. I was much too hard on the kid this morning."

"You're just worried about Carl and Jack. I'm sure Xavier understands. He's just about to lose his mind for the role he played in their present circumstances."

Niles placed his thumb on the I.D. reader and the doors hissed open. "By the way, how did Mr. Personality take his orders to accompany Will to South East Asia?"

They both entered the cleanroom and then started placing the paper protectants over their clothes, shoes and heads.

"Oh, he cursed, threw a few things, but calmed down when I explained the situation."

"Calmed?" Niles asked.

"Well, for the Master Chief it was calm. We have to replace his office door window."

Compton opened the automated doors to the interior cleanroom and entered with Virginia close behind. "Make sure the cost of the window comes out of his pay."

Virginia smiled and said nothing as they approached Xavier Morales who was concentrating so hard with Europa that he failed to see them enter the cleanroom.

The Cray computer's protective core doors were open, and both Virginia and Niles watched as the 'bubble' memory system that drove the Cray 'Blue Ice' system was in full swing. They could see that Doctor Morales was pushing the system to its limits. The three thousand clear glass tubes were multi-colored and were in full activation as some bubbles rose and others fell. The large bubbles rising were programs being utilized by the paraplegic computer genius and the ones falling to the bottom of the eighty-five-foot tubes were programs that had already been used and were in the process of being stored.

"You cannot tell me that!" Xavier said into the microphone at his station. There were places for five other personnel at the long table facing the massive computer system. Xavier was all alone. Whenever he was pressed for time, the good doctor always worked alone, much like their old friend and deceased member of Department 5656, Pete Golding.

"Regardless, Doctor, the tracking device is not currently emitting a trackable signal."

Morales slammed his palm against the table's top at the Marilyn Monroe voiced response. "There has to be a reading one way or the other. If the Colonel is dead, we should be able to see his vitals. It's a nuclear-powered device, for Christ's sake!"

"Still can't trace Jack?" Virginia asked as she pulled out a rolling chair and sat.

Morales jumped at the suddenness of the enquiry. "Doctor Pollock, I'm sorry, I didn't see you there." Morales turned and that was when he saw the director leaning against the wall watching them. "Director...I, uh...," he stammered.

"Continue, Doctor," was all Niles added.

"Europa, display Captain Everett's trace parameters please," he said as he rubbed his eyes.

On the clear glass window facing them and separating them from Europa's brain systems, a hologram appeared on the thick glass. The numbers and icons were all green and blue in color.

"As you can see, Captain Everett's vitals have improved. I think maybe he's gained some form of consciousness. Heart, respiratory and brain activity has been steadily improving over the past three and a half hours. Still no location for the Colonel," Xavier said and then turned toward the glass. "Europa has yet to locate him," as if accusing her in a sarcastic tone of voice.

"You've been able to pinpoint the Captain's precise location?" Virginia asked.

"Europa, display the area of Captain Everett's current location."

The hologram changed and then a street map of Ho Chi Minh City stretched across the glass. In the far upper right corner, a small red blip appeared and then the map changed to bring that area into close detail.

"The area is called, unofficially of course, 'traitors alley'. District four in the city. Most residents there were of the Southern persuasion during the war years. Europa surmises that this area may be the only part of South East Asia that could possibly help the Captain if only for old time's sake. His transponder readings and improving health may bear that theory out."

"Doctor Morales, I have picked up a trace signal from Colonel Collins' transponder. It is very weak."

Xavier brightened and sat up immediately. "Location?"

"Current location is approximately one hundred and thirty-two kilometers from Ho Chi Minh City. The Laos province of Hai Lap Hue. Current evaluation of health is unclear. The transponder appears to be moving north toward Cambodia."

"Damn it," Niles said as he began his usual pacing when thinking.

"What is it?" Virginia asked.

"The damn Golden Triangle is what it is. Most of the world's heroin comes from there. In other words, it's not the safest place for Jack to be, especially without any form of backup."

"One thing is for sure, if he knew Carl was alive he never would have left him hurt and lost," Virginia said.

Niles stopped his pacing, much to the relief of Xavier and Virginia. "Okay, Xavier, I want to clear the board of all operations in Asia for the time being. The furthest out I believe is Captain McIntire's team in Mongolia. Their field report says that Europa was mistaken in her evaluation of the satellite images. So, bring them out, now."

"Sarah's team is currently awaiting pickup for their return home," Virginia offered.

"Don't wait for their scheduled pickup. Get an Air Force aircraft in there now. I want Ryan to join with Will's team when they land in Vietnam. They'll need him."

"Europa, let's give Captain McIntire a heads up."

"Incoming communications packet from Captain McIntire has arrived."

"Fortuitous," Virginia said as she watched the hologram in front of her.

Instead of a voice communication, it was a video that Sarah sent.

The three sat in silence as they watched the experiment Sarah had conducted in the Gobi. There was no sound, so they all surmised it was taken by a weaker cell phone camera instead of a video cam. They watched in awe as the experiment went off. They could see the detail and the strange ore Sarah had used. They watched it no less than six times trying to figure out just what it was they were looking at.

"Europa, dissect the video from Captain McIntire and estimate speed of travel of object in video."

"Calculating."

Doctor Morales impatiently drummed his fingers on the steel table-top.

"Due to low grade quality of visual, I am unable to estimate exact speed."

Xavier rubbed a hand through his dark hair in exasperation. "Damn it, give me your best guess Europa!"

Virginia stood up and patted Xavier on the shoulder, trying to calm the young genius.

"Since precise visual trail of exhaust is lost at approximately thirty-three-thousand feet, I can only estimate from time of explosive outgassing of object as it leaves the desert floor."

"Oh, come on Europa, you're killing me! Estimate of speed!"

"Speed of object is estimated at six-hundred-thousand miles per hour."

The cleanroom became silent. The only sound they heard was the air in the vent system that constantly scrubbed the air of germs and microscopic particles.

"My God, I think they found something better than copper and zinc out there. What in the hell is that ore?" Virginia asked.

"Europa, contact Captain McIntire immediately for clarification," Niles said as he leaned over the table and spoke into the microphone. They waited.

"There is no verbal response at this time. Europa is currently recording a malfunction in the transmission signature."

"What malfunction?" Xavier asked incredulously.

"Non-verbal communication established."

"What do you mean non-verbal communication? Let's hear it," Xavier said as he gripped the rails of his wheelchair spokes.

All three heard it. It came out loud and clear over the speaker system. The series clicks, and blips was loud and clear and Xavier and Niles knew its meaning. ... -- ..., it repeated twice more and then ceased suddenly.

"Morse Code, Doctor," Europa said.

"Morse?" Virginia asked aloud.

Niles again started pacing.

"Well, what did it say?"

Morales started punching in data to retrieve Sarah's exact location but paused long enough to answer Virginia's question.

"It was an S.O.S. Doctor. Captain McIntire's team is obviously in some form of trouble."

CHAPTER THREE

**Allal Mountains,
Outer Mongolia**

"Doc, do you mind very much getting your skinny ass out of my face?"

"Oh Lordy, sorry," Ellenshaw said as he scrambled off Jason after landing on him.

Ryan rolled over and got the breath back into his lungs after having it knocked out from the thirty-foot fall from high above. Jason looked up and saw the hole they had fallen through and was curious as to how they could have even fit through the small opening. He shook his head and hissed in pain.

"You didn't break anything, did you?" Charlie asked as he too was looking at their entrance portal far above their heads.

"Yeah, something's broken. Besides my dignity," he reached for the back of his belt and pulled the small walkie-talkie from its holder, happy to feel the Glock nine-millimeter still in its holster. The radio fell into three pieces and he allowed them to fall through his fingers. "I hope you have yours, Doc."

Charlie grimaced and then hissed. "Uh, yeah, about my radio, I uh—"

"Left it back in camp," Ryan finished his sentence for him. It was a practiced exercise that Ellenshaw had to be constantly reminded about field team practice and directives.

"Sorry, I didn't think I would be gone so long."

Ryan eased himself to his feet and brushed himself off. He once more examined the cave they had fallen into. He again checked his belt and was happy to feel that the small Maglite was unbroken. Charlie also had his in the same condition, and they both turned them on at the same time.

The cave was immense. A sharp smell of dampness permeated the air.

"There must be a source of moving water somewhere close by," Ellenshaw said as he moved the beam of his light from one end of the cave to another.

"What makes you say its moving?" Jason asked.

"The air, don't you feel it?"

Ryan paused as he took in Charlie's point. The air did have a freshness to it he hadn't noticed before. He shrugged. "Well, let's just hope we're not stuck in here long enough to need it. Come on Doc, let's see if we can find a way back to the world."

Charlie watched as Jason started moving from one side of the cave to other, looking for hand and foot holds to climb back out. His light was picking up nothing but smooth walls all the way to the small hole above.

"Damn," Ryan hissed under his breath, "one thing's for sure, we're not getting out the way we came in. Unless Sarah and Anya show up with some rappelling gear, which was mysteriously left off the logistics for this mission, we need to find another way up."

"Oh, my goodness," Ellenshaw said, ignoring Ryan's concerns of escape.

Jason turned and saw Charlie looking at something on the cave wall. He added his light to Ellenshaw's and his brows rose.

"What in the hell is that doing down here?" Jason asked as he stepped closer to see the image Charlie had illuminated. "What is it, a dinosaur?"

Charlie snickered. "No, no, my dear boy. That is a dragon. A depiction of which I have never seen before." He moved the light from the maroon painted dragon to Ryan's face. "And as you know, I am an expert on such renderings from our own cave systems in America, and those cave paintings in France. Yes, I am quite sure this is a dragon. And rendered in such a way that I have never seen before. Very precise for a mere cave depiction."

"Yes, amazing, Doc," Ryan said as he eased the flashlight away from his face. "But unless we can ride on the back of that beast, we need to find a way out."

Charlie looked disappointed. He moved the light back to the artwork that he estimated to be no less than ten thousand years old.

"Commander, I think you fail to grasp the significance of this find."

Ryan shined his light back at the unmoving Charlie. The crazy-haired cryptozoologist finally turned and faced the small naval officer. "Yes, I am indeed failing in that regard, Doc."

"You see, Dragons did not appear in Chinese lore until about 1375 B.C.E. Oh, there may have been fanciful depictions before that, but never in the way the more modern Chinese nation used them. This rendering is about seven thousand years too early."

"Seven, huh?"

"Yes indeed."

"That is enthralling on so many levels, Doc. Maybe we can discuss this at length when we climb out of here. Deal?"

"Oh, yes, yes of course. You lead, I'll follow."

Ryan gave Ellenshaw one last look with slatted, suspicious eyes and then waved him forward.

A few minutes later, Charlie asked worriedly; "You are aware we seem to be traveling at a precarious downward angle, Commander?"

"Really? What gave it away Charlie, the downhill trail?"

For the first time, Ellenshaw really concentrated his light on their footing. That was when he noticed, as Ryan already had, that they were walking on a well-worn pathway.

"Goodness. It looks as if this could have been tread upon by a million sets of feet."

"A million pairs of feet, huh, Doc?"

"Yes, from the look and size of the trail I would say at least a million."

Ryan stopped their downhill tread and faced Ellenshaw. "Not bad considering this godforsaken country has less than three million total people in it. And as old as this trail looks, they must have had major conventions down here for thousands of years in order to get this deep and very well-trodden trail."

"I see your point." Charlie looked around, suddenly anxious. "Maybe we should have stayed by the hole we fell through. Perhaps young McIntire and Anya will be able to follow us here. You think?"

"For once, Doc, I think you're right. This place is creeping me out some." Ryan turned and bid Charlie to follow him back up the trail.

As they moved, the going was harder because of the incline. Then it was again Charlie who pointed out the problem.

"Mister Ryan, I don't want to place added worry onto our situation, but when we started back the incline was what you would expect. But now—"

"Come on Doc, what is it?" Ryan snapped.

"We seem to be traveling downhill once again."

Jason looked down and the trail ahead had a distinct decline as it meandered further. He shined the light around. "I'm sure we came this way. Oh, come on, we were only walking for fifteen minutes when we stopped and turned back. No one could ever get that lost."

"Did you say fifteen minutes?" Charlie asked as he shined his own light onto the wristwatch he wore.

"Yeah, no more than that."

"When we fell through the hole I checked the time. It was ten thirty in the morning. Now look at your watch."

Ryan did with a shake of his head as he thought Ellenshaw was having another Crazy Charlie moment, which he remembered, he had a lot of.

"Shit," Ryan said as he tapped his watch with the tip of the flashlight. "According to mine we've been down here for five hours."

"Uh, let's go back the other way," Charlie said, nervously looking about and shining his light everywhere. Then the circle of glowing light stopped. "Ah, ha! There's the dragon, we must be close."

Charlie started to move forward toward the maroon colored dragon, and that was when Ryan reached out and took the older man by the arm.

"What, we must be close to our starting point."

"Doc, look," Ryan said as he adjusted his own light to an area to the left and then to the right of the red dragon.

"Oh, my."

Instead of the one dragon, they were now looking at several. At least fifty of the winged creatures were drawn over an area about the size of a large living room wall.

"Okay, that just about does the twilight zone thing. Let's get the hell out of here," Ryan said, and then took Ellenshaw by the arm.

They turned as one and suddenly came face to face with what they had been staring at for the past few minutes.

The dragon was blocking their way forward.

Charlie stood motionless. "Oh, crap."

As the circle of men surrounded and moved into the small camp, Sarah saw at least three of the Mongolian guides that had stolen their Land Rover earlier. They were all three flanking a large man in native dress. The long robes and head coverings told Sarah that these were the real princes of the plains in this area. These were actual Mongols, and their guides were a part of this group. They did not look friendly, and the fully automatic AK-47s the hundred men held accentuated that point. They started rummaging through the camp, smashing and removing things of value.

Sarah looked at Anya with anger etching her face, as one of their captors pushed her to the ground and searched her. Then the brute of a man removed the small satellite phone from her pocket. When they had found themselves surrounded, Sarah knew she couldn't raise the phone to her ear without being filled with all kinds of holes from the approaching men, so she had hit the auto-relay button that would connect her to Europa. She had started hitting the transmit button over and over again, hoping the super-computer could interpret. After being searched and basically felt up by the Mongol guide that had just been in their camp that morning, Sarah and the others were allowed to stand up.

"You can tell them to stop playing their little games now," Anya said as she turned to face the man impersonating Professor Anderson. "Its obvious these pirates work for you. And ask them if our friends are still alive."

"Sorry to disappoint, Major Korvesky," Anderson said as he slowly stood up from the brutal search of his body, "but these surly looking gentlemen are most assuredly not with me."

"I personally love the irony here, old man," Professor Birnbaum said, "the back stabber stabbed in the back. That fact almost bloody well makes this situation worthwhile," Professor Birnbaum said as he spit a mouthful of blood out onto the sand after being backhanded by one of the Mongols when he hadn't moved fast enough for his taste.

"May I suggest no further antagonistic moves toward our captors. They are notoriously ruthless in their methods. Quite unreasonable at times actually," Professor Lee said as he slowly moved his eyes about the camp. "They usually do not kill outsiders unless they have reason to. Let us just hope that our colleagues are a-foot, and not dead. If we cooperate, all we'll have after this is a long walk out of here. Do not and we'll be no more active than the American pilot we discovered this morning."

"Wonderful choices you give us, Lee old man," Birnbaum said with a sarcastic nod of his head.

"No talking!" a small man with a fur lined hat said. He eased up to the very much larger Birnbaum and slapped him across the face, which made the large Australian take a sudden step forward.

Anya jumped up and knocked Birnbaum down before the small man could shoot him.

"He's sorry, he won't do it again," Anya said as she lay across Birnbaum.

The Mongolian took an angry step forward but was called back by the large man who seemed to be leading this group of thieves. He kicked sand at the two prone scientists before moving off. Sarah stepped forward and helped both to their feet.

"Alright you two, I think it best we adhere to Professor Lee's advice about these people. They seem to be very experienced at what they do."

"We may not be in this situation for very long," the man claiming to be Professor Anderson said. "My associates have a very long reach. The information I sent to them will be seen as valuable enough to retrieve at all costs. They shouldn't be long."

It was Sarah who saw the Mongols stop their pillaging then congregate in a circle. Every now and then she saw one or another look their way and she didn't like the smiles of anticipation on their faces.

"I believe they could be in the next valley over, and still not make it in time, Comrade whatever your name is."

"It most assuredly is not Comrade, Captain. And why would you say that?"

"Because they are in the process of deciding to shoot us here, or," she turned and looked at the mountain rising above them, "up there."

At that moment, the circle of Mongols broke up and they moved toward the group of geologists.

"I guess they decided," Birnbaum said as he prepared himself to fight.

AS RYAN TRIED TO KEEP HIS TESTICLES IN PLACE AS HE CAME FACE TO face with the dragon, it was Charlie who saw that it was a man in a mask and red garb. He slowly placed a thin fingered hand on Jason's shoulder and eased him back three steps. He placed another hand on the nine-millimeter Glock semi-automatic pistol that Ryan had a hand on in the back of his belt.

"Easy, Mister Ryan, it's just a mask."

The seven-foot giant took a menacing step toward them.

"Okay, how about that spear?" Ryan asked with his eyes and flashlight on the immense curved blade at the tip of the eight-foot shaft. The sharpened edge was pointed in their direction.

To Ryan's surprise, Crazy Charlie Ellenshaw moved his body from around Jason to stand in front of him as if in guardianship.

"Hello," he said as Ryan rolled his eyes.

The massive figure in front of them tilted its large head before looking from Charlie to Jason. Then the monster leaned the spear against the cave wall. Its large clawed fingers reached up and lifted the edges of the mask.

"Do you mind shining that light someplace else?" the figure said in perfect English. Charlie was speechless, and Ryan amazed when the mask of the dragon was lifted free of the wearer's head. Jason moved the light to the right of the figure before them. "Thank you."

The two Americans watched as the figure exposed a well-trimmed head of black hair. The man, more of a boy in Charlie's estimation, removed the large gloves that had crystal-type claws sewn onto its fingertips and rubbed his right hand through his wet hair.

"You're Americans from the geological survey in the valley? We were told that you were leaving this morning. Perhaps you should have."

Ryan was surprised. The large figure before them was just a boy. He could be no older than seventeen at the most. He watched as the young Chinese kid reached into the satin-like cloth of his disguise and placed a pair of wire-rimmed glasses over his eyes before fixing the two strangers with a curious look. He could see that neither man was willing to speak. The tall figure moved to a large rock and clumsily sat down. He lifted the long skirt that covered his legs and shook off a pair of long stilts. The kid wasn't a giant, nor a dragon as first suspected. He was a teenage boy with a colorful mask and leg stilts used for height.

"Excuse the dramatics, but the local indigenous population are terrified of the old legends of these mountains."

"Uh, uh, who are you?" Charlie stuttered the question. "I mean, is that a British turn you have in your accent?"

The boy moved the mask from his lap and placed it on the ground. He stood and stretched. "Perhaps so, we pick up habits from wherever we are sent to school. I am currently enrolled at Cambridge."

Ryan and Charlie exchanged confused looks.

"My brother, Che Li, has the more barbaric slant to the English language, he's at Princeton."

"Just who in the hell are you, and why are you living in a cave?" Ryan asked, stepping back around Charlie.

The boy laughed as he peeled the rest of the satin cloth from his body. Both men saw that, underneath, the kid was wearing what looked like blue jeans and a white button-down shirt. He was also sweating profusely.

"I've probably said too much already." The boy moved to retrieve the mask and the spear as he bundled the clothing into a ball and then faced the two Americans.

"At least tell us your name," Charlie said as he again stepped around Ryan.

"My name is Che Lao, and I've got to get back, so I can hand this off to my relief. There seems to be too many houseguests above, so we have to have people in all of the tunnels."

"Houseguests?" Ellenshaw asked.

"Yes, your group and the bunch of thieves about to murder them."

"Sarah and Anya," Ryan said as he fixed the kid with an angry look.

The boy saw Ryan's reaction and then smiled. "No, not murdered by us. Come on, let's get back and someone with more authority will explain things far better than myself." He placed the bundle and mask under his arm and then pointed with the spear. "This way."

"No, no, we have to get back to our friends, they're just geologists," Ryan said, unwilling to follow the kid anywhere. Both he and Charlie didn't think the boy heard Ryan's concern, but he answered as he walked.

"Your friends are soon to be in the hands of the most capable man on the face of the Earth. Perhaps its time for you to worry about your own fate, Mister Ryan."

The boy vanished around a bend in the trail. Ryan looked at Charlie.

"He knows your name, Commander," Charlie said as he shined the light onto the trail where the stranger had disappeared.

"And yours, Professor Charles Hindershot Ellenshaw III. I've read your work, well, not all of it, but some. Very interesting theories you have, Professor, on many varying subjects," the voice echoed. "Now, we can either talk or you can get answers. Up to you. But let me warn you, if you strike out on your own you'll never get out of here. If you noticed, time has a strange way about it the further down you go. As far as I know," the voice was growing fainter the further the kid got, "only one man ever made it out of here, and that was by pure luck."

The last words were almost so faint that they were hardly understood.

"Perhaps we—"

"Yeah, let's go," Ryan said.

The two Americans followed the stranger into the bowels of the Allal Mountains.

SARAH STOOD NEXT TO ANYA AS THEY WERE HERDED TOWARD THE FACE of the lowest mountain rock.

"Where in the hell is our security element?" Anya asked as one of their captors poked her in the back with the barrel of his AK-47. "Ow, do that again...please!" Anya hissed as she suddenly turned and faced the bearded brute. The man smiled and then raised the muzzle of the weapon toward Anya's face.

A sudden burst of Mongolian stopped the man from his premature carrying out of Anya's execution. The beast of a man took a step back.

"Look, I have many soldiers coming, they can pay you a lot of money," the imposter posing as Anderson said.

The group of Mongols didn't respond. The last of the group, about thirty of them, had finished loading their plunder into the backs and onto the roofs of the stolen Land Rovers.

"I don't think they really care, Comrade Anderson," Sarah said as she tried to muster all the courage she could, assisted as she was by seeing someone else more frightened than herself.

"Regardless, when they do arrive, they will kill every one of these thieving bastards!" he shouted at the Mongol facing him.

"I suspect so. But let me say this, I respect these assholes far more than you. At least this is their way of life. You do it because your masters in Siberia and Moscow say to," Sarah said, stepping away from the rock wall so Anderson could see her face. She was immediately and unceremoniously shoved back by the muzzle of a weapon.

"Before I get shot, I would like to know just one thing—WHO IN THE HELL ARE YOU PEOPLE?" Birnbaum screamed the last few words.

"We are all people that should have left when our geological survey came up with little of value," Lee said as he eyed the men lining up before them. "I should have insisted this morning we be out by nine. Man, I won't ever live this down with the Master."

All sixteen sets of eyes from the survey group leaned forward and stared at the diminutive Professor Lee. He smiled with his hands and arms still in the air.

"Oh, come on, mate, you too?" Birnbaum said with incredulity edging his question. "Is anyone here who they claimed to be?"

"Why yes, like Sarah here, I am an actual geologist. Master's degree from Edinburgh."

The Mongols lined up in front of them. The fifty or so loaders of plunder stopped their movements in order to watch. The other thirty or so stopped digging what would be their shallow grave.

"The one time we leave without Carl and Jack's planning, we get shot and killed," Anya said with faint sarcasm lacing her words.

Mongolian orders were shouted and the AK-47's were raised.

Sarah took Anya's hand and they both looked defiantly at their line of executioners.

Before anyone realized what was happening, a sprig of fresh, cool air whipped the area in front of the line of condemned. The Mongols seemed not to feel it. The breeze freshened into a light wind as the weapons came to a stop after being raised. They aimed their rifles at the group. The wind increased dramatically and this time the line of executioners looked around as small pellets of sand started to strike their faces. Sarah turned her head away as some of the particles struck her own face. It was at that time that she saw Professor Lee lower his hands and then examine his watch as if he expected something to happen at this time.

More angry shouts sounded in the Mongolian language as men started turning away from the pelting they were getting. To the amazement of all, the sand directly in front of the geologists sprang into the air. It looked as if the wall of dirt and sand were more than a thousand, small tornado-like shapes as they spun and moved left to right in front of them. They all turned away as the sand spun off the funnels. The wall climbed higher and then even higher. The wall of sand was solid as the group looked and could see none of the Mongols who had lined them up for execution. Sarah managed to raise her head as did Anya as the wall of swirling sand rose still higher. They could see nothing but heard the shouts and screams of the Mongols they could no longer see.

"What is this?" Anya shouted as loud as she could as the wind now forced them all to the ground. They heard the rending of steel and even more distant shouts of men. Still the wall grew higher, higher and even more so. The group would later comment that the wall looked as if it stepped from the film sequence of an old Cecil B. DeMille motion picture.

As Sarah and Anya covered their heads, silence immediately engulfed them as if by magic. They looked up just as the last of the sand fell away into a cloud of moving dust. They heard the sound of engines, and as they slowly rose to their feet they saw the trail of dust from the Land Rovers as they sped away. All started to brush the sand from their hair and clothes. Most were in shock. Birnbaum was being helped up by the much smaller Lee.

"Are you okay, Professor?" Lee asked Birnbaum, who could only stare at the devastation of their once orderly camp. Lee stepped away from the Australian when he saw the man was too shocked to speak. He looked up at the rock wall they had been lined up against, and then angrily shouted to the now clear skies. "Do you think that was funny?" he screamed as they all looked at Lee as if he had lost his mind. "Oh, I get it, you wanted to make an example out of me, is that it? It wasn't my fault that they found that skeleton. You yourself told me how resilient Ms. McIntire and her friends were!"

"Lee, who in the hell are you speaking to?" Sarah asked as she and Anya approached, ready to subdue the obviously insane geologist.

Lee brushed more sand from his clothing and then noticed that he was being spoken to.

"And why is it you know so much about us?" Anya asked.

"Because I told him."

Sarah heard the voice as well as Anya. The others outside of Professor Lee hadn't heard a thing. Sarah slapped the side of her head next to her ear. The voice tingled as it traveled through her inner ear to her brain.

"Did you hear that?" Anya asked as she too shook her head as if to clear it.

"Ignore it, he's playing games with you. It seems he's also angry at you as well as me."

Both Anya and Sarah looked over at Lee who stopped slapping at his clothing in an effort to get the sand out, and then looked at them and shrugged.

"Who's playing games?" Sarah asked. "And I also noticed you have lost your Chinese accent, Professor."

Lee just pointed out of the camp to the north. They saw a small figure walking, no, they thought, the lone person looked as if to be strolling along the flattened sand.

Sarah and the others saw the dark figure as it approached and then they turned away to look at Lee who was just replacing his glasses. "Lee, who is that?"

After the question had been voiced, Sarah turned back to the person slowly walking their way. Whoever it was had gone from five hundred yards away to only a few in the time it took to turn away and then back. It was a man in a black sport jacket and white shirt. His shoes were shined, and his glasses were expensive. The small man removed his bowler hat and then half-bowed to the group of five men and women.

"I am Li Zheng," the man with the gold rimmed glasses said as he too brushed some sand from his lapels. "I am your host, possibly for the rest of your lives."

Professor Lee stepped forward, and just when the rest of the stunned geologists thought the younger man was going to strike out at the older, he instead hugged the strange newcomer. He finished with his greeting and then turned to the others.

"My father, Master Zheng, he can be a real jerk sometimes."

Phnom Penh, Cambodia

THE DARK-HAIRED MAN SAT AT THE SMALL TABLE AND WATCHED THE rain falling on the capital city of Phnom Penh. His blue eyes scanned the streets below as was his habit. His gaze searched out the busy street and decided the safehouse was well out of the way of the Russian embassy. Thus the surveillance of all foreigners was limited to an accidental sighting by forces contrary to his new position in the deep cover operations of the Siberian Group.

The stout man reached behind him and pulled a silenced Russian manufactured RSh-12 pistol from the waistband of his slacks, before placing it on the table before him. With a gentle nudge, he moved the long cylindrical silencer toward the door, and only then did the man relax. He rubbed the three-day old growth of beard and waited. The wait wasn't long. There *had* been eyes on him, but those eyes leaned more toward the friendlier side of the equation.

He eased his right hand over and cocked the pistol but left it resting on the table's scratched and filthy top.

"Come," he said, his hand never more than a few inches from the deadly weapon.

The door eased open just a foot. "The cold in the Ukraine is as bad as reported."

The man with the black hair shook his head at the dramatics he had to endure. "Those reports are greatly exaggerated," came his response.

The door opened wider and the large, rotund man framed the doorway with his bulk. He smiled and stepped into the room. Doctor Leoniv Vassick, a man who rarely, if ever, traveled away from the dark borders of the new Russia, eased into the shabby apartment and removed his fedora. He nodded at his host, who upon seeing the newcomer only hesitantly eased his hand away from the powerful handgun, and then made to stand up but was waved immediately down by the heavyset man.

"You look tired, my friend," Vassick said as he turned and closed the door. He came closer and placed the wet hat on the table, covering the weapon the dark-haired man had waiting as a reception for anyone that did not address his opening statement with the 'key phrase' password offered at the outset.

"Traveling in these backward nations is not comparable to the ease we use while traveling in Europe. Here, all 'round' eyes are under deep suspicion from the moment they enter."

The man removed his overcoat that was still dripping water and tossed it on the filthy bedspread on the fold-up bed. "For me it is quite a bit easier." He moved to retrieve the only other chair and then placed it across from the man. "I just look them in the eye and they automatically turn away. It's a quite useful trait and talent. Perhaps it stems from the old days and their natural fear of us."

"Perhaps," the man said, remaining seated as the large man eased onto the rickety chair.

"All went well in Vietnam?"

The man was silent, looking at his employer as if evaluating something. "Why have you come?" His blue eyes remained fixed on the heavily jowled man before him. "After all these years, you take a chance on us being seen together?"

The old man smiled and then shook his head. "Operational planning has changed, along with your orders. Now, you had no problems in Vietnam?"

The man removed the fedora from its place over the pistol and placed it next to it.

"Yes, our friend went into the river with more holes in him than he had the day before."

"And the other?" The old man had noticed that the hat had been removed from its place over the firearm.

"He's being held, awaiting transport to Siberia, as ordered."

The older man looked more closely at the long sleeve of the man's left arm. The blue eyes of the rugged looking man saw this and, with a shake of his head, removed the cufflink and rolled up his sleeve. He extended his forearm. The gray colored eyes saw the small, round bandage and then nodded his head.

"Good, I see all the bases have been covered, as our American friends would say. Unless our counterparts in Nevada have been watching their electronics closely, we should have been successful in fooling them." The old man cleared his throat. "Your most challenging test will come sooner than expected, and from another area of interest other than the field mission to Mongolia. Same profile, different mission. I hope your skills are up to the standards we have seen in the past, because they will be tested far beyond what they have been." He reached into his dress jacket and removed a small electronic pad. "This is everything we have on the personnel you will be encountering with this new direction we are taking. Let's call it, 'a target', or dare I say, 'targets', of opportunity. We have made your travel arrangements. You will not be accompanying our military element into Mongolia. What is the old poem, ah, many miles before I sleep."

The man picked up the small device and entered his security

code. Several pictures with a small dossier appeared in rapid succession for each target.

"You will have plenty of time to study the details on the flight. This mission has become one with the highest priority. I dare say it may change the world as we know it, the parameters of which are encoded in the mission order. As I said, your past studies will be put to the test." He reached into his coat pocket one last time and tossed several small items on the table. "Your adjusted passport and travel papers to Hanoi, and then to your final destination."

The dark-haired man smirked. "I take it that the mission parameters have changed without authorization from our superiors in Siberia?"

"Since you were able to secure the tracking device, we'll call this a target." He smiled wider. "Or should I say, targets, of opportunity. We cannot pass up this challenge. A strike here will set this Group back decades. We must take the chance. When all is said and done, Siberia will see my reasoning."

The old man smiled, stood and then retrieved his hat and coat. "You had better be on your game, old friend. The test is upon you." The large man eased into his overcoat and then stopped before opening the door. "Our military forces are preparing for immediate operations in Mongolia. The prize there, an important prize to say the least, will keep our superiors in Siberia occupied long enough for you and I to change the dynamic of our own Group for fifty years." He turned for the door. "Good luck, I know the detailed training has prepared you well for changing the world. Dasvidanya, Colonel."

The man watched as the head of Russia's version of Department 5656 left the room. He then eased the second, much smaller pistol from under the table and placed it next to the silenced weapon. He stood, went to the door, listened for a moment, and then turned away and sat once more. He again started going through his mission orders on the small electronic device he had been given. He studied the first photograph in the dossier. His smile grew as he took in the unsmiling features of the man he had studied many times during his training in operations began over fifteen years before.

The dark-haired man switched off the electronic device and then started cleaning his powerful weapon—the same one he had used to kill his best friend, Captain Carl Everett, just three days before in Laos.

Colonel Jack Collins smiled as he paused. He would indeed study all of the faces of his many friends while awaiting his ride, and then the longer journey to his final destination. He may very well perish on this change of orders, but it was a risk worth taking. His smile grew in anticipation of possibly eliminating everyone on his list in one fell swoop.

For the next two hours, he studied the dossiers of the men and women he knew better than any in the world—members of Department 5656, the Event Group.

United States Air Force C-130
'Hercules', somewhere over the Pacific

THE LARGE INTERIOR OF THE 'HERKY BIRD' WAS JAMMED WITH EIGHT crates of the new 'Patriot Six' missile defense system negotiated between the Vietnamese and the U.S. State Department for deployment to Hanoi. They were a replacement for the Russian system that the government was taking offline due to deteriorating relations with Moscow. The Air Force technical support element, for its installation, lined the aircraft's interior walls as most slept. All, with the exception of two.

"Here we go, Master Chief. We have the location pinned down to the square inch."

Master Chief Jenks leaned over in the canvas covered, uncomfortable seat, and looked at the locator icon that appeared on the Europa link Major Will Mendenhall was holding.

"I'm thrilled beyond all imagination."

"You need to temper that enthusiasm, Master Chief," Will said as he turned off the portable Europa link he had been issued. As for

Jenks, he just leaned back in his seat and placed the Air Force issued baseball cap over his eyes.

Jenks reached down and grabbed the area between his legs. "Temper this, Major Fuck-head."

Mendenhall smiled and shook his head. It was always pleasurable traveling with the Group's newest engineer. "Bad memories of this place, Master Chief?"

"No, it was all dancing in the mountains with Julie Andrews singing Kumbaya type memories," he said without removing the cap covering his eyes.

Will decided he couldn't push the Master Chief on the subject of Vietnam too far. He knew Jenks had two tours under his belt as a navy SEAL, beginning at age nineteen in 1970. He had been in on the Son Tay raid as a kid in that same first year of 1970. That raid was code named Operation *Ivory Coast* and was a mission conducted by United States Special Operations Forces and other American military elements, to rescue U.S. Prisoners of War during the Vietnam conflict. It turned out to be a highly successful operation. There was only one problem with the plan—the prisoners of war had been moved a few days before their rescuers had arrived. Other than that, Mendenhall knew Jenks had lost many pals during the evacuation of Saigon in 1975. It was soon afterward that the Master Chief was done with killing for King and Country and went into engineering, where he proved to be one of the brightest men in the field.

Will was just leaning back to close his own eyes when a small chirp sounded. Even Master Chief Jenks roused and looked at the Europa link as it chimed a message. Mendenhall placed the small laptop on his legs and opened it. He read the flash encoded message from Europa and Niles Compton in Nevada, as relayed through the supercomputer to their KH-11 satellite, *Boris* and *Natasha*.

"Well, Army, what in the hell do they want now, to send me to hell to rescue the devil?" Jenks snickered at his own snide question.

Will's eyebrows rose. "No, change of plan. You are to meet our contact in Hanoi."

"What about Toad?" the Master Chief asked, referring to his nickname for Everett, that he earned in SEAL training for his ability to jump at the softest of explosions.

"It says other arrangements have been made for the Captain's recovery and debrief." He read on silently. Again, his brows rose, and a worried look crossed his features.

"Look, just say it, don't tease me like a damn cheap hooker in downtown Bangkok."

Mendenhall closed the laptop and then fixed Jenks with his ever-present worried look. "It seems Jack and Carl aren't the only ones having trouble with their transponders. Sarah, Anya, Doc Ellenshaw, and Ryan's location and health monitors just went offline. Our orders have been changed. You are to meet your contacts and then head out to Mongolia. The director has warned us that NSA has confirmed that area of the Gobi is receiving a lot of attention from many different players. Our Russian friends are among them."

Jenks finally removed the Air Force cap and sat up. "The hell you say?"

"The Director says to watch your asses after you meet up with these mysterious contacts. He and Virginia believe that Russian Black Group is making some sort of play here. Now we have the Chinese sitting up and taking notice. Damn, I wish I was going with you. I want a shot at those assholes from Siberia. I guess I was lucky enough to travel with you this far. The Director expects me back in twenty-four hours."

The old and angry look crossed Jenks' hard features as he stood and retrieved his travel bag from under the seat and started rummaging through it. He pulled out his own nine-millimeter Glock and then made sure his extra clips were inside the bag before sitting again.

"Well, I'll shoot one of them for you, how's that? Those murderous sons of bitches are about to see how the U.S. Navy likes to play the game. Tell that goddamn Air Force puke pilot to goose those damn engines and get me to Hanoi. It's about time we settle up with those Russian bastards!"

The C-130 made a steep bank as the first United States Air

Force transport plane since the Vietnam-era prisoner of war exchange, which happened over forty years before, started its landing procedures to bring Americans down into the heart of Vietnam.

The United States was back in South East Asia one more time to do harm to an enemy.

District Four, thirty miles Northwest of Ho Chi Minh City

DOCTOR HÙNG QUOC VƯƠNG WAS JUST RETURNING FROM HIS SMALL kitchen, with a hot bowl of rice and chicken broth, when he saw his new charge standing next to the rickety cot trying to pull a blue denim shirt over his bandages. He hurriedly placed the bowl down and ran to the large man just as he lost his balance and fell back, half on, half off the bed.

A solid stream of Vietnamese language was hurled at the American for attempting to undo all the medical work that the doctor had done. He tried to push the old doctor's hands away as he attempted to rise from the cot. He again failed as he fell back. Hùng angrily tore the shirt away and then reached down and pulled Everett's legs up to rest on the bed.

"You...Americans are as stubborn...as I...remember you...being," he said as he admonished his patient. "You have sixteen stitches... holding you...together and one very deep void where a bullet rearranged your...insides."

Captain Carl Everett shook his head as he tried to make sense out of just where he was.

"Where am I?" his eyes fixed on the small frail doctor, "Who are you?"

"I am...the man...who risks his...life for a very...stupid man."

"How did I get here?" Carl asked as he finally allowed gravity to settle his question on the subject of if he could get up. "I do admit I hurt some."

"Another...very...foolish man found you...in the Mekong. He brought...you here."

Carl finally felt he could keep his eyes open long enough to evaluate just where he was and study the man before him. "Where is here?"

"Here...is District Four, Ho Chi Minh City." The doctor reached down and felt the Captain's head. "You have...to excuse my English...I have not had...need of it since...1975."

"Your English is far better than my Vietnamese." Carl raised his head, before the small man angrily pushed it back down on the pillow that seemed to have only five or six feathers remaining inside.

"For now, you need not...use English at all." The doctor looked around his tiny apartment. "These and...many other walls...have ears. You may be in...friendly territory, but there...are many here who...have long memories."

Carl felt helpless. In a rush he raised his left arm up and looked at it. He relaxed when he saw the small bump just under the skin. The new transponder was still there. He felt the doctor push his arm back down and, soon after, a cold cloth was placed on his forehead.

"Thank you," Carl said as he allowed his eyes to close.

"Do not thank...me. It was...an old...friend who...brought you here. He and his family risked all...to save you. Do not waste the... kindness of...very frightened people...and pull those stitches." The doctor retrieved the bowl of soup. "You have to eat...I have no...intravenous fluids...to give...you." He fed Carl for the next ten minutes and unbelievably he felt better.

"Thank you," he said.

"Old...habits," Hùng said as he removed the bowl and then pulled the thread-thin blanket back up to Everett's shoulders. "Now...before you lost consciousness, you...claimed a friend...did this...bad thing...to you."

Carl was silent as he tried to bring back into focus what he remembered. "Yes." Carl fixed his eyes on the doctor.

"I have no...phone...for you."

Everett smiled at the old man. "You have done enough. My

friends know where I'm at." He closed his eyes and thought about Jack. There was a problem with the image he remembered. He did know and see in his mind's eye, Jack raising the pistol just after he had dispatched the Russian with the knife. When he had seen Collins come to his rescue, he was relieved. Relieved that is, until the memory flashed forward to his best friend shooting him. Carl knew his cloudy memory was failing him. There was something wrong with the memory. The image itself was accurate. He had the bullet wounds to prove it. It was the way he was shot. He just couldn't place it. He concentrated. Something was off in the memory. He saw Jack. It was most assuredly him. He saw the pistol being raised as he thought the Colonel was covering something he himself could not see behind him. Then the shock of the gun going off and the memory of the bullets impacting his body. He did remember looking at his face and seeing no sympathy, no friendship there. The eyes were Jack's eyes. *No*, he thought. That wasn't the issue. It was something that lay just beyond his brain's ability to focus on.

His attention was drawn away by movement in the apartment. He saw the lights dim and the old man move to a window and pull back the blinds that were missing at least half of their slats. He watched as the doctor froze at a sight he was seeing down below. Hùng moved away from the window and quickly went to Carl's side.

"We may have visitors...I am not sure. My...landlord is...below. Her attention...is focused on my home. There are two strangers with...her."

Hùng started to assist Carl off the bed. Before he was able to fully sit up, a pounding sounded on the door. Both Carl and Hùng froze as the door opened, suddenly casting the room with light from the alley below. The figure was backlit to the point they couldn't see who was there. Simultaneously, they saw the saucer cap that was clearly part of a uniform and their hearts skipped a beat in tandem. Hùng allowed Everett to slide back to the bed as the old man partially raised his hands in the air. He saw the Vietnamese army uniform and knew that his freedom, along with his life, may have just been placed in forfeit—that was the confusion in modern Vietnamese society these days—are we friends with the Americans or are we not? The figure came forward into the room.

Before the newcomer could say anything, the voice of the old lady sounded behind him. The rapid-fire Vietnamese bounced from wall to wall and Carl could tell it had an accusing tone to it. Before he realized what was happening, the voice was silenced by a large hand that snaked around the small woman's head and placed something over her mouth. Then came the mumbling, and Everett saw the property owner collapse as the man behind her saved her from falling. He moved the old woman inside and laid her on the floor. Both Carl and Hùng saw the first man in uniform come closer and Carl smiled. Then the second well-dressed man came into the light. He frowned at seeing the second.

"Do not say a word. I am here for only a moment. After this, our friend here can handle things," said the tall blonde man who had allowed his hair to grow past his collar, of which was a tuxedo shirt with formal jacket over it. It was obvious that the man had been someplace other than Southeast Asia when he had been contacted by Niles and Morales.

"Hello, Henri," Carl said with a contemptuous look at Colonel Henri Farbeaux, and then he nodded his head at Van Tram, the Group's old friend.

Sergeant Nuong Van Tram smiled and removed his saucer cap and then held out his hand to Everett who gladly took the offered greeting.

"Will you be able to handle that?" Carl asked as he nodded at the old lady after releasing Tram's hand.

The Vietnamese Special Forces sergeant turned and looked at the old woman lying on the floor. "Yes. It seems our landlord here is dealing in stolen video discs outlawed by the new intellectual property agreement we just signed with INTERPOL. She will claim she is innocent, but if pressed, with the overwhelming evidence, she will cooperate."

"That's what delayed our arrival here," Henri said as he moved the old lady to a chair by the lone table. "It seems the sergeant here has learned a little too well from your Group, Captain. He planted a few boxes of the worst movies you have ever heard of in her basement. I don't think we'll have a problem there."

Hùng was staring at Tram with wide-eyes until the sergeant shook his head, and instead of shouting at him for disobeying the law, patted the old man on the back. He spoke softly in Vietnamese, and the doctor relaxed and collapsed onto the foot of the bed. Tram turned to Everett.

"Can you travel, Captain?"

"Your English has vastly improved, old friend," he smiled at the much smaller sniper. "But as Jack once said, I think there is more to our sergeant Tram than meets the eye," Carl said, as he held out his hand once more for Tram to assist him to his feet. He slowly helped Carl up, then reached down and placed his large hand on the Doctor, who was still in shock as he stared at the unconscious form of his nosey landlord. "Thank you. You saved my life. I can never repay your kindness."

The old man stood and then half-bowed his head and shoulders. "It made me feel like a...doctor again. Thank...you."

Carl smiled and then partially collapsed in Tram's arms.

"We have to get you to a hospital," he said.

"The Director has forwarded new travel papers, and our devious little sergeant here has come up with, what do you Americans say? A doozy of a cover story. It seems you were mugged by criminals in District Six, where you were conducting your John Deere tractor business. As I said, our good sergeant has learned his lessons well."

"No hospital. We have to track down Jack."

"Not possible in your condition, Captain," Tram said as he moved Carl toward the door. "I will assist in finding the men who did this to you, but since you are not willing to go to the hospital, I will accompany you to your final destination in Hanoi to make sure you and who you meet are safe. Then I will return here to find the Colonel."

"Tram, it was Jack who shot me and threw me in the river."

Van Tram stopped and looked at a now smiling Henri Farbeaux who obviously thought the comment extremely humorous.

"Oh, so the friends had a falling out. This story must be heard," Henri said, and then smiled more blatantly than the moment before. "Do you plan on payback, Captain?" He gestured toward the door, indicating for Tram and Carl to exit first.

"Why are you smiling, Froggy?" Carl asked Farbeaux.

"No reason at all."

CHAPTER FOUR

Allal Mountains,
Outer Mongolia

The four geologists could not take their eyes off the small man in the black suit and bowler hat as he and his son spoke softly out of hearing range. Professor Lee, who as it turned out, was not the man they thought he was, was gesturing from the group, and then back to his father as the older man listened patiently.

"As I asked before, how many of you are not who they say they are?" the rotund Australian, Birnbaum, asked as he sat on a large rock while watching the two men before them.

"Does it matter, Professor?" Anya asked, as she sat next to Sarah, who was still eyeing the men arguing over their fates.

"I believe I would like to know exactly who I am to be buried with when they come to some form of conclusion over there."

Sarah stood and, with a wary look at Lee and his father, faced the Australian. "I am Captain Sarah McIntire, United States Army." She gestured to the seated Anya. "Major Anya Korvesky, attached to same." She stepped in front of the man known to them as Anderson. "This man, obviously Anderson is not his real name as we surmised earlier when he was holding a gun on all of us, is your typical Russian asshole." The man smiled up at the diminutive Sarah. She kicked out with her boot and caught the man squarely in the testicles, sending him sprawling onto the sand with a laugh coming from Anya. "That's for scaring these poor people, Comrade."

Anderson lay moaning as he tried to keep the contents of his stomach from spewing out onto the warming sand. The move had caught the attention of both Professor Lee and his father, Li Zheng. They watched as Anderson rolled on the ground. The older man smiled and the younger looked shocked.

Anya slowly stood and brushed sand off her pants and then started to assist Anderson to his feet, who gratefully raised his hand for Anya to grasp. When he was off balance, she let go and he fell back to the ground with an *'umph'* sound.

As Sarah and Anya moved away from the agonized Russian agent, the older man and his son slowly approached.

"Before you do to us what you plan to do, what word is there on our twelve colleagues who left earlier this morning?" Sarah asked while holding both men's eyes.

"I was not able to help them. I am sorry for that. None of this was supposed to occur," the man introduced as Li Zheng replied with true sadness lacing his words. "When it was discovered that there were no minerals in the mountains for your governments to profit from, my son was supposed to lead you all out of this valley." He half-turned and faced the very much younger Professor Lee. "Instead, he indulged his natural arrogance to assist in showing you what you never need know."

"Excuse me, mate, but you lost me somewhere back there," Birnbaum said as he finally stood and faced the smaller men. "You know about that strange ore we found?" His angry look went from Lee to his father.

"Yes, my father and I disagree on many things. The mineral is one of them." He turned to face the man who just stood and watched. "This is our main point of contention. He moves at a snail's pace while the world destroys itself."

"And my eldest son still has not learned the shared lessons of our past, and wants to rush headlong into a world war if our ore is discovered."

Anya was watching the oldest story in history. A father's disappointment in his son and vice versa. "Excuse me, us, here, prisoners?"

"Yes, I am sorry," the older man said as he stepped past his son. "You are our guests and we should not be so rude. You are not prisoners. But," he frowned, "your associate there has contacted his superiors and now I am afraid we will have to wait for the next move in this game of chess."

"A game? We lost twelve very valuable scientists to this game of yours," Anya said as she stepped toward the two men. "If this is just a game, you play by very strange rules."

The older man smiled. "Chess is not a game, young lady. Chess moves are what we call life here in the Gobi. Now, I am sure you are curious as to what it was you have discovered. We may as well show you since my son has failed miserably in keeping it quiet. Now we have you, and possibly the outside world, closing in on that secret. This we cannot have." He gave his son a stern look, which looked out of place on the man's gentle features.

"You know our names and why we were here?" Sarah asked.

"Oh, very much so, Miss. We have bumped into your organization," he looked without smiling at the Russian, Anderson, "and his, from time to time. When we learned the Americans had satellite intelligence on this region, possibly pointing to a new mineral source, we knew this to be a lie. My son is a geologist. He knows there are no minerals here worth the trouble. So, we surmised that you Americans were possibly onto something other than your cover story. It has to be the ore that your magnificent machine..." He looked perplexed momentarily. "Ah, yes, Europa, had found that no other system in the world could have detected. Amazing stuff." He again angrily faced his son. "Another example of someone being caught unawares."

"So, there is more of this strange material here?" Anderson asked haltingly as he eased himself back to a sitting position while still holding his stomach in check.

The old man nor his son answered the strained inquiry. Li Zheng just turned and started walking.

Sarah watched Lee as he gestured that they should follow. "The locals scare easily, my friends. But make no mistake, they will be back. You have the choice of going with us and learning some of the deepest, darkest secrets of the world, or stay here, eventually walking out and running into the indigenous population once more."

"What about Charlie and Ryan?" Anya asked.

Lee just smiled and turned to follow his father. "Stay or follow, the choice is yours."

"That's bleedin' great, mate, follow you to possibly get murdered or stay here, and definitely get murdered," Birnbaum said as he started to follow the two men. "Hell of a choice."

Sarah and Anya looked from the men's retreating backs, to each other. They turned to also follow. Anya on her way by, kneed Anderson one last time, sending him sprawling once more.

"Very professional, real professional," he called out as he haltingly rose once again.

THEY WALKED ABOUT A MILE. OR WAS IT TEN? SARAH AND ANYA WERE having a hard time keeping track. They both looked at their watches and saw that neither one was sharing the same time information as the other. Finally, Li Zheng stood facing a stone wall. The old man held his arms out to his side and slowly raised them. His son, Lee, shook his head as if in exasperation. He half-turned and faced the four people following.

"He can be the most irritating man on the planet. This is all for show, you know."

"What is?" Sarah asked as she stepped closer.

"This Merlin crap. He doesn't get to show off much to outsiders. I admit, it's his only vice handed down over the generations, so, we allow him this one small deceit. I mean, with his ability he could enslave the world, so we give him this. The world's a happier place with his abilities in check."

"Abilities?" Birnbaum asked as he saw Anderson step up next to him. He moved away out of distaste.

There was no answer as the old man turned his head toward them and then smiled as his arms and hands came to their pinnacle. Before anyone knew what was happening, the rock facing at the end of the small box canyon started to shake. The sand and dirt that lined the area between the stones started to sift through the cracks and the old man curled his fingers into balled fists. Lee rolled his eyes and shook his head. Suddenly, the entire facing of the wall shot upward. The stone, at least one hundred and thirty tons of it, hovered over a darkened hole. The black area inside the mountain was not able to be penetrated by the four strangers as they stepped back a few paces, as the tonnage above them wavered, rolled in the air, but held firm directly above them.

"This is our eastern gate," Lee said as Li Zheng waved his fists around, as if keeping the massive stones in the air by wind power. "We better go through. It would be our luck the old fool has a stroke before we move out from underneath."

"I heard that, my son," Li Zheng said as he continued to wave his arms and balled fists.

"Well, it would be the first thing you heard me say since my birth." The younger man angrily waved their guests through the strange portal. As soon as they were through, Li Zheng slowly lifted off the ground and, as if he were being carried on a gentle swell of tide, came through. He lowered himself to the worn ground beneath his feet and then closed his eyes. They all screamed and jumped back when the rock facing outside came crashing back to the box canyon outside.

"Jesus Christ, this is too bloody much," Birnbaum said in the darkness of the cave they found themselves in.

"Does anyone have a flashlight?" Sara asked.

Before they knew it, a small glowing light filled the darkness. They turned and saw, not Li Zheng, but his son, Professor Lee, as he swirled his hands in front of him. The ball of light grew brighter and Lee allowed the swirling mass of sparks to rise from his hands.

The ball grew as it rose into the damp air of the cave. Then the swirling ball slammed into the stalactite covered ceiling and the ball of electrical light spread as if it were water breaking upon a shore. The cave was now alight as if the sun had risen inside the mountain.

"Wow," Sarah said as she held her gaze upward, as if in a trance.

Anya for her part, was staring at young Lee. He smiled and pushed his glasses back up on his nose. "That is the shit," she said with mouth ajar.

"That's it for me. I'm what you would call a 'one trick pony'."

"Well, that's one hell of a one trick, laddie." Birnbaum's eyes went from the brightly illuminated electrical storm above their heads over to a smiling and embarrassed Lee. "What in the hell is he?"

Lee snorted. "He is an elemental."

"An ele-what?" Birnbaum asked.

"Air Bender, my friend. He is the last of the Air Benders."

Li Zheng snickered as he walked past the observers and down the trail they were on. "He's a slow learner, my son is. That name is a misnomer. I am but a man. The real magic is a false one. You will see."

Sarah and Anya saw the younger man shake his head in exasperation as he started to follow his father, as he was strangely snapping his fingers and looking high above them as he walked. Just before Li Zheng vanished around a bend in the trail, he raised his right hand and snapped his fingers as his son was attempting to do. The brightness above flared out and then spread even further to cover the part of the trail they were on.

"As I said, my son is a slow learner."

"Asshole," Lee said as he again shook his head.

AFTER AN HOUR, OR WAS IT SIX, MAYBE EVEN LESS THAN FIFTEEN minutes, the group stopped at another blank wall of rock. The light from above still followed the deeper they traveled. Li Zheng turned and faced the newcomers to his desert.

"Welcome to our home," he said, as he and his son both faced the group.

"Not much to look at," the Australian said with a smirk.

Li Zheng smiled and then turned and faced the second rock wall. He simply raised his left hand and swiped at the damp air in front of him. With their mouths wide open in stunned silence, the rock slowly evaporated right in front of them as if a movie projector had been switched off. Sarah estimated that the open space was no less than a mile wide as they stared out onto a sight they could never have imagined.

"Oh...my...god," was all Anya could get out of her mouth before the beauty of the view took her words away.

It was an entirely new world before them as they all looked down from a height of three hundred feet. The green colors are what sapped everyone's desire for further questioning. Trees. Grass. A valley of life that stretched out for miles upon miles. Pagoda-style buildings. Towers of red, green, and gold stretched to the top of the most enormous cave system ever seen on Earth. Water was every-where as many rivers flowed down below them. They meandered with a soft glow of movement as two rivers curled around the settle-ment. Magnificent stone statuary lined the rolling hills of the valley. Birds sang. A cry of a cat sounded somewhere in the hills surrounding the settlement. They saw figures walking, playing, and working the fields far below. As they looked up, it was if they were looking at blue skies. It was an illusion they soon discovered. What-ever it was, was based on the same principle as the ball of electric light used in the cave. The laughter of children sounded, a bell tolled, and cows and chickens moved about in their daily routine.

"This is impossible," Sarah said as she felt her knees grow weaker by the moment.

"And yet, here it is," Birnbaum said as he felt he should close his mouth before anyone saw the drool that wanted to escape from his mouth in the most desperate way.

"Welcome to our home," Li Zheng said as he again stretched out a welcoming hand toward the valley below.

"Ahh," was all the false spy, Anderson, could mutter as he took in the most impossible view imaginable.

"Where in the hell have you taken us?" Anya mumbled, finally losing her ability to stay on her feet, collapsing to the soft green grass of the trail.

"Hah, I told you!"

All heads turned to see three men who had come upon them unnoticed above their position. Sarah smiled when she saw a young man holding a bundle of clothing and a large spear, and then they saw a surly Jason Ryan and an ecstatic Charlie Hindershot Ellenshaw III, smiling on the trail just above them. Charlie slapped Ryan on the back as he took in the view and their friends down below.

"Welcome to Shangri-La, you silly unbelievers!"

Pi Biehn, Laos

THE AREA WAS DARK. NOT ONE SLIVER OF LIGHT PENETRATED THE INKY darkness. The thick walls kept sound all but muted, and the smell was one of dampness and mold. A large and very thick door opened, and a large, rotund man stepped through, and closed the door, immediately plunging the stone prison once more into satin blackness. The man found a switch on the wall. He waited momentarily until his pupils adjusted to the new illumination. The man removed the same fedora he had worn when he had met his contact in Cambodia that very same morning. Doctor Leoniv Vassick saw the folding chair next to the door and hefted it and then walked the few paces toward the only cell hidden away down the long, damp corridor. He placed the chair down and sat. His gaze saw the figure on the bare-springs cot. He placed his left leg over the right and then the fedora was rested in his lap as he cleared his throat.

"It is good to see you once more. We had such a short visit aboard the battle cruiser *Simbirsk* last month."

Silence from the figure on the cot. No movement, no words.

"You have my condolences on the premature death of your

associate. It was unfortunate that we ran into you in this unlikeliest of places. Laos is a hell hole of the worst kind, but very valuable in the field in which we are endeavoring to make a mark in. Unlike your own entity with its massive budget, we must procure resources where we find them." Still no movement. "I admire your ferocity in continuing a search for the killers of the innocents aboard the *Simbirsk*. We have never seen such devotion to justice before, especially from a professional killer such as yourself. But, as they say, curiosity killed the kittens."

"Cat, dumb shit. Curiosity killed the cat." The voice was deep and absent humor.

"Ah, a little flair of life.'

Vassick finally saw the dark figure move. The man sat up on the squeaky springs of the cot and faced the Russian. He was battered and bruised, but the life shown in his blue eyes were visible even from the distance they had between them.

"I just came to say farewell until our next meeting. Your new home awaits, and we have many, many questions to ask you about your organization." Vassick pulled out a pocket watch and clicked the lid open, studyingthe time. "But alas, that can wait," he said as he stood and replaced his hat on his balding head. "I just wanted to say to you that it was a shame you murdered your best friend. A situation like that may spark a self-righteous reaction from a man like you. But revenge should not be your priority. What *must* be your priority, is the fact that we got to you and your friend rather easily and set in motion a plan that has taken many years to prepare. Do you think that we cannot get to others, even more important people in your life? I dare say we can. In fact, we are currently tracking four of them as we speak." Vassick stepped toward the thick bars that separated him from one of the most dangerous men in the world. "Be very fruitful and talkative when you get to my homeland. You may find your cooperation will save many lives." He turned away from the man as he rose and stepped toward the bars. Vassick stopped and turned to face the bearded man. "Goodbye, Colonel."

Colonel Jack Collins watched the darkness close in once more.

His blue eyes were ablaze with anger, self-loathing, and hate. He had to concentrate. He knew the most important field team at the moment was in Siberia. Is that the target of their next murderous act? He shook his head, knowing all he could do was wait for an opportunity.

PART II
WHITE MAGIC

"I can feel white magic burning inside of me just waiting to burst out and eager to be used..."

~ Alejandra Moreno
From the poem, White Magic

CHAPTER FIVE

Reunification Express Train, (Vietnam Railway)
Nearing Hanoi, Vietnam

C arl was watching Colonel Henri Farbeaux. The Frenchman never ceased to amaze the American for his ability to blend in with any nationality in the world. Jack once declared, in a security brief at the complex, that this was the reason Henri had been so adept at gathering the antiquities he had acquired. He made those he met feel comfortable and confident in his kind nature before stealing everything they had entrusted him with. At the moment, that seemed not to be his main goal as he was toying with the four-year-old Vietnamese child in the seats in front of them. Henri would raise his head above the seat-back and then lower it again quickly when the child would peek. This would bring giggles to he and his mother. The game ceased when the mother and child got off at the stop before reaching the Vietnamese capital.

"Okay, Henri, what did you steal from that kid?"

Farbeaux sat back in the bench-seat of the oldest train he had ever traveled upon. He didn't favor Carl with a look. Unlike Colonel Collins, there was very little grudging respect the navy SEAL had for Farbeaux, or vice versa. While Jack could see some form of virtue in Henri, Carl could never find any. He figured the Frenchman was always in it for himself. Perhaps Jack understood that and used Farbeaux's greed to the Group's benefit. Everett just couldn't put aside the affronts that he had committed in the years gone by to Department 5656.

"Since you refused Tram's advice about that hospital, perhaps you should rest, as I suspect you will need it."

"Henri, why in the hell are you even here? You did the favor for Director Compton and assisted Van Tram in locating me, so why travel north?"

"After all of these years, I thought that would have been obvious." Henri leaned back and closed his eyes with that irritating smile stretched across his face.

"Sarah. You think that if I kill Jack for shooting me, you have an open road."

"Okay, Mister Everett, there are two reasons that should be obvious."

"What is the second?" Carl asked as he eyed the Frenchman.

"Because I gave your Director Compton my word. That is one resource I try to keep intact." He finally opened his eyes as the ancient train started to slowly leave the last stop before Hanoi. "You know, it is the opinion of that little Vietnamese friend of yours that you have to be mistaken about who put those bullets into you."

"It was Jack. But there is something that I can't put my finger on that has me doubting my memory."

"And that is?"

"I don't know. I said I can't put my finger on it."

"Wishful thinking on your part, Captain?" Henri chuckled and that irritated Everett more than anything. "I think your Colonel Collins just may have hit, what we black operatives call, the breaking point. It happens to the best."

Carl sat up so fast that he winced at the pain in his abdomen. He slowly sat back. "It wouldn't happen to Jack and you damn well know that."

"Break those stitches open and we may have some explaining to do to the local authorities. However, I believe you are right, my backward friend. There is something amiss here."

Carl waited until the pain eased somewhat in his belly. He took a deep breath and he turned to face Farbeaux. "Well?"

"The Collins that I have come to know would never have made that one mistake," he turned and looked at the larger American. "He would have never left you alive to even ponder the possibility that he had a breakdown." Henri smiled at the consternated Everett. "I must admit that your friend has a few admirable qualities. One is the fact that outside of your African American buddy, Mendenhall, and that little Vietnamese fellow, Van Tram, Collins is the best shot with a firearm that I have ever seen." His smile grew. "Besides myself, of course."

Carl didn't respond. He looked out of the window at the seaside as they sped past. Henri was right. That was the one fact that had fled his memory. Jack would have placed at least one of those bullets directly into his heart, or right between his eyes. The man that shot him had been far more erratic than that. Even when hurried, Jack never missed.

"Your friend, Van Tram, what is it he hopes to accomplish? He refused my help in investigating this event about you and Collins. He looked suspicious when you told him about your friend shooting you. It was if it was not quite a surprise to him. Even though he professed not to believe your account."

"Tram did enough as far as I'm concerned. He needs to stay out of this. Vietnam may be progressing in relations with the U.S., but they still have a way to go. He could have been shot for helping me. It was hard enough to talk him out of traveling north with us."

Farbeaux was quiet as the train started to slow and the announcement was made concerning their next stop—Hanoi. Carl had his eyes still fixed on Henri. "What's going through that warped mind of yours?"

"I was thinking about my intelligence days back in France. We uncovered an old program the Soviets had going in the late sixties. Though our old contacts—"

"You mean before the Vietminh handed France their walking papers after Dien Bien Phu in 1954? You Froggies got your asses handed to you on that one."

"Always ready to point out my countries deficiencies, aren't we?"

"Always," replied Carl.

"As I was saying, the program revolved around look-alikes. Doubles. Since the men you are chasing seem to be of the old Soviet guard, I was wondering if they may have reinstated the program."

"It would explain a lot. But in the light of day, very farfetched. The man was identical to Jack. Facial scars, his manner. Perfect. No, it was Jack."

"Yes, but as you said, it would indeed explain a lot, Captain."

They fell silent as the train pulled into the new station inside the capital city of Hanoi. Everett's hackles rose somewhat as he realized he was now inside an area very few Americans had ever seen, unless they were flying above it during the war years, or worse, dressed in little striped pajamas at the Hanoi Hilton as a prisoner of war. A feeling of unease came flooding into his soul.

Henri was smiling again. "Don't feel bad, Captain," he said as he stood and retrieved his coat from the overhead, "I get the same jitters when I visit. Believe it or not, they despised us far more than they did your nation."

"Yes, I find that hard to believe." Carl slowly stood.

"Well, we should know in just a minute if Compton and Van Tram's little skullduggery has worked. If we see more than six uniformed police officers on the platform, we can probably say Tram's plan to get us to Hanoi didn't pass muster, as you Americans would say."

They waited until most of the passengers had moved out of the car before they slowly started walking down the aisle, looking through the filthy windows as they did. For Everett, he suspected the whole of the Vietnamese intelligence arm would be waiting for them instead of the mysterious contacts they were to meet. He paused at the doorway as the train whistle blew.

They stepped off the train and started to walk. Everett thought he could feel every eye in the capital on them as they slowly moved toward the terminal and hopefully some familiar faces. So far, he was only seeing happy, pleasant people as they moved about.

"Hey!"

Carl's heart froze. Even Henri saw his life pass before his eyes just before he realized that the call-out was spoken in English.

"Toad!" came the deep and gruff, and for Henri, the most irritating voice that he could ever have heard. "You son of a bitch!"

Carl turned and saw the short, stubby man in the grey overalls. "Master Chief?"

"Yeah, and sidekick, Poncho," Master Chief Jenks bellowed as he pulled an embarrassed Will Mendenhall out in front of him.

The Master Chief came up to Everett and took him into a bear hug. Carl felt his insides explode with pain from the assault. Jenks finally put the very much larger man down as he saw the form of Henri Farbeaux.

"You're keeping very salty company these days, Toad."

"It is good to see you also, squid-head," Henri said as he shook hands with Will while ignoring the Master Chief's greeting. He and Mendenhall had faced death together in the Antarctic and had come to a grudging admission that they both liked each other. A very rare event with any member of the Group, besides the feelings of Sarah McIntire.

"Captain, you had everyone at the complex somewhat concerned the past few days," Will said as he shook hands with Everett.

"It has been eventful." He looked from Will to Jenks. "What's the story so far?"

"As soon as we put you and me on that C-130 back home, the Master Chief is heading to Mongolia with an Air Force commando unit. It seems Mister Ryan and Sarah's field team have gone offline. Their new implant transponders ceased operation twelve hours ago." He turned to Henri. "Colonel, the director wished me to express his gratitude for assisting us. He offers you a ride home—free of charge, courtesy of the U.S. Air Force."

"And I was only supposed to help retrieve you and King Ground Pounder get the hell back home. Now I'm off to the land of nothing... goddamn sons of bitches, that damn Compton was just looking for a way to shove shit down my pants," Jenks mumbled.

All eyes went from the Master Chief to Farbeaux, as Carl actually held out a hand. "Thanks Froggy. You'll have the C-130 all to yourself. I may not be able to help Tram find Jack, but I still have friends lost out there in the Gobi some place."

Farbeaux took the offered hand and, as Jenks looked on in distaste, shook it.

"Always a pleasure to see you writhing in pain, Captain. Call me again the next time your best friend places some bullets into you. That is always of interest."

Henri half-heartedly saluted the three men and then disappeared into the crowd.

"I don't know why you people put up with that guy," Jenks said as he popped a cigar into his mouth. "And you, Toad, there's no way you can travel to bum-fuck Mongolia in your condition," he spit onto the platform which elicited a severe look from an old peasant woman as she boarded the train south. "Why don't you head back to the States and I'll take the new Major here with me."

"Master Chief, I believe you are a civilian engineer. I am a Captain in the United States Navy, who, at last report, out-ranked you anyway. So light up that cigar and shove it up your ass, will ya? And if the Director wants Will back home, he's got to go. If what we discussed on the train is a possibility, this killer is targeting the field team. And I won't miss that. So, cigar, up ass, that's an order."

Mendenhall took an involuntary step back as he had never seen anyone speak to the Master Chief in the manner Carl just had.

"Okay, okay, you don't have to get pissy about it, Captain shithead."

"Gentlemen, I hate to bring this reunion to a conclusion, but you two have another train to catch. Last report from Morales and

Compton said that some kind of Russian operation is gearing up north of the Mongolian border."

"Gearing up for what?" Everett asked.

"Not sure yet. But *Boris* and *Natasha* are picking up heavy military movement at the border."

"What kind of activity?" Everett asked as Jenks sent another stream of spit onto the tracks the south bound train had just left.

"Europa thinks it the 59th Black Sea Regiment."

Jenks finally removed the cigar from his mouth. "Goddamn killers are what they are. Aren't those the bastards that attacked those kids in Syria with nerve agent?"

No one answered his question as they knew very well who the 59th was and what they did for Vladimir Putin. They did the ugly stuff, and the Director and Europa thought they may be headed southward from the Russian border into the Gobi Desert.

Jenks shook his head and then gestured toward the terminal and the street beyond. "Well, we better get our asses off to the land of Genghis Khan, Toad, we wouldn't want to miss all of the fun. I love traveling with you slack-jawed gurus, you're always so much fun."

Major Will Mendenhall felt absolutely worthless as he said his goodbyes to his friends. His new duties were killing him slowly inside. He watched as Everett and Jenks, with Henri moving away in another direction, head off to the real world—a world that was no longer Will's.

THE DARK-HAIRED MAN WATCHED THE AMERICANS LEAVE AND THEN waved his car to the curb. Once in the blue colored Citroen sedan, he checked in electronically with Director Vassick to inform him that the Americans had arrived and were now on the move north.

"Where to, sir?" the driver asked his new boss.

"The airport. I have a date in a different desert."

After fifteen years of studying the enemy, the reborn Jack Collins had a very important mission to fulfill, and it was time to get serious.

Headquarters MI-6, 85 Albert
Embankment, London, England

THE HEAVYSET MAN WITH THE BOWTIE GREETED HIS ASSISTANTS IN THE outer office with his gruff 'good morning' as he had every day, six days a week for the past eighteen years. As always, his head was angled downward in deep thought as he read a communique from his operations department. As he strode into his modest office, he waved his assistant in without looking up. She knew the mood immediately. The head of the intelligence arm of Britain's MI-6 was worried about something he had been informed of at home earlier that morning.

"Would you like tea, Lord Durnsford?" she asked as she came in with her archaic notepad and pen.

"If I had wanted tea I would have procured it for myself," he grumbled as he placed the report down on his desktop and then waited for her to take a seat. "Put away that pad. Nothing of this goes to paper, is that clear, Ms. Jennings?"

Without answering, she simply placed the notepad on her lap and folded her hands over it.

"I am about to commit a crime."

The assistant had worked for Lord Durnsford even before the *Overlord Operation*. Durnsford had overseen the United Kingdom's end of things as he worked closely with other officials from every nation. Durnsford had been instrumental in forming the alliance that had virtually saved the world from the Gray invasion with the Overlord plans in Antarctica. The event had aged the old gentlemen countless years, and those years were now well-worn and etched deeply into his face. With his statement about committing a crime, the assistant was nonplussed. Lord Durnsford committed crimes every day of his professional life in order for him to cut through the red tape and the bureaucracy of intelligence gathering, with a government that was prickly when it came to what Her Majesty's forces were up to in the world of espionage. In other words, what the Prime Minister and the Queen didn't know, surely would not hurt them.

Durnsford reached into his top drawer and dialed in a code for his combination lock for the small safe. Before he pulled out the small, black notebook, he looked up at Ms. Jennings. "I'm sending you on a field assignment."

The woman's eyes lit up. "Is it dangerous?" she asked with mock excitement.

"Only if you are observed. Then if you are, I will strangle you myself when you return. So, yes, it could possibly be dangerous."

"I see. I'm meeting someone you want no record of meeting."

"I knew there was a reason I keep you on. Precisely."

"Parameters of said assignment?" she asked.

"You are meeting a man for lunch at an Indian bistro. You know him, we have worked closely together before. After you finish your lunch, order the chicken curry by the way, it's very good, then after you finish your curry, you will stand up as you make your goodbyes to the gentleman, lean in and whisper, and I mean whisper mind you, *the Khan has awakened.*"

"The Khan has awakened," she repeated.

"Leave the bistro, return here." He started to reach for his small black phone book. He stopped and looked up over his half-moon bifocals. "Well, that is all."

She stood with her notepad and then looked at Lord Durnsford. "Should I go armed?" she asked with hope brightening her blue eyes.

Durnsford took an intake of breath, exasperated. "Woman, this is Great Britain, not bloody Syria. The man is a Colonel in the SAS. I don't think he will be inspired to shoot my assistant. That would not be a well thought out career move, now would it?"

"Let's just hope he loves his career," she said as she turned and walked out of the office disappointed.

Lord Durnsford shook his head, but he did offer a smile at the enthusiasm of some of his people. He removed the black book from the safe and then flipped through the pages. He found the number he was looking for. He picked up the phone and then punched in one number.

"*This is the Router,*" came the squeaky voice on the other end of the line.

"Secure for overseas."

"Yes, you have a secure line. Use number five-oh-six."

"Thank you," Durnsford said as he punched the button indicating 506. When he heard the scrambler squeak and squeal, then the dial tone, he knew his call was as secure as MI-6 communications could make it. He punched in his chosen number and then waited.

"Gold City Pawn," came the voice from over five thousand miles away.

"Yes, I would like to speak to the manager about a silver tiara pawned last year."

"Was this a pawn item, or a sell item, sir?"

"Pawn," came the coded reply.

"One moment please, I'll connect you with the manager's office."

Lord Durnsford smiled at the simple way the Americans had of security. Rather antiquated in his opinion, but he knew the man he was about to speak to never trusted in the technology concerning the protection of his most obscure and top-secret agency. He heard the chirps and clicks as the phone was sent to the man's private and scrambled line.

"Compton," said the voice of the man Durnsford had become very close to over the years.

"Niles, old boy, good to hear your voice," Durnsford said.

"Lord Durnsford, you're in the office a bit early today."

"You and I never really leave our offices, old man, you of all people should know that."

At the Event Group complex underneath Nellis Air Force Base in Nevada, Niles Compton couldn't stifle the yawn. *"I take it you have had the same results on your end about this Russian shadow government as I?"*

"Niles, at least you got a chance to get into the Oval Office and speak your piece. I was turned away from 10 Downing after only twenty minutes of debrief with the Prime Minister. Our official government stance going forward is...well, we have no official stance. No proof, no stance."

"We're just two voices crying out in the wind. Oh, the C.I.A. and N.S.A.

believe us, but without proof any Senate oversight would butcher them if they go after Russia with what we have."

"Same here, old boy." Durnsford cleared his throat. "Uh, Niles, that's not the real reason for my call. It seems one of my people has gone and got himself lost."

"I know the feeling," Niles said as he was starting to suspect that Durnsford had eyes on the situation thanks to placing a tag on his own Department 5656 personnel.

"The Mongolia thing, well I—"

"Oh, for Christ's sake, Willy, you tagged my field team in Mongolia, didn't you?"

"You know the game, old man. We have never been impaired with an overabundance of trust. But no, my man is there on his own. He has no idea who your people are. Or he didn't to being with. No telling what he knows now. I don't employ idiots, as I am positive you do not. Nonetheless, we have lost contact with our boy."

"Well, join the club. Our tracking and health implants on our people have gone offline. How many tags do you have with the field team?"

"Just the one. Very experienced, and a man who knows his limits on who are the bad guys and who are the good."

"That's good to know, you sneaky ghost bastard."

"I'll take that as a compliment. However, to the point. Our man's signal ceased at 0125 this morning. Yours?"

"The same. I believe we can safely say our field team has been discovered."

"Yes. Now, may I assume your team was there for the same purposes as our man?" He again cleared his throat. "What I mean to say is, it had nothing to do with the mineral content of the Gobi Desert?"

"Only one mineral, to be specific."

"Then your satellites picked up the same buried secret as our own?"

Niles was silent for a moment. He toyed with a paperclip on his blotter as he thought. Durnsford was a close friend, but as a friend he had learned to keep his Lordship at arm's length. He made a quick decision.

"We suspect that our Slavic friends may have also penetrated the geological dig, but for other reasons, at least at first. Europa was able to use Boris and Natasha to track the Russian's communication from the mountain range the field team is at. You can guess where that communication ended up. And one hint, it wasn't Newark, New Jersey."

"Ah, this would explain our current situation somewhat."

"This thing just may blow up in our faces, Willy. I've spoken to the president. He's ready to send a SEAL team in with an Air Force commando unit if necessary. But, I have to find my people first."

"Yes, I am in the process of doing the same. I'm putting Colonel Mayfield on alert notice and getting he and his Special Air Service team into Ulaanbaatar within the day. I will not lose one man to those imposter bastards in Siberia. After what they did to that innocent Russian cruiser crew, I don't care if the Queen orders me bloody-well hanged."

"Okay, First Lord. I'll ask the President to get our teams coordinated and they can rendezvous in the Mongolian capital of Ulaanbaatar. Sometimes it pays to have a lame duck president in office. He doesn't really care who it is he pisses off. He's kind of like Jack Collins on that one. I take it that your superiors will not be so pleased if your S.A.S team were discovered invading Mongolia? May I suggest our teams coordinate, that way you could possibly use us backward Americans as your excuse for being in country?"

"Understood, old boy. Not a good plan, but when it comes to cover-ups, I'll go with the American angle most times." He paused a moment. "I have one more subject to broach. May I take it you received the same video feed from Mongolia that we received?"

Niles wanted to chuckle. Lord Durnsford and his people were light years ahead of the rest of the world when it came to intelligence gathering. He knew if someone had a secret, that very secret would be on the desk of Durnsford within the day.

"Yes. Virginia ran the numbers with Europa for estimating the speed demonstrated in the video. I'm hesitant to describe her words and theory."

"Which one, Ms. Pollock's or that damnable criminal element you call Europa?"

"Both. They can be that irritating."

"Then I take it your analysts have come to the same conclusion as our physics boys?"

"Faster than light space travel."

"Now we know why our semi-red friends are interested."

"Explains a few things, yes."

"We'll speak again, Doctor, when our forces mop up in Ulaanbaatar."

Lord Durnsford hung up the phone and checked his watch. He shook his head as he realized the world's most dangerous game was once more afoot.

The race for a possible fuel source that could create faster than light space travel had begun.

**Altai Mountains,
Mongolia**

SARAH FELT HER KNEES GO WEAK. SHE ALLOWED HER LEGS TO DO their own thinking as she slowly eased herself down onto the soft carpet of grass that lined the well-worn path leading down into the hidden city. She stayed that way while Professor Birnbaum made his way toward Anya who could not take her eyes off the scene far below.

"Can you bloody well believe this? A garden of Eden hidden underneath the most inhospitable desert on the planet. This is the most spectacular sight I have ever seen."

Anya felt the words she wanted to speak stick inside of her closing throat as the view below overwhelmed her senses.

"This will change the world as we know it," Anderson said as he finally felt his insides straighten themselves out after Sarah and Anya's assault.

Li Zheng looked at his son just as Anderson put words to his astonishment. The rebuke was apparent, and the younger Lee could not hold his father's eyes.

"Somehow I believe this unfortunate outcome may have been perpetuated by you, my son. Could it be your youthful exuberance and natural instinct for rebellion has brought our people to this? The outside world has now invaded the sanctuary that was the hope of our and their futures," he nodded his head at the circle of newcomers to his city. "We needed time to acclimate the planet to our existence. Now we have no time. I believe you have achieved the outcome you have argued for since you were but a child. That outcome may have destroyed not only our home, but the people in it."

Professor Lee lowered his eyes.

"Your silence speaks volumes, my son. We will speak of this later." Li Zheng turned and walked away down the grassy path just as twenty children from the city ran up to greet him. The younger Lee watched as the love of Li Zheng's people was apparent.

Sarah felt two strong arms lift her up from the trail. She stuttered at first when she saw Jason Ryan.

"You don't need to say anything." Ryan steadied Sarah as he turned and looked down into a valley that could not possibly exist in natural geological terms. "Hell, what could you say? How do you explain this?"

"The truth about the myth of Shangri-La, is that the legend itself always defied a scientific explanation. Never once did any ancient people or nationality actually lay claim to the story." Sarah turned and saw Charlie as he stood with hands on hips as if he were surveying heaven itself. He reached up and pushed the Pith helmet back on his head as he surveyed the scope of the valley through his bottle thick wire-framed glasses. He looked up and saw the unnatural sunlight as it was seemingly being filtered through solid stone. Stones, giant boulders, that had been laid as if by the hands of an ancient master-builder. There was not one inch of open space between the placements. It was if he were looking at a giant geodesic dome a half a mile above their heads. He finally looked at Sarah and Ryan as Anya joined them. "You non-believers constantly forget the lessons that were taught to you by the two smartest people on the planet. Every myth and legend have a basis steeped in fact. If you forget that, you lose the very science that you seek."

Sarah remembered the words of not only Niles Compton, but the man who taught the director those very same words, Garrison Lee. Now the truth of that statement was staring her right in the face.

"I apologize, Charlie. I for one will never laugh at one of your theories again. This...this...I can't begin to tell you how impossible this is, even though I am looking straight at it. I am a geologist and I can say with no doubt in my mind at all...this cannot be here. Yet—"

"Here it is," Ellenshaw said as he smiled and then nudged Ryan out of his way as he placed his thin arm around Sarah's shoulder and hugged her. "Now, shall we do what we do best?"

"If you mean we are free to pee our pants, I've already accomplished that," Ryan said as he was still looking up at the impossibility of the ceiling structure high above his head.

"No, no, my boy. Shall we head down there and ask a few questions on just how this could be?"

The four Department 5656 personnel, with Birnbaum and Anderson following, started down the trail into the mythical city of Shangri-La.

THE FIVE WATERFALLS THAT RINGED THE CITY BROUGHT FRESH WATER from someplace that Sarah knew to be geologically impossible. The water tables of the Gobi could not support such a volume of liquid water. She suspected it may spring from giant pockets of trapped ice. Very few people knew the Gobi, while hot most days of the year, could be brutally cold during some of the rainier months. Any rainfall could be theoretically trapped in the substrata and then melt to create small falls of water. But the size of the five surrounding waterfalls vehemently denied that very theory. The volume was just too great.

The group of newcomers watched the citizens of this underground metropolis as they came forth from their daily chores to greet

Li Zheng and his son. Special attention was paid to Lee as the group supposed he had been gone the longest. The people looked happy for their return. The colors and manner of dress was astounding. Simple robes of red, orange, white, blue…rainbow colors of homespun-weave that looked as if they were a throwback to ancient Chinese culture. Some men were shaved bald, and Charlie suspected a religious group of some kind. While others had long, short, even braided hair, it seemed that many Asian cultures were represented. The children were laughing, and the newborn babies looked content in their mother's arms. There were vendors, where it was noticed by Professor Birnbaum, that no form of monetary compensation was offered for the fruit, or the jewelry, nor even the abundance of western goods, like T-shirts or jeans, as the people gratefully just gave these things to the passerby in exchange for something as small as an apple, or a bag of what looked like sugar. The professor figured they were on the simplest of monetary systems here—the time-honored tradition of bartering.

Teenage children approached the visitors and then stood surrounding them in a circle. The move wasn't hostile, just one of curiosity. One girl about the age of thirteen approached Sarah and Anya and reached out and felt the denim jeans they both wore.

"These are Wranglers. 714s? They're not supposed to be on sale for another year," she said as if jealous of the advanced styles the two women were wearing. The girl with the most beautiful dark eyes they had ever seen, smiled, and then moved off as other teens came closer. They had beautifully designed glasses and they held them out to the newcomers.

"Beer," Professor Lee said, as most of the citizens of this magical place moved off to finish their days' business. "Brewed from an ancient Chinese recipe."

Ryan accepted the offered crystal blue glass from a young girl who was as beautiful as any young woman he had ever seen. He sniffed the beer and then tasted it. He made a satisfactory 'ah', and then smacked his lips. "I sense the Heineken company may have a beef with your brew-masters over proprietary property."

"We pay little attention to the worlds legalities here. What was it Captain McIntire called you? Oh, yes, Commander Ryan," Lee said as he gave Jason a wry smile and then moved off.

"If I'm not mistaken here, pal, I don't think we're the only ones not being entirely straightforward about certain truths."

Lee still had the smile on his face as Jason spoke.

Anya reached out and pulled Charlie Ellenshaw's arm down as he started to consume his third glass of beer, as five or six of the small children and teens laughed and giggled almost out of control at the tall man's funny hair and even funnier headgear.

"You need to slow down, Professor," Anya said. "I think you need to eat something before you get totally shitfaced."

"I'm facing our circumstance the best way possible for the moment," Ellenshaw said as he pulled the glass back and drained it.

"Circumstance?" Professor Birnbaum asked, quite enjoying the beer himself.

Ellenshaw finished the glass and then handed it over to a waiting teen to take away. "Yes, circumstance. How do you think this society has kept the largest secret in the history of the world for so long?" He saw the questioning faces around him and then shook his head as he finally removed the ridiculous Pith helmet. "Our circumstance surrounds the fact that we will never be allowed out of this valley alive." Crazy Charlie smiled at each shocked person in turn, and then happily snatched another beer from a passing teen. "Cheers."

They watched Ellenshaw drink his beer as they realized the crazed, white-haired cryptozoologist was right. Ryan quickly lost his appetite for the dark brew he held and allowed it to pour from his glass.

"I miss Mendenhall. Charlie is becoming a little depressing these days."

"All of this...all of it, will not be able to stand up to the brutal force my country can bring to bear. They will have little choice on whether to cooperate with the modern world. You can feel the raw power here in this place. An ancient power, possibly an unstoppable force."

Sarah was getting tired of the Anderson imposter and his bravado. "Its amazing that you overlook that very same power you speak of," she said as she watched the citizenry close shops and started to wander off to their carved-out homes of stone and wood surrounding the city center. She was amazed that the trees were even waving in a breeze that could not possibly be here inside the most immense cave system in the world. "Do you think that this society, that has lived under the noses of one of the most powerful nations in world history, did so by just asking to be left alone?"

"Obviously they use some form of illusionary science, young lady," Anderson said. "Perhaps the Chinese don't even know they are here. They can't see or detect them."

"I think Sarah just made her point, you Commie prick," Anya said, as she once again pulled another glass of beer out of Ellenshaw's hand, much to his consternation. "If they can hide this magnificent city from Chinese, American and Russian satellites, not counting Mongolian hordes and peasants, what chance do you think your people have of finding them?"

Anderson lost the confidence in his argument as he looked around at the ten-mile-long and half mile-high structure. He could not hold the looks of the others as his plan for glory just evaporated with the Israeli woman's words. Sarah and the others moved off to follow Professor Lee to whatever fate these amazing people had waiting for them.

It was Ryan who had just caught the reference as he ran to catch up with the others.

"Commie prick? Uh, did me and Charlie miss something?"

CHAPTER SIX

Pi Biehn, Laos

After meeting with a contact inside Ho Chi Minh City, the small man had pulled what strings he could to get a special operations helicopter for a covert joyride into a foreign land. The French-made Aérospatiale Gazelle flew low over the fast-flowing Mekong River. The man in the Gazelle's co-pilot seat sat in deep thought. The information he had received from an old combat friend from special operations had made very little sense until he dug a little deeper into the area he was headed. His friend had informed him of a drug cartel's safehouse in Pi Biehn, Laos. The safehouse was also used by Vietnam's former ally against the Americans, the Russians. After reading the report and the description of the area Captain Everett had described, Van Tram had concluded that the safehouse may be his only lead.

The Vietnamese sniper was out on a limb and he knew it. If it was discovered that he had gone rogue in his investigation, no matter how the Vietnamese government was trying to modernize and change to the point they could join the west in shaking off the yoke of communism, he could very well have that limb he was out on cut away, sending him to a firing squad, national hero or not. He knew he was not very well trusted after his dealings in working with the Americans in the planet's war against the Grays. Heroism only goes as far as loyalty. Right now, he was torn between two loyalties; one was to his struggling nation, the other to the man he most respected above all others—Colonel Jack Collins. Sometimes there was an even higher calling than patriotism. Not only did the world owe the Colonel, Tram personally was a deep debtor to the man.

That was not the only concern that Tram was in deep thought about. It was the second item he had discovered in the Vietnamese dossier on the area he was headed into. When he had examined what he had thought was the file on Jack Collins, he was shocked to find out it wasn't his friend's dossier, but his father's. The confusion was spreading in his mind as he failed to see the reasons why his government would have a file on Jack's father. After an hour of heavy reading, he soon discovered the reasons why. Collins senior was a very important Special Forces operative for the Americans. Captured in 1972, the Vietnamese government had turned him over, at special request, to their Russian allies. The reason for this was not explained in the short dossier. It was obvious that, with the American combat forces pulling out of the war, his own government found very little interest in keeping the young American Captain, so they instead turned him over to Russian intelligence. The exchange was done at the location he was now trying to get to. Not because of any intention by the Russians, but for the lone reason it was their only safehouse in Laos for conducting the Russian drug trade out of Laos and Cambodia. It was the Russian Golden Triangle connection. That was his only lead in finding his lost American friend. That and the location as described by Everett.

The pilot spoke to the sergeant through his headphones as the Gazelle shot low over the dark waters of the Mekong. "We have a Laotian river garrison coming up in three miles. If they detect us, we'll have to turn back."

Tram looked at his old friend who was the most experienced

insertion pilot he had ever known. "If they detect us, you return, my friend. As for me, I will have to swim."

"If they detect us, we'll both be swimming, which is a good thing since the fires covering our bodies would be put out when we go diving into the Mekong." The pilot looked over at his friend and smiled, easing Tram's apprehension about his private invasion. "By the way, it is not like you to go anywhere without that damn American antique rifle."

Tram offered the pilot an irritating look as the Gazelle swung lower to the river. His gift from Jack Collins, while on attached duty to the American field teams down in South America, had been an ancient World War II weapon that Tram had fallen instantly in love with. The venerable M-14 Garand rifle was so inaccurate for most soldiers at along distance, that very few had ever mastered the weapon for anything other than close-range fire. But Collins' gift was one Tram loved. Instantly he had become the most accurate sniper in the world with a weapon without a scope. He treasured the Garand as much as his friendship with the American Colonel.

"I may have to egress out of Laos rather quickly. My weapon would have slowed me down. I may be able to blend in out of uniform, but even in the Golden Triangle it's not too healthy to be seen armed amongst the drug killers of the region."

"Well, I hope you have that pistol ready, because we are being painted by the damn Laotians."

Tram glanced over and saw the red flashing warning light and the direction the radar 'paint' was coming from.

"Hover and I will jump from here. You need to escape."

"And ruin my reputation as the greatest pilot in all of Vietnam? My friend, just tighten your harness and watch what magic your friend can provide to your criminal enterprise."

Before he moved the collective to the left to avoid the sweep of the Laotian radar, bright red tracers lit up the darkening sky. Tram involuntarily ducked as the rounds came within feet of the helicopter's canopy. The pilot jerked the collective to the left and went so low to the Mekong that his left landing skid skimmed the water.

"Where did you learn to fly this way?" Tram asked as he held on for dear life.

The pilot swung the black helicopter back to the left as the tracers found them. The four-bladed bird again skimmed the water as Tram felt three or four bullets impact on the airframe.

"American war movies."

"You mean the war against us?"

"Of course, we use them as training films at the academy. What better helicopter pilots to learn from than the very men who invented air assault methods?"

The Gazelle suddenly climbed up and over an almost solid line of tracer fire. Finally, Tram felt relieved as the Gazelle broke out over open jungle and the Laotian fire was left in their wake.

"Now, who's the best pilot you know?"

Tram was about to say something totally different than what the hot shot helicopter pilot wanted to hear, but he decided to keep Commander Jason Ryan's name out of the conversation for political reasons. "You're definitely the craziest."

"I'll take that as a compliment."

Tram saw the lights of Pi Biehn ten miles ahead. He reached into his civilian coat and brought out a small electronic pad and clicked it on. The pad had been another gift from the Event Group when he had been assigned to them in Antarctica for mapping purposes, and Tram had kept the system as he had nothing like it in his own army. He held the pad out to the pilot.

The small glowing circle was highlighted. "That's damn close to the center of town."

Tram smiled as he finally saw worry in the arrogant pilot's eyes. "It's a small park just on the outskirts. Twenty minutes' walk to the location of the Russian safehouse."

"Okay, I hope there are not a lot of telephone and electrical lines in the area."

"This is Laos, not Paris."

The pilot reached out over his console and turned off the Gazelle's anti-collision lights. Tram was now worried that they would snag an electrical line as they sped toward their destination in total blackness. Suddenly the pilot pulled back on his collective as the rear landing assembly snagged one of those nonexistent powerlines. The line grew taut, and then the wheel simply rolled over it with only a small slowing of speed from the French-made bird.

"That was close!"

"There's the park," Tram said pointing down below. "Looks empty."

"Until the drug dealers start to get curious," the pilot said as he started to ease the Gazelle down onto the sparse grass of the park.

Tram didn't waste time on goodbyes to his friend. He slapped him on his right shoulder and was out of the door before the helicopter's skids touched down. The Gazelle sprang back into the air as its turbine screamed in protest. Van Tram moved quickly away to get shy of the park's only two tower lights as he sped for the tree line that surrounded the small town. He knelt down and again looked at his mapping pad. The small glowing circle was only two miles distant. He replaced the notepad and then checked his only weapon—a small and very lightweight Ruger EC9s Semi-Auto Pistol. It was light for a reason—it only held seven rounds in a clip, plus one in the chamber. Tram didn't like pistols, but knew he needed a light one. He checked it and then slid it into the back of his belt as he started to move away from the park.

After an hour and a half of ducking for cover and avoiding anyone on the dirt roads of the town, Tram was able to find a safe spot across from his objective. He reached into his coat and brought out a small pair of binoculars and scanned the property. It was a rundown three-story structure made of tin and clapboard. As he spied the building, he saw several windows aglow with light. There seemed to be no movement on any of the floors. He was starting to become concerned when he noticed no guards of any kind roaming the property. Tram lowered the glasses in deep thought. If Jack was here, it would seem the Russians who held him were not that concerned with keeping his location secured. He looked around the surrounding buildings. None looked to be occupied. He was just thinking of moving his vantage point to the front of the dilapidated structure when he detected movement to his front. He brought the small field glasses back to his trained eyes. He smiled. He saw one man step out onto a back-porch area. The large man relieved himself off into the bushes below and then stepped back inside. He again lowered the glasses. The man was at least six feet five inches, a little too large for a Laotian. He counted the steps to the back-door area and saw that he could get to the area without much risk of discovery.

Tram made ready to move when he saw the sensor in a tree not fifteen feet from him. He shook his head, angry at himself for being naïve enough to think that a Russian drug cartel would have human security only. He recognized the heat sensor and night vision camera system. The camera was remote and thus far he hoped he had not set off a Russian security man's curiosity. He waited. Finally, the camera and sensor moved to the right, away from his location and Tram was able to breathe once more. Still, he thought he could time any movement to the angle of the system. He heard a snapping sound behind him and he drew his Ruger and waited. The noise did not occur again. A cat, he suspected. He looked up and then, when the camera and sensor moved left, Tram sprung through the scarcity of trees and squat-ran to the concrete steps of the back-porch. He slid onto his knees and knelt in the dark. He froze as the rear door opened once more and the light was cast outside. He held his breath as a stream of urine splashed down right in front of him. He shook his head at the undignified greeting he was receiving. So much for the glory of rescuing a friend. The flow of urine ended, the sound of the door opening came once more and then the light was again drawn back into the safehouse. He took a deep breath. It seemed this may not be the way inside. If every guard was close enough to the door for restroom purposes, the odds were against his using that way as gaining entrance. He was about to move back into the tree line when he saw a light come on in a basement window.

As Tram thought, he knew the odds had again swung back into his favor. The basement would be the logical location for any prisoner to be found. He may have caught a break. He slowly moved to the small frame of the window and tried to look inside. The yellow tinted light was right in his eyes, and as a sniper he knew that the night vision he so craved was momentarily lost to him. He leaned back away from the small portal and laid back against the clapboard wall. He was now realizing his plan had major flaws. He needed intel from the inside that he was not going to get. It would be like sneaking into a beehive. It just couldn't be done covertly.

Tram was trained as a stand-off weapon. He could kill from up to three miles distance with the right weapon. He looked down at the small Ruger and shook his head. He had been so anxious to assist his friend that he had not thought out his plan. He moved back to the safety of the lee of the porch and went again to his knees. He had to think. His eyes roamed the perimeter of the grounds. There were three old and rusted out Citroen sedans from the old French years in the region, and also several rows of old tires stacked, and it was these that acted as a barrier of sorts that guarded the safe house from neighbors' prying eyes. He was growing frustrated at himself. He was now starting to believe he would need at least a squad-sized assault team to get inside and accomplish what it was he set out to do. He saw the camera and sensor in the tree where he had been moments before. He listened and heard the whine of the small electric motor as it moved. Then the idea hit him. He could at least get a count of the number of men in the back portion of the safe house. He again reached into his jacket and this time he brought out the only accompaniment to his Ruger—a small cylindrical tube that he screwed onto the muzzle. His weapon was now silenced. He aimed.

To the trained Tram the weapon didn't seem to be silenced at all. A very loud 'clack' sounded as the small Ruger discharged and then recycled another round into the chamber. Then it was the extremely loud whine and the impact of the bullet as it struck the camera and sensor. He winced as the pieces of the assembly fell to the ground. He lowered his head and waited for the enemy to pinpoint his precise location.

The back door soon opened, and he heard words being spoken in Russian. He understood very little of the language but knew he heard the words *'damn kids'* in there somewhere. Evidently, the safehouse had problems with local neighborhood hooligans. At least he hoped. He heard the footsteps of two men as they descended the concrete steps. There were curses as Tram saw the Russians up-close for the first time. His eyes widened when he saw the true height of these men. To Tram, they were like giants as they moved toward the tree line to examine the damage. He saw the two men start to look around as one of them picked up the smashed camera lens.

"That's two. How many more?" he whispered to himself. He knew the action was a bad idea.

The two men stood after examining the damaged camera and sensor and both drew from their jackets two of the largest handguns Tram had ever seen before. They started to look closely at the darkened area around them. He made a decision. He suddenly stood and turned for the stairs as stealthily as possible. He grabbed the handrail and started to pull himself up to the first step when he slammed face first into a solid brick wall. The pistol was knocked from his hand and he was grabbed by the collar and lifted free of the concrete step.

"Что у нас здесь?"

Van Tram was looking into the most heavily scarred face he had ever seen. The old wounds crisscrossed the brown visage of the man holding him three feet off the step. His words were not recognizable to his ears. The man shook him three times in rapid succession. He again asked his question and again Tram only stared, wide-eyed.

The English language came from his left, but he failed to see who spoke it.

"He said, what have we here?"

The large man turned with Tram still held tightly in his clutches. Tram's heart skipped a beat when he saw one of the two men sent to find out the problem with their security system. The man reached out and picked up Tram's pistol from the dirt. The Vietnamese sniper remained silent as if he didn't understand English.

"Don't tell me that the Laotian police has become this brave?" the man said with a smile. "You should have possibly checked with your superiors before snooping around our property, officer."

Tram was still too busy looking at the gorilla of a man attempting to strangle him and throw him to the moon in the same action, to really care about what was being said. All he knew at that moment was the fact he had failed miserably at what he was trying to do.

"Take him to the cages. We'll inquire as to his curiosity inside."

The large man just seemed to tuck Sergeant Tram under his arm as the world once again flooded with light from inside the Russian safehouse.

Sergeant Van Tram's mission to save a friend had turned out to be a bust, and now he faced the same fate as the very friend he had been trying to rescue.

Atal Mountains, Mongolia

SARAH AND ANYA HAD DECIDED TO TRY TO GET A HEAD COUNT OF THE population of the underground world Charlie Ellenshaw had dubbed, Shangri-La. The task was made easier since every evening meal was done communally. The setting for these meals was a visually stunning sight to the unbeliever. The long tables were set against the backdrop of the four waterfalls that surrounded the city center, with dugout housing in the cliff facing rising up to and over the falls themselves. Sarah thus far had counted over thirty-five families on her side of the divided-up place settings. She glanced at Anya who was in deep conversation with a family of five as she sat next to them. She saw Sarah looking her way and she held up ten fingers. With Sarah's count, the city seemed to have no less than forty-five separate families living in the underground world.

"Your count will not be accurate, I'm afraid," came the familiar voice behind her. Sarah turned and saw the old man, Li Zheng, smiling as he waved a hand. "May I join you and Professor Ellenshaw?"

Sarah looked at crazy Charlie as he was toying with a small girl child of about four years old with the old 'pull off the thumb' trick.

The girl was not as confused as Charlie was making out. "Please do," Sarah said.

Li Zheng who had changed into orange and white robes, eased in to Sarah's left. His smile never wavered as both women and men delivered the meal of braised chicken and steamed vegetables. Sarah saw the joy the old man had at being with his small group of citizens. Pitchers of the cleanest water Sarah had ever seen before were added and the citizens of Shangri-La talked and ate. The newcomers were spared little curiosity and were basically ignored. Ignored, except for Jason Ryan, who was wooing some of the older girls at the far end of the third table with fanciful tales of his aviation exploits. That was until he looked up and saw Sarah's warning look. He was garnering a few angry looks from the fathers of those girls to go along with Sarah's non-verbal warning.

Li Zheng saw who Sarah was looking at. His glance over at Ryan, while not angry, seemed 'knowing'. "I like your young naval aviator. I have known many men such as him. One who thinks his power over women is complete. All the while that very same man is terrorized by rejection. I, and my son, had the same difficulty. But my son, as myself, were taught many lessons about the appropriate way to regard women. May I?"

Sarah, with a glance toward a smiling and confident Jason, and then with a growing smirk on her face, nodded her head.

Li Zheng stood from his chair and then closed his eyes. Without looking, he turned toward the first of the four waterfalls near Ryan's position. He held out his hands, palms up. Then lowered them quickly. "Sometimes it takes a reality check to bring a young man's thoughts from the gutter."

Ryan was paying special attention to a young woman of about twenty when the waterfall directly to Jason's left acted as if the water flow had been cut off from above the cliff-line. The cessation of falling water took everyone's attention away from familial conversations as the citizenry understood that something was about to happen.

Before Jason knew what to think, the water reappeared. Only it wasn't exactly water. The giant dragon sprang from the dry bed of the falls and sprung down to the tables below. As the girls ran off screaming and laughing, Ryan was frozen at the table. As the water-based image of the giant dragon sprang downward, the maw of the beast opened wide as it plunged onto the main city center. Ryan ducked and screamed as the water giant slammed into him, swallowing him whole as the image of four-foot-long teeth encompassed his small form.

Sarah smiled as the scream from Jason resounded over the meal. The water dragon slammed into him and knocked him from his seat. Then the water splashed up and rebounded to the small, easy flowing river that circled the city center. Ryan spit out water and then looked around him in near panic as he sat in a small lake of water trying to figure out what it was that just nearly drowned him. Everyone was laughing. Even the once angry fathers of the girls assisted Ryan to his feet with uncontrollable laughter. Giggling girls brought Jason rags to dry off. As for the dragon, it was now a peaceful and light rumbling waterfall once more. Ryan finally shook his head and then sat once more. Sarah could see that the most arduous talent of Ryan's was now under control. Jason had just learned first hand about the magic of *Air Bending*. The citizens smiled and applauded as Li Zheng laughed, before sitting once more next to Sarah. Charlie was clapping his hands wildly as he made sure Ryan saw his extreme pleasure at the example made by the Master of Shangri-La.

"Albeit you may be good at embarrassing strangers, even those who deserve your humorous attention, may I ask Master Zheng, are we guests of your marvelous city, or are we your prisoners?" Sarah asked as she settled in and sampled the chicken.

Li Zheng poured her some of the fresh water, never losing his smile. "I have not decided yet, Captain McIntire. A few of you may be welcome here." His eyes wandered over to his right and a smiling Charlie Ellenshaw, then his gaze wandered to another table and the visitors there. "While others may have to stay with us for a while."

Sarah knew Li Zheng's look fell squarely on Jason, Anderson, and Birnbaum.

"You know, where we work we have heard the legends of Northern China and outer Mongolia for decades. The history of the first sovereign emperor of China never once mentioned he had a half-brother."

Li Zheng sipped his water and tasted his chicken. "I dare say you could fill the world's libraries on what's not recorded in history books, young lady," he said as he assisted a small boy in pulling apart a large piece of chicken. He smiled as he finished and looked at Sarah. He held her eyes for the longest time before finishing his statement. "It would seem to me that your organization would have come to that very same conclusion many years ago."

"Now, about my organization. How in the world would a man hidden deep in the wilds of Mongolia know about Department..." she caught herself, "...about my employer?"

"When I was but a boy, many, many years ago, I met a man not long after the world war...let me clarify that, the first world war," he saw the stunned look in Sarah's eyes, but continued, "I had traveled to America with my father to examine choices for college. Princeton was where he graduated from. So, my choices were very nearly limited. My father—"

"Also named Li Zheng?" Sarah interrupted.

Again, the wide smile. "Are you accusing my family of not being very imaginative when it comes to naming our offspring, Captain?"

Sarah only returned the smile.

"The name is more of a title now days. To continue. My father had an old friend who was dying. A man he met while attending Princeton University. He was so ill that only my father was allowed inside his dying room. I, in the meantime, was entertained by this man's wife. A very nice lady who had stepped into her husband's business shoes, so to speak. After the meeting with my father and his friend, we left. I chose another venue for my higher education against my father's wishes. So, that was the last time I ever went to America. Can you guess the name of the friend he visited, Captain McIntire?"

Sarah thought and then shook her head in the negative.

"You see, quite of bit of history has been neglected and left to

vanish in the winds of time, even in your..." the deep smile again, "...
Group." Again, Li Zheng paused to assist the boy child out of his
small chair and then swatted him playfully on the butt as the boy ran
to his mother's arms. "My father and this American man were very
close. He conferred with his friend on one last bit of business this
friend had to accomplish before he joined his ancestors in the afterlife. Business this man dreamed about for the many years they were
together in college."

"The Event Group."

"You see, you know more about history than even your memory is
aware of. It just takes time to think things out."

"Your father's friend was President Woodrow Wilson, and the wife
you met was Edith Wilson. The one person the President trusted to
run the government when he fell ill."

"Rumors surrounding the events in the Ottoman Empire and the
finding of that magnificent archeological vessel at Ararat many years
before, had haunted Mr. Wilson from the time he learned of that
mission in his youth to his dying day. Thus, the charter was finally in
place to create an organization that investigated what those history
books may or may not say."

"Department 5656 of the National Archives."

Li Zheng nodded his head as he finished his meal. To Sarah, it
was as if that explained everything for her. She was not satisfied.

"Master Zheng, that doesn't explain how you know about the
present Event Group."

He kept smiling, but was mute on the subject, allowing Sarah to
think it out for herself.

"You've got a person...," she returned the smile with an accusing
glare, "or persons, inside the Group."

"Don't think unkindly on our motives, Captain. We are always out
to protect that which is ours. The way your Group functions, they are
one of only two entities on the planet that could cause our little secret
to escape these mountains. Now, wouldn't you seek inside assistance
to protect what's yours?"

Sarah thought about Jack and what she would do to protect him.

She didn't agree, but she also remained silent on the subject. Instead she asked; "The other Group you speak of?"

"Ah, the real point is voiced on the subject of why you may never be allowed to leave these mountains." He lost his smile as he glanced toward the end of the long table as many of the citizenry were standing and assisting in gathering the dishes from the meal after the last item, rice, had been consumed. She also saw the playful way everyone laughed and patted Jason Ryan on his wet back. Li Zheng's eyes fell on the man posing as Professor Anderson and the large man next to him eating, Professor Birnbaum.

"The Russian connection?"

"The Russians. A very old and refined people. It is a pity that the men and women representing them have very little honor. It seems it's been that way since they were but a tribe of people." He placed his small arm around Charlie Ellenshaw for a moment and then faced Sarah again. "Secrets about history can be told to men such as this," He said, indicating Ellenshaw. Charlie smiled, unknowing what the conversation was even about. "Men such as this would go to their deaths in protecting that which needs protecting. Most in your Group are that way. Honorable. Sometimes to a fault. Here I speak of your Colonel Collins and Captain Everett. Many reports tell me that their unbending ways compromise your organization. Honor sometimes can be a...what do you Americans say? Ah, yes, a pain in the ass."

Sarah knew exactly what Li Zheng was saying about Jack and Carl, even herself at times. She decided to move off the sore subject of personal thoughts instead.

"What we found in the sand this morning, this—"

Li Zheng laughed, cutting off Sarah's question. "Mineral?"

"Yes, the mineral. Do you have any idea the potential power source this could give the world?"

Sarah could see that Li Zheng knew exactly what power was based inside of these mountains. His look never changed.

"Oh, he knows exactly what benefits the ore could bring to the world. But as always, he thinks he knows best what's good for the planet," a voice said behind them. "Arrogance has always run very deep in my bloodline."

Professor Lee was there with a small woman at his side. Sarah saw that the girl was very much pregnant. She looked to be about ready to pop at any moment. Sarah stood as the woman was embraced by Li Zheng. Obviously, the girl was Lee's wife and Zheng's daughter-in-law.

"Captain McIntire, this is my wife, Mei Sung," Lee said proudly. "She was also educated in the west. She has a doctorate from M.I.T. Her idol is your Director. She studied the works of Doctor Niles Compton for her thesis into his relativity work as a follow-up to Mr. Einstein's work."

The shy woman half-bowed to Sarah, and she in-turn reached out to stop her from doing so. For Sarah, she would never want another woman to have to bow to her. "Please," Sarah said as they were joined by Anya, "it's nice to meet you." Sarah introduced Anya to Mei Sung.

"You'll have to excuse my wife, she has a million questions she would like to ask about Director Compton," Lee said with a sour look toward his father.

"I am sure Captain McIntire has a few she would like to ask us also," Li Zheng said with his ever-present wry smile. "That is what you would call a quid pro quo, I believe."

"To tell you the truth, if the questions I ask are going to get my friends killed, or be the cause you won't let us go, I think I would rather stay ignorant."

Anya nudged Sarah, wanting her to ask the questions. Sarah waited for Anya to pick up the questioning. She finally caught on.

"The world already knows about this place. Well, the mineral and its possibilities at any rate. So, why don't we start there?"

"It was my son and his arrogance that has brought this to my people. He refuses to see the wisdom of his ancestors. He knew when I sent him to be a part of your expedition that the results of your cover story for getting here wouldn't hold."

"Father," Lee said as he pulled his wife in closer. "I did not lead

Captain McIntire to a corpse that has been buried since 1945. She recovered the mineral, what was I supposed to do, murder them all?"

The old man's silence was somewhat unnerving for Sarah and Anya. Even Charlie caught the last few words of Lee as he joined the group.

"In my belief, I think you saw the opportunity to bring our world into the present with a marvelous gift to the planet. The exact same argument I had with my father, and the same he had with his father before him. On and on the argument goes throughout the centuries. The young are always eager to bring the world back from the brink with white magic."

"And what is wrong with that?" Sarah asked as Charlie reached out and tried to stay her. A soaking wet Jason Ryan was curious as he also joined them while he finished toweling off. Then Anderson, and then following him, Professor Birnbaum. "We have a chance to bring the world together with this find. Can you imagine the chance we have here for the possibility of going beyond our own solar system?"

"Its not only that," Lee's small wife interrupted, shaking free of her husband's restraining hand. "I am an engineer," Mei Sung continued, "there is even far more beneficial properties to the asteroid than that of deep space travel."

"What do you mean?" Anya asked when she saw that even her husband Lee frowned at her and her exuberant science background.

Mei Sung looked happy to speak her piece. Sarah and Anya were starting to suspect that Lee's wife was also in on Lee's plot to bring this mineral's value to the world. But of the possibility of her exposing more than her husband about the true nature of the properties of Dragon's Fire, was dangerously close to unveiling too much to the strangers.

"You have only witnessed a small part of what that mineral is capable of."

"What mineral are we talking about?" Ryan asked, trying to slap some remaining water from his left ear. Charlie had caught on, but the naval aviator was somewhat slower to get the point.

"The mineral that can turn flowing water into a giant aviator eating Dragon," Anya said as Charlie began laughing once more, to Ryan's chagrin.

The father, Li Zheng, nodded his balding head at his daughter-in-law for her explanation to continue. "Shall we walk with our guests while you talk, my dear?"

Without comment, Mei Sung happily took Sarah and Anya by the hand and started walking toward the large civic building in the center of the city, as people went about their night routines with smiles on their faces. Li Zheng and his son waited until all were following and listening. The old man, instead of angry silence toward his only son, placed his arm around the boy as he also listened to the excitement of his daughter by law.

"Dragon's Fire has so many benefits to our peoples. Do you know, your experiment this morning as explained to me by my husband, is only the tip of the spear. The exhaust of the mineral that propels an object at such a high rate of speed, creates more of the mineral. Instead of consuming, the residual leftovers of the mineral actually doubles and triples in nature. If you could recover your steel table from, well," here she giggled like a school girl, "space, or wherever it vanished to, you would find double or triple the amount of the mineral used for propulsion. An amazing recyclable material that, as of right now, many of our scientists cannot explain."

"Wait," Ryan said as if he got the whole of the science as explained thus far. "Dragon's Fire?"

Sarah rolled her eyes.

"Yes, it was named that by my ancestors. I think you can imagine the horror they must have felt the first time someone actually got this material too close to a fire, thus the name," Lee answered for his wife. Ryan saw that the mention of the name made Li Zheng smile even broader.

"As I was saying, there are properties far beyond that which you witnessed. For example, can you imagine chemotherapy without the side effects of radiation. I have done the tests in Europe, it works. Can you also imagine developing the human brain to use much more of its potential? Why Master Li Zheng can use—"

175

"Again, you'll have to excuse my wife, she tends to get overly excited about her work with Dragon's Fire." Lee shot her a warning look.

"It's all right, I think we saw a little of that this morning," Sarah said as she slowed enough for Lee and his father to catch up with the group. "Didn't we, Master Zheng?" Sarah crooked her eyebrow. "What would your brain scan say? Fifty, sixty percent of your brain? It would have to be at least that for your abilities of Air Bending, correct? You send your young people out into the world to learn just what it is you have here, don't you?"

"Whoa, wait a minute," Ryan said with his hands up in the air. "Air Bending?"

"Oh, that's right Jason, it was Air Bending that ate you for dinner tonight. I forgot you missed the excitement this morning when you and Charlie were lost. Master Li Zheng lifted up half the desert floor this morning just to protect us. I believe he can do much more than that."

The three Shangri-Lasians just stood and listened to Sarah's story.

"You mean you're a mythical Air Bender?" Charlie Ellenshaw asked with his wide eyes amplified by his thick glasses. "An actual Elemental of legend? I thought the water dragon was more like a David Copperfield thing."

Li Zheng smiled and then half-bowed to Charlie, before gesturing that they should continue walking. The group moved into the mouth of a cave with two young men standing guard. Sarah saw that they were only sort of guarding it because they were playing handheld video games on two small devices. They stopped when they saw their Master approach, and quickly stood up. Ryan gave the Dragon masks and clothing a wide berth as they entered the large cave.

"Does everyone here have the elemental, or air bending ability?" Anya asked.

"To one degree or another, yes," Li Zheng answered. "But the proficiency in Air Bending springs stronger in my bloodline than others. My ancestors discovered this place over three and a half thousand years ago. The secret was kept until the original Li Zheng and his mother were captured by Qin Shi Huang a thousand years after that."

Charlie leaned in to Ryan. "The first Emperor of China. Boy, this is a history lesson, wouldn't you say?" Charlie's sharp elbow jabbed Jason in the ribs, resulting in a watery 'squishy' sound.

"Why have you kept this a secret for these many thousands of years?" Professor Birnbaum asked, as he continued to keep a close eye on Professor Anderson.

"Many have tried to find out the secret, but we have an ability to cloud men's minds," Li Zheng said.

"Like The Shadow," Jason volunteered, then lowered his head when Sarah gave him that look again.

"I used to love that radio program, yes, very much like The Shadow," Li Zheng, said giving Ryan a chance for a return smirk in Sarah's direction. Then Jason's face went slack as he had just caught the 'radio' aspect of the conversation and he stopped in his tracks. "You mean you heard recordings of the radio show, The Shadow, right? I mean, we're talking about the 1930s."

"I'll explain later, fly-boy," Sarah said with a knowing smirk.

"Can this ability be used by outsiders?" Birnbaum asked, continuing his line of questions as they found themselves delving deeper into the cave system under the mountain.

Charlie Ellenshaw was just about the only one to notice that they were being led somewhere dark and dank. Anya also felt her hackles rise when she too noticed.

Silence met the Australian's enquiry.

"I have studied the impact that the asteroid has had on our people. We, as a group, are never ill. The cancer rate is at zero and our life expectancy, with respect to my father-in-law, who is much different, is near twenty-seven percent longer than the planet's normal."

Anya saw the way Mei Sung deferred to Li Zheng. "Just how old are you, Master Zheng?" she asked.

"At dinner, Master Zheng told me he was a small boy when he went to the White House and met President Wilson's wife," Sarah said, retelling the story as told by the old man.

"That does it, I'm sitting at the adult table next meal," Ryan said, not exactly joking.

"That's why he knows everything about us, is that it?" Anya asked.

"My father was in on the creation of the very charter your organization abides. He believed that one day we would need the assistance of outsiders." He turned to his son. "You see my boy, we all have our moments of rebellion against our ancestors. Even myself."

"What do you mean?" Sarah asked.

"While we choose not to bring in outsiders and bless them with this other-worldly power, we do try occasionally to assist the world in other ways. For instance, regardless of what my young people believe, we were heavily involved in the war against the Grays. Do you think that the British government just happened upon an ancient archeological site in Antarctica by chance? Out of the thousands upon thousands of square miles of frozen earth, do you believe it was sheer luck that an expedition uncovered an ancient extra-terrestrial battleship under the ice?"

"You mean you led them there?" Anya asked.

"Not myself, no. I had three graduate students enrolled at Cambridge. They all specialized in sonic recording of ice covered geology, thus, they hinted at something buried under the ice. This led to your amazing plan against the Gray invaders."

"But you could have assisted the planet in other ways with just your abilities of Air Bending. Do you realize that millions upon millions of men, women and children, plus the hundreds of thousands of soldiers, died in the Gray assault?" Sarah asked, growing angry at the old man's flippancy about his abilities and his not sharing it with the rest of the world.

"I know of where your anger springs, Captain McIntire. I know you lost very close friends in the war. One very special small, green friend as I have come to understand. But you must understand, what we have hidden in these mountains would make the assault by another world pale in comparison if this ore and its possible science fell into the wrong hands." He held up his palm when Sarah started to protest. "Perhaps you will understand when I show you what is really the true secret of the Gobi." He gestured for the group to follow his son through a giant hollowed out portal of stone. "Please, this way."

Ryan pulled on the ecstatic Charlie Ellenshaw's arm and the others waited. He was looking wildly at the darkened area beyond the portal.

"Deep, dark, dangerous, and everyone is just willing to walk right in there?"

"Mister Ryan, that is what we do," was all crazy Charlie said as he smiled and started to follow the others.

As they neared the portal, four men stepped out from the darkness. These men were not what they were used to seeing inside of the magical city. These men were wearing desert camouflage fatigues, or BDU's, and each carried an automatic assault rifle. These guards were not smiling and were most definitely not as accommodating as the other citizens of Shangri-La.

"Here we will ask that if you are carrying anything that could cause a spark...matches, a lighter, anything, please give them over to the guard. Also, any electronic devices that may produce a static discharge."

Each person was checked. Even the old man, his son, and his daughter-in-law.

"Now, shall we show the outsiders what they have come to see?" Li Zheng asked as he gestured for them to step through the ancient portal to another time, another world.

"For someone who refuses to allow the world to know about Dragon's Fire, he sure does put on a performance, doesn't he?" Lee whispered to Sarah and Anya. Mei Sung smiled and nodded her head vigorously as she also knew her father-in-law very well.

Before the last two men entered the long, dark tunnel that had been carved out of solid rock many thousands of years before, Professor Birnbaum pulled Anderson aside. "Now, I don't know who you work for exactly, I only have Sarah and Anya's word for it, but if you make a wrong move inside there, I will kill you myself. I may be just a slow-witted Aussie, and the only one in this group that isn't a bloody spy, but make no mistake, this is science and if you do anything to endanger us learning from this, I'll crush your bleedin' skull," the large man said as he smoothed out Anderson's collar from where he had grabbed it.

"Is there a problem?" asked Sarah, who had lagged behind when she had noticed their absence.

"Just explaining to our Russian friend here the consequences of embarrassing us westerners in there."

"Professor, steer clear of him. This new threat this man poses is something we are yet to fully grasp in our business."

"Me? I'm just a bloody pussycat." With one last hard look at Anderson, Birnbaum moved off.

"Keep that backward man away from me," Anderson said as he rubbed his throat.

Sarah fell into step with Anderson as they followed the others. "What is your real name? I mean, Anderson just isn't cutting it any more. It's a little ridiculous at this point to keep your real identity secret, isn't it?"

"In my world, Captain, names mean nothing. It's what you believe in. I believe in my cause. My country's cause. The name Anderson will suffice for now."

"We witnessed your country's cause in the Atlantic last month." Sarah stopped in the darkness of the tunnel and placed a small hand on Anderson. "Professor Birnbaum would be the least of your worries if you cause trouble here. The odds are that this secret will be buried with us when all is said and done, and no matter what they decide, your group must answer for the murder of your own sailors on the *Simbirsk*. Our organization now have the smartest men in the world that will see to it you and your asshole cronies are held accountable." Sarah smiled and then patted Anderson on the arm. "In other words, behave."

Anderson held back a moment, and then followed.

They saw Li Zheng stop in the darkness ahead. They heard what sounded like a giant gate being raised in front of them. The group continued forward, not seeing anything to their front. When the noise stopped, Li Zheng waved his left hand and then twirled his fingers in front of him. Before anyone realized what was happening, the underground world came alive with brilliant light. Not one person in the group of newcomers were able to believe what it was they were seeing. They were standing on a ledge, they had no idea they were even near, in the dark and, after walking through the largest steel gate any of them had ever seen in their lives, were astounded. A thousand feet down was the Dragon's Fire asteroid. Again, they watched as Li Zheng swung both arms this time and the roof of the expanse of cave came alight with a greenish illumination. Li Zheng had excited the ore to give a glowing cloud of light that covered the entirety of the asteroid. It stretched for what looked like miles. The ancient celestial body was gigantic. It was covered in green mold and even had small trees and bushes growing from its exposed surface. Anya tugged on Sarah's arm and pointed far below.

"Yes, it is only partially exposed." Li Zheng gestured to his son and daughter-in-law to continue as he sat on an outcropping of stone. To Sarah, it looked as if his magic with Dragon's Fire had taken something out of the old man.

"We estimate that the Dragon's Fire asteroid came to Earth long before life sprang up on the planet. A billion years possibly. Its impact created these mountains and, over the eons of time, became buried deep beneath the Gobi. My wife has advanced the theory that it very well could have assisted in multi-celled life to be created on a world where no life existed."

"I don't bloody well know how modern science is going to take to that theory. To discount five thousand years of research into how life started here, may cause trouble in our simple world," Birnbaum said, stepping forward to get a better view of the asteroid.

"How much Dragon's Fire do you estimate is here," Anderson asked with a glare from Sarah, Birnbaum and Anya.

"We have excavated a mile down and finally found the initial impact point. So, based on measurements, the best we can come up with is that the asteroid is four-point-six miles long and three wide,"

Mei Sung said as she gestured toward the expanse of green ore. "The weight is unmeasurable."

"The silver streaks in the mineral, what are they?' Sarah asked as she had never seen any natural or unnatural mineral with the brilliancy of colors before.

"Ah, the very dangerous aspect of Dragon's Fire," Professor Lee said as he stepped forward. "It is a very strange mix of the purest silver I have ever examined, and mercury. Naturally occurring. For many years, the ancient emperor thought the mercury was the key source of our people's powers. Thus, he filled his tomb and many monuments with the killer element. We still do not know how many thousands of workers Emperor Qin Shi Huang killed with this foolish theory. It's not like the silver that naturally occurs here." Lee reached down and over the ledge and felt for something. He stood back up and held out his hand, so the others could see. The material looked to be some form of moss, or even mold. Sarah started to reach for it and then she hesitated. "It's safe. It grows on the green sections of the asteroid. My wife has the theory that this may be the very first extra-terrestrial life ever to arrive on Earth.'

"It feels like...like...cotton," Sarah said as Anya, Charlie, and Birnbaum each felt the moss Sarah held out to them.

"It has," Mei Sung looked at her father-in-law and he nodded his head only slightly for her to continue, "a vitamin content that we just cannot identify. It provides a growth factor for life that is astounding. Our food comes from deep underground near the bottom of the asteroid. We planted simple foodstuffs, like rice. There is so much water below that we have surmised that the Dragon's Fire body smashed into an inland freshwater sea when it came down. The rice grows nearly out of control. Corn, sixteen times the size of normal ears. And wildlife. That is one of the reasons we must keep control, as Master Zheng says, and one of the few points upon which my husband agrees. When animals feed off the mold that grows from the asteroid, they become enhanced in size and intelligence. Very problematic if this ever gets into the wild. As of now we can control the aggressiveness of what Earth elements live below, but if this product escapes our control, that could mean a war with an out-of-control ecosystem, and a war that would make the Gray invasion pale in comparison."

"Are you saying we have monsters down there?" Ryan asked as he leaned over the edge and looked down.

Professor Lee smiled at the uncomfortable way Ryan asked about the life in and around Dragon's Fire. "Insects, small rodents, the usual cave dwelling life you would find in most cave systems the world over."

"Excellent," Ellenshaw said as he joined Jason at the ledge. He placed his hand on Ryan's arm to steady himself and Jason jumped, angry that Charlie almost unbalanced him.

"Uh, where is the light disappearing to?' Birnbaum asked looking around.

"Unlike in the city above, only my father's power has the ability to alight such an expanse of area. He is growing weak. We must leave before the light is completely gone. Please, follow me."

Mei Sung and Sarah, with Anya helping, assisted Li Zheng to his feet.

"His weakness is only temporary. He will regain strength with rest. The elemental action this morning, added to his illumination of the caves and Mister Ryan's little encounter with the waterfall, has drained him. He will recover just fine. Now, we must hurry."

Just as Ryan stepped back from the ledge and just seconds before the light from the mineral content of the cave vanished completely, Charlie Ellenshaw let out a scream as his Pith helmet went flying off his silvery hair as a large amount of wind flew past he and Jason. The unexpected wind was so powerful that Ellenshaw lost his footing and fell. Just as Ryan reached down to help him up, the giant bat flew past once again. This time there was more than one scream as they saw the local animal life for the first time.

"Jesus!" Jason yelled as he and Charlie stood and then made a dash for the gate.

The bat came down on the very ledge that they had been standing on. Its wingspan was close to sixteen feet. The teeth were razor sharp. But that wasn't what scared everyone, so much as the bat's color profile. The fur was white, and the eyes were pink in color. The giant hissed and flapped its wings to steady itself on the small ledge. Before they realized it, the four guards they had seen earlier rushed past them and covered them as they escaped from the cave. Soon, the guards came back, and the giant gate was once more lowered.

Ryan placed his hands on his knees as he tried to get his breath and his heart rate back under control. Charlie Ellenshaw did the same.

"I swear to God; how many times are we going to run into this crap on field assignments? My mom once told me that there were no monsters in the world, but every time we go on a mission there they are. I hate my mom." He slid to the floor of the cave and threw his hands up in mock surrender.

They heard the laughter of Li Zheng. It was a hearty sound in the darkness of the tunnel.

"For every blessing the Gods bestow on us, there is also a curse." He laughed again and then quickly calmed. "There are many more undesirable curses far below in the depths, Commander Ryan." Again, the laughter came.

Professor Lee looked down at Jason to see if he was all right. He finally caught his breath. The small man helped the even smaller Ryan to his feet.

"Your father has the most bizarre sense of humor I have ever seen."

"You should see the old man on a good day. And evidently, your very own mother had the same traits."

Charlie smacked Ryan on the back as he moved past him in the dark.

"Don't you just love this job?"

CHAPTER SEVEN

One Hundred Sixty-Eight Miles
East of the Altai Mountains

To keep out of the sixty mile an hour slipstream headwind that slowed its progress, the United States Air Force C-130 *Hercules* lowered its altitude to only eleven thousand feet. The Mongolian government sanctioned flight from Hanoi had been a bumpy one, but luckily for the twenty-two Air Force commandos, and for Master Chief Jenks and Carl Everett, the flight crew had just returned from a tour in Afghanistan, where flying a *Hercules* was one of the more dangerous professions in the world, as blasts of winds across a runway were the least of your problems, as heat seeking missiles were quite often chasing you through those winds.

Jenks was sleeping and, sitting next to him, Carl was in deep thought about the circumstances that led him to be flying over Mongolia. If what Henri Farbeaux said was true, the problems the Event Group faced were far beyond the pale of the attempted murder of himself by a man he thought he knew above all others. However, if true, what were the plans of this Siberian group as far as the field team in Mongolia was concerned? Was it Jack, or an imposter that tried to kill him? Everett suspected the man responsible for him ending up in the Mekong River was on a mission to discredit operations in the Gobi or possibly just a kill raid against Department 5656 personnel. He was so deep in thought, he failed to hear the signal tone from the Europa link left to them by Will Mendenhall at the train platform in Hanoi before he left for home.

"Hey, are Toads deaf?" Jenks asked without raising the Air Force baseball cap from his eyes.

"What?" Carl asked as he looked around and saw nothing but dozing commandos.

"The nerd brigade at Nellis is trying to get a hold of you."

Carl looked to his right and saw the small flashing light on the larger than normal laptop on the canvas seat next to him. He reached for it as a few of the Air Force Special Operations men roused as the *Hercules* climbed back up to two thousand feet more of altitude after discovering a patch of smoother air. He waited until the men turned their attention to waking, and then as they began opening the box lunches the Air Force supplied the team for their long flight. He finally picked up the link much to Jenks' liking. The Master Chief looked none too concerned about the reasons for the call from Group. Everett opened the top and entered his coded response and scramble. A face soon appeared, and it wasn't who he had expected.

"Virginia."

"Captain, its good to see you active once more."

"Okay, it's not Niles yelling at me for disobeying orders, so it's the old sugar before the bad tasting medicine thing, huh?"

"I'll take that as a compliment if the meaning being I am the sugar aspect to your query."

"Always."

"Well, to a point you're right. Niles is not happy with your decision to risk the flight to Mongolia. We both thought the sacrifice of the Master Chief would have been sufficient."

"I heard that, Skinny," Jenks said without moving the cap from his eyes.

"Yeah, well you should have had the common sense to keep Carl out of it. He's been shot, you know."

Finally, the Master Chief raised the baseball cap from his eyes and was about to retort to Virginia's verbal abuse but stopped when he saw her arched eyebrows. She was just waiting to cut into him, but he knew that look very well. He decided to let it go.

"Any news from Sergeant Tram?"

"Not since Will reported that he left you at the train station in Ho Chi Minh City. Doctor Morales and Europa are monitoring every channel for any news." Virginia hesitated a moment and then said, "There is a reason for my call. Carl, you may be heading into a full-blown international incident. Minutes after you left Hanoi, the government of Mongolia officially closed its borders."

"Why would they revoke our status?" Everett asked, sitting up a little straighter. "They do know we have a sanctioned field team in the mountains, don't they?"

"Our good friends the Russians are gathering a strike team along Mongolia's northern border."

"Yes, Major Mendenhall informed us in Hanoi. Its about what we expected them to do. Does the Mongolian government know the difference between saber rattling and the real thing?"

"If its saber rattling, they know how to rattle. The 59th Black Sea Regiment has been joined at the border by the Russian Special Operations Command. Those are the boys credited with taking control of eastern Ukraine during the Russian's non-invasion."

"Yeah, we've heard about them," Everett said recalling the dossier he and Jack had pored over after the *Simbirsk* mission. These were the men that they suspected of eliminating the Russian cruiser crew. "The operational standard of those yahoos doesn't scare me much, but their usual support elements do."

"Well, it should. The whole gang is lining the border. They are bringing with them the MI-8MTV transport support helicopter group. And, I'm afraid, the entire 23rd Aviation assault Regiment."

"That means over thirty-five MI-8AMT-Sh armed assault choppers. Jesus, those are ground troop killers. What in the hell are they playing at, a full-scale invasion of a neighbor?"

"Its not like they haven't done it before."

"The Mongolian response?"

"The better question to ask is about the Chinese response. Something just short of a division is moving into place. Including an entire armored regiment."

"Damn. All of this for that mineral Sarah and her team uncovered?"

The silence on the other end of the Europa link disturbed Carl to no end. His military hackles rose.

"Oh, God, what is the Pentagon's stance?" he finally asked, terrified of Virginia's answer.

"They are seeking permission from Uzbekistan for overflight permission for our stealth bombers to supply support for you and your team. The find in the Gobi Desert is that important to every government on the planet."

"I suspect the Mongolians won't give their permission, thank God. This thing could escalate beyond all control if we start using strategic weaponry. Has anyone explained that to the brass-hats at the Pentagon?"

"Niles has been in conference since four A.M. this morning with the President. After the *Simbirsk* incident in the North Atlantic, the President isn't keen on losing anyone in Mongolia. But as of right now, we have no alternative but to match move for move with the Russians and Chinese. Even our cousins, the British are moving in several Chindit Special Operations units from India. No orders to move in yet, but that could change at any moment."

"Well, we have no choice but to figure this thing out in the Gobi."

"Carl, can Tram track down Jack?" Virginia asked with worry on her face.

"It's his part of the world, Virginia. If anyone can, he can."

"Captain, I know Niles is mad at you for not following orders, but inside he knows you'll bring everyone back home. He's counting on it."

"Oh, now you have the all the confidence in the world now that Captain America is on the job, is that it?"

Everett glanced to his left and then gave the Master Chief a dirty look.

"You're nearing your destination. Don't you special-operations-types usually lighten the planes load before landing. You know, jettison excess weight? Like about two hundred pounds of Master Chief?"

"Let us know of any changes, Virginia." Carl closed the laptop's lid before the love spat could gain any more momentum. He fixed Jenks with that angry look again. "You know, some night she's going to just lean over while you're sleeping and slice your throat?"

Jenks placed the ball cap back over his eyes. "What makes you think she hasn't already tried?"

Everett was about to say how lucky the Master Chief was that any woman could even tolerate him in the same room, much less love him, when the *Hercules* unexpectedly went into a nose dive, and then just as rapidly turned to the left. Carl quickly placed the headphones over his ears as Master Chief Jenks went flying from his seat. The rest of the commandos were attempting to grab handholds for support against the forces now pulling at them.

"*...we are under attack, I repeat, we are under air attack!*" came the calm voice of the co-pilot as he tried to get off a radio message. "*Four missiles are tracking. Radar and heat guided!*"

"Paint my ass red and call me an orangutan, those sons of bitches are as brazen as they come!" Jenks cried out as he too was fighting to get back into his seat.

The C-130 banked hard to the right when Carl heard the chaff and flares go off in the tail boom of the *Hercules*, spreading a line of burning flares to distract the heat seekers, and aluminum chaff strips to confuse the radar guided missiles. Everett knew that when those things popped off, missiles were in very close proximity. He also knew from Ryan that missile deterrents never usually worked.

Everyone inside the cargo hold was hanging on for dear life as the giant *Hercules* fought to out-maneuver missiles that were designed specifically to kill them.

The impact of the first missile strike must have been a heat-seeker. They felt the strike against the left side of the C-130 as several panels of aluminum skin tore free, and the next thing they knew the aircraft was filled with every imaginable piece of debris. Carl had a hard time seeing as he tried to pull the Master Chief back onto the canvas seat. Luckily the pilot already had the *Hercules* below eleven thousand feet or they would now either be suffocating for lack of oxygen, or many of them that hadn't been strapped down in their seats would have been sucked out of the gaping hole that took up most of the aft side of the aircraft.

Just as the Master Chief managed to get into his seat, another, heavier impact happened toward the back of the aircraft. The loading ramp was now partially blown off its hydraulics. Three men and a pallet of equipment flew from the damaged area and into the blue skies of Mongolia.

"Beijing Center, this is American Air Force Flight Bravo 210, we're going down, I repeat we are going down! Our position is—"

The transmission was cut off as the headphones were ripped free of Everett's head by the forces of wind and turbulence.

"I knew the damn Air Force would kill me someday! It wasn't enough the bastards sent me to space, now they're going to attempt to kill me in bum-fuck Mongolia!"

Carl failed to hear the Master Chief as the first contact with the ground came suddenly. He closed his eyes and waited. The wait was blessedly short in duration.

THE C-130 STRUCK A SAND DUNE AND THEN REBOUNDED INTO THE AIR. The starboard engines were ripped free of the wing as the giant aircraft nearly started to cartwheel before the second impact with the Gobi sent it sliding to the right. Then the right wing was torn free as the aviation fuel exploded, taking out six more of the Air Force commandoes seated on that side. Again, the C-130 rebounded into the air after leaving the starboard wing behind this time. Finally, the *Hercules* came to rest on the sparse scrub of the oldest desert in the world. Then the remaining fuel in numbers one and six fuel tanks erupted.

The C-130 *Hercules* was left to burn on the desert floor thirty-four miles short of their destination.

Pi Biehn, Laos

TRAM WAS UNCEREMONIOUSLY THROWN INTO THE DARKENED CELL. HE hit the slime covered floor and slid into the cinderblock wall. He immediately came to his feet and tried to charge the large Russian who awaited the challenge at the cell door. Just as Tram reached it, the large gun was produced, stopping the small Vietnamese sergeant cold in his tracks.

"You should have stayed home, small man," the Russian said with a menacing look. Then he quickly reached out and popped Tram on the forehead, sending him once more to the cold and damp floor. The cell door closed and Tram, wiping a smattering of blood from the gash in his head, continued to stare at the retreating form of the brute.

"You have to learn to pick your moment," came a voice from the darkness.

Tram wiped some of the blood from his head to his trousers as he peered into the blackness of the cell. The voice had a familiar ring to it and Tram took a tentative step forward. He saw a grey form lying on a shabby bunk with no mattress. His eyes went wide as he could not believe his luck. He immediately charged the prone man who jumped to his feet to defend himself from the new visitor to his imprisoned world. He raised both fists and took up a defensive stance. Instead of a series of blows, of which he expected, the smaller stranger wrapped his arms around him. The man tried to step back but was held firm.

"Hey, hey, take it easy." The man was finally able to push a small space between him and the newcomer that was trying to squeeze the breath out of him.

"You have many friends worried about your situation, Colonel."

Jack Collins had always tried to keep any surprise with orders or circumstance from his initial demeanor or response, but when he realized who it was that was thrilled to see him, he smiled and patted Tram on the back.

"What in the hell are you doing here?"

Tram finally released Jack. He shook his head and then wiped more blood from it. "Looking for you."

"Well, sergeant, you seemed to have found me." Again, Jack showed his affection by taking Tram by the shoulders. "Where are the others?" he asked with hope highlighting his question.

Tram became quiet as he tried to get a good look at the Colonel in the dim light being cast from the end of the hallway outside the cell.

"You're alone?" Collins asked as he finally released him.

Tram only nodded his head. "This was a gamble. I have heard rumors of this house from my contacts in the drug enforcement bureau. I came alone."

"Have you heard from Carl?" Jack asked as the worry was evident in his voice.

"He is well. We found him in Ho Chi Minh City." Tram became silent and turned away for the briefest of moments before he turned back and asked the question that many wanted to know. "The Captain says that you shot him."

"Shot him?" Collins asked incredulously.

"Yes."

"He believes that?" Jack asked as he turned and then sat on the bare springs of the cot.

"He is not sure on many points but is quite sure on that one." Tram sat next to Collins and then shook his head. "I don't believe it. He must be mistaken."

"To tell you the truth, Sergeant, I don't remember much after someone cracked me over the head. We were just following a lead on a Russian Group out of Siberia. We had no idea we had walked right into a nest of the same bastards we were hunting."

"You should have contacted me. I could have been beneficial to your search," Tram said, finally looking over at Collins.

"I'm not in the habit of getting friends shot for aiding a foreign power, Sergeant." Jack slapped him on the left leg. "Especially very good friends."

Tram felt his heart warm over the comment that the Colonel thought that highly of him. He was never sure because of the history of the Collins family line about how the colonel really felt about he and his countrymen. He knew Jack's father never returned home after his final tour during the Vietnam war. He watched in the dark as Jack stood and paced to the cell door in thought.

"Colonel, why do they keep you here?"

"From what I understand, I won't be here that much longer. It seems I'm in for a debrief in Siberia."

"Do these backward people believe that your Group would ever stop looking for you?"

Jack didn't answer as he thought out the question as posed to him. He turned and faced the sitting Van Tram. "You say Carl was convinced that I am the one who shot him?"

"I believe 'convinced' is too strong of a word. He was almost as confused as you were when I informed you."

"But he's all right?"

"Yes, I believe he is now on his way back to the States." Tram stood and paced, as Jack had a moment before, to the other side of the small cell. "Colonel, I am a fool. No one knows of my activities on this matter. I thought it best to continue covertly. Captain Everett, besides one other, are the only people who know about my quest. My government cannot help us as they know nothing of this incident."

"Don't be too hard on yourself. Sergeant, we all think we can go it alone sometimes. If you were under my command I would chew your ass off and then we would move on. If you noticed throughout my career I have left pieces of my ass all over the world."

"Still, I should have been better prepared."

"You mentioned two people knew your intention?"

Tram again shook his head. "Yes, Colonel Farbeaux assisted me in locating Captain Everett."

"Henri?"

"Yes, he was very helpful."

"What did he get out of it?"

"Nothing I believe." Tram smiled. "I think he may be afraid of Director Compton."

Jack also smiled for the first time in what seemed ages. "Hell, we're all afraid of the Director. Where is the Colonel now?"

"I am afraid his obligation to the Director only goes so far."

"Henri has never been on the stupid side."

"Colonel, we must get you out of here. Perhaps we could—"

"We do wish you would try some of your American heroics. Thus far we have been vastly disappointed after receiving warnings about your prowess as a soldier from our superiors."

Jack was caught off guard by the voice. The Russian guard had never left. He had stationed himself by the doorway well out of sight. He took a step away from the bars as the largest Russian Collins had ever seen approached. He tracked him by the guard's heavy footfalls. Collins knew that his abilities had been diminished since he had been deprived of light and sound for so long.

"But, we will be moving very soon."

"My government is well aware of what you are doing here," Tram said, coming as close to the man beyond the bars as he could. The look in the small sergeant's face seemed determined to make the Russian believe he was telling the truth.

"One thing we have learned about the Vietnamese, little man, is the fact that you, as a people, have no idea how to bluff an opponent. You are as alone as our American Colonel here." The Russian stepped closer to the cell just into viewing range. "Now, small man, can you tell if I'm bluffing when I say that, when we do depart with Colonel Collins here, that you will still be breathing five minutes after?"

Silence greeted the question.

"Do not play games with Russians, my small friend. The Americans think they understand us, but as time proves repeatedly, they know little."

The man turned on his heels and walked to the door at the far end. It opened. "As you see by the predicament that your American Colonel is in, there are very few heroes left in the world." The laughter followed the Russian out of the door like a train of sour breath.

Jack's eyes narrowed. "Well see, Ivan."

THE DRUNK MAN STUMBLED TOWARD THE LINE OF HIGH-STAKED TIRES IN the back of the safehouse. He tripped, stumbled, and then righted himself.

"What is this?" the smaller guard asked as both Russians laughed at the bumbling fool from the higher vantage point of the raised porch.

"It seems we have a European who is not used to sampling Laotian drug wares."

"He must be Dutch. Their consulate is not that far away," said the fattest of the two as both men laughed at the idiot who didn't know the power of Southeast Asian drugs. They laughed far more loudly when the tall man finally lost control and fell onto his back less than thirty yards from the porch. "Come, if Yuri sees this we'll be the ones sprawling on the ground."

Both men took the steps down the porch and started walking while watching the man writhe in the dirt. Before they realized what was happening, the smaller of the two Russians seemed to stumble and then went to his knees holding his throat. The more rotund man laughed at his companion until in the light of the floods he saw blood spurting freely from the man's throat. He immediately reached for his own weapon inside of his coat when another 'pop, clack' was heard. He felt the bullet enter his head, but his brain continued to function. His hands didn't however, and the Makarov pistol fell from his grip as he turned and faced the threat like a disoriented zombie. The man was now standing and walking his way.

"You Russians are too stupid to realize that you have been shot in the head," the tall, blonde man said as he stepped up to the overweight Russian and then placed his free hand over the brute's heart, then with a gentle shove, sent the man falling backward into the dusty ground. He hit with a 'plop' sound as the man barely spared him a glance on his way toward the porch. He went quickly up the stairs with the still smoking and silenced pistol aimed at the doorway.

THE THREE MEN FINISHED THEIR SNACK OF CHINESE TAKEOUT AND THEN the large Russian looked at his watch.

"We must go. We have to meet our consulate staff at the airport for our little human smuggling operation," he said in heavy accented Georgian. "As soon as we remove the Colonel, it will be my pleasure to shoot the little yellow man. I wish the American to witness his friend's death. Then I can leave you men to do your very distasteful work in this backward country."

"Yes, Yuri," both of his subordinates said as they tossed the remains of their takeout and then followed the larger, well dressed man downstairs.

JACK AND TRAM HEARD THE FAR-OFF DOOR OPEN AND THEN THE laughter of the men who entered. Tram backed up three steps until his back was against the damp wall. Jack took up station beside the cell door. They had both decided that they would go out in a way of their own choosing. Jack knew he would die before he allowed Tram's life to be taken by men who were nothing but unconscionable pigs. And also, because he hated the cold and Siberia was just not in his planning.

"Colonel, please step away from the door," came the same voice as before. Then the hallway lights flared to full brightness. Collins and

Tram both knew they had just lost any edge they had before the lights came alive. Collins didn't move.

The pistol came up and it aimed through the bars of the cell. It was sighted directly at Tram.

Three things happened at once. There was a loud popping sound, quickly followed by the 'clacking' of a weapon being recharged. Then another pop. Then one more. The largest of the Russians still had his pistol pointed in the cell when his eyes widened as the third pistol shot struck him in the side just below his hip. Jack quickly reached out and took the Makarov and twisted it until he heard the man's wrist break. The Russian screamed in pain and anger as his eyes betrayed the fact that he was still confused on just what was befalling him. The Russian went to his knees as Jack aimed the pistol at him. Then they heard a man whistling.

"I seem to come upon you in the strangest of places, Colonel."

Jack felt his limbs almost go weak at the voice he so readily identified. He shook his head and then tossed the Makarov pistol to Tram.

"And you always seem to take your good time in deciding if you're a good guy or bad guy, Henri."

"The jury is still out on that one. You and your associates seem to have an adverse effect on my personality," Henri was finally seen in the full light as came forward into view and easily reached down and felt through the angry and hurt Russian's coat pockets until he came up with the key. He kneed the man away who yelled at the pain in his wrist and hip as he sprawled onto the filthy floor. "Excuse me," Farbeaux said as he inserted the key in the ancient lock and then opened the door. "Shall we go?"

"Henri, did you happen to notice there are more men up there?" Jack said as he awaited Tram to exit.

"Oh, they were hungry, at the moment they are both eating dirt." Farbeaux's smile came.

"I do love your attention to detail, Colonel." Collins looked down at the man on the floor hissing in pain over the hole in his upper leg and at his broken wrist. Jack's eyes met those of Sergeant Tram. The unspoken thoughts of both were very apparent as the Colonel turned and shook Henri's hand as both men turned for the door.

Tram stood over the man that had only an hour before clubbed him in the head and tried to humiliate him. He felt the weight of the heavy Makarov in his hand, and then turned his back on the Russian, who closed his eyes in silent relief. Then they widened when Tram turned back to him with the pistol raised.

"You are right, we Vietnamese are only just now learning to bluff. For instance, like when you thought just now I was leaving you here to live a full and meaningful life." He fired twice into the large Russian's head, blowing the back of his skull away. "That is a Vietnamese bluff." He turned to follow Jack and Henri toward freedom. "We do learn quickly."

Farbeaux paused at the door and looked from a smiling Tram to Collins.

"What was that about?"

"Karma, Henri, Vietnamese Karma."

United Nations, New York

Since the democratic wave of 1990 ousted the long standing communist rule of law inside the borders of Mongolia, the new state had struggled to maintain their sovereignty against its larger neighbors—Russia to the north, and China to its south. Its small armed forces have tried to join the modern part of the world in joint operations that mutually benefitted them. They were heavily involved in the United Nations effort to oust terrorism from the world. They had gained massive support from the west and had thrown relations with its neighbors into turmoil.

Now, on the floor of the United Nations, Mongolia was asserting its right as a new nation, and several security council signatories were trying to flex their veto power after Mongolia's address to the world on the main floor, which had called for all foreign entities to leave the borders of Mongolia. The most discouraging part of the day was the fact that, after Mongolia placed its dissent over its own border security, they were left out of the United Nations Security vote on the matter.

"We have very strong evidence that Mongolia has been, and is even now, in the process of developing a possible weapon of mass destruction inside an Altai Mountain research complex," said the man representing the Russian delegation. "This we cannot allow."

"We have gathered the same evidence as your government and our findings tell us we have yet to come to that same conclusion. A possible beneficiary ore, maybe, until our science teams examine the find, we just don't know. But a weapon of mass-destruction? That's broadening the picture a little too much. Assumption, sir, is the mother of all miscalculation." There were several hand slaps on the table tops by mainly western powers.

"You are out of order, sir, the representative from the Russian state still has the floor," said the Indian chairman at the head of the large conference table. Still, the Ambassador from the United Kingdom continued.

"Of which he will continue to pontificate their so-called findings until we all die of either lack of oxygen, or dare I say, boredom," said Sir Jeffery Kinsley.

"Russia does not have to sit here and be bombarded by British humor, or lack thereof. We have a right to defend our southern border, and no entity on the face of the Earth can deny us that!"

"And yet we still await this so-called Russian evidence," interjected the representative of China.

"Gentlemen, you are all out of order!" called out the chair from India.

"What is in order is the fact that the United States is more than willing to defer our lost field team and its safety, to the government of Mongolia, and we also call for the cessation of saber-rattling from all parties before the situation becomes untenable. I believe that China will concur on the point of standing down all activities inside of Mongolia and allow the government of that nation to conduct a search for our missing field elements. Only then can we talk about the benefits or the dangers of what will be found as far as the new discovery is concerned," said Ambassador Fred Whiting of the United States.

"Until such a time, China must concur with the ruling body about standing all forces down until an agreement can be reached on this new material," he paused with a skeptical look at the Russian team, "if there is this magical ore that all nations seem to now know about, but few have evidence of." All eyes went toward the usually quiet representative of China. "China must insist that Russia stand its forces down and withdraw from the border with their neighbor. If not, we are building a sizable force in the south to confront any and all incursions into the nation of Mongolia."

The gavel slammed down three times to regain order, as the Russian delegation stood from the council table. The ambassadors from the United Kingdom and the United States exchanged worried looks over the comment by China. On the outside, it looked as if the largest nation in the world was siding with them, but they knew China was also playing the situation to their advantage. In other words, they were using Russia's actions as an excuse to carry forward with their own goals in the matter—the possible procurement of the new material for China could be their end game.

"Until such a time that this body regains its senses, Russia uses its veto power over the proposal by the United Kingdom. The State of Mongolia has twenty-four hours to produce the material that has caused this problem, so it can be determined of its weaponization possibilities."

The ambassador from the United States stood, along with the representative from the United Kingdom, and, over the slamming of the gavel, stated their response.

"At the request of the Mongolian nation, the United States will assist that nation in repelling any incursion by outside influences into the Gobi."

The security council flew into shouts of anger and yells of right-eous indignation over the Russian stance and the outright declaration of the west to meet them in the field. It seemed many more politicians than first thought had taken the claims of Department 5656 and that of MI-6 far more seriously than even Niles Compton had assumed. The turmoil was so great inside the chamber that few noticed the Chinese representative step aside and gesture to an assistant with a preconference signal. The aid pushed a single button on what looked like a normal cell phone. Looking normal was the optimum point. The coded signal went all the way to Beijing. Twenty minutes later, the entire 15th Chinese Peoples Liberation Airborne Corps went on full alert. The material the Chinese governments had been searching for the past two thousand years was now found. The decision had been made, three days before, that this motherload of fortune would not go anywhere but into Chinese hands. That meant that the 15th Airborne division and its six airborne brigades would kill any foreign entity trying to recover it.

The world's governing bodies were being forced to war on rumor, greed, an outlandish legend, and innuendo.

Event Group Complex,
Nellis Air Force Base, Nevada

ALICE HAMILTON WATCHED THE TIRED EYES OF NILES COMPTON AS HE slowly hung up the phone. He removed his glasses and, for the fiftieth time that night, rubbed the bridge of his nose before placing the eyewear back on. Virginia Pollock and Alice exchanged worried looks over the director's short and brutal conversation with the President.

"The Russians will not withdraw," Niles said, and then he looked straight down the table at the youngest member of the hierarchy of the Department 5656 management, Xavier Morales. "Doctor, please tell me that Europa has had success in establishing contact with the field team's location and health and welfare implants?"

"None. Here's what we have, the situation is changing rapidly, and we are close to losing control from the standpoint of searching here in Nevada. It seems the transponders for Captain Everett and Master

Chief Jenks are signaling that they are on the ground. Far short of their destination. Their health and welfare signals are intermittent and inconclusive. This coincides with the Mongolian air traffic report of a Mayday that was sent by the C-130 that they were under aerial attack."

Niles looked over to his left at Virginia, whose face remained neutral at the news that Master Chief Jenks may either be dead, or at the very least hurt.

"Jack?"

"Better news on that front. It seems Sergeant Tram and Colonel Farbeaux secured Colonel Collins inside a Russian safehouse in Laos. While we didn't speak to the Colonel, Tram reports that the Collins and Farbeaux will be heading back to the States on the next available transport. I explained to Tram that it was of the utmost importance for the Colonel to be debriefed immediately over his situation. His explanation and debrief on what befell him and Captain Everett is of paramount importance to the theory of what government entity we are truly facing in Siberia."

Both Alice and Virginia looked at Niles who was shaking his head in the negative. The three highest members of Department 5656 knew Jack Collins all too well.

"And he was briefed on what's happening in Mongolia?" Niles asked.

"Yes, sir. Although I did not speak to him, the word was passed on by Sergeant Tram," Morales said from his wheelchair.

"And what follow-up questions did the Colonel ask through Tram?" Virginia offered.

"None, he seemed satisfied with the orders to return home, ASAP.'

Alice couldn't hold back. The eighty-five-year-old laughed and shook her head at the naivete of the young computer genius.

"What?" Xavier asked when Virginia also smiled.

"He lied to you, Doctor. He's going to Mongolia. Did you express concern over the fate of Captain Everett and the Master Chief, and the fates of the initial field team of Sarah, Anya, Charlie and Ryan?"

"Yes, I informed Tram and he in turn filled the Colonel in on all aspects of what we think is happening in Mongolia."

"Jack is heading for Mongolia. You'll learn that the Colonel will not allow what's happening there to jeopardize any of his field teams. It's not your fault, we just know him better than you. You'll learn. Besides, he has the bad influence of Henri Farbeaux to mine the anger aspect of Jack's concerns." Niles watched as the overly-excited Morales protested.

"This time even Colonel Collins cannot lie. Europa has picked up his transponder and he is already airborne for the States."

Silence greeted his statement.

"He's on his way back home. Europa is not wrong about that."

CHAPTER EIGHT

**Altai Mountains,
Eastern Mongolia**

Sarah and Anya were up late. Most of the citizenry had gone to sleep in their naturally carved-out cave quarters. They had no guards on duty to watch them. The only sound this late at night was the splashing of the four waterfalls surrounding the city center. The sound would have normally been a sleep-inducing treatment but, for Sarah and Anya, it only reminded them they were very far from home and the people they loved. For Sarah it was harder as the situation between her and Jack did not allow for peaceful rest of any kind. Anya's sleeplessness sprang from missing Carl.

"Damn it, even my small fingers can't get to the screws!" Sarah said in exasperation. She placed the broken satellite radio on the table's top and then rubbed her red eyes. "Why don't they make these things more durable?"

"You mean boot and heel proof?" Anya asked, and then a smiling Sarah allowed her anger to fade along with the hope of fixing their communications link with Europa.

"Look, I don't think these people are a cruel sort. They just don't trust the world. I can honestly say that we both love men with the same exact attitude about that world." Anya patted Sarah on the back after she realized that the subject of the men that they loved was still a little hard on her friend. Anya knew why Jack had tried to separate his feelings from Sarah. She knew because, as an ex-Mossad agent, she understood the routine of cleaning up your life just before you went off on a mission there was a high probability you would not return from. Carl had tried the same with her, but she knew the game and would have none of it. Sarah was different, from a very different world of order and study. It was harder to understand the mindset of men like Jack and Carl.

"I just hate being out of communication. I know these kind people will eventually allow us to leave this place, but we need to update Niles."

Anya again smiled. "That's not why you are trying to fix the radio, dear. You want to know about what our male friends are up to. You're just afraid of what we'll discover when we get home; that's worrying you."

Anya was attempting to ease Sarah's mind but before she could speak more on the matter, she saw a strange sight. Jason and Charlie were standing by the center-most waterfall. They were watching something, or someone, from a distance. It looked as if Crazy Charlie was trying to persuade Ryan to do something. He was tugging at his sleeve and looking very nervous. Anya lightly tapped Sarah on the shoulder and nodded toward the two conspirators. Sarah saw the same thing. Charlie looked reluctant about something, and Ryan determined.

"This cannot be good," Sarah said as she replaced the pieces of the broken phone into her back pocket and then stood. "If he's chasing women again I swear to god, I will write his ass up. He doesn't know this culture and what they would do to him if he's caught trying to play playboy pilot with one of these girls."

As Sarah stood, they saw the two glance around one last time, and then vanish into the spray of the falls. Sarah and Anya went after them.

Once the two women made it to the falls, they saw the wet sets of footprints leading beyond the back of the spray of water. Sarah was about to follow when Anya tugged on her sleeve to stop her. She nodded toward the wet footprints. Sarah was confused at first, and then she quickly saw what it was Anya was pointing out. Not only were there the sets of both Charlie and Ryan's prints, but those of another. The third set was made by someone not wearing shoes. They were about to continue to follow when they heard a commotion in the cave system further back from the falls. It was the sound of Charlie shouting. Then they heard a struggle and they both ran to the sound of commotion.

"Who are you and why were you spying on us, thief!" came the questioning voice of an angry Ryan.

"Mister Ryan, you're scaring him!" said Charlie. "Come on, he's an old man."

Sarah and Anya rounded a bend and that was when they saw that Jason had someone on the cold stone floor and held him by the shoulders. The wild hair of the man covered most of his face, but they could clearly see that the man Ryan and Charlie had cornered was old. Very old. The man held his hands in the air in subjugation as Jason threatened him.

"Jason!" Sarah said loudly enough that Ellenshaw jumped into the air. "Stop scaring that man!"

Anya rushed ahead and with a foul look, passed by and around a scared Charlie. She eased Ryan's hand from the man's shoulders and that was when she saw the shaking and very frightened gentleman. He was bearded and wore the usual clothing associated with the citizenry of Shangri-La. He had on the white undergarment with the flowing orange robes. His feet were bare, and his hair was even wilder than Charlie's. She could see the man held what looked like a small necklace. She jumped back when she felt Ryan's hand shoot past her and snatch the item from the old man's trembling fingers. Anya angrily shoved Ryan out of the way and assisted the crazed old man to his feet.

Ryan was about to say something to a very angry Sarah when Charlie attempted to explain.

"We were sleeping when we heard someone enter our quarters. I didn't know what was happening until Mister Ryan shouted, and then before we knew it we were outside chasing the intruder. He stole something from Mister Ryan."

Sarah turned angrily to a subdued Jason. "Well, mister wonderful, what did this threat to society steal from you?"

Ryan held out a set of dog tags on a chain. Sarah immediately understood. Ryan would never have gone after an old man for something as trivial as a set of tags, if it had been his own that is, but Sarah knew he carried a very special set of military I.D. tags. She knew them to be special to him. The set belonged to Ryan's old flight-leader aboard the U.S.S. *Carl Vinson*. The pilot was lost in the now famous UFO encounter over the Pacific that eventually led Jason to the Event Group. The friend was killed, and Ryan was given his dog tags after the F-14 Tomcat's pilot's body was recovered. They were precious to him. Now she understood why Jason took it personally that someone would attempt to steal them. McIntire just nodded her head that she understood. Instead of haranguing him further, she patted him on the shoulder and then joined Anya and the man she was helping to his feet.

"I...I..." The old man started to speak but lost his words. Instead his eyes went from Sarah to Anya. He hesitantly reached out and touched first Anya's, and then Sarah's shorter hair. Both women exchanged curious looks as the man rubbed their hair and smiled a toothless grin.

"I am Captain McIntire, this is Major Anya Korvesky. We're Americans."

The old man heard the introduction and then his eyes widened. His hands shot away from both women as he placed his back as far against the wet wall as he could. In the dim light from the softly glowing mineral, they could see that the look was one of more shock than fright. The man, it was finally noticed, was from the west. They could see that at one time he had been a very large individual.

"I am Professor Charles Hindershot Ellenshaw III," Charlie said as he stepped forward and held out his hand in greeting.

"Charlie...Hindershit?"

Charlie pulled his hand back in terror at the butchery of his name as Ryan laughed. This seemed to break the tension somewhat.

"Ah, no. Hindershot. You know what, just call me Doc," Charlie said and once more held out his hand.

The old man, his eyes darting from one person to the next, finally held out his hand and Charlie vigorously shook it.

"Why did you steal Mister Ryan's dog tags?" Ellenshaw asked as the old man shook everyone's hands with great enthusiasm.

The old man, instead of saying anything, reached into the folds of his robe, and happily brought out his own set of dog tags. These were far different from the ones Ryan had, or any current form of military I.D. tags. These were round and made of brass and not tin. They were connected to a broken chain. He held them out for Sarah to take. He was smiling and nodding his head as if the offering would explain everything to them. Sarah held them, and then after she saw the toothless smile, leaned into a section of the wet tunnel next to one of the mineral lights and examined his peace offering. Sarah's look told the others immediately that she was stunned.

"Douglas Pierce, Major, United States Army Air Corps, serial number 512348789."

"Yes, yes, yes, yes, Old 'Slick Willy' at your service...yes, that's right, 'Slick Willy'!"

They smiled as the old man clapped his hands together and then did a dancing jig. Charlie looked at Ryan who seemed to understand why the old man's excitement had flared.

"He's crazy," Ellenshaw whispered.

"No," Jason said, now feeling absolutely ashamed for chasing and then threatening this man who was now happy as a lark. "His aircraft was called the 'Slick Willy'. They all named their ships back then, before the war department got all uptight about nose art."

"Yes, sir!" The old man stopped rotating as his dance came to a breath-catching halt. He bent at the waist and tried to catch his breath. "Old Slick Willy's not as young as he used to be," he said, finally getting his breathing under control.

"My God," Anya said. "You've been here all of this time?"

The old man scratched his beard and then his head as he looked the two women over. He first pointed at Sarah and tapped her shoulder. "Captain?" Then his skinny finger jabbed Anya. "Major?"

Both women nodded their heads.

He smiled as broadly as any of them had ever seen anyone stretch their lips, as he again scratched his head. "The Air Corps has changed a bit; Slick Willy is impressed!" He danced a jig again and the others watched and smiled in the green-tinted light. He stopped and fixed them with a serious look. Then he sidled up to Jason and whispered in a conspirator's tone. "Does old Curtis know about this? I mean, the man doesn't like anyone, much less women in uniform."

Anya and Sarah smiled. Charlie explained to Ryan. He mouthed the name Jason was searching for in his military memory: 'General Curtis LeMay'. Jason also smiled.

After everyone realized that the old pilot of the B-29, 'Slick Willy' was speaking about General Curtis E. Le May, his old commanding General, Sarah asked the most pertinent question of all. "Do you know what year it is?" as she tried to get the old flier calmed down enough to answer some questions.

"Of course, I do, madam. Or Captain. It's...it's...1973?"

Everyone exchanged looks but all decided on their own not to comment on the correct year.

The old man suddenly sat hard onto the cold, stone floor. "One tends to lose track of time here." His eyes refused to look up into the visitors' faces.

"Where is the rest of your flight crew?" Ryan asked, as he slid in beside the ancient bomber pilot.

His look was one of pain and sorrow, and Jason felt that maybe he shouldn't have asked. He patted the old man's leg and then started to stand, but the hands of the old man held him place.

"The Japs got...got..." He looked up in shattered memory. His eyes filled with tears. He looked from person to person as if guilty of something horrid. "I can't remember those kids' names." His shoulders hunched as he lowered his head and began to weep. Then, just as suddenly, his head popped back up and his eyes were wild. "We were going home. Going home. Going home." His eyes almost looked as if he were pleading for the newcomers to understand. "Then he betrayed us all." He placed his thin arms around his knees and started rocking back and forth. "That bastard didn't give them any choice. None were to be trusted after that."

"Who?" Ryan asked, as he placed a far gentler hand on the old man than he had before.

His head suddenly came up and his eyes were anything but calm. "I gave them my word as an officer in the United States Army Air Corps." He slammed a weak fist onto his knee. "That son of a bitch, Krensky lied to me, to my crew, and to them," his finger shot straight out toward the falls and the city beyond. "Lied, lied and lied. He stole away into the night, not caring what became of his friends. He lied, he lied, he lied!"

The dawning of understanding hit Sarah like a sledgehammer to the face. "The body we found, Captain Everson Krensky, the mineral in his leather pouch. He stole it from here and left these men in Shangri-La."

"Master Li Zheng kept you here?" Anya asked, now following Sarah's logical course.

"Yes, yes, yes, the 'Slick Willy' boys were not to be trusted." The old man looked so apologetic that the four of them had to look away. "The Master does not trust you either. Be careful of your friends. The ore has a way of confusing the truth here."

"We don't understand," Sarah said.

"They sense evil in your company. Very big evil." His eyes once more became wide. "I hear things when they don't think I'm listening. They are very smart people. They are hard to fool. They suspect that you are in league with..." He leaned over and from his sitting position whispered, "...Emperor Qin Shi Huang." His eyes looked around as if he was in danger of being heard by ears that were not friendly.

"The first Emperor of China?" Charlie asked with a snicker. "He's been dead for over two thousand years."

The old pilot started to laugh. His laughter was loud and looked to be out of control. He stopped suddenly and then fixed them all with a crazed look.

"Yes, yes, dead. Very dead. There's only one problem with that." Again, the eyes went from person to person. He sat down and said nothing.

"Problem?" Ryan asked.

Pierce jerked as if shaken from a doze. "He's coming for Li Zheng. The brothers will collide, and the world will tremble, and millions will die."

"You're not making a whole lot of sense here, Major," Sarah said.

"I see it was a mistake to allow you the freedom to roam the city," came a voice from the dark. They all turned, and Major Pierce screamed out a hoarse cry, and then jumped up and ran off further into the tunnel behind the falls.

"You kept that man a prisoner for all of these years?" Sarah asked angrily.

"We prefer the term, *guest*."

The young professor Lee stepped from the shadows and confronted the four.

"I'm sure you would. We like the more accurate term of *prisoner*. Where are the rest of that man's flight crew?" Sarah asked as she stepped forward toward Lee who held his ground.

"Captain McIntire, the man is ninety-two years old. Where do you think the rest of his crew is?" Lee shook his head. "You understand nothing. We thought you would be more informed because you work for a man the Master holds in high regard in your Director Compton. He has obviously made a mistake."

"What does Major Pierce mean when he says that Emperor Qin Shi Huang is coming for a man that's been dead for over two centuries?" Sarah persisted, no longer taking Lee nor his people at face value.

"This day has been coming for precisely that long, young lady."

They turned and saw that Master Li Zheng was standing by the far wall. His son turned, and half-bowed to his father.

"What's coming?" Ellenshaw asked, not willing to put his theory on the line just yet.

"The day I have warned about since the beginning. He now knows exactly where we are, and he *is* coming. There is now nothing we can do about it. For two thousand years we have avoided this confrontation. We will now be forced to go to war, and the world will suffer for it."

"You're him, aren't you?" Charlie asked with incredulity etched on his face.

"*Him*?" Ryan asked.

"You didn't tell us the truth, did you?" Charlie said as he stepped closer to the father and son. "You're him. You're the real, and very much original, Li Zheng, aren't you?"

Silence from the two men.

"What are you suggesting, Charlie?" Sarah asked, confused as ever.

"The first Emperor of China, Qin Shi Huang, wasn't interested in the power of the mineral for its military value. It is a historically documented fact that he was possessed with the possibility of immortality. That's why his tomb was filled with Terracotta soldiers. He was preparing for a life beyond his own death, which if he had the mineral only his brother possessed, he wouldn't need protection in the afterlife, because he would live forever, just like his half-brother, Master Li Zheng. Oh, he knew the asteroid could give him the power of Air Bending like his brother and his followers, but that wasn't his main interest was it, Master Zheng?"

"I told you not to underestimate Professor Ellenshaw. My wife told you his work in Cryptozoology was beyond reproach," the young Professor Lee said to his father. For his part, Ellenshaw smiled and nodded that, yes, indeed he was exceptional.

"Immortality is the sole reason for keeping the mineral secret. Not its power, but its life-extending properties." He looked from Sarah to

Anya, and then to a skeptical Ryan. "This whole community has been subjected to this wonderous material."

"Are you even more crazy than we thought, Doc?" Jason asked with his suspicious eyes going from Lee to his father.

"I do not deny my mental disposition in your description, Mister Ryan. However, I do not hear any denials coming from that part of the cave. You *are* the half-brother of Emperor Qin Shi Huang, aren't you?"

"Yes."

With that one-word answer, the world had suddenly changed for the members of the Event Group.

This was not the Shangri-La of myth and legend. This was a city of immortals, and they may have unwittingly led a not-so-dead ancient Emperor straight to his prize.

Six Miles Away

MASTER CHIEF JENKS PULLED ON THE ALUMINUM SHARD PINNING THE Air Force commando to the left fuselage. As hard as he could pull, he found the resistance was just too great. The boy stopped screaming as Jenks reached behind the injured man and felt around. The aluminum had bent after piercing the commando's liver. Jenks knew he would have to straighten the bent piece before he could pull the young air commando free. He removed his hand and focused on the boy's eyes which were closed in pain.

"I'm not hurting you on purpose, airman. But I have to straighten out the aluminum that went straight through you." Jenks watched the boy's eyes flutter open and a grim determination filled his blue eyes.

"Yes, sir," was all he could get out before a spasm of pain shook his body.

"That's it, Master Chief. Six live bodies accounted for. I've got the healthier ones trying to pull apart the cockpit to get to the pilots. It doesn't look good."

"Come on, Toad, I need a hand here," Jenks said as he shook the fingers of his right hand free of the dripping blood. "We have to get this kid out of here."

Everett saw how the boy was speared to the damaged fuselage. He moved and stood next to Jenks. "What do you need?"

"Just lift him enough to take the pressure off while I try and bend that piece straight, so we can pull him free."

"Got it," Carl said, as he reached down and placed his hands on the boy's shoulders. The Master Chief nodded his head and Everett pulled up as gently as he could. The commando squeezed his eyes closed as the searing pain took hold.

"Damn it!" Jenks said as he tried desperately to bend the shard that pinned the kid down.

"Master Chief," Carl said as he saw the relaxation of the kid's extremities. He let go of his shoulders and Jenks cursed that he didn't have the room to straighten the aluminum. "Master Chief, damn it, listen to me."

Jenks stopped his cursing and then looked up at a blood-soaked Everett.

"He's gone."

"Ah, damn," was all the Master Chief said as he looked at the kid's serene face. He reached out and closed the boy's eyes and then placed a bloody hand on his own face and rubbed at the growth of beard there. Then he stood up and looked around at the damaged C-130's interior. "What's the situation outside?"

"Out of the twenty-two commandos, we have six. The rest were either lost when the fuselage blew apart in the air, or they died on impact." Carl shook his head and then surveyed what was left inside. "The six are in varying states of injury. Cuts and bruises for the most part. Everyone on the starboard side of the Hercules didn't make it."

"Yeah, that's where the damn heat-seeker hit. It had to have been a Russian built weapon. The Chinese missiles aren't that damn accurate." Jenks cursed again and then plopped a cigar into his mouth. "Well, what's the plan, John Paul Jones?"

"As close as I can figure it, we're about six miles from the field team basecamp."

"Communications?" Jenks asked, and then quickly saw the sour look on the Captain's face. "Don't tell me, everything was on the pallet on the starboard side."

"That means what's left is spread out over approximately twenty square miles."

"The Europa link?"

Carl looked to his left and Jenks' eyes followed. The laptop was on the floor of the aircraft in several pieces.

"Well, I can honestly say that when we fuck it up, we do it with style," he said as he wanted so badly to light up his cigar, but the smell of aviation fuel was still too strong. "Can those boys out there walk?"

"They don't have a choice. We'll have tribesmen here at any minute to scavenge anything they can get their hands on."

"Captain, we got the two pilots and the crew chief free."

Carl looked at the Air Force sergeant and saw the negative look on his face. Everett shook his head. "Tell the men to gather up anything useful. Rations, weapons, and then destroy anything we cannot use. Master Chief, I need your expertise here. By the smell, we have plenty of fuel left in the inner wing tanks. Burn it all, leave nothing for the tribesmen to get."

"That I can do." Jenks turned his attention to the young Air Force commando. "Bring the bodies inside."

"Inside, aren't we going to bury them? They deserve at least that."

Jenks started to shout at the young sergeant when he received the look from Everett and his raised brow. He took a breath and faced the kid. "Son, there isn't a soldier that has died in the line of duty that doesn't deserve to be buried with honors, but that option isn't available to us. Bring the bodies inside."

Everett slapped the sergeant on the back. "Now, sergeant. We have ground to cover and a short time to do it in. We're going to have some very unfriendly company very soon. Burning the bodies is the only way we can guarantee that Mongol tribesmen don't strip them and leave them for the buzzards. Okay?"

The young sergeant seemed to come to his senses and then abruptly turned to follow his orders.

"You come in handy, Toad. I never got the knack of trying to calm down scared kids."

Everett reached down and picked up a discarded M-4 assault weapon and then made sure the magazine was full. He charged the weapon and then fixed Jenks with a knowing look. "Not true, Master Chief. I remember a young SEAL frozen in terror in his first assault in Panama. Hell, I was just nineteen and was about to shit my pants when the bullets started coming our way. I remember this gruff bastard talking softly to the kid that I was that he had to move or die. Then you pulled me to my feet and shoved me out of my safe cover. So, you do know how to speak to scared men."

Jenks removed the cigar from his mouth. "Hell, Toad, by the time of the Panama invasion, I was just an instructor. I was the scared one. And the only reason I pulled you from cover was to use your dumbass as a human shield to get me the hell out of there." He smiled and then plopped the cigar back into his mouth. "Now, shall we see if we can get our asses out of another god-forsaken desert?"

"Asshole."

Hong Kong, China

TRAM AND JACK WAITED FOR FARBEAUX TO RETURN FROM THE CHARTER office. A bearded Collins slapped Tram on the back and then looked honestly into his eyes. He smiled as best as the situation would allow.

"Here's where we part company, old friend."

Tram looked momentarily confused as they sat on a wooden bench outside of the office. He tilted his head as if he wasn't understanding. Tram was wearing civilian clothing for the first time Jack had ever seen. The small man looked to be the most normal of civilians, but he also knew Tram to be a dedicated soldier and by far the best shot with a rifle he had ever seen. Now that the time was upon them to part, Jack felt sick that he may never see his friend again.

"It's time for you to go home and leave this mess to us. You've done enough."

"Cannot go home."

Jack was caught off guard by his simple comment. "What do you mean you can't go home?"

"I have made my choice, and that choice does not coincide with my soldiering duties."

"What damn choice?"

"We all have to make choices in our lives, Colonel. You know this better than most. I have made mine. I am now a criminal in my government's eyes."

Van Tram had disappeared for about two hours while Henri and himself purchased clothing and, after visiting one of the Frenchman's contacts in Hong Kong, procured weapons. He never asked where Tram had vanished to and now he thought he knew."

"How do you know this?" Jack asked, growing angry at a man he most respected from another military organization.

"A contact I have here checked in back home. An arrest warrant was posted three days ago. I am being charged with assisting a foreign power inside Vietnam. You see, I am now a man without a country. After I assist you, I will surrender to my government."

Jack stood and slapped his thigh. He started pacing. He stopped when the answer came to him. "No, say what you will about me, I have friends in high places. This will not stand. Even the President of the United States knows who and what kind of soldier you are."

Tram bowed his head at the compliment. Then he looked Collins square in the eyes. "It's because of this praise in your reports from the field that I was placed on a watch list by my government. They thought I became a little too close to your government during the war with the Grays."

"And you still chose to put your neck on the line for me?"

"This is what one does, Colonel. I have learned many things in our time together. One of them is that you take risks to save friends."

"Damn it."

"Mongolia seems the place to be for my immediate future," Tram said, and then saw Henri exit the charter office. He stood.

"Inform Doctor Compton he now owes me fifty-two thousand dollars."

"Jesus, someone saw you coming and raped you on price!" Jack said.

"It seems on my last visit I chartered a plane, and well, failed in my obligation to return it." Henri handed Collins a receipt. "By the way, that receipt is only for the previous charter. They failed to renew any continuing service agreement with me."

"So, you're out over fifty thousand dollars, and we still don't have a way to get there?"

Henri smirked and then produced a set of keys. "Airstream, tight and cramped, but it will get us there."

Tram smiled as he watched the banter.

"From a soldier to a pirate all in one day," Jack said as he looked at the smiling Tram.

"What, now he's coming too?" Henri asked as he was tossing the keys up and down as Tram reached out and plucked them from the air. "I guess so."

"There is an American sporting goods store nearby. I need a weapon and ammunition," Tram said as he started walking. "The receipt you can give to me."

"You know Colonel, I once thought of myself as a devious person, but since I met you and your organization, I could take lessons."

"Let's go procure what Tram needs. I have a feeling we're gong to be happy he's along."

"Happy? You?" Henri snorted laughter.

"Yes, this is my happy face," Jack said, as Henri took an involuntary step back as Collins passed by him and started following Tram.

"That's not comforting at all."

Xinjiang, Eastern China

THE SIX TANK REGIMENTS SAT AT IDLE ON THE NORTHERN BORDER OF Xinjiang Province, situated on the northern border. The assault element was prepared. The air Assault helicopter units were gathered nearby at Nanjing. They would delay their assault while waiting for the tanks to get through the mountain pass leading to the Altai Mountains in Eastern Mongolia. At the moment, the entire division was facing only a token border security unit of the Mongolian army.

The commanding armor general, Wei Li Cheng, looked at his watch inside his command vehicle.

"If we delay too much longer, the Mongolians will reinforce the border. Then we will have a battle on our hands before we even enter Mongolian territory."

His adjutant, a full colonel, sat at the map table and then looked up at his commander. "Why are we delaying, sir?"

"We have orders to await a person from Beijing. He and his personal detachment will arrive shorty. We are to commence operations after he arrives."

"Does Beijing know the current border situation?" the colonel asked.

The general finally stood and then climbed to the upper hatch and opened it. He took his field glasses and scoured the men and equipment of his command.

The division had been newly formed since the disaster of the Gray invasion where over seventy-five percent of the Division's armor was lost in the streets of the capital. Now he hoped this unexpected delay would not cost him unnecessary casualties before they even started their mission in full.

He turned when he heard the sound of several helicopters. He tried to focus on the clear blue skies overhead. "I told the aviation battalions to stand down and not to give any indication of their positions. It's imperative we keep some of our aspect of attack to a minimum."

"Western outposts report civilian aircraft heading in this direction, General," the colonel called from below. "Six choppers in all."

"Civilian?" he asked while trying to punch through the glare of the clear day. Then he saw them. As he focused on the lead heli-copter, he saw the gleaming and colorful livery colors of the birds. They were bright red and blue in paint scheme. He saw that the others following were also the same colors as the first. He lowered the field glasses and then went below into the troop carrier. "Let me see the communique once more, Colonel."

The man handed the general the teletype message received earlier that morning. He read the flimsy for the fourth time.

'Expect private executive group to join you. Their health and welfare are of the utmost priority. All accommodation will be accorded this group, and their orders will supersede previous orders if detailed.' Signed; Xi Jinping, President, PRC.

The general handed the message back to his adjutant and then went to the rear door of the personnel carrier and opened the hydraulic system, exiting with the colonel following close behind. The first five very expensive French-made *Dauphin EC155* executive helicopters settled to the earth just south of the Great Wall. Men in black Nomex assault BDUs exited and surrounded the choppers. The sixth and final bird didn't start descending until the others were secured. The *Dauphin* slowly settled into the circle formed by the other five helicopters.

"Is this what we have become?"

"What is that, General?" the adjutant asked.

"Tour guides for Hong Kong playboys come to enjoy the sight of men in battle?"

The adjutant didn't respond as three men exited the last heli-copter and then opened the rear door. A shapely leg was seen, and then the beautiful woman they were attached to was then seen by every man watching. She carried a briefcase and stood and eyed the men and land around her. The sunglasses she wore covered most of her face, but her demeanor told everyone who saw her that she was very important. The General noticed she was awaiting someone herself. Finally, a man stepped from the plush interior of the heli-copter and then slowly buttoned his suit jacket. The black attire was immaculate, and he wore no tie. He was sporting a nicely trimmed beard and his black hair was exactly combed. He placed a pair of sunglasses over his eyes, and then as the woman pointed their way, the man nodded his head and started forward. He was followed closely by his black-clad security detail.

The man smiled as he confronted the general, who stood at rigid attention and then half-bowed to the man and woman. He then straightened and started to salute, but thought better of it.

"General—" he started to say by way of introduction.

"Wei Li Cheng." The man didn't take the offered hand of the general and received a look of pure disgust from the tall woman next to the well-dressed man. "I have read your file, General. I approved of your command in this operation."

"Approved?" the stunned officer asked.

"Yes, we have followed your career from even before the defense of Beijing last year," the woman said for the man, who walked past the general and his adjutant and examined the row upon row of tanks lined up behind the Great Wall. The general ignored the woman and turned to confront this civilian interfering in his operation.

"Sir, may I ask of whom I am addressing?"

The question was ignored as the newcomer jumped upon the first Type 99-A-2 main battle tank. The crewmen watched as the immaculately dressed man rubbed a loving hand over the 125-millimeter smooth bore main gun of the most advanced tank in the world. He turned and smiled at the woman, who approached the tank and waited as the man hopped down from the chassis and whispered something the general couldn't hear. The woman smiled at what he had said, and then she turned to face the general.

"Mr. Chang is most impressed with the status of your equipment. He wishes to say that he hopes your command fares well in the upcoming unpleasantness. He is most hopeful you succeed. He has waited many, many years for action to be taken against the backward country to the North." She smiled, and then finally held out a hand as her boss continued to examine the General's men and equipment. "My name is Lisa Chow, special assistant to Mr. Chang. I will be your liaison from now on. Mr. Chang will remain behind the Great Wall until your breakthrough is achieved. When you have approached the mountain, stop and await orders."

"Orders?" The general looked from the smug woman to the man he had waited upon for life and death in the coming days.

"Yes, you did receive the message from the capital, did you not?" she asked as she removed her sunglasses and faced the general down.

"Yes," he said as he bowed to the stranger.

"You will run into more opposition than you were briefed on from high command. The Russians are prepared to stop any incursion of that mountain range at any cost. You will also be facing American and British personnel. Are you prepared, General?"

"You have said you have examined my personnel file, so you understand that I am always very well-prepared Ms. Chow, that is when I am given *all* of the details of my mission parameters."

"Very good, General. You have all the information you need for the moment. One point you may not have is the fact that Mr. Chang will not tolerate hostilities once you have captured that mountain. Is this clearly understood?"

"What if attacked? You cannot order men not to defend themselves."

"I most certainly can, General," said the man in the black suit as he approached with his hands placed firmly behind his back. "The prize we have sought can be damaged. This cannot happen. Every man in your division is expendable toward that goal. Am I understood?"

The man and woman didn't wait for an answer, they just turned away and went toward the campsite his security detail was setting up. The general watched them go until the smallish man turned back to face him.

"Once more I am placing my trust in a General." He placed the sunglasses back on. "Do not disappoint me, or I will see to it that every man in your command never sees his homeland again." He smiled and then turned away.

"Who is that?" the adjutant asked.

The General felt the chill course down his spine when the question brought to the forefront of his thoughts on the strange little civilian.

"Did you not feel it, Colonel. I think I have avoided evil men for most of my life. But that man is just that. Evil."

Ulaanbaatar, Mongolia

THE CAPITAL HAD AWAKENED TO A RAIN STORM THAT DRENCHED THE city. In Ulaanbaatar, the news was coming so fast that the population had very little time to digest it. The prevailing thought among the populace was the fact that there were two different armies seemingly ready to invade their country. After the United Nations debacle, the president of Mongolia strengthened his border guards. However, the soldiers placed there were out-numbered by close to six thousand to one.

The current president of Mongolia had been elected on a democratic platform, thus distancing his government from their once close ally; The Peoples Republic of China.

"Yes, Mr. President, my orders will stand. Any assault by Chinese forces across our southern border will be met by Mongolian patriots. Any outlaw move will cause considerable trouble as my people are virtually unanimous about the correctness of my decision. I thank you for your call and it is my sincere hope beyond measure that you heed my warning."

The president hung up the phone and faced the large, rotund man in the chair in front of his desk. Doctor Leoniv Vassick nodded his head, indicating in his opinion, the message was well put to the president of China.

"You do realize my meager forces cannot begin to even delay the Chinese forces if they move past the southern wall?"

"They will be delayed by many hours trying to breach the passes through the Altai Mountains. Dirt trails and harsh terrain is not a friend to heavily armored vehicles." Vassick stood up and presented the president with a small envelope. "This will go a very long way in supporting your new infrastructure bill in your government."

The president opened the envelope and examined the card inside. There were several sets of numbers and a monetary amount that eased the conscience of the man only two years in office.

"Your assistant can verify the payment to your treasury through electronic means. All roads that would lead to our assistance have been well covered," Vassick said as he returned to his chair.

"I will give the order to my northern command to not interfere with your crossing of the border. My official statement, regarding the volunteer Russian forces here to assist in preliminary mining operations, is already been sent to the press. I do expect very angry complaints from other members of the United Nations Security Council over this decision."

"The council has always been a toothless tiger, Mr. President. You will have little trouble with them, our people have seen to that. They have muddied the waters so much that it will take weeks to figure out our play in this matter."

With little remorse, the president of Mongolia placed the envelope aside and commenced setting his nation on a far more prosperous course for their future.

He may have felt differently if he had seen the smug look on the Russian's face as he left the presidential office.

CHAPTER NINE

Altai Mountains, Mongolia

It had been a sleepless night since the revelations from Master Li Zheng. The Group had many questions to ask, and that is what cost them all needed sleep.

As Sarah and Anya watched from the high vantage point where they were quartered, Shangri-La was just beginning to wake from its slumber. They watched through glassless windows, three hundred feet up overlooking the city center, at a few of the populace as they started their day. They watched men in ceremonial garb come and go. To the trained eyes of Sarah and Anya, these men and women looked to be soldiers.

"What we were told is hard to believe," Anya said, as she finally turned away from the window and poured herself a glass of water from an ornate glass decanter.

Sarah was about to comment about the lessons the Event Group had learned over the years that nothing, not even immortality, could be shrugged off as legend, but stopped her rebuke when a light knock sounded on the thick wooden door. Sarah moved from the window and opened it. She saw Master Li and another ornately dressed man with a feather plumed helmet, standing there. The colors of the cere-monial uniform were, at the very least, impressive with their brightly hued blue and red leather and steel armor. The man had a heavy beard and stood rigid next to his master. The long sword was secured by jeweled leather. The two men stepped aside as several young women entered with steaming bowls of food.

"I have taken the liberty of bringing you breakfast," Master Li said.

Sarah and Anya heard grumbling coming from behind the two visitors to their quarters. The saw Li Zheng gesture for someone to enter before him. Shaking her head at the cursing coming from outside, she was not surprised to see Jason Ryan, flanked by a sleepy Charlie Ellenshaw, as they came into the room.

"Also, I took the liberty of asking your friends to join us." Both men followed a complaining Ryan and Charlie inside. "Please, sit."

Sarah, Anya, Charlie, and Jason sat at the large round table. Li Zheng and his guest stood for a moment until all were settled. The steaming bowls of rice and eggs were ignored for the most part.

"I don't suppose you have anything other than tea?" A bleary-eyed Ryan asked as he sniffed at the tea pot placed in the center of the table.

"I could use some coffee myself," Charlie added.

Ryan looked at Charlie indicating maybe something a little stronger. He figured he needed a few shots of alcohol after the ridicu-lous claim made last night by Li Zheng.

The Master nodded his head at the last young lady placing food on the table. She bowed and was back two minutes later with a pot of coffee served in a beautiful pot that had to be at least five hundred years old. This small detail was readily pointed out by an ever-schol-arly Charlie Ellenshaw. Ryan poured the coffee for all. Both Li and his guest deferred to their tea.

"Where are Professors Birnbaum and Anderson?" Sarah asked as she sipped the rich coffee, grateful to Ryan for asking for it.

"I believe they need not be a part of our discussion," Li said, as he too savored his own drink.

"I am sure you have many questions, and in the short time available to us, I will attempt to answer them."

"You can say that again," Jason said sarcastically as Charlie lightly elbowed him in the side.

"There is an old saying, I believe by Winston Churchill. Americans, after doing everything the wrong way, will however, eventually come to the correct conclusion."

"Not an exact quote, I believe," Anya said, as she sampled the rice and eggs. "Although the Israeli government professes the same belief, just not in those words."

"And just what are we slow about concluding?" Sarah asked.

"That there are forces in the world who have no goals, desires of land, ideology, or even of property. Americans believe that everyone has a goal, or dare I say, a plan."

"Don't they?" Charlie asked, stirring far more sugar into his coffee than anyone had ever seen before. Including the man sitting next to Li. He eyed Ellenshaw and quite rightly decided that the man was very strange.

"Professor, this is not the conclusion I have come to after four thousand years of study." Master Li Zheng leaned forward like he was about to deliver the largest conspiracy theory in history. "It is my conclusion, after many thousands of years, that some men just want to watch the world suffer."

"Are you saying that we, the United States, have that tendency?" Ryan asked, growing angry at the way this bizarre explanation had started.

"Not at all. I accuse you and many others of trying desperately to draw conclusions as to the *why's* of evil men. Take Hitler, he had no desire to help his people. He had a natural hatred of those he could not control. That is not a plan, Mister Ryan, it is insanity. You," he looked from person to person, "all of you, try for a reality check on that insanity. What is the purpose? The reasons are simple. There are men and women in the world that defy explanation as to that insanity. They just like to watch things burn. This is what you are up against with this new threat your organization now faces. The men you pursue are those that want the world to burn so they can rule from the ashes they themselves have created. You have to fight them accordingly."

"You sound like a couple of men we all know," Sarah said, shaking her head.

"Ah, yes, Colonel Collins and your," he looked at Anya, "Captain Everett. I and my General have read their reports on this Siberian Group. They are not far off the mark in their general conclusions. Only their report did not go far enough. They too search for logical explanations as to this group's aims. There are none. At least *my* antagonist has a clear goal."

"And just who is that antagonist?" Charlie asked while chewing some rice.

"Over two thousand years ago, I died for the first time. It happened on the banks of a river where I made a stand to finally deliver my people to their new home here in the mountains of Mongolia." He placed a hand on the shoulder of the man to his right who was slowly drinking his tea. "I was pierced by so many arrows, I actually felt the relief of death. This man, disobeying his orders, came back for me. His intent was to bury me in my homeland. He brought me back home to the mineral which sustained for two thousand years before that fateful day. I was reunited with my wife and newborn child, my son, Lee." Li Zheng stood and turned to the window and watched his people starting their day far below. "My first conclusion was as your Colonel Collins. I believed there was a purpose to my half-brother's murderous attempts on my life and those of my people that stemmed from avarice, or a military goal. Not at all. His was to extend life beyond the borders of death. I had two sons, Lee, and one other, the youngest, Tai Li. This boy was captured three hundred years after my death at the river. This led to a betrayal of all that I loved. My wife, driven mad by the circumstance, offered Emperor Qin Shi Huang that which he sought, the mineral in a large shipment, for his life beyond death, as ransom for my child. He showed his gratitude by murdering my wife and my son." He turned back to face the others. "This is how I know that such men have no desire for the future. They just wish to watch the planet burn for their own enjoyment. Now Qin Shi has that ability at hand."

"Why the object lesson?" Sarah asked.

"No lesson, just a warning. There are forces that are gathering to destroy what it is we have here. Your Professor Ellenshaw calls it Shangri-La, while not quite the vision of beautiful mountains and serene valleys of legend, we are still quite fond of our home. I am here to tell you that all of this will be destroyed within three days."

All four Event Group personnel didn't stir as the room fell silent.

"This is General Chang. My oldest and dearest friend, and the man who saved this immortal's life. He will explain why, after two thousand years of life, my city will be destroyed."

Chang stood up and then half-bowed to Li. He removed his helmet and placed it on the table as he faced the four visitors. His demeanor told them that the general believed all of this was set in motion by the men and women before him that day.

"Since your incursion into our country, forces are swelling that will spell the end for us. Out of our long history, this is the greatest threat we have ever faced. Forces of which Master Li has told you about are gathering to strike at the heart of this city. We cannot defend it. Russians to the north, Chinese to the south. The Russians believe that, with the mineral, they can make the world burn. The Chinese? They are mere puppets to the man that has been, since his birth, the greatest threat to human existence in history."

"Who?" Anya asked as she was starting to get the military chills.

"My half-brother, Emperor Qin Shi Huang," Li Zheng explained.

Charlie spit out his coffee. "You mean the first Emperor still exists?"

"Long ago he claimed his prize for long life, now is his time for military conquest since he now knows the exact location of our home. A home he failed to find for over two thousand years. Thanks to your expedition, he has done just that. With the Dragon Asteroid, he can rule with very little effort. He can expand, as you have proselytized Captain McIntire, beyond this solar system with the power supplied by the Dragon Mineral. This we cannot allow. Our time is over, and we need your assistance to ensure the mineral from this asteroid is destroyed."

"We can't even convince our own government about this Siberian conspiracy, much less that a four-thousand-year-old wizard needs our help. They would laugh in our faces," Sarah said, shaking her head. "Besides, you are correct, the only way to make sure this doesn't fall into the wrong hands is to destroy it. But as I'm sure you know, introducing an explosive composite to the Dragon Mineral very well could blow this portion of Asia to bits."

"General?" Li said.

"In my studies in foreign lands, I have come to the same conclusion, Captain. Any composite explosive will set the mineral off, resulting, in my calculations, in a million times more powerful a detonation than the bomb dropped on Hiroshima. The explosion would set off a chain reaction that would ignite the Pacific Rim. My figures have been verified by Professor Lee, Master Li's son. This was the reason he lured you here. I was not in favor of it, as well as Master Li," he looked over at his old friend, "but we were wrong. The evil men he spoke of are even now upon our doorstep, thus we must assure the mineral dies with us."

"Until we learn how to destroy the Dragon Mineral without explosives, we will have to delay those forces with everything we have. Women, children, myself, my son, his wife, will meet the Russian and Chinese barbarians at our gate. All the powers of Air Bending will be needed. This will give you time to aid us in our quest. This you must promise."

Sarah looked at Li and shook her head. She turned to Anya. "Any thoughts?"

"Yes, evacuate instead of fight. No matter what answers we find, there is no way to completely destroy the mineral. Even upon detonation, there will be enough material to survive that this exercise would be a complete waste of time. They will still get their hands on it no matter what we do."

Li lowered his head. "Then all might truly be lost." He thought for a brief moment, and then faced the group once more with a sadness that was clearly seen on his soft features. "If you wish, you may leave our city." He turned, and the General stood to exit with Li.

"Perhaps since the gig is up here, we can take Major Pierce back home. I mean, why force him to stay if all of this is about to end?" Ryan asked as he thought about the brave and crazed B-29 pilot.

Li stopped and turned. "Forced?"

"Yes, you made him and his crew prisoners to keep your little secret," Ryan said.

Li Zheng and the General Chang exchanged questioning looks. "Major Pierce was never a prisoner here, Mister Ryan. He kept his word about not betraying us. His crew, not just the man you found in the desert, left here after breaking their oaths about the mineral. Major Pierce stayed of his own accord."

"Why would he do that?" Sarah asked, shocked that they had assumed all along that he was being kept here against his will.

"One month after the Pacific war ended, we received word from one of our family members studying in the States, that Major Pierce's wife had left him for another man, taking his two children with her." A pained look crossed Li's face. "You see, his wife thought him dead after your government informed her of his being shot down. A little bit of the Major's mind left that day and never returned. It was his choice to stay."

The shock was on everyone's faces.

"You never had any intention of keeping us here?" Charlie asked, with the coffee cup halfway to his mouth.

"We as a people, do not take prisoners and never have. The choice to betray us has always been in the hands of those who know the secret of the mineral. Maybe by sheer luck, or divine provenance, have we not been discovered. Every year we have expected it all to end. Now it has. Please, take Major Pierce with you if he wants to leave. The mountain is no longer anyone's home."

The two men left without another word after their hopes for a solution failed to materialize. The room was silent momentarily as everyone thought about what had just occurred.

"Well, we as a group finally did it," Charlie said as he sadly placed his cup down on the table.

"What?" Ryan asked.

"The Event Group's quest for knowledge and understanding of our history, our world, has undone a civilization that didn't need anyone other than themselves."

"Charlie, what can we do to repair what we've done?" Anya asked.

"Send that damn asteroid back to whatever distant universe it came from."

"And how do we do that, Doc?"

Charlie turned and faced Ryan. "The only people and entity that I know of that can possibly have an answer is seven thousand miles away. Only there is no way to get in touch with them, or *her*, at the moment."

"Damn it. Who, Charlie?" Sarah asked angrily.

"Niles, Virginia, Xavier and—" he started to say, but Ryan cut him off when the answer struck him.

"Europa."

Novosibirsk, Siberia

NOVOSIBIRSK IS THE LARGEST CITY IN SIBERIA AND THE THIRD LARGEST in all of Russia. The city goes by unnoticed by most citizens who are far more concerned with what is currently happening in a city further away—Moscow.

Much of the world, including the citizens of Russia, don't understand the city of Novosibirsk. Most are under the illusion that the city is unbearable and inhospitable. In actuality it is beautiful, and at the very least, misunderstood. The city on the Ob River is friendly and, for the most part, goes about its business in quiet slumber.

The façade of quiet slumber belies the fact the city of Novosibirsk has a secret buried deep under the Ob River in a complex that was built ten years before, right under the noses of its citizens. In all of Russian history there has never been a more secure site. The populace did not know that, for every ten dwellers of the city, there were two security men to match their numbers that guarded this strange facility. The complex was built a thousand feet under the Ob River and five hundred beneath the old Royal Conservatory. During a massive renovation of the three-hundred-year-old conservatory, after the fall of the old Soviet Union, the construction of the complex was well hidden amidst the renovation.

The complex comprised a mere seventeen levels that housed the secret that the world's intelligence organizations were just becoming aware of but could not prove. The Siberian Group. The group comprised the old guard of the extinct Soviet Union, from the highest ranks of government to the hundreds of KGB, science and military men and women displaced after the fall. This was where the real power broker of the Russian government was housed. The falsity of the man that occupied the Kremlin and the one that heads its government was one chosen by this council of patriots. Vladimir Putin was an original member of this group but had gone astray in his illegal endeavors on behalf of the new Russian oligarchs, of whom few found favor with the secret organization, which set up Putin to lead the nation with their blessing and guidance. This, of course, did not happen. Unbeknownst to the general population, Putin had been eliminated and replaced by an unknown twin brother who had been kept hidden from the world by this Siberian group as a fallback to the known avarice of Vladimir Putin.

The conference room on level eight of this mysterious complex was full, for the first time in years, as the group gathered to follow the operations in Mongolia. This was a situation they initiated and one of which would fulfill their destiny of regaining the power and prestige that was lost when the Berlin Wall came tumbling down. The council had all sixteen members present. The true power in Russia.

Names of this group were never permitted to be spoken aloud inside the complex, nor even through open phone lines. Extraordinary precautions were taken to keep the ruling body safe from any wanting intelligence groups. They were called by number, and those numbers were assigned accordingly for the power the men held.

The man holding the title of 'Number One' almost never spoke in these gatherings. While occupying the center position behind the 'U' shaped conference table, he sat in shadowed silence as reports were given. The only seat unoccupied that day was the chair of the man who held the rank of 'Number Eleven'. Number One scribbled a note and slid it down to Number Four. All Number Four saw was the tailored sleeve of their leader as the hand pulled back into darkness.

"What is the disposition of Number Eleven and his team?" asked Number Four.

"Sir, Professor Vassick—"

The man reporting stopped talking when Number One cleared his throat at the mention of Vassick's name.

"Sorry, sir, Number Eleven. His latest report signals that his operation is going forward with all deliberate speed. The targets in Laos were either successfully targeted and eliminated or captured by your order. The American and Chinese field team in Mongolia will soon meet the same fate. Number Eleven has reported one change in his overall plan however. What that change was he failed to elaborate upon."

"Does Number Eleven understand that the American field team is not his number one target? That it is just a target of immediate convenience and not strategic in nature?"

The man reporting remained silent as he really did not know the answer to the query.

The man holding the Number One chair spoke for the first time in three conference meetings since the plan for the Mongolian campaign began a month before. "We all know and appreciate Number Eleven's obsession with this Department 5656 inside the American government. And while many of us at this table can see his anxiety about a group that mirrors his own, many of us agree that it blinds Number Eleven to the real purpose of his mission. He does understand that we accepted his explanation for the elimination of the two American soldiers in this American group. They were a threat thanks to their involvement in the *Simbirsk* affair, which was poorly handled from beginning to end in the opinion of many here today. And we even accepted his estimation of the dangers of the American involvement in the field team regarding the Mongolian operation. But that is all we approved. I truly hope that Number Eleven's ambitions have not gone astray. Operations by his team inside the United States are absolutely forbidden at this time while the spotlight is on Mongolia. Is this clear?"

"Yes, sir," said Number Four.

"Now, we are grateful in his handling of the Mongolian President. Number Eleven truly has talent in the area of bribery. But make no mistake what the prize here is. The mineral is to be recovered. No other factor, including this...this...Event Group, is to stand in the way of that. Communicate our concerns to Number Eleven immediately."

"He has gone off the grid, sir. He has not communicated since his appointment with the Mongolian President this morning. Our intelligence arm has been trying to locate him in order to debrief him on his meeting." Number Four looked uncomfortable. "He has vanished."

The conference room became silent as Number Four sat down.

"Since we have invested many billions in the personnel Facsimile Program, and given him a valuable asset for his own goals toward the eventual destruction of this American Group, perhaps we should give Number Eleven the benefit of the doubt?"

The man who spoke was the exact duplicate of his older brother, the now deceased Vladimir Putin. He was number fifteen in the hierarchy and not very well trusted in most matters. His job was to do the Council's bidding in open governmental affairs.

Again, silence from the shadowy figures. The identical twin brother of the former Russian President cleared his throat and slowly sat down.

"Yes, Number Fifteen. The Chairman and most of us can see your point. You were a part of the planning for the strike using our Facsimile program against this American Colonel and naval Captain, am I correct? Even so far as to continuing the operation against the field team in Mongolia, is this not also a fact?"

"Yes."

"Very ambitious of you to show your wisdom and bravery. You seem to be gaining valuable insight to just what our long-range plans are and are willing to now start taking chances and thinking, what do the Americans call it? Oh, yes, thinking outside of the box. We commend you on this. However," said Number Two from the shadows of his chair, "since you are so close to Number Eleven, we will agree that his end result and your fates are tied together."

Number Fifteen, the double for Vladimir Putin, frowned and felt a chill travel up his spine. Perhaps he had allowed Professor Vassick to talk him into too large a risk. The council was very unforgiving of mistakes. He just nodded his head and sat.

"Now, have we commenced Operation *'Assisted Dynamic'*?" asked Number Two.

The man occupying seat number six stood and proudly went to attention. "Operation *Assisted Dynamic* entered Mongolia territory one hour ago."

"And the Mongolians have been confirmed to have stood down their border forces?"

"From all reports, they waved their small Russian flags and Mongolian banners as our element crossed. Of course, the news outlets were forewarned and the cooperation between Russian and Mongolian nations was well covered and well received by all accounts. The Chinese, Americans and British have no option but to remain silent. Any incursion on their part will be perceived internationally as aggressive moves against a friendly nation. Peace on Earth through cooperation and partnership. As ordered."

"Number Fifteen," said Number Two, "you did a fine job in preparing the world's news organizations to cover the friendly crossing."

The Putin look-alike stood, and half bowed to the men around him, finally happy that he received praise instead of threats. "Thank you, Number Two."

"Let us hope that the exuberance of Number Eleven does not cloud your efforts in this matter."

Number Fifteen sat, losing all of the exhilaration of praise given just a moment before. Now he only hoped Professor Vassick wasn't setting them both up for a disciplinary action against them by the council. He was worried as the meeting broke up to await news from Mongolia and the recovery of the mineral, which had the possibility of sending the new Russia soaring into the future as the leading power in the world.

The only two men that remained seated were Numbers One and Two.

"Professor Vassick, while seemingly indispensable, and a natural resource for our committee, he worries me about this obsession with this American National Archives Group."

Number One listened to his second in command and sat silently for the briefest of moments.

"Professor Vassick is right on the one point, that this Group and its capabilities are far more of a threat to us than either the American CIA or MI-6. Their investigative capabilities cannot be underestimated. This man, this Doctor Niles Compton, is the larger threat. Vassick by all accounts, is right about that."

"Perhaps Professor Vassick's goals and ours are one and the same then? Maybe his first suggestion that he be allowed the use of the Facsimile Program to be used on this troublesome group's home territory is the correct course?"

Number One smiled. "A strike against their complex would receive too much attention, and at the moment an operation such as that would not be beneficial to our cause. Limiting Vassick to a strike on their personnel was one thing but cutting the head off this particular snake could be an attention-getter we do not need. After all, this Compton, as I understand it, is extremely close to the outgoing President of the United States and was the main reason even ourselves listened to his council during the brief war with the Grays. This Compton may be even more worthy of our attention than we initially thought. But Compton and his strange Group can wait. Let us just hope Vassick stays the course and keeps to his limited schedule. Find him if you can and remind him of the confidence the committee has in him."

Number Two saw the right brow of Number One raise, meaning many differing things to some. But for him it was a warning about the fate of men that failed to follow instruction, no matter how brilliant they are.

Altai Mountains,
Eastern Mongolia

GENERAL CHANG HAD CHANGED OUT OF THE CEREMONIAL WARRIOR garb of that morning. He was wearing American made desert BDUs of multi-patterned browns and grays. His bush hat was placed to cover his eyes against the harsh sun as he sat upon the rocks overlooking the valley far below.

"General?"

Chang took a breath and then turned and saw a figure backlit by the afternoon sun. He recognized the voice.

"Young Master."

The small man edged in next to the general and sat.

"Don't call me that. You of all people place to a standard I do not deserve. Boy would be preferable, or even Professor."

Chang continued to watch the desert floor hundreds of feet down the mountainside. "You are Master Li Zheng's only son, my respect for that position is my duty and honor, not a mere standard."

Professor Lee removed his wire-rimmed glasses and followed the general's eyes to the valley floor.

"My father is keeping his views to himself. He has vanished amongst the tunnels and will not share his feelings with me."

Chang smiled and then removed his sunglasses. He faced the young master. "This has not changed in two thousand years. You know, when we first arrived here, in this place, we all expected to die.

Instead we were given the greatest gift on Earth, well, it turned out not to be from Earth at all, but a gift nonetheless."

"More of a curse actually," Lee corrected.

"Well, it started out in the good category anyway. Now, the gift is about to be taken, and do you know something, young Master?" Chang looked closely at Lee. "I am not sad."

"What do our eyes and ears at the border tell you and my father, is it that bad?"

Chang laughed and replaced his sunglasses. He pointed to the north. "The Russians will come from that direction. They have the support of our friends in the Mongolian government. They will strike in the early morning hours, both from the air and from the ground. Their intent after recovering the Dragon Asteroid is clear. Our friends from that American Group are right. These men in Siberia are bad men, but also men with a plan. But that is not the real threat. Russians playing games will be petty to the plans of the evil one. His forces, or the Chinese element if you prefer, will strike from the mountains above us. They are taking their armored division over the old pilgrim trail from the south."

"I have brought this doom upon us with my arrogance in my belief that the mineral belonged to the world, not just us."

This time Chang's laugh was genuine. "Do you know how many times Master Li wanted to give this gift to the world?" He shook his head in wonder. "Too many times to count. Perhaps every other year for two thousand years." He slapped at the dust on his BDU pants. "No, young Master, things are happening now that were preordained many years ago. The Americans are right on one point."

"What's that?"

"The Dragon Asteroid is not a natural element to our world. It does not belong. It should have destroyed this planet when it first arrived, but our science says by fluke alone it did not. The world will be a better place without it."

"Then General, is it not best to evacuate the mountain?"

"We have much work to do here first. We cannot allow the evil one to get his hands on the mineral. Any of it. Just three small bags of it extended his life force. Think what a ton could do for his filthy aims. He has waited over two thousand years in his patient ambition to rule the entire world."

"Hi," came a voice from behind.

General Chang smiled as he didn't even turn to see who had come upon them. He knew military men and Jason Ryan was one. He wasn't just out sightseeing, he was there to formulate an arrogant plan to get his people off the mountain, if and when it came to that.

"Join us, Commander Ryan."

"Hope you ground-pounders don't mind a navy man sitting in?"

"The navy, I never had much use for the sea," General Chang said. "No offense."

"None taken." Ryan sat and then slapped both palms on his knees. "So, what are we talking about?"

"Life and death, Commander," Professor Lee said.

"Whoa, heavy."

"Yes, quite so," Chang said as his attention bored in on something in the far-off distance. His eyes remained there as Ryan spoke.

"As a navy man, most infantry-types don't regard my opinions on battlefield maneuvering as educated. But as I see it, and from over-hearing your conversation earlier, which I apologize for by the way, I see no other option than to get the hell out of here. Blow the damn asteroid back to whatever hell it came from and run like hell."

"Mister Ryan, I am well versed on many of your exploits during and before the war with the Grays. Your opinion in normal circumstances would be most welcome. But we must remain here to stop the man from the south from getting the Dragon Asteroid."

"General, throughout all of the years you have served my father, why did you not attempt to kill the Emperor?" Lee asked.

Again, another small laugh from Chang. "Emperor Qin Shi Huang is a ghost. When he realized his immortality could become an issue the world would notice, he had the foresight to die, at least in the public eye. Make no mistake, he has ruled from afar for many hundreds of years. He is the most formidable man I have ever known. My brother, General Kang, served him until the great battle at the riverbank. The Emperor has instincts beyond that of nature. As I said, formidable. He would have seen me coming and any attempt by us to kill off this evil would have led him to our home." He faced Lee and Ryan. "And this we could not allow."

"Well, it sounds like the asshole's instincts are coming into serious play now," Jason said as he saw the general concentrating on the expanse of desert below.

Lee laughed at the simple way the American naval aviator had of looking at things.

"So, when are you going to evacuate these women and children?"

"The children are already moving through the tunnels to the Great Wall, the rest will stay."

Ryan stood and looked at the relaxed way the General just condemned the menfolk of Shangri-La to death.

"Hey, General, I hate to break it to you, but the fanatics on their way here don't give a god damn if you meet them with all honor. They will kill everyone here to get their hands on that crap buried in that mountain. Hell, I wouldn't even trust my own government with that much power."

"Distrust is an assurance against corruption, Mister Ryan, you are to be commended for that. However, we will stay and fight."

"Jesus, you're just like Colonel Collins. Don't worry about me, I have a death wish anyway. Damn!"

"Mister Ryan, behind you there are several weapons, bring three of them, please."

Both Lee and Ryan watched as General Chang stood and then used a set of binoculars to view the desert terrain below. Ryan did as asked and recovered the three AK-47s hidden behind them.

"What is it, General?" Lee asked, feeling uncomfortable about holding a weapon.

"Come with me."

"What is it, Indians?"

Chang stopped and turned and faced Ryan. "Indians?"

"He means hostiles, General," Lee said by way of explaining the American's comment.

"Yes, hostiles. Normally I would not take notice, but these tribesmen seem to be chasing a ground element on foot." The General tossed the binoculars to Jason who stopped and focused on the rising dust cloud in the distance.

"You've got to be kidding me!" Ryan said as he handed the glasses to Lee who took them and saw what Ryan and the General had.

Several men were running on foot. One looked injured, as a burly little man was assisting him. The rest were taking a rearguard action and firing on the Mongolian tribesmen and the vehicle they were in, when the ATV would swerve for cover, the rearguard would cease fire and then catch up with the first two.

"Now who in the hell are these guys?" Lee asked, finally lowering the glasses as Ryan started to run to catch up with General Chang. "This place is becoming more popular than Piccadilly Circus!"

"A couple off assholes who don't understand they're too damn old to be out here!"

THE MASTER CHIEF LOWERED EVERETT TO THE GROUND BEHIND A small dune as the six Air Force commandos set up a minimal perimeter to the left and right of the slight rise in terrain. The old navy man took a moment to catch the breath that had escaped his lungs after the mad dash, just after a hail of bullets announced in no uncertain terms, that they had just met up with the indigenous population of the Gobi Desert.

"Damn, Toad, but you're one heavy son of a bitch!"

Carl shoved a full magazine of 5.56 rounds into the Master Chief's chest. "Yeah, I'll go on a diet if we make it out of here, you old bastard. Now, why don't you try and place some of those rounds downrange, or are you going to cuss them to death?"

The six commandos were having difficulty defining targets of opportunity. The tribesmen had dismounted their vehicles and were dodging from dune to dune in an attempt to make the Americans waste their ammunition.

"Cease fire!" Carl called out from his back as he himself slammed a magazine into an M-4. "Wait till you have a clear target, we may be here for a while."

"Listen," the Master Chief said as the tribal return fire dwindled down to nothing. Jenks cocked an ear. "Damn, our luck continues to go our way," he said as he ducked behind cover once more after peeking up and over the small rise. "I think the rest of the Backstreet Boys have arrived."

Everett took a chance and raised his head up and looked just as three more all-terrain vehicles started disgorging more Mongolians who ran for cover. Everett ducked back under cover and shook his head.

"Damn, they have enough men now to outflank us." He leaned as far forward as he could. "Sergeant, take two men and cover our rear, they'll try that avenue first."

"Why maneuver when they can just charge us?" Jenks asked as he started placing magazine after magazine into the sand in front of him for easy access.

"I suspect these guys have been doing this since the dawn of time. I don't think they're stupid."

As the area quieted, they heard the sound of at least three more large vehicles as they joined their friends.

"These bastards are going to 'Custer' our asses," Jenks said.

"Well, we'll have to try and make it too expensive for them, won't we?"

Jenks looked at Everett like he had lost his mind.

He smiled at the Master Chief. "We'll have to do the one thing Custer didn't do."

"You've got to be kidding?" Jenks said, as he felt like screaming, crying, or even fainting at what the Captain was suggesting.

"Sergeant Wilkes?"

The black commando appeared with a belly crawl as a few of the tribal rounds 'zinged' overhead. "Sir?"

"If we stay here, we're going to be picked off piecemeal. Suggestions?"

The Air Force commando looked at the determination in the navy

SEAL's eyes. He hadn't asked the question in the normal sense. He was speaking his thoughts aloud so that the other men could come to the same conclusion as he.

"Let's see if we can put a fright into them."

"Is the Air Force ready to make a cavalry charge, Sergeant?"

"Yes, sir. I think I'll get two of my men to lay waste to their transports. We have fifteen M-79 grenade rounds for party favors. That may convince them of their folly if they're on foot."

"Good thinking. Get your men ready. The Master Chief and myself will take the center. Tell everyone to stay low. Let's see how determined these people are."

Carl looked at Jenks as the commando scurried off to issue the order.

"Hey look, my chest is still a little sore. You have to use that bully voice of yours to make the call. Loud as you can. Make these jokers think the devil himself is coming for them."

"I want to know just who in the hell taught you this shit!"

"Well, he kind of looked like you. Ready?"

Jenks came up to his knees. He placed his two small fingers at the corners of his mouth and blew. The whistle was piercing in the late afternoon air. Suddenly, the six commandos, followed quickly by a limping Everett and a flustered Jenks, stood to charge the tribesmen.

They all stopped in their tracks as the echo of the whistle died to nothing.

"Okay, that just about covers the cavalry charge, Toad. Any other brilliant military maneuvers?"

Carl stopped counting the tribesmen when he reached close to a hundred. They were now confronted by every Mongolian in the desert, that was his closest estimation. At least two hundred men and weapons had arrived. They were now totally surrounded.

The man leading the Mongolians stepped forward. He wore a wrapped turban and had the lower half of his face covered. He held an old Thompson submachinegun and looked to be a not-so-friendly type. He slowly raised the ancient American made weapon in their direction.

Before any man, either tribesman, or American, saw what was coming, the few clouds covering the late afternoon sky started roiling and swirling above their heads. Carl pulled an amazed Master Chief to the ground before one of the Mongolians placed a bullet into his thick head.

The wind picked up from nothing to what Everett estimated at sixty to seventy miles per hour. Sand and dirt pummeled them as the few clouds started to expand. Then bright flashes of lightning started to extend downward from the circling clouds that had gone from white and wispy to dark and foreboding in a matter of seconds. The tribesmen were caught off guard as many of the legends they were told as children came flooding back into their memory. Many went to their knees as their bodies were pummeled by piercing sand particles, while others tried to turn and run. Streaks of chain lightning started to reach for the ground.

The Air Force commandos hit the sand as the world started to come apart around them. Rain began falling sideways as the winds took the moisture and whipped it into a frenzy of storm waters such as you would see as a hurricane started reaching landfall. Still the wind speed picked up in volume as it started to rip the scrub brush from their rooted places in the ground.

"Jesus!" Jenks cried out as he attempted to shield his head and face from the buckshot-like sand as it tore into everyone and everything.

Carl tried his best to brave the wind and look to see just what the end of the world looked like. He was nearly decapitated by an M-4 as it shot across his vision. In the briefest of moments, he saw an entire three-hundred-foot square of earth and scrub, with at least fifty of the tribesmen upon it, rise into the sky by a minimum of sixty feet, and then, before being blasted apart by the winds, a lightning bolt hit the raised portion of earth and the area just exploded, to be swept away by the wind and then rain.

Jenks reached up and pulled Carl back to the ground. "You crazy bastard!"

Hail started falling as the winds increased even more. He heard men being hit by softball-sized hail. Still, there was more thunder, followed immediately by lightning, which struck six times in less seconds than it would take to describe. The Earth around them shook and rolled as if a wave-like earthquake struck. Carl felt his stomach reel at the motion. The roll continued from there to snap tribesmen into the air like a blanket being whipped over a bed for straightening. The hurricane force wind claimed the men and they vanished into the blackness that had become more night than day.

"Good God!" Jenks cried aloud.

Several of the all-terrain vehicles, with men hanging onto the four-wheeler's running boards and top, started moving. Before they got a hundred feet, a wave of sand that was higher than any tsunami recorded struck. The wave came on and there was no escaping its wrath. The base of the wave hit the three vehicles and shot them into the air. The mammoth wave of sand and rock crested and then rolled over the tumbling cars and screaming men.

Then there was nothing but silence. It was if the Americans were buried alive in the total absence of air, wind, and rain. All noise had ceased and, even before Everett could raise his head, he felt the warmth of the sun once more heating the back of his neck. When he did finally gain his feet, the view looked like something from an old moonscape photo. There was absolutely nothing to see. The sand had been so thoroughly scrubbed clean that only hard dark earth could be seen. This was earth buried under rolling sands for fifty million years. There was not one standing bush or tree. Even the rocks were gone, all the way to the base of the mountain a mile away.

"Okay, that just about does it for me," Jenks said as he joined Carl to view the devastation around them.

Everett checked to see if the commandos were all accounted for. They were. They were digging themselves out of piles of sand so deep that it covered them to their hips. Carl nudged the Master Chief in the side and made him examine the ground they stood upon.

"Just stick a banana in my ass and call me a monkey," was all he said as they both looked at what had happened.

The ground they stood upon was now twenty feet higher than it had been before the strange storm. It wasn't a mountain rising from the earth, it was because the sand and earth around their position had been so thoroughly scrubbed clean by the wind, that it only looked to be rising. They were now on an island of untouched sand that rose above the Gobi.

"Thank you, thank you, we'll be here all week!"

Carl and Jenks turned to see Jason Ryan walking toward them. He was accompanied by two men. Neither Jenks nor Carl had words.

Just as the remaining clouds overhead dissipated to a mere five or six white, unthreatening clouds, they heard Ryan laugh.

"Brothers, you ain't seen anything yet."

Thirty-five Miles East

"Hey look, while I'm trying to avoid slamming us into the Mountains, tell your small friend back there that accidentally shooting the pilot is not a good thing."

Jack looked from Farbeaux and then turned his head to see Tram cleaning and fiddling with the new toys that Henri had procured for him on the black market in Hong Kong. Jack smiled as he remembered Farbeaux's harsh criticism when Tram had chosen an old American made Winchester model 70 scoped hunting rifle over the new, far more modern sniper rifles flooding today's world's markets. Tram had the Winchester's receiver apart and was adjusting the over-travel spring and the trigger-pull weight adjustment.

"He's just adjusting the weapon to his own specs, Henri. He hasn't loaded it yet."

"It's not the Winchester that worries me," Henri said as he adjusted the course of the twin-engine Bonanza they had stolen twenty-four hours before in Hong Kong.

Collins looked back one more time at the cased specialty weapon that Tram looked upon as if a child had just received the greatest Christmas present he could have been given. The case was sitting on the left seat next to Tram and looked deadly even without being seen.

It was a Barrett M-107 Anti-Material fifty caliber rifle. Jack had to laugh inwardly as he knew the weapon was more like a portable artillery piece than a sniper rifle. It was designed to not only take out an enemy with extreme prejudice, it was also designed to take out the very vehicles they rode to war in. It was the scariest anti-personnel system Collins had ever seen. He understood Henri's nervousness about it. Just a single fifty caliber round going off would destroy in total the interior of the Bonanza. He turned back to face Farbeaux.

"Hey, you're the one that spoiled the kid, not me."

Henri snorted. "And then I would have to look at the disappointment on his face, no thanks."

The drone of the engines lulled Jack into thinking about Sarah. And it was this that made him give the Frenchman another hard look. He knew exactly why Farbeaux was on this merry little trip, and that reason was the small woman they both loved. These thoughts drove Jack mad after the way in which he and Sarah had parted. He now knew it was a mistake. Since he and Carl's journey had started, he had concluded that these Siberian Russians were far more out of his league than first thought. He needed to be ruthless and that trait was just no longer in his DNA. The Event Group and the friends he had made there had changed him forever and he was just now realizing it. He had decided he would now embrace that change if he found everyone still alive. He had abandoned them when they needed he and Carl most. He felt like a heel.

"According to my calculations, we should be coming up on the last fifty miles or so," Henri said as he manually adjusted his flight navigation. He looked out of the Bonanza's window. "I wish we had a better radar."

"Hey, you're the one that stole the plane. It was your choice."

Farbeaux looked to his right with a scowl. "I guess this is blame the French day."

"Always."

"Sometimes I think you and that crazy man Everett are blood kin."

Before Jack could agree, the twin-engine Bonanza was rocked.

The blast was so powerful that both men thought they had been struck by an air to air missile. The plane rolled and came close to flipping over as the aircraft was caught in a vortex of swirling air.

"Missile?" Jack asked as he fought to hold onto the flight console.

Henri fought the wheel until the Bonanza righted itself and then he pushed the control wheel into the down position and dove as if he were piloting a fighter jet.

"Not exactly!" he cried just as Tram pointed out the left rear window.

As both Jack and Henri looked, the nose of a shark appeared and came level with the propeller driven Bonanza. The Russian made Stealth Fighter eased into position next to them.

They heard another rumble and turned and saw an equal terror move into position to the right of the Bonanza. The first fighter which had buzzed them a moment before had turned and was now flanking the aircraft.

The SU-57 was a fighter for the Russian air force that replaced the MiG-29 as the fifth-generation fighter of that nation's air force. With the exception of the new American built F-22 Raptor, the new king of the skies had arrived.

"Can we get low enough to give these boys a hard time?" Jack asked as he could see the masked faces of the two Russian pilots as if they were merely looking into his living room window.

Before Henri could answer, the fighter on the left rolled slightly to its right as the bright red star of the Russian Air Force became visible. Then the pilot made sure the Americans could see the heat seeking and radar guided missiles inside the now opened and recessed weapons bay of the stealth aircraft. The Russian rolled back to level and pointed with a gloved hand to the north.

"I think he's inviting us to go north," Jack said thinking furiously about what their options were.

"You think?" was all the Frenchman said as he raised his left hand from the flight wheel and flipped the Russian the finger.

The stealth fighter jinked to the right suddenly, coming mere feet from the left wing and fuel tank of the Bonanza.

"I think he knows what that gesture means, Henri. It pretty universal by now."

"Well, do you have any options other than to join the Russian Air Force?" Farbeaux asked.

"Look for a soft place to sit this plane down."

Henri looked in his mirror and Jack couldn't help but turn and face Tram who was busy.

"Excuse me?" Henri asked, incredulous.

Without speaking, Tram tossed Jack a steel-jacketed round. Then he reached for the cased Barrett fifty caliber rifle.

"Colonel, take your knife and split the tip of that .30-06 round by about a third of an inch, and cross the cut, please," he said calmly as he uncased the Barrett. "You have to use much pressure to split the steel jacket."

"Uh, may I ask just what it is you are doing?" Henri said through the side of his mouth as he turned and faced the Russian fighter to their left and smiled widely.

Tram didn't answer as he brought up the Barrett, which he barely had room in the backseat to maneuver with. Jack finished cutting the .30-06 round and then handed it to Tram who laid the Barrett aside and chambered the slit round into the Winchester.

"I will take the left aircraft first," he said as Henri felt the blood drain from his face. "Colonel, please use your nine-millimeter to shoot out the left-side glass back here. The bullet would lose too much velocity going through the plastic, and I will need all of the energy the grains can provide me."

"What about the right window?" Jack asked as he made sure his Glock was ready.

Tram just smiled as he took a firm hold on the Winchester and deftly removed the scope from its mount.

"Colonel Farbeaux, please hold the plane as steady as possible. We must strike before they realize they are under attack."

"Under attack? Have you lost your little communist mind? Did you happen to notice the missiles in that bay? And possibly the twenty-millimeter cannon at its nose?"

"They were rather hard to miss, Colonel. Ready?"

"Not at all!" Farbeaux yelled.

Jack nodded as Tram kept the sniper rifle only inches out of sight of the Russian pilot to their left.

"Let us just hope that this one is the flight leader, that could also help us in the confusion."

"Oh, you damn people!"

"Now, Colonel!"

Jack took quick aim and the next thing they knew the cabin was filled with a blast of wind. Tram didn't hesitate, he pulled the trigger. The .30-06 round went through the hole Collins had just made and the next thing they knew a perfect hole punched through, the SU-57's canopy. The round expanded as it 'flowered' as it struck the pilot's helmet. The pilot slumped forward in his ejection seat, and then the fighter rolled lazily to the left and started spinning out of control.

Tram didn't hesitate, he discarded the Winchester and immediately brought the heavy Barrett up. He hadn't enough room to bring it to his eye level for aiming. Just as the weapon came up, they saw the pilot commanding the second fighter hurriedly start a right turn to peel away from the sudden threat from the twin-engine Bonanza.

Tram fixed on a spot he thought most vulnerable—the left engine. He pulled the trigger and the world inside the Bonanza exploded with a roar. The fifty-caliber round punched into the left engine compartment before the Russian could fully turn away. The engine burst into flames with fuel shooting out of its interior housing. The aircraft rolled hard onto its top as it rolled away.

"Damn," Tram said.

"Is that all, just damn?" Henri said as he too rolled the Bonanza to the left, diving for the desert below. Farbeaux brought the small plane down to eight hundred feet and then started scanning the skies.

He was about to start cursing Tram when they felt the impact of twenty-millimeter rounds as they struck the rear of the Bonanza. Then the heavy caliber projectiles ran a perfect line of holes all the way to the left mounted engine, blowing it into a thousand flying pieces of steel. The disruption caused the wing tank to shear away, along with two feet of aluminum wing tip.

"Hang on, we're going in!"

The Bonanza struck the desert floor just as the Master Chief and Everett's C-130 had the day before. It hit and skid hard into a small rise and then rebounded into the air before settling once more to the sands of the Gobi.

A moment later the smoking SU-57 turned north to report his kill.

PART III
DRAGON'S FIRE

Earth provides enough to satisfy every man's needs, but not every man's greed."

~Mahatma Gandhi

CHAPTER TEN

Altai Mountains, Mongolia

The man the Event Group personnel knew as Professor James Anderson watched the two young men who were assigned to watch *him*. Something had occurred outside the hidden mountain fortress Crazy Charlie Ellenshaw had dubbed Shangri-La, that had put the city on edge. The two guards seemed to be occupied with the news and were not paying close attention. Anderson allowed himself the time needed to make the armed men comfortable about his docile actions thus far. He knew when it would be time to move. The one man who seemed inordinately preoccupied with him, even far more than the young men watching him, was the Australian, Birnbaum. Every time the man went wandering the city, he would check on him as if he knew something the others did not. It would seem normal but for the clear problem that Birnbaum was not like the others in the field team, as they had already declared that they were there as spies. Birnbaum had made no such confession or admission. He was supposedly what he claimed to be, a professor of geology.

Anderson watched the two men who were not paying him close

attention. Several young girls walked by and coquettishly flirted with the boys. He had come to know them as two students who had just returned after three semesters at universities across the globe, who were put out that they were assigned watchdog duties when they could be out with the young girls, like the ones they were now speaking to. The rest of the field team was off learning all they could about the mystical city and the people who occupied it. The inhabitants were in the process of trying to decide how better to defend their fortress. This was his chance. The only one he may ever get.

There was a commotion from across the city center as General Chang had returned with Professor Lee and the American Ryan. The two young guards, along with the four girls they were flirting with, moved off so they could determine what all the fuss was about. Anderson did not hesitate. He stood from the small alcove table he had been sitting at and swiftly vanished into the crowd of citizens moving toward the General. He ducked quickly into the first open tunnel entrance he came to. Once in the dark, he removed a small compass and flashlight from his pocket that he had managed to hide from his watchers, and checked the heading. He moved off further into the inky blackness.

EVERETT, JENKS AND THE SIX REMAINING AIR FORCE COMMANDOS could not believe what they were seeing. They had been led by a smiling Ryan and his two friends into the side of the mountain, through an entrance Carl believed he never could have found on his own. It was like all of the entrance points were so well hidden or disguised that it was near magical in its camouflaged ingenuity.

"Well, butter my ass and call me—"

"Master Chief, really, enough with the metaphors," Carl said, as he finally saw the face he was looking for. Even Jenks had to smile.

Anya Korvesky shot through the crowd of onlookers who were more interested with General Chang's presence than that of the newcomers. She jumped in the air and Carl caught her with a loud 'umph'.

"Hey, take it easy on my patient, he's still a little gunshot."

Anya ignored Jenks as she kissed Carl all over his face as the large man was finally forced to sit her down.

"You don't know what horrors I was thinking since you and Jack left," she said as she couldn't resist kissing Everett over and over.

"Master Chief," Sarah said as she stepped up and held out her hand.

"Well, Tiny, you and your antique diggers had a few people out in Nevada worried," he said, as Sarah could see he was genuinely glad to see her.

"Where's Jack?" she asked, as Jenks released her hand.

The Master Chief looked uncomfortable as he placed the weight of one foot over to the other. Sarah saw this and faced Carl, who had finally managed to disentangle himself from Anya.

"Carl?"

"Is there somewhere we can talk?"

Sarah felt her heart sink to the bottom of her chest as she read Carl's eyes. She merely nodded that they could sit at one of the community tables nearby.

Crazy Charlie smiled at the Master Chief, genuinely happy to see the gruff old sea dog.

"Well, I guess this place puts your panties in a bunch, huh, Doc?" Jenks said as he plopped a fresh cigar into his mouth and shook Ellenshaw's hand. He normally wasn't this friendly toward the eggheads in the department as he called them, but he didn't want to overhear Carl telling Sarah about Jack shooting him. He could bear a lot, but not that.

"Yes, isn't this place the cat's pajamas?"

Jenks got a serious look on his face at the comparison to 'cat's pajamas' but shook Ellenshaw's hand nonetheless.

"How did you get here?" Charlie asked, as Ryan walked past to join Carl, Anya, and Sarah.

"Doc, I would love to sit here and tell you it all went according to plan, but the Air Force seems to have forgotten how to land planes safely. But for now, I think these kids are hungry and need water and rest."

Charlie looked at the six young Air Force commandos just as Professor Lee joined them.

"Please, will you follow me? You can clean up and eat."

"Nice friendly folk you found way out here, Doc," Jenks said as he lit his cigar. "Any reason why they chose to live in the largest desert in the world?"

As Jenks and the men fell in behind Lee, Charlie became excited as he started to explain.

"IMPOSSIBLE," SARAH SAID, AS SHE TURNED HER BACK ON CARL, AND even Anya looked angry that Everett could have been so badly mistaken.

"Before the bullets hit me I would have said the same thing. Even when I was found, my mind was so cloudy I thought I had to have been delusional. Since then my memory has become far clearer. It was Jack, Sarah."

Sarah was speechless as she turned and faced the center-most waterfall.

"Captain, maybe we should wait to hear from the Colonel. I'm sure he has some logical explanation for what you believe. Sarah's right, that's not in his makeup."

"I hope so, Mister Ryan. But my mind is clear on that point."

"Okay, so where is Jack now?" Sarah asked, turning away from her thoughts. Her eyes went straight to Carl's.

"The last report we heard from Doctor Morales was that Jack's transponder was still operational, meaning he's alive. That's all we know right now."

Sarah seemed somewhat relieved. She knew she could not press Carl on his memory on that night, so she would let it go. She would never believe Jack could shoot his best friend.

There was more commotion from the citizens as another man joined them. The crowd parted and General Chang and another man that Carl didn't know stepped up. Everett stood also and held out his hand.

"I didn't get a chance to say thank you for whatever happened out there. You saved our asses."

General Chang looked at Carl's outstretched hand and then refused to shake. Everett lowered it slowly.

"You'll have to excuse the General. He's concerned about the popularity of our desert of late."

"Carl, this is Master Li Zheng," Anya said and then paused for dramatic effect. "He's the half- brother of the first Emperor of China."

"The hell you say!" Jenks said as he faced Ellenshaw. "Bullshit," was his answer to Charlie's statement about the age of Shangri-La and its leader, Li Zheng.

Ellenshaw only smiled.

"If they're immortal, this place would be busier than Times Square," he removed the cigar and spat, forcing several women who were serving the hungry men a meal to place a look of horror on their faces. "Hell, if no one ever dies, life would suck."

"No," said Charlie. "Once they're of age, they are sent out into the world to watch us. Learn our faults, our truths, and to protect us in small, sometimes undefined ways."

"Doc, sometimes you truly have earned your nickname."

"No, crazy is the fact that you repaired the very battleship they found for the British. That's right, they help us when they can without the world knowing who does it."

"Bullshit. Just like out in the desert, we were saved by a freak blow of wind, that's all."

Charlie shook his head, knowing he could never convince the Master Chief of the truth of Shangri-La without another powerful demonstration.

Ellenshaw was about to attempt another chance at telling Jenks what was really happening in Shangri-La, when they saw several men in battlefield BDUs come running from the entrance they had just used.

"This cannot be good," Charlie said.

"WE ARE GETTING READY TO EVACUATE THE CHILDREN AND YOUNG ones," Master Li said looking at Sarah. "I would suggest you go with them through the tunnels to the Great Wall. Soon our home will become untenable."

"How will you fight them?" Carl asked, looking from the stern General Chang, to Master Li. "From the last report we received, the Russians are headed here with some serious firepower."

"Yes, and that is not all," General Chang said, finally breaking his silence but not relenting on his unspoken distrust of the American. "Chinese forces may even now be crossing the divide."

"Jesus," Everett said. "I respect the powers that Sarah and Anya say you possess, but wind, water, air, and sand cannot stand for long against armored vehicles."

Li nodded his head that he understood the American's warning. "This is a fact. White magic cannot be our only avenue. No matter what becomes of us, these ruthless men cannot take the Dragon Mineral," he looked directly at Everett. "Any of these men. The asteroid must be destroyed."

"According to our experiment, just set fire to it. Something not very welcoming to either the Russians or your brother will be the end result," Sarah explained.

"I admire your theory, Captain McIntire. If that were the case, I assure you we would have blown the asteroid up many millennia ago. It will not burn as a whole. Only the dust creates the explosive outgassing effect." General Chang went silent after the explanation.

"Then create the dust needed," Sarah said.

"The green substance in the bulk of the asteroid prevents fire from taking hold. It will only produce a toxic gas. Not that much of a deterrent against aggressive men who have technology on their side,"

Li said. "No, evacuation is our only course. The elders among us will attempt to make taking the Dragon Mineral too expensive for them."

"The Russians don't usually let expense get in their way," Everett said, seeing the fright the situation was placing upon their hosts.

"Nor your brother, Master Li," Chang added.

To the Americans, it looked as if that point was a bone of contention between the two ancient friends.

"Still, I advise that you and your friends join the evacuation," Li said as he started to turn away. "You may take Professor Birnbaum and the Russian spy with you."

"Look, the way Sarah and Anya explain it, you have a powerful brother. Your point about making recovery of this mineral too expensive for a hostile force to take has merit. The same it seems would apply to the Chinese. No matter how rich and powerful your brother is, the Chinese government can only go so far in supporting his cause."

Li turned. "My brother is the Chinese government. Always has been, and he, most assuredly, always will be."

"You cannot give up on this city," Sarah said angrily. "Look, from what I can tell so far, you are good people. Your continuing existence is important to the world. We have to try something."

"And as far as ordering us out of here, no." Everett looked from face to face. Ryan, Sarah, Anya. "We don't run from a fight. The Russians headed your way are under the orders of a maniac group. Sarah says you know about them. So, you must understand that no matter who gets their hands on this mineral is equal in menace. We'll stay." Carl stood and again held out his hand to General Chang. "Show us how we can help." Again, Everett's hand hung in the air.

This time the General took it and shook. "Gather your men, Captain, we will show you what we are up against."

"Slick Willy...Slick Willy...Slick Willy. Buried alone, all alone, all alone."

Carl released the general's hand and looked up to a high ledge where the voice sprung from.

"Take no notice of this man. He is ill," the General said, pointing to his temple, "up here."

"I will get our friend," Master Li said. "I will try and convince him to go with the young ones."

Ryan explained the situation with Major Pierce. Carl was aghast that the man had remained as sane for as long as he had.

"Slick Willy has all the answers, all the answers...all the answers."

"Poor bastard has really lost it," Ryan said, as Li moved off to try and silence the man before he had all the children scared to death.

"Ignore Slick Willy at your own peril!" Pierce ran off into the darkness of a tunnel. "Your own peril!" The words echoed off the barren walls of the darkened tunnel.

"This is by far the most interesting cast of characters we have come across," Carl said, as he placed an arm around Anya.

"Yeah, besides the little green alien who was our friend for years. Gray beings who wanted to eat us, traveling through time to get you back from a lost world…, or even stranger, the man I love and the one who saved you in Antarctica trying to kill his best friend. Yes, interesting to say the least." Sarah moved off to be alone.

Carl wanted to go after Sarah, but was held back by Anya, who just shook her head no.

"Give her time to absorb what you told us. She needs it."

"By the look of things," Carl said as he eyed more young men and women in battle BDUs and armed with automatic weapons arriving in the city center, "she doesn't have a lot of time to come to grips with it. In case you didn't notice, these gentle people as you describe them are going on a war footing."

JACK, FARBEAUX, AND TRAM WATCHED FROM COVER AS THE SIXTEEN parachutes eased to the desert floor only a mile from the position they took in the foothills of the large mountain. Jack handed the Winchester with the scope attachment back to Tram. From its lens, Collins saw in clear detail the Russian uniforms of the elite 2nd Guards Unit of special air assault.

"Scouts."

"They'll be on our position in only minutes, Colonel," Henri said as he was also looking at the far-off unit coming closer. "There can be no way to warn the field team in time from here. And they are going to cross right into the path we would have to take to get to Sarah."

Collins noticed there was no mention of either Anya, Charlie or Ryan, just Sarah in his worrisome observation.

"I see your point with one exception, Colonel. Those scouts aren't headed in the direction of the last transponder coordinates of the field team. They're heading directly for the mountain."

Henri gestured to Tram and the Vietnamese sniper handed him the Winchester. Farbeaux looked through the scope for a moment and then gave it back.

"The report you said initiated all of this, you explained it was just a cover story to explore the region for an unknown mineral source that your criminal computer said is possibly here someplace?"

"From my understanding, yes."

"Could that be what the Russians are really interested in?"

"Possibly."

"I hate to suggest this, but maybe they already have your field team. Maybe that's why they are not going in that direction. You are right, they seem to be far more interested in the high ground than the lower."

"No communications, no sign of anything. We're as blind as bats out here." Jack turned and looked up to the lowering sun in thought.

"Get down!" Tram yelled as he placed his weight on Farbeaux and pushed him to the ground.

Just as the men went to ground and hid, two jet fighters flew low over the desert scrub toward the men moving toward the mountain. Jack rolled over as Tram explained what was happening as he looked through the scope.

Suddenly the 'burupp' sound of a twenty-millimeter minigun canon sounded and echoed off the desert floor. As they watched on, geysers of dirt and rock flew skyward as heavy weaponry tore into the Russian scouting party.

"What in the hell is going on?" Jack asked as he rolled over and tried to get an identification of the aircraft he had initially thought were Russian.

Just as the second fighter jet rolled in to finish the job his wingman had started, Collins saw the unique shape of the fighter's configuration. The 'Delta' wing and the twin-canards at the nose of the plane identified it readily for the Colonel. They were Chengdu J-20 fighters, NATO designation, 'Flounder', China's newest, most advanced fighter aircraft. The second Flounder struck the hillside as the Russian scout group was decimated by the twenty-millimeter canons of both jets. As soon as the attack was over, the fighters climbed high into the skies and vanished.

"Well, that solved that immediate problem," Henri said as he joined Jack in standing to see the destruction just a mile off.

"This is great, now we have China poking their noses around," Collins said as he saw the far-off bodies torn to pieces by the heavy assault.

"Yes, and they would not send their top line fighters if they were not serious about this area of the world," Tram said as he moved ahead of Jack and Henri. "We must examine the bodies for any information they have."

Both Collins and Farbeaux watched the Vietnamese sergeant take the lead.

"I get the distinct feeling our friend Mr. Tram hates the Russians and the Chinese equally."

Jack smiled as he started to follow.

"They're not a very trusting people, the Vietnamese."

THE BODIES WERE TORN TO PIECES. THE FIRST MAN THEY CAME TO WAS sliced neatly in two parts, where a twenty-millimeter round hit him in the torso, as Tram went through his pockets. The third Russian commando had a map. He was also still alive.

"What do we do about him?" Henri asked, as Tram straightened and unfolded the map.

"Shoot him," was all Tram said.

Henri hesitated. This was not his usual attitude when it came to enemies and Jack was curious as to how he would react. He didn't.

Tram lowered the map and then pulled out his nine-millimeter pistol and shot the Russian in the head with no thought whatsoever. He went back to looking at the map. "They would not have given you such mercy, Colonel."

Henri looked from the man examining the map to face Collins.

"Bastards get little sympathy from me," Jack said in all seriousness.

Farbeaux shrugged his shoulders as Tram brought the map over to them. "They seem to be interested in this area of the mountain, Colonel," Tram said as he held out the Russian made map. "The highlighted area."

Jack looked from the map and then adjusted his line of sight to the mountainside.

"It looks like a barren side of a mountain to me."

Tram folded the map. "Perhaps we should check these men for a functioning radio. It would seem that Director Compton needs to be filled in on what is transpiring here."

"I knew there was a reason we brought him along," Henri said as they moved off.

High overhead Russian and Chinese fighters started to gather and, as the three men moved off, they started hearing explosions deep inside the valley that led to the mountain from the south where the Chinese expeditionary force was cutting a trail large enough to get through.

The Gobi Desert was filling up with bad people and, after four thousand years of existence, time was finally running for mythical city of Shangri-La.

CHAPTER ELEVEN

Event Group Complex,
Nellis Air Force Base, Nevada

Niles Compton placed the phone down and took a breath. His call with Lord Durnsford had not gone well. MI-6's man ensconced on the international field team in Mongolia, like his people, still had not been located. Compton was even far more worried than the British Lord, due to the fact that the British agent had only failed to check in. Niles' concern was the fact that he knew the situation was far worse than even MI-6 believed. The transponders of his people had been completely dark for the past two days.

Also discussed was the fact that, no matter their concerns over their operatives, the entire Asian continent seemed close to a real shooting war. If their people were still alive, they were about to be right in the middle of a possible World War III scenario, where the British and American governments were stuck on the sidelines.

Alice Hamilton knocked on the door to the conference room and entered, followed by Virginia and Xavier Morales. They saw Niles was deep in thought and, knowing the Director as well as they did, they sat silently and waited for him to come out of his concentrated silence. Xavier started to give his only good news, but just one look from Alice stilled his voice. Niles finally removed his horned-rimmed glasses and placed them on the conference table.

"I have had two conversations in the last hour, neither was the bearer of good news." Niles took another deep breath. "There was an incident in Mongolia. The Air Force admitted to the President that Captain Everett's transport went down somewhere in the Gobi, location unknown."

Xavier and Alice glanced momentarily over at Virginia Pollock. She gave no hint as to her feelings about Master Chief Jenks. Her face was serene as she remained as she always had, poised.

"Europa hasn't seen any alteration in their health," Xavier said, hoping to give Virginia a little reassurance.

"MI-6 still has no word from their man," Niles said avoiding the subject of Everett's and Jenks' transponders.

"Europa has also been monitoring all military communications in Mongolia," Xavier added.

Niles looked up and then placed his glasses back on and waited for Doctor Morales' report.

"It seems the Russians dropped a squad of commandos in the desert near the spot of our field team's last reported position. Europa monitored radio traffic from a Chinese source. A flight element reported a target destroyed at that same exact location."

"Europa's conclusion?" Niles asked.

"Her estimation is that the shooting has already started. She clandestinely heard radio traffic from Chinese forces closing on Sarah's last reported position, claiming a Russian ground incursion has been halted by deadly force. CNN will be breaking the story in about fifteen minutes, and they will cite Chinese sources for their reporting. It seems China isn't concerned with the implications of firing the first shot."

"Prepare a briefing package for the President's eyes only. Send it to his Europa link. Suggest, and only suggest, that the same report go to National Security Advisor Caulfield. This may go a long way to getting some of our forces into Mongolia to get our people the hell out of there."

Xavier wrote down his instructions without a word being said.

"I have never felt this helpless," Niles said, standing up and pacing.

"I do have some good news," Xavier said. "Major Mendenhall just landed at McCarran airport, he should be back in an hour. Perhaps then we can get a clearer picture of Captain Everett's intent."

Niles stopped pacing and nodded his head. "Colonel Collins?"

"His transponder says he's close to home, somewhere over the California coast. I estimate he'll arrive at the complex in two hours."

"I just pray Jack can shed some light on what in the hell's going on."

"Sitting here and fretting about what we can do nothing about will do us no good," Alice said in her calm voice. "You better start thinking about how you're going to tell Jack the answer's 'no' when he pitches his plan to go after his people."

Niles didn't respond, as he was feeling the plastic walls of the complex closing in around him. He sat once more and collected himself.

"Once Jack and Will arrive on station, call a full managerial meeting of all departments. I want scenarios on what we do if the real shooting starts. I need recommendations from our end that we can advance to the President. As far as I can see it may not do that much good, because if the real shooting does start, old animosities will come to the forefront between Russia and China. This may lead to a wider conflict. As of now, the President has ordered the Seventh Fleet to clear the area. He obviously expects the worse-case scenario." He shook his head in despair and looked at each worried face. "Thank you, that will be all for now. Alice, as soon as Will arrives at the complex, send him to me."

Xavier and a silently fretting, Virginia Pollock started to leave, and Alice, always worried about how much Niles was taking on, stood and squeezed his left shoulder.

"Your people are good, Niles. They don't need Jack holding their hand. They'll get through this somehow, they always do."

Niles reached up and took Alice's hand as she stood over him.

"Sooner or later we all pay for past sins. This may be that 'later'. I have pushed the luck of my people to the breaking point." He finally let go of Alice Hamilton's hand. "Somehow I have let escape the real reason for our existence." He stood up from his chair. "We're not a spy agency, we're scholars trying to figure out what in the hell is happening to us. We don't predict, we estimate, solve and report. There are no real truths that we have learned concerning today's problems. The only truth that we have come across, that is not diametrically opposed to human existence, is the fact that the world is consumed with greed and blowing ourselves up. We have to get through this and get back to learning, not spying." He turned and faced his oldest friend in Alice Hamilton. "I need my people back."

"Get some rest and I'll have the chef bring you in something to eat." Alice started for the door.

"Alice?"

She stopped and turned. "Would Garrison have allowed Jack free reign to go after this Siberian Group?"

She smiled and shook her head. "Niles, Garrison would have been leading the charge. But you're not Garrison Lee, are you? That's why you were chosen. You outthink Garrison every inch of the way. He knew what kind of man it would take to lead the department in us stepping into the future. That man is you, the opposite of him." Alice smiled and nodded and turned once more for the door but stopped. "Garrison was a stubborn man, but he was smart when he admitted to his limitations."

Niles nodded his head in thanks and then went to his desk and sat.

Despite Alice's reassurances, the world was spinning out of control and no matter what, he felt responsible for it.

Los Angeles International Airport,
Los Angeles, CA

THE MAN CAME THROUGH CUSTOMS AND PICKED UP HIS ONE BAG. HE moved easily through the airport until he came to the baggage pick-up area where he was met.

The large man in a sweat suit held out his hand as if in greeting and the two shook. Then the larger of the two nodded his head and left, without saying a word.

The dark-haired man felt the locker key in his palm and moved quickly to the left and the ten rows of long-term locker rentals. He found the correct locker and inserted the key and saw the large black leather case inside and took it out. It was heavy and filled with the tools of his tradecraft. Once he closed the door, he moved off to the helicopter charter area of the airport.

He was nearing the end of his fifteen-year journey and felt absolutely nothing. Once he did what he came here to do, there would be no glory, no medals, and most assuredly, no greeting from his superiors. He would be dead. The fulfillment of years of training led him prematurely, by a chance opportunity, to clear the slate of his own department and that of its head, Leonid Vassick.

Jack Collins moved off to charter the helicopter that would take him home to Nevada and the men and women that were weighing heavily on his mind, and what was needed to fulfill his mission.

The elimination of the brain trust of Department 5656—the Event Group.

Tai Yin Valley (Valley of the Lion)
Southern Mongolia

THE GENERAL WAS GROWING IMPATIENT. THE COLUMN OF ARMOR HAD been halted for the past hour as the engineers tried to clear the game-trail his tank division was attempting to use as a bridge to their target. He slapped a hand down on the steel turret of his armored personnel carrier, as the engineers struggled with their C-4 charges. He was impatient because, at last report, the battle for the mountain had already seen its first shots fired by air power. The Russians were moving faster than expected.

The sound of a helicopter came unbidden into his headphones. "Colonel, who in the hell is that?"

The colonel didn't say as he came to the ladder. His non-voiced answer told the general all he needed to know. He nodded his head just as the *Dauphin* EC155 executive helicopter flew over their position and then hovered over the blockage in the road far ahead momentarily, before turning back and settling to the ground only yards from his command vehicle.

"I believe, if I'm not mistaken, we are about to be micromanaged."

Once the blades of *Dauphin* had stopped their spin, a woman in black Nomex clothing, with a ballistic vest covering her torso, stepped out. It was Lisa Chow, special assistant to Mr. Chang. Gone were the fine dress and high heels. She wore a black baseball cap over her dark hair and replaced the heels with polished combat boots. She came over to the general who hopped hurriedly down from the personnel carrier.

"Ms. Chow?"

She ignored the General and went to view the engineers just ahead of the column.

"Your advance has fallen behind, General."

"This trail was never meant for armor. It will take time to clear the sides, so we can squeeze past. As it is, we will be vulnerable to air attack while bunched together."

"You have fallen behind our planned schedule, General."

He looked at her with concern etched on his face. It was as if the woman hadn't heard a word he had just said.

"I am here to make adjustments."

The general was tempted to move his hand toward the holstered pistol but refrained doing so over the imposed threat.

"Please order your engineers back. Tell all personnel to enter their vehicles and to button up."

"But—"

"I am not used to issuing orders twice, General."

In frustration, the General nodded his head toward his second-in-command to do as she asked. He started to inquire as to what her plan was when she started walking toward the retreating engineers and the blockage in the trail three hundred yards away.

"That order also includes you and your command element, General," she said without ceasing her walk.

The General angrily nodded his head toward the command vehicle and went inside with his command team. He buttoned down the hatch as was his order just as the assault element did the same.

Special Assistant to the immortal Emperor, Lisa Chow, examined the blockage in the road. It had been a landslide that happened somewhere around the time of Moses' exodus from Egypt. The blockage was obviously placed there on purpose. She suspected she knew who had done it four thousand years before.

She turned to make sure there were no spying eyes to see. She knew that, after tomorrow, there would no longer be a reason to hide the abilities her Master had bestowed upon her in 1932. It wouldn't matter by then because the plan of two thousand years was starting to unfold before the very eyes of the world. She removed her hat and then slowly untied her boot laces. She removed her socks and then stood rigid as she faced the fifty-five tons of boulders in the path of the armored unit. She closed her eyes. She felt the warmth of the earth beneath her bare feet and the light breeze on her face. Her hair, which had been done up in a bun, fell and the strands started to slowly swirl as if caught up in an electrical field. Her hair waved in and around her face as her arms slowly came up, with the palms facing the falling sun.

There was a rumble as the first of the boulders moved, as the air around became alive with static electricity. Dust and sand swirled in small vortexes as the rest of the blockage started to lose the weight of its mass. She slowly started to raise her arms higher, and then even higher. The first line of tonnage started to shake as the air began to force the boulders off the ground.

The wind picked up around the tank column in a tornado-like torrent. The men inside felt the heavily armored tanks tilt on their treads as the forces continued developing around them. The general and his men felt as if their personnel carrier was in danger of tipping over and they hung on. His only thought was: are we being attacked?

Ms. Chow had every boulder blocking the pass a thousand feet in the air. Her eyes were still closed but she felt the power of the mineral flowing through her very soul. In her minds-eye, she saw the floating tonnage as it drifted lightly on the blinding wind she had created. With the power the Emperor had bestowed on her many years before, she moved the boulders to the side, and then with a mighty move of her swinging arms sent the mass high into the air to crash down a mile away from the advance. Her eyes remained closed as she once more started the natural forces of Air Bending to finish what she was sent here to do.

Before anyone in the tank column knew what was happening, the winds stopped and, as they were just getting ready to exit their vehicles, black clouds and lightning pierced the skies for miles around. With each crash of thunder sounding like artillery going off around them, the tanks shook on their heavy chassis. Then all became silent as the skies cleared and the peace of the eastern Mongolian mountains returned.

The general slowly jumped from his vehicle as the last of the clouds dissipated to allow the day's last rays of sunshine to show through. He raised his binoculars and examined what had happened. With men streaming from their tanks and pointing, they all saw the trail had not only been cleared but had also been widened. It seemed the electrical strikes had blown open the trail for as far as the eye could see, as smoke was still rising from the expanded area ahead. He lowered his field glasses when a small figure walked toward the column through the settling dust. Her hat was missing, and she carried her boots in her hand. Her hair was wild with static electricity that only calmed the closer she came to the General.

"My God, what did you just do?" he asked her as she slowly moved past toward her transport.

"What I did was put you back on a very tight schedule, General," she stopped and, without facing him, whispered her threat. "Don't make me come out here again. Get to your target area quickly, General."

He watched her move off toward her helicopter and climb aboard.

"Order all forces forward, Colonel."

"General, what is happening here?"

The commanding officer hesitated a moment as the tanks in his brigade started their engines. He finally spared the colonel a worried look.

"Something we are going to regret being a part of, Colonel."

He tossed the binoculars to the colonel and then mounted his personnel carrier.

"It seems the old world is interfering with the new, and no one will be the winner."

Altai Mountains,
Eastern Mongolia

THE MAN KNOWN AS ANDERSON MOVED EASILY THROUGH THE DARKENED tunnels. The course he set was leading him straight to the asteroid buried two thousand feet beneath the mountain.

When he arrived at the heavy iron gate, he knew he had a problem. There was no latch or winding gear to raise it. This meant one thing to him—the only man capable of raising it was the Master himself. He checked the only weapon he had on him, a knife. He stuck it into the rusting gap of iron and stone. He pried but nothing happened. He tried again, but this time the knife snapped in two and the blade fell to the dirt floor. In exasperation, he cursed his luck.

"I thought in your line of business, mate, you were supposed to be able to improvise, adapt, overcome?"

Anderson turned. In the dark, he saw the outline of a large man standing against the stone wall of the tunnel.

"Somehow I knew it would be you," Anderson said as he reached down for the broken knife blade.

"I never called men in your line of work stupid." Birnbaum moved into the weak light cast by Anderson's small flashlight.

"All along I thought it was someone in the American camp I had to face down. Captain McIntire, that little fool Ryan maybe. Anya Korvesky was my first choice. But now I see that I was overlooking your power of deception. Very well played, Professor."

"In our professional lives, we make very few mistakes that we are allowed to get away with, mate."

Anderson moved to his left, but Birnbaum deftly mimicked the move, blocking his way.

"I think you can drop your pretense of being Australian, Professor."

"It was pretty good, huh?"

"You even fooled a Mossad agent, so yes, I guess you did a good job."

"Yes, it's a shame you won't be able to get back to those fools you work for to explain just how good I truly was."

Anderson saw his chance and charged Birnbaum with the broken knife blade. He came up with a thrust toward the large man's belly, but the move was blocked. Then Birnbaum brought the rock down onto Anderson's head, bringing his attack to a stop. He fell and that was when Birnbaum stepped up to him and raised the rock.

"Easy, Professor, we'll take charge of the Russian from here," came a voice from behind him.

Birnbaum lowered the rock before he could finish off Anderson. He turned and saw Professor Lee standing there with four BDU dressed guards.

"Thank God. I'm not sure I could have handled a professional like him. Good to see you, mate."

"Professor, there was no need for you to take matters into your own hands. My guards, as young as they are, never ceased their watch on Mr. Anderson. You were lucky he did not kill you."

"You're bleedin' right about that, and I apologize."

The four guards moved in and picked up a moaning Anderson and straightened him up. They moved off ahead of the others. Lee turned to face the Australian once more.

"With our current dire situation, may I suggest you stay with the other members of your field team? And may I also suggest you join the evacuation of the women and children?"

"If it's all the same to you, mate, I think I would like to hang around and share the danger with my associates."

Lee watched as Birnbaum moved back into the darkness of the tunnel. He remained for the longest time as he thought through what it was he had just witnessed. With a curious nodding of his head, Lee moved off to prepare for the final battle of the Air Benders.

CARL FACED SARAH AND ANYA. CHARLIE WAS ALREADY SHAKING HIS head no.

"Shove it," was all Sarah had to say. She was still put out over Everett's conclusions on Jack.

"That's an order, Captain. The same goes for you, Major Korvesky. Charlie, I don't even want to hear anything out of you. You proved your point about your lost civilization here in Mongolia. Its now time to leave. You three will escort the women and children out of the mountain and get them to safety. Mister Ryan, the Master Chief and myself will stay and lend a hand."

"Look, if you're staying, we're staying," Sarah said as if broaching the subject again would be fatal to Carl's future.

"You see, darling, you haven't a choice. You can very well court-martial our asses when we get home, that's your prerogative. But for now, get it out of your head," Anya said, crossing her arms in defiance.

The door opened, and Master Chief Jenks was there.

"Toad, General Chang says we have company coming."

"Russians?" he asked.

Jenks was hesitant to speak as his eyes roamed over to Sarah.

"Well, Russians or Chinese?" Everett insisted.

"That sneaky ass ground-pounder, Colonel Collins, and two others somehow got past their guards and entered the mountain."

Carl stood and faced Sarah. With his eyes boring into hers, he charged his nine-millimeter and then turned to leave.

Sarah ran after him as did the others.

CARL, ANYA, RYAN, CHARLIE, AND THE MASTER CHIEF CAME UPON THE General with six of his guards. Standing next to them was Master Li himself. Beside him, squatting and rocking back and forth was Major Pierce. He seemed to have calmed somewhat from his earlier explosion of rambling about the 'Slick Willy'. They were all watching something far below near the hidden entrance to the mountain, which these men had somehow found.

"This man is very resourceful," Li said to the General. "I suspect this may be the famous Colonel Collins." He turned to face Everett. "Perhaps he has come to finish the task he started in Laos?"

Carl didn't say anything as Sarah stepped up beside him and looked down into the darkness, which highlighted Jack and two others with the weak lights of battery power.

"That's Jack," Sarah said.

Carl remained silent as he turned and looked at Anya. With a simple head gesture in her direction, she took Sarah by the arm. "Maybe we should let Carl handle this."

"And let him shoot first and then ask?" She shook off Anya's tight grip. "Jack didn't shoot you!"

Before another word could be said, ten bullets ripped into the wall behind the group of onlookers. They all hit the dirt flooring of the high gallery. Just as Carl was about to raise up and see what was happening, another five bullets struck just to his left. All the rounds made perfect circles only inches apart. Master Li did raise his head and a bullet ripped into his feathered hat and he ducked back down.

"Hah, he missed!" Jenks cried.

"Master Chief, I hate to burst your bubble, but whoever that is down there has hit everything he's aimed at," Carl said as he held Sarah in place with his weight.

"Yes, a very accomplished marksman," Master Li said, removing his round hat and examining the feather that had been professionally cut in half. He placed the hat back on his head and looked at the General. "Perhaps you better take the situation under control, General."

General Chang gestured toward his prone men. "Move cautiously and use silenced weapons. Do not give away your position, as this man down there will exploit your folly rather quickly."

The first guard sat up, barely clearing the small rise of rocks with the very top of his head. That was when the next bullet struck him in the cap he wore, sending it flying. The guard once more threw himself to his belly.

"Captain, I think I will leave this in your capable hands," Master Li said.

"Jack?" Everett shouted.

Silence from below.

"Jack, tell whoever that is to cease fire before he hurts someone!"

The comment echoed off the stone walls of the immense space.

"Carl?"

"Don't shoot, I'm standing up!"

"Slow, Sergeant Tram has you lined up."

"Tram?" he turned and faced Sarah and shook his head in confusion.

He stood along with Sarah. "You stay here, I'm going down."

Sarah wanted to refuse the order, but with one look into Carl's eyes, she saw at last the relief that Jack was at least alive, and the great mystery of his possible attempted murder was near an end. She nodded, placing her trust in the many years of friendship between the two men.

CARL AND RYAN APPROACHED CAUTIOUSLY FROM ON HIGH. THEY MADE their progress down the ledge as visible as possible. They both knew how expert the Vietnamese sergeant was at correcting a failure in judgement. They both raised their hands into the air.

"Jack?"

They saw three men rise after they had looked he and Ryan over thoroughly. Ryan lowered his hands, but Carl made him raise them again. Trust had yet to be earned.

"My advice to the sergeant was to kill first, then we could interrogate."

"Jesus, I thought you went home with Will," Carl said, finally lowering his hands.

Farbeaux's laughter seemed to shake the open space they were in. "And miss this? Not for the price of King Tut's headdress, my friend."

Tram stepped forward and opened the bolt on his Winchester. He was smiling. Collins moved forward, also grinning his pleasure at seeing Everett. That was why it shocked him when Carl brought up his Beretta. Jack froze and Tram, who started to move to close the bolt on his rifle, also stopped moving when Ryan aimed his pistol at him. Farbeaux continued to smile, then stopped when Carl's aim adjusted to him.

"Perhaps I should step aside while you gentlemen converse?" Henri said as he moved a step to his left but stopped when Everett's aim continued to follow him.

"You wouldn't have been lying to me as to the possibility that you were working with Jack all along would you, Henri?" Carl asked, not smiling any longer. "I mean, just showing up like that in Ho Chi Minh City like you did."

"What in the hell are you talking about?" Jack asked as both pistols moved to him.

"Colonel, he believes it was you who shot him in Laos," Henri said, slowly raising his hands in the air.

"Me?" he said, looking at his friend. "You think I would shoot you?"

"Believe it? Yes, it was you."

"Stop this right now!"

279

Everett didn't have to take his eyes off his targets to know who was behind him.

"Sarah, I said to let me handle this," Carl said as Anya also came up from the back.

"Hey there, short stuff," Jack said in relief at seeing her alive.

Sarah didn't respond, she only smiled, and then forcibly made Carl lower the weapon. She also gave Ryan a look that could kill until he followed suit.

"Now, talk," she said, looking at Everett.

Carl thought long and hard. "Jack, we became separated in Laos. We were apart for two days while chasing the Russians to their drug compound. Where were you all that time? The next thing I know, you found me on that bridge and shot me."

"Carl, how could I shoot you when I was whacked on the back of the head the last night we were together and held someplace until Tram and Henri found me. I did not shoot you."

Everett ran a hand over his face in frustration. Then he made a decision. "Okay, Colonel. The first day we met inside the complex twelve years ago, we ate lunch. Tell me what happened there that changed your life?"

Jack smiled. "Easy, I met Sarah."

Sarah smiled at the memory of Jack almost running her over, barely missing her head by swinging his lunch tray over her. She started to move forward, but Carl's hand shot out and stopped her. "Not good enough. Perhaps that story is a little too widespread."

"Oh, this is such bullshit," Sarah said.

"I agree," Anya added. "You guys are dicks!"

"Alright assholes, you want to play word games? Try this on for size."

"Sarah, don't do this," Jack said, sparking the interest of everyone around.

"Kiss off, Jack. You two are about to make total fools of yourselves and blast each other for nothing. So, let me handle this. If this doesn't convince these idiots, nothing will, and then they can just go ahead and shoot me too."

Henri was smiling out of control and Tram was just as interested. Master Li and General Chang were watching the scene like it was the cliffhanger to an old soap opera. Ryan was just moving his head from man to man in a confused state.

"Jack, we went to Reno last month, just after you returned from the Atlantic. What song did we last dance to?"

Collins looked around at everyone present. He slowly shook his head in the negative. This meant to Carl that he didn't know the answer, so he prepared to shoot the man who he once thought of as his best friend. Sarah stayed his arm from moving. Jack lowered his head.

"*Beyond the Sea*, Bobby Darin."

"Maybe you were spied on in Reno. Someone could have seen you dancing and what song was playing."

Sarah looked at Everett like he had just lost his mind. "Why is that song so important to us, Jack?" she asked, still looking at Carl. Her eyes slowly filled with tears as the question was asked.

Jack moved from foot to foot. He looked at Henri and he couldn't help it. The pleasure he was about to receive from the look he knew he would get from the Frenchman, made his day and year.

"Jack?" Sarah prompted, finally releasing Carl from the evil look she was giving him.

"*Beyond the Sea* was our wedding song."

The bullet Ryan had chambered went off by accident, accentuating the conclusion to the tale and also erasing all doubt about Jack's real identity.

Of all the myths, legends and historical mysteries they had uncovered over the years, there was no more shocking news.

"I'll be dipped in whale shit!" was all Carl could say, as he quoted one of Master Chief Jenks' most despised metaphors.

As for Henri Farbeaux, he had vanished.

CHAPTER TWELVE

Altai Mountains,
Eastern Mongolia

For the Event Group staff, there wasn't much time to congratulate Sarah and Jack. They all knew that, once word got out, one of the career military officers would have to resign his or her commission. As for Jack and Carl, they had spent the better part of an hour comparing notes on just what happened in Laos. As for Shangri-La, the entire city was mobilizing for both defense and retreat.

The one hundred and thirteen children under the age of fifteen were standing in line, receiving documents and new identity papers. They would be disbursed throughout the world and live among their own kind who were already established in nations throughout Asia, Australia, New Zealand, the Americas, and Europe. Saying goodbye to his young people was the most heart-torn day in Master Li Zheng's long life. As he said goodbye to the last child as the boy joined his parents to be escorted from the mountain, Professor Lee joined his father.

"I have caused you and our people the greatest of sorrows, father.

I am the architect of this disaster because I thought I could bring our magic to the world. After your refusal to assist the world in their fight against the Gray invasion, I became despondent and angry. But for this to happen will be my eternal disgrace." He went to his knees in front of his father.

Li Zheng quickly took his son by the shoulders and made him stand. "In our long history, we made a vow never to bow to any man. This will continue. I cannot blame my son for the very sins of his father." Li Zheng smiled. "You are me, and I am you. Stubborn, and very most likely, insane. Insanity must run in our bloodline for the arrogance we have shown throughout our history for believing we could live apart from our world. This, my son, was wrong." He swept his right hand over the saddened citizens of Shangri-La below in the city center. "We had no right to think the Dragon's Fire Asteroid was meant only for us. Now, it is too late to bring justice to my decisions. Instead of bringing this gift to the world slowly, with trace amounts, we chose to hide it. No, my son, this is what was meant to be. Now go and organize the withdrawal of the children. Professor Ellenshaw has graciously offered to assist the exodus of our people."

With tears flowing from beneath his glasses, Lee moved off to follow what would be his father's last instruction to him.

"It's a hard thing, isn't it?"

Without turning, Li Zheng knew who it was that was addressing him. "Colonel Collins." He turned and faced Jack just as Carl joined them. "And Captain Everett." He took a deep breath and then removed his hat. "In answer to your question, Colonel, yes, it is the hardest thing I have ever had to do. But it must be done."

"Sarah explained the power of the mineral you protect here in this mountain. She says you cannot blow it up in place. Is this correct?"

Li Zheng toyed with the damaged feather of his hat. His beard trembled as he stood before the two Americans. "It would burn with the fires of hell only. Possibly eventually sinking to the core of our planet. At least, that's what my children have told me after their tours among the educated of the world. Your Captain McIntire's experiment is misleading at best, Colonel. She missed one valuable aspect to her brief study. The sample size of the asteroid. It had access to air, or oxygen, if you prefer. The air is what gives the mineral its power. While in its natural state below, it is a whole, not a sliver where air can get to its interior. Thus, it cannot be destroyed in place."

Jack and Carl exchanged anxious looks. "If we had an operational radio, we could get advice from some very smart people."

"Ah, yes, your Doctor Compton. Or perhaps your great machine, Europa?"

Jack only smiled. He had been told earlier that Li Zheng had at least one Event Group staff member working for him. The information hadn't frightened Carl, so he let it pass.

"Radios do not work here, Colonel. The content of the asteroid forbids radio signals from escaping the interior of the mountain. And I am afraid I forbid their use at any rate. Radio signals can be tracked and, in my criminal pursuit of keeping secrets, I outlawed them in and around the mountain. Fool that I am."

Jack rubbed his two-week growth of beard and thought. "From my observations outside, we have about three hours before your home comes into artillery range. Your plan is to fight with the abilities of your people?"

"Yes, we are all expendable in that pursuit. We must make taking this mountain too expensive. The Russians may fold, but the man coming from the south will not. I will have to face my one-time brother myself."

"From what Charlie Ellenshaw says, the first Emperor doesn't have it in him to face you down. The Doc says its not in his personality."

"If all goes well, I believe I can force his hand. I outran the man for two thousand years. I believe I still have few tricks, as you Americans say, up my sleeve."

"What can we do to help you draw him out?" Jack said.

Li Zheng thought a moment. Then he replaced his small, round hat on his head. "My people are not strategists, Colonel. They can strike with their abilities, but—"

"They just don't know where to strike," Carl said for him, seeing Li Zheng's problem right off.

"Genghis Khan began his takeover of the known world from here. He used the rolling terrain of the Gobi. I think we can use that to our benefit," Jack said as he turned away to think.

"An excitable boy he was," Li Zheng said.

"What?" Collins asked upon hearing the implied claim as he turned back around.

"Long story, Jack," Carl said, knowing that the man standing before them actually once knew the boy that became Genghis Khan.

"If I had a terrain map, I could place your people at strategic locations." Jack fixed the Master with a hard look. "No matter what we come up with, many of your people may die. Russians in the field are formidable. If we can bloody their noses, it may give you a chance at your brother's forces, where the attack will be much harder than the Russian attack coming from the Gobi."

"As long as the children and the young adults are safe, we are all expendable, Colonel. We have lived off the charity of the Dragon Mineral for thousands of years. It's time we pay back the Gods for those long lives by sacrificing our own."

"Noble, but if we can plan this right, we can at least give you a fighting chance at your brother. We Americans don't say it's an honor to die for your country, sir. You make the other poor son of a bitch die for his. Russians have one thing we can count on. Their soldiers are never too thrilled to fight for anything other than their homeland. Everywhere else they grow weary and timid very quickly."

"I will bow to your knowledge on the enemy, Colonel. Now, you said you need a terrain map?'

"It would help."

Master Li Zheng used his sandaled foot to scrape the sand he stood upon smooth. Then he closed his eyes just as Carl pulled Jack back. Li Zheng swirled his hands in front of him as both Jack and Carl felt the breeze freshen around him.

"I think you're going to see a smaller version of Air Bending, Jack," Carl said as both Americans stepped back to allow Li room.

The sand at their feet swirled into a small vortex, freshening the breeze a little more. Li squeezed his eyes tightly closed, picturing his home around the mountain he had occupied for close to four thousand years. He slowly raised both hands, palms up, as he concentrated. Then he swirled his hands and the whirlwind of sand fell back to the earth. When the breeze had stopped, Jack and Carl saw small mounds of sand. The largest was an exact copy of the mountain they were inside of. The rest were the small rises of land that comprised the Gobi for at least thirty miles around. It was detailed in its small scale.

"I don't believe it," Jack said, as he examined the magical terrain map before him. "Man, you could find work anytime at the U.S. Geological Society."

"I find myself wondering why I hadn't chosen a different career path myself, Colonel Collins, believe me." Li turned to walk away. "Perhaps as an ice cream vendor, or a clerk at a children's school," his voice was slowly fading away. "I hope the map helps, gentlemen. You have less than two hours before the Russians arrive."

Jack leaned over and examined Master Li's map. He started pointing out choke points the Russian armor had to traverse.

"Pssst," came a hissing noise from the dark.

Both Jack and Carl straightened to see Major Pierce squatting in the dark near the center waterfall only fifty feet away. They walked over to the old flier and it looked as if he were frightened and ready to bolt as they approached. Carl had explained earlier about Major Pierce and his circumstance. As they stopped in front of the frightened man, he stood and started to run, scared to death after making an attempt to talk to them. Jack knew he had to try something.

"Stop, Major!" he said in a loud and commanding voice.

"Turn about and stand before the Colonel, Major!" Carl said loudly, picking up on Jack's approach.

Peirce did stop as his arms went straight to his side. He placed his right foot behind his left and expertly did an about-face, and then he stood at rigid attention. His gray and silver hair wild, and his old

286

jumpsuit torn and threadbare. He was at attention with his hands along the seams of his pants.

"Report to the Colonel, Major Pierce," Everett said.

Pierce tried to speak but it seemed his voice was blocked as if he forgot how to do even that.

"At ease," Jack said in a calmer voice. "Do you have something to report, Mister?"

Pierce allowed his body to go lax as he attempted to place his hands behind and at the small of his back but failed miserably as he leaned too far to his left and started to go down. Jack sprang forward and arrested the old man's fall.

Jack looked back at Carl. "How old is he?"

"Ninety-seven."

"Jesus, I can't imagine what he's been through."

Pierce looked at Jack and then raised an old and wrinkled hand toward Collins' face. He lightly touched it and then gave Jack a toothless smile.

"Sorry...Colonel...I...don't...know...what's...wrong...with...my... legs...they...don't seem...to...work."

"You don't have to explain anything to anyone, Major."

"Slick Willy is ready and waiting, Colonel, sir. She's been waiting for...for...for—"

Carl and Jack watched as a single tear flowed down the cheek of the old bomber pilot. Collins turned to look at Carl. He mouthed the words 'the name of his B-29'.

"Report the status of your aircraft, Major," Jack said, as he eased the old man against the wall.

"The Slick Willy and her crew are...down...went down...down... down...down." Pierce suddenly looked around him as if he were afraid of being overheard. "Can't let the natives know...no...no...no."

"Know about what, Major?"

"Camera plane...she went down...first...." Again the look around him. Even Carl was getting the creeps at his weird eye movement and crazed look. "Then...the Japs...the Japs...they got...our weather plane...got her...got her...got her good."

Jack looked back up at Carl as the navy man shrugged his shoulders as he didn't know what the pilot was saying either.

"Hey, what's up?" said a voice behind them as Everett nearly jumped out of his tighty-whities.

"God Ryan, you nearly made me—"

"It is very unusual for a bomb-run to include a weather platform and a camera aircraft."

Carl and Ryan turned as Jack looked up to see the large Australian, Birnbaum.

"I don't know that much about wartime bomb runs in the forties," Jack reluctantly admitted.

"The Thin Man...the Thin Man...oh, a powerful old boy he is... long, tall, drink of cool water he is."

Pierce seemed to be losing what little mind he had left. Jack shook his head in the doubt the old fella knew anything useful.

"Who is the Thin Man?" Carl asked, seeing Jack's hesitation at grilling the old man further.

"Oh, he's the big brother...yes, yes, yes, the biggest brother."

"Brother to who?" Ryan asked.

"Oh, that's a secret...big secret...," Pierce's eyes bugged out. "Old Curtis Le May said it's big...top secret...yes," he leaned into Jack. "The Biggest secret."

Jack shook his head as he eased the old man up. He made sure he was stable and then faced Carl, Jason, and Professor Birnbaum. "We don't have the time."

All four started to walk away.

"The big brother...he is...the biggest brother...yes, oh, yeah."

They didn't slow or turn as Pierce leaned against the stone wall with mist from the falls dampening his old jumpsuit.

"The Fat Man is nothing, just like Little Boy is nothing. Oh, not compared to the Thin Man."

They all four stopped in their tracks. Jack slowly turned to see a smiling and conspiratorial Pierce looking at them. Again, the man came to attention and this time he saluted.

"Fat Man and Little Boy?" Jack asked, as he slowly approached Pierce so as not to frighten the crazed old man away.

A frightened look came over the Major's face. His head looked left, and then right. "You're not an agent for Tojo are 'ya?"

Ryan started to say something, but Jack held up a hand to stop him. Pierce had to say this alone. He had to come to grips with something that frightened him.

"Tojo was hung, Major. We got him," Jack said, as if the execution of the Japanese Prime Minister for crimes against humanity happened only the week before.

A shocked look came over the Major's face. "Really?" He lowered his head and the next time he looked at Collins, his face was a mask of anger. "Then why were my boys sacrificed?" He again lowered his head as if his mind was clearing a seventy-five-year fog. "My wife and kids, do they know?"

"Yes," Jack said. "But Major, the fight's not over.'

"Yes," he said as if he just remembered the point he had been trying to make. "Bad guys coming, huh?"

"A lot of them, Major. We need help."

"The Thin Man...Slick Willy, reporting for duty!" Again, the rigid stance of attention.

"So, there was Fat Man, Little Boy and—"

"The Thin Man. No glory, just a test where no one can see its power." A strange look came over his face as if he was confused once more. "No glory for Slick Willy...just another bomb-run."

"Major, report the condition of your aircraft," Jack insisted.

"Slick Willy has been laid to rest...yes, sir, laid to rest...I follow orders, Colonel Sir...yes, I follow orders. I stayed with Slick Willy as ordered...watched..." His eyes bulged out again as he once more looked around as if spies were everywhere. "Stayed behind...as ordered to do, sir...Slick Willy is buried and no one knows but me... and now..." He looked hard at Jack. "You."

"Do you know where Slick Willy is?"

"I can show you."

They turned and saw Professor Lee. He was standing with his hands full of new papers for the last of the evacuating children.

"I am the one who saved Major Pierce and his remaining crew. A little wind and air pressure can go a long way in easing a falling plane back to earth. It's buried about three miles from here."

"Jason, get Professor Lee since he knows this area better than us, and take Major Pierce with you and find that bomber. Tram will go with you as cover. Be careful of what's inside," he said as he gestured for Carl to come with him as he started to leave the area.

"Mind if I tag along? I feel like a bloody seventh wheel here," Professor Birnbaum said.

"More company can't hurt," Ryan said. "By the way, Colonel, just what in the hell are we looking for out there in the sand besides an old bomber?"

Jack stopped and turned to face Jason and the others.

"You're looking for the big brother of Fat Man and Little Boy that Major Pierce says is out there. It can only be one thing, Commander."

"Well?" Ryan persisted, angered he wasn't catching on as had the others.

"Mister Ryan, Major Pierce was on a special operations mission. One that was never meant to see the history books, or one they deemed important enough to make a movie about," Carl said. "The Manhattan Project designers were so afraid that their so-called 'Apparatus' would fail, they had a third bomb specially designed for a test run. That test run was over the unoccupied portion of Mongolia."

"Major Pierce was the pilot chosen to drop the first of three Atomic bombs, Jason. You're going on the hunt for The Thin Man—the big brother of the two bombs dropped on Hiroshima and Nagasaki."

Pierce cackled like a hen laying an egg as the stunned men moved off.

"Big Boom!"

SARAH, ANYA, AND CHARLIE HAD BOTH JACK AND CARL CORNERED. IF men could be murdered by just eye contact, both men would have been dead by now.

"After all of this time together, I really thought you had lost your macho-man attitude toward women in danger, Jack," Sarah said angrily.

"And I don't even know where to begin with you," Anya agreed, poking a sharp finger into Carl's chest.

Charlie Ellenshaw took a step back as he saw the look of murder in the former Mossad agent's eyes.

"Perhaps I should wait outside," Charlie said timidly, but Jack took him by the arm and held him in place.

"Stay right here, Doc, I have instructions for you too."

Crazy Charlie looked deflated.

"Jack, when I get back to Nevada, I am resigning my commission anyway, so what makes you think you can bully me away from what I see as my duty?"

"Okay, you two, listen to me, and Charlie you file this away for any future field related work. You three are here to follow the orders of a superior officer. What makes you think I will let you stand here and squabble about what orders you will or will not obey. I can see you have a growing attachment to the situation here. These people have made the hardest decision in what amounts to close to four thousand years. We will honor that decision. Now, I am going to do something for the first and last time. I will explain to you why you have to go. Sarah, you know the strata of this mountain almost as well as the people who live here. Guide the children south to the Great Wall. Anya, you speak fluent Chinese, and that just happens to be the language they speak in China. You show up on China's back porch with a bunch of children you may have to explain. Charlie and Anya will act as security."

"Jack, what about one of the Shangri-La adults, they can guide the children to safety," Sarah said, folding her arms.

"For the next hour until you leave, it's Colonel, not Jack, Captain. When we get home, you can give me the silent treatment for as long as you want, but for today, you will follow my last orders to you. Is that clear, Captain McIntire?"

Silence.

"Look, Li Zheng said he needs every young and older adult to slow both factions down enough until we can see if we have a shot at destroying that thing down there. I'll take him at his word. You three are about to see young children and babies being separated from their parents and they will be terrified. Parents will be saying goodbye and knowing the odds are that they will never see their families again. And you two are complaining about how life is not fair because you've been ordered out?"

Both Anya and Sarah could not hold either man's eyes. Sarah cleared her throat. "Jack, you once told me that when Douglas MacArthur was ordered out of the Philippines before the fall of Bataan, you said that would have been one order you would have had to refuse. You said you believed it was a blot on MacArthur's legacy because he obeyed a Presidential order. Why do you expect us to have a different attitude?"

"Because MacArthur wasn't responsible for an army full of children. At least he left behind men. Now get the hell out of here."

Sarah, while not surrendering, walked up to Jack and laid a hand on his chest. "Yes, sir," was all she said as their eyes met.

Anya just smiled softly toward Carl as she grabbed Charlie by the arm and pulled him away.

"And Mrs. Collins?"

Sarah smiled upon hearing her new last name spoken aloud in front of others for the first time, but then erased it from her lips before she turned back to face Jack.

"In a couple of days, we'll have breakfast in Hong Kong, deal?"

Her left brow went up in the way that irritated Collins to no end.

"Oh, you think it's that easy?" She turned away and then stopped and turned to face him once again. "See ya, Jack." She turned and left with a smiling Anya and a frightened Charlie Ellenshaw following.

Both men watched them leave with sadness clouding their minds. Then Carl cleared his throat.

"Jack, in case you hadn't noticed, ever since you told the world about your clandestine marriage, no one has seen or heard from the Frenchman. The Master Chief has also vanished."

"I noticed. Its always nice having a wild card in the deck, and now we have two. For Henri, he just may have lost his warm and fuzzy feeling for our little band of merry men. As for that mean bastard Jenks, maybe he met one of those large spiders, or even a giant bat that is maybe just as mean as him. In either case, those two can take care of themselves."

They heard a moan come from the small dwelling next to their quarters.

Jack and Carl went through the door and saw three women coming from a room with bowls of water and bloody rags. Jack and Carl exchanged looks. Jack placed his palms together and then placed them in the prayer position as the last woman came by. He half-bowed. Then to the surprise of Carl, Jack asked her, in what Everett thought was passable Chinese, who was in the room lying injured.

The young woman looked at Jack and then back to the room confused. Then she smiled. "You can speak English, Colonel, as I am fluent in sixteen languages. Perhaps you should brush up on your Chinese. You asked who we were eating inside."

"Good one, Jack," Carl said, trying to stifle a laugh.

"Shut up, smart ass."

"He is Professor Anderson. He no longer needs a guard. He is dying. Brain hemorrhage, I believe," she said and then walked off.

"The Russian agent," Carl said as both he and Jack stepped inside to see the prone man on the bed of feathers. His forehead was covered with a bloodstained wrap and his eyes were moving fast behind his lids. "Well, that Birnbaum fella really cracked him a good one, didn't he?"

Collins got a curious look on his face. He moved further into the room. He practically ran the few feet to the bed. His mouth was ajar as Carl followed him inside.

"You say the Australian followed him into the nether regions where the Dragon Asteroid is buried, and hit him with a rock just before the guards showed up?"

"Yes, that's what Professor Lee said at any rate. What is it, Jack?"

Collins sat on the edge of the bed and then eased the thick bandage and wet cloth up that partially covered the man's eyes.

"Oh, no. Harry," Jack said as he raised one of Anderson's eyelids. "Harry, Harry Thompson, it's me, Jack."

"Harry?" Carl asked, astounded that Jack would know this Russian agent.

Jack reached out and took the cloth from the bowl of cold water next to the bed. He placed the cloth on the man's forehead and then wiped his face and head. "Come on Harry, wake up."

"Jack, the man's done for. Half of his head is caved in."

The dying man's eyes fluttered open and then closed. His hand reached out just as Jack thought he had died. His hand took Jack's.

"Jack...Jack...you damn well took...your sweet...bloody time... getting...here."

"Harry, what in the hell is going on?"

"Lord Durnsford said not...to trust...anyone on the...field...team. I didn't...know...it was your...people." The man that Jack knew as Harry, sat up and took both of Jack's hands. "That little Geologist... and her...gangster Mossad...friend, are...rather rough on...people... they don't...like. I think Sarah broke at least...three of my ribs."

"Harry, why in the hell did MI-6 attach you to the field team?"

He squeezed Jack's hands even tighter as a bolt of pain shot through his head. Collins stilled him with kind words.

"Our analysis...of the satellite...data confirmed...the instability of the mineral." He was wracked once more by a spasm of pain. He again calmed. "My orders were to...confirm...and if possible...destroy it..."

"Harry why—"

He sat up further and took Jack by the collar. "Birnbaum...he's...he's..."

The man known as Harry slumped forward into Jack's arms. Collins laid him easily back on the bed and then quickly saw that his pupils were fixed and dilated. He cursed, checked his pulse to be sure, and then pulled the silken sheet over his head.

"Jack, who in the hell is this?" Carl asked. "I mean, Sarah and Anya were convinced he worked with this Siberian Group."

Jack finally stood. He looked from the covered body to face Carl.

"Harry Thompson. MI-6 and former SAS Captain. We trained together in the old days. He was once the best man in the world when it came to intelligence gathering in field operations. He helped track down Bin Laden toward the end. He was a good man. So good that our friend Lord Durnsford basically retired him after 2014. I guess this mission was supposed to be a cake walk." Jack bit his lip as he thought things through. "If Harry had orders to destroy the Dragon Asteroid, the British may have known about it for years. That's the way Durnsford plays. He had little trouble sacrificing lives during the Gray invasion, as you remember."

"That means the Australian Birnbaum is not what he claims to be."

Jack turned and started for the door. "And he's with Ryan, Professor Lee, Tram, and Major Pierce!"

Carl started after him. "It seems we may be getting a little slow on the uptake lately, Jack."

"That's a situation we are about to remedy."

CHAPTER THIRTEEN

Altai Mountains,
Eastern Mongolia

As Ryan eased past Lee, he saw the valley stretching out before them. He was on his belly as he examined the terrain below. Tram was doing the same through his scope. The heavy Barrett fifty-caliber was still cased and was being carried by Birnbaum to ease the load on Tram. Major Pierce was laying beside Ryan with the fingers of both hands in circles over his eyes, just as if he were looking through binoculars. Ryan looked over at him and shook his head. He handed Pierce a handkerchief.

"Better clean your lenses, Major," he said, and then winked at the old flier.

Pierce looked at the handkerchief and accepted it, and then acted as though he were wiping down the lenses of a pair of field glasses.

"I don't see any distinguishing features that would belie the fact there's a seventy-metric ton bomber buried out there."

Lee looked at Ryan. "Nonetheless, Commander Ryan, it is there."

Jason looked over at Tram, who had stopped searching for any tell-tale signs in the sands and was just looking at Major Pierce, who was once more looking though his circled fingers and then looked as if he were adjusting the lenses. Tram looked from the bomber pilot to Ryan with a confused look on his face. Ryan tapped his left temple and Tram thought he understood.

"Hee, hee, hee," Pierce laughed as he lowered his imaginary binoculars. "Told you, told you Slick Willy was here!" he rolled to his back and then saw Tram looking at him. Major Pierce got a suspicious look on his face as he quickly sat up. He eyed Tram who only looked more confused.

"He's from Vietnam, Major, not Japan," Lee said, shaking his head.

Still, the suspicious and half-closed eyes stayed on Tram.

"Son of a bitch, mate, the old fool seems to know of what he speaks," Birnbaum said pointing. "Quarter mile, see," he said pointing.

Ryan focused on the area. He saw nothing at first but a small rise with scrub growing from it. Then his eyes focused on a gleaming object at the top of that mound. He adjusted the glasses and that was when he smiled and rolled over and sat up. He patted Major Pierce on the back, causing him to finally move his eyes from the obvious Japanese spy he saw in Tram.

"Your damn glasses are better than mine," Ryan said.

As the others looked, they finally saw what Pierce had seen. The very tip of the giant tail of the B-29 was visible. Almost everyone in the world knew that all Boeing bombers of that era had the largest vertical tail stabilizers in service. 'Slick Willy' was giving them the exact location of her burial site.

"Slick Willy is ready to play," Pierce said as he stood and jumped up and down and danced a jig, causing Tram to back away a few more steps.

Suddenly, Ryan pulled the old man back to the ground just as four Chinese fighters screamed overhead. They were the stealth variant of their new SU-57. Ryan cursed their luck as the battle for the skies of eastern Mongolia was commencing, meaning the Battle for Shangri-La would soon follow.

As they watched, another flight of fighter-bombers came in low from the west. They were nearly hidden in the setting sun. Before they knew it, the darkening skies were illuminated with streaks of fire as Russian and Chinese pilots triggered off missile after missile. Explosions shook the world around them as two fighters slammed into the valley floor, creating a wave of superheated air and a river of fire.

"Look!" Birnbaum said pointing to the north.

When they turned, they saw the first armored forces of the Russian attack group as they came into the nearly sunless valley. The attack helicopters were soon to follow. Fighter after Chinese fighter made attack runs on the armored column. Missile strikes lit up the ground as infantry started to track the Chinese. Small ground to air missiles launched high into the sky as the battle started in earnest.

"Well, we better get down there before the neighborhood becomes untenable," Ryan said as he stood and quickly started down the slope toward the 'Slick Willy'.

CHARLIE HAD TWO SMALL GIRLS IN HIS ARMS, WHO CLUNG TO HIM tightly as the last goodbyes between mothers, fathers, and children were made at the north underground exit to the mountain. Tears flowed freely and Ellenshaw was having a hard time reassuring parents that he would guard them with his life.

Master Li Zheng was standing on an archway above the moving children. With a last look, they saw their Master as he slowly raised a hand in a sorrowful goodbye. Sarah and Anya waited to see if Jack and Carl would see them off, but after the bombing began outside, they knew that would not happen.

"Let's get these kids out of here," Sarah said resignedly.

There were about two hundred children and young teens in the exodus and, to a child, they were angry at what was happening. As the first aerial bomb struck the side of the mountain, not one of the children screamed. They just moved off as they were told. Each had a backpack full of what Master Li thought important. There were names and addresses of Shangri-La citizens already in the world, who would raise the children in their own homes. Once in their new environments, they would be schooled and loved just as if their parents were raising them. Each child would have three hundred thousand dollars in gold for their education and support. Once they became young adults, they would enter the world and blend in as much as they could. They would all have the duty of making the planet a better place.

Sarah and Anya came to the cave entrance that would lead them through the tunnels and then upward to the world that was now exploding overhead. As they approached, they saw a lone figure who stood ramrod straight as the children moved past him. The man would touch each child on the shoulder as they looked up at him with love and admiration. As they came upon him, it was Charlie who was the object of the man's immediate attention. He held out both hands and General Chang took the two girls from Ellenshaw's arms. He hugged them tightly and that was the first tears they had seen the children shed as their father said his goodbyes. With one last hug, the ancient man handed his two girls back to Ellenshaw.

"I will be forever grateful if you would see my two children to safety, Professor. Can you do this for me?"

"I will guard them with my life, General," he looked at the long line of children ahead of them. "All of them."

General Chang saw the sad determination in the crazy haired man's demeanor, and then he half-bowed to the man known as Crazy Charlie Ellenshaw. Just as Charlie was about to move off, the General held something out for Charlie. It was his lost Pith helmet he had dropped over the ledge in the Dragon Asteroid chamber.

"Your Tarzan hat. May it bring you good luck."

Charlie accepted the helmet and the smiling girls placed it on his head as if it were a crown.

Sarah and Anya stepped up and the General again bowed. "May the Gods of luck guide your way."

"They will. Protect those idiot men out there if you can, General, we've become quite attached to them."

The General smiled and bowed again. "The men you associate with have the 'Chi'. I will send them back to you if possible, in this you have my word."

Sarah nodded her head and Anya said goodbye by placing her hand on the General's ceremonial armor.

He handed both women two AK-47s and four bandoliers of ammunition. "Stay clear of the lower passages. Bombs and the animal life that dwell in the lower reaches of the mountain do not coexist well. They will be moving away to find safety."

"Oh, that's good. Now we have monsters again," Anya said, as both women nodded their thanks and moved off with the children.

General Chang watched them leave just as he was joined by Li Zheng. He could see that the Master had been crying over his farewell to his children.

"Well, my old and faithful friend, shall we go and greet my brother?"

Chang slowly drew out his long sword and then brought it to his forehead. He again half-bowed.

"For the last time, let us do battle with the dark one, Emperor Qin Shi Huang!"

JACK AND CARL SAW THE LAST OF THE CHILDREN LEAVING. THERE WAS no sign of Anya and Sarah. The adults had gathered and were awaiting their order to leave the mountain. Jack came to a sudden stop as he eyed the milling adults of Shangri-La.

"Why are we stopping?" Carl asked. "Ryan and Tram don't know what they're facing out there."

Collins continued to see the bravery around him as the citizens gathered. No complaining, not even a frightened face. Even the older teens, dressed in ceremonial armor with their long spears of gold plated blades, watched Jack and Carl. He could see they were clearly awaiting the order to advance and to die if necessary.

"Mister Ryan is on his own. We're out of time here, buddy."

Carl also looked around at the anxious citizens. He saw their determination. He just nodded.

Suddenly, the noise of the city center muted as if by a magic switch. All eyes turned to the top of the four waterfalls. Li Zheng, with General Chang beside him, was there. The Master held up his hands as a gong sounded from somewhere, demanding the attention of all. It thronged three successive times until all attention was on the Master.

"Our time, our home, is at an end. But our lives will continue through the minds and memories of our young. Our sacrifice will give them a chance to join the world that I led you to forsake. They will disburse their knowledge throughout the entire world and seek the forgiveness of mankind for our..." He hesitated and then corrected himself "...for *my* mistakes. Many of you will not believe the power that each one of you has. You will have to become one with the earth around you. In this, I have no doubts. I have brought this upon our people. I beg your assistance of setting the world right again. Give those outside, seeking an answer in how to destroy the Dragon Asteroid, assistance and time. Help our American friends slow the Russian advance. The General and myself will do battle with our real foe, Emperor Qin Shi Huang. He seeks to gain the military power offered by the Dragon Mineral. He will not succeed. For our ancestors he murdered, to the Great Wall he built to keep us in, it all ends this day!"

The men and women of Shangri-La cheered and threw up their hands in tribute to the man who had led them through two thousand years of hiding. It was now time to reveal the truth of the ages. It was time for war and their final stand against the Emperor. The General stepped forward and held his long sword high into the air.

"Kāi Zhàn!

With the General's shouted words, the three hundred men and women broke out running from the city's center. Jack and Carl felt the fervor and started to follow, to hurriedly issue their instructions and emplacement orders.

"What does kāi zhàn mean, Jack?"

"To War!"

Event Group Complex,
Nellis Air Force Base, Nevada

WILL MENDENHALL WAS WELCOMED HOME WITH SO MANY QUESTIONS that his head was left spinning. The grilling about the Colonel was the harshest he had ever endured and made his thoughts on the drawbacks of commanding security that much more evident. He hadn't even had time to take off his ballistic vest since he landed, much less eat and shower.

The only conclusion to the question of was it truly Jack that had shot Captain Everett, was that they would have to wait for the final report from either Collins or Everett themselves. Mendenhall just didn't have the answers they were seeking. It was the general belief among the staff that it could not have been the Colonel, that Carl had been mistaken in the confusing moment of trouble.

A knock sounded on the security door as Will was just coming to grips with his jetlag. He looked up and at that moment felt his face flush. Colonel Collins was looking straight at him. He was leaning in the doorway and smiling.

"I can see you made the right decision on returning to your duties here?"

"Yes, sir, I did feel a little guilty about leaving." Will was trying to study Jack's face without making it obvious. He could see no difference in the Colonel's features nor his demeanor.

"Any word from Carl and his team?"

"Not for the past twenty-four hours. Since the report from the Air Force saying they lost their transport over the Gobi, nothing."

Jack came inside the office and sat on the edge of his old desk. "Well, if anyone can pull off crashing into the desert, it's Carl."

"What happened in Laos, Colonel?"

Collins placed his hand at the back of his neck and then rubbed out the kink there.

"I wish I knew. One minute we're chasing down the lead on Russian drug running, and the next thing I know I'm whacked on the head and wake up in a cell. It took me two days to escape. That's all I know. I figured I could accomplish more here than Laos. At least I have you and Europa to fall back on."

Will watched Jack move over to his locker and unlock the combination lock. As he had his back to him, Will continued to study the man. There was no difference at all as far as he could see. Mendenhall shook his head to clear it of his suspicions. He was starting to stand and excuse himself to shower, when he heard the locker close behind him. The tone from Europa sounded, indicating a full meeting of the Event Group departments had been called. Mendenhall allowed his disappointment about not showering to show through with the deep breath of disappointment he took.

"The director is calling an emergency staff meeting, probably about you and the Captain." He stood and stretched and then started to turn around. "We better get—"

The nine-millimeter was pointed right at his chest.

"I think you can skip the meeting, Major," Jack said, as he raised his eyebrows at the stunned look on Mendenhall's face.

The three silenced shots struck Mendenhall in the chest, sending him flying over the chair he had just risen from. His head hit the corner of the desk, and after that he felt no more pain from the bullet strikes.

Demi Blintnikov, a former Captain in the Siberian Group's 'Dirty Tricks' department, was a man who had spent the past fifteen years learning everything there was to learn about Colonel Jack Collins, even going as far as having ten plastic surgeries to duplicate every scar, every blemish on his body. The Russian duplicate placed the silenced weapon into the back of his waistband and made sure the sportscoat covered it well.

He looked down on a motionless Will Mendenhall. He knew from the Colonel's dossier that the man he had just murdered was one of Collins' protégés. He smiled at his first target as mentioned in the dossier that had been forwarded by Vassick. Now to face the other targets. Luckily, they would all be in one place. He smiled down on the second of his targets.

"He should have taught you better, Major Mendenhall."

JACK WAS GREETED WARMLY BY THE SIXTEEN MEMBERS OF THE managerial staff as he entered the conference room on level seven. Director Compton stood and made his way to the front and took Jack by the hand.

"Good to see you home, Colonel. We would take more time showing our appreciation, but things are developing rapidly in Mongolia. I know you want to be there, but we need you here for right now."

"Good to see you, Jack," Alice Hamilton said as she placed her arms around him and hugged.

Jack didn't say anything, he accepted the greeting stoically just as his double would have. He winked as he held her at arm's length and smiled.

"Sit down and we'll get started. Where's Will?" she asked, returning to her normal spot beside Niles.

"You caught him showering. I sent a man to get him."

Collins looked around in amazement as he moved to what he hoped was his seat. The odds were with him since there were only two empty chairs around the giant conference table. He tried to keep his head from swiveling as he took in the main conference room. The technology on display was something he had never seen before. Hologram maps and other mystical devices held sway over the most covert group in the world.

"Welcome back, Colonel," Niles said. The men and women around the table lightly tapped their palms in tribute. "Take your coat off, Jack, we will be a while."

Jack removed his sports-coat and then placed it on the back of his chair and sat, not exposing his back to the men and women waiting on him.

Xavier Morales was the only one to notice the small bandage on the right forearm of the Colonel. His eyes went to Niles Compton, but he couldn't get his attention. He made sure not to look the Colonel's way again. He eased his hand down to his lap and opened the small device he used while circumnavigating the long hallways of the complex. He used it to keep a direct link to Europa when he wasn't in the comp center. He bit his lower lip as he started typing Europa a message.

'Status on Colonel Collins health and welfare implant. Non-verbal answer only.'

Xavier looked up as Niles continued giving the Group the latest update on what was happening in Mongolia. Morales allowed his eyes to wander to Jack's side of the table. He was watching the Director closely. He chanced a look down on the small cell-like device in his lap. The answer came fast.

"Implant indicates nominal health status at this time. Elevated heart rate and body temperature, health studies have indicated that is considered normal after long flights."

Xavier started to punch letters at a lightening rate of speed.

"Pull up records of blood type of Colonel Collins and compare to current status." Morales swallowed as he waited.

"Doctor Morales, hello, are you with us today?"

Xavier nearly jumped from his wheelchair when Virginia's voice broke through his speeding brain. His eyes went from Virginia first, and then for the life of him he couldn't figure out why they went directly to the man under suspicion. Jack Collins was staring right at him.

"Excuse me, I uh...uh...what was the question?"

"Explain the armor movement by the Russians and how far are they from the field team's last reported position," Virginia said once again.

"Europa and *Boris* and *Natasha* say they are currently within two miles of last readout."

Again, the chance look into his lap. He felt his heart skip and almost stop. The answer was there.

"The subject that checked into the Complex at 0725 is not, I repeat, is not Colonel Collins."

The men and women around the table were awaiting Xavier to expand on his report, but watched instead as his head slowly turned to Jack Collins. Jack was smiling. He winked at the paraplegic computer genius.

Xavier froze at the worst possible moment as Collins stood suddenly from his chair.

Morales broke the trance he found himself in and rolled as fast as he could toward the director, who was amazed at the speed of the young computer whiz. He was about to say something when Xavier's chair slammed into him, sending the director reeling into Alice Hamilton and they both fell to the floor.

Collins shot twice, striking the wheelchair in its leather back. Xavier was thrown violently forward and onto the carpeted floor as both men and women around the table jumped to their feet. When they looked again, Jack Collins had aimed his silenced weapon at the group.

Silenced shots started to ring out.

Altai Mountains,
Eastern Mongolia

RYAN FELT OVERLY EXPOSED AS THEY SLOWLY MADE THEIR WAY TO THE raised mound. It seemed as if all hell had broken loose in the desert surrounding the mountain. In the distance, Russian armor was burning and aircraft debris littered the sands. As Ryan came to a sliding stop on his belly, he spied even more Russian assault troops parachuting into the war zone. These hit the ground with the intent of charging the mountain under the cover of Russian armor. The naval aviator knew their time was short to the extreme.

"Sergeant Tram, get on the far side of the knoll and set that Barrett up. If those assholes get close, explain to them in no uncertain terms they're not welcome here."

Without saying a word, Tram belly-crawled to his new position and uncased the Barrett.

"Professor Lee, we don't have the time it would take to dig this big bitch out of this sand."

"I believe I can assist with that," Lee said.

"What are those things?" Major Pierce asked, as again he was using the circled fingers of both hands as binoculars.

As Ryan chanced a look, he saw the Russian built assault helicopters striking near the mountain passes behind them. The MI-28 'Havoc' was an air superiority chopper that could lay waste to any armored column they faced. Some reports said it made the Apache Longbow seem meek in comparison. The Russkies were chucking everything they had at the Chinese advance. Ryan looked at Pierce, who was lowering his fingers and staring wildly at things he had never seen before. There were sixteen of them making missile and cannon runs on someone very high on the mountain's top.

"I think we are about to be surrounded. Professor, you're on!"

As Ryan, Pierce and Birnbaum watched, Lee braved the fire around him and stood. He closed his eyes and started to relax his brain. He slowed his breathing just as he had been taught by his father, Master Li Zheng. He prayed to a long dead mother and praised his people in a silent thought. Then he started to swirl both fingers of both hands in a circular motion while they were still at his sides. He began circling his fingers faster, and then even faster. He raised his head, eyes still closed to the heavens. Then his arms started to rise, slowly at first and then faster as the wind picked up to a briskness until Ryan felt the stinging grains of sand as they started to assault everyone.

"Cover, cover, cover," Ryan shouted as loud as he could.

Soon, the small rise of the elevated mound was inundated by the swirling tornado of sand and rock. The storm picked up in intensity. Static electricity shocked Tram so hard he dropped the fifty-caliber weapon and covered his head. Birnbaum was struck by a tumbleweed that nearly decapitated him. Jason began to feel the earth around him move and was amazed at how Professor Lee could keep his feet during the assault of the elements. Even the sound of the raging battle less than two miles away was unable to penetrate the vortex of noise and the movement of sand and earth.

Suddenly, it was over. Ryan raised his head, shedding a hundred pounds of sand as he did. When he opened his eyes, he saw Lee moving his way. The small man seemed unfazed by what had just happened.

"Well?" Ryan said as he shook himself free of sand.

"Oh, she looks beautiful!" Pierce said, just as twenty-millimeter rounds stitched a pattern of flying earth high into the air as one of the Russian assault choppers had viewed the disturbance on the ground and attacked that position. The pilot had peeled off from the assault on the Chinese column above them to strike at what he had seen.

Just as Ryan pulled the crazed pilot to the ground, they heard the loud pop of something behind them. Under the cover of the piled sand that had just been created by Lee, Tram had targeted the assault of the Russian helicopter. As Ryan braved a look, he saw the engine compartment of the twin turbo-powered MI-28 start to smoke. Then another loud 'pop' sounded, and the canopy in front of the rear-seated pilot exploded inward, killing the Russian immediately. The 'Havoc' spun out of control and then slammed into the desert only a hundred feet away.

When he turned back, he saw the result of Lee's air bending. The 'Slick Willy' was totally uncovered. Its gleaming silver fuselage shone bright in the setting sun. Rays of the dying orb bounced off what looked like brand-new aluminum. The giant tail of the bomber was now sticking up so high it could have been used as a sign post directly leading to their location.

"I wish we would have thought to bring a camouflaged tarp along," Jason said as he scrambled into the large circular pit caused by the uncovering of the B-29. Again, he had to pull Major Pierce to the ground as he was saddened by the damage done to his beloved aircraft. The wingless giant looked forlorn in its sandy grave.

"What did I do?" Pierce said, as he came to a stop just outside the old pilot's compartment. The glass in the nose was mostly still intact but the main fuselage was bent as if a giant hand had swatted it out of the sky.

"At the time I brought it down as gently as I could," Lee said sadly.

"What you did, Major, was bring your aircraft down with no wings. As a pilot myself, I would say that may be the single greatest accomplishment in aviation history."

Pierce looked from Ryan to the wingless 'Slick Willy'. He smiled and then puffed out his chest in pride. A change seemed to come over him. He started to move toward the open crew hatch beneath the cockpit, but Jason stopped him.

"Professor, did your people recover the crewmen killed in action when you found the Major?"

Lee's silence told Ryan what he needed to know.

"Major Pierce, I need you to stay here."

"But...but...that's my aircraft, it...it's...my responsibility."

As Ryan looked from Pierce to the ghostly body of the 'Slick Willy', he shook his head no.

"They're my boys."

Ryan closed his eyes. He knew he didn't have the right to keep Pierce out. He himself would never have allowed it. He nodded his head and Pierce scrambled forward, expertly lifting himself up and into the plane near the faded nose-art of the cartoon character 'Slick Willy' dropping bombs on a fleeing Tojo's head. Ryan, Lee, and Birnbaum followed suit.

The interior was blasted to bits and the men had a hard time moving past the dislodged wires and cables. Over the seventy-five years of its interment, sand had filtered into the bomber to create soft flooring in the old pressurized compartments of the Boeing plane. As they moved forward, they saw the first of the crewmen. Given the dryness of the desert, and the fact that air could not get to it, the body looked as if the young man had died only months before. The dried and leathery skin looked peacefully asleep. Pierce saw this and went to his knees in front of the splayed body in the old gray flight-suit. Ryan had to turn away as he had experienced the same remorse over lost friends. Pierce picked up the thin dry fingers of the young boy who never went home after the war. Ryan placed a hand on the shoulder of the grieving old pilot.

"His name was Sergeant Jimmy Blackwell. He loved baseball and wanted to try and go pro after the war. His mama lives in Muncie, Indiana." He pulled the dog-tags free of the boy's chain and then, without looking, held them up for Ryan to take. "Take these to his mother, will ya Navy?"

Ryan, Lee, and Birnbaum were shocked at the change in Pierce's demeanor. Gone were the quirky little movements and the crazed look of the eyes. Jason, knowing the kid's mother was long dead herself, accepted the tags and then nodded yes, he would most definitely do as asked. Pierce nodded his head and then patted the dried-out corpse of his old crewman on the shoulder and then with determination stood up.

"This way, gentlemen."

As they moved toward the bomb-bay compartment, they began to see things not normally associated with a B-29. Electronic monitoring devices, long dead, lined both bulkheads as they progressed. Pierce pulled wiring from their boxes in an angry tirade as he was anxious to get to where he was determined to go. Finally, he stopped as more bodies appeared. A gloved hand sticking through the sand here. A broken form of a leg there. Pierce was no longer concerned with the dead as he went to his knees. Ryan at first thought that the Major was losing control of his senses again, when he suddenly started to dig. Ryan, Lee, and Birnbaum also went to their knees and started scraping the sands of seventy-five years away. Then they heard the hollow sound when Pierce struck steel. He dug more fiercely than before. Then there it was. The bomb-bay compartment door. Pierce, with the help of the three others, lifted for all he was worth.

Every man got the chills when the door was thrown wide. The 'Thin Man' was there, and it looked menacing with its wires and its gauges exposed for the first time in close to a century. The bomb itself was elongated, very much different than either Fat Man or its cousin, Little Boy. It was at least ten feet longer and took up the entire bomb-bay compartment. The three men jumped when Pierce began to speak as if he were giving a lecture. They could tell he had been taught every aspect of the bomb from the people at White Sands proving grounds, who had instructed him in India. Ryan saw the intelligence of the pilot, as he had obviously been picked because he was the best there was at one time.

"Gentlemen, we will be dropping the first atomic bomb ever used in warfare. The 'Thin Man'. Fifteen thousand two hundred pounds in weight. Length, one hundred and seventy-two inches, with a diameter of ninety-three inches. Far larger that its brother apparatuses. Its payload is plutonium based. Gentlemen, this weapon has a blast yield of twenty-five kilotons. It has six contact fuses and a mercury-based altimeter trigger. In other words, people, it is designed to ruin your whole day."

They watched as Pierce smiled and looked down at them. "I remember everything about this damnable bomb."

"I can see you have the same attitude about these things as a friend of mine," Ryan said, remembering Will Mendenhall's hatred of anything nuclear. "He thinks they handed these damn things out like the album *Frampton Comes Alive*." Ryan smiled at his small joke as he looked at Professor Lee. The small man raised his brows as if Jason had lost it just as Pierce had gained some of his sanity back. "You know, the old joke that it seemed the post office mailed everyone a copy of that Peter Frampton live album in the seventies, because everywhere you went someone was playing it?"

Blank looks all around.

"Forget it, barbarians."

"How do you suppose we get that big bastard out of there?" Birnbaum asked.

"Any ideas, Professor?" Jason asked.

"We must use the air to get it inside the mountain."

Just then they heard the discharge of the Barrett as Tram was increasingly engaging targets.

"Oh, Lord," Birnbaum said, as he held out the satchel Sergeant Tram had given him. "I've got his ten magazines in here."

"Well, you better go get 'em to him," Ryan said. "Sounds like some very bad company is right around the corner.

TRAM SIGHTED ON THE LONE ARMORED PERSONNEL CARRIER TO ADVANCE within range of the Barrett. He shook his head in wonder at the bravery of the Russians, and also their stupidity and arrogance. Why commanders always had their heads sticking out of the small turret was beyond him. He sighted. He eased the trigger back as he held his breath, and then slowly exhaled half of what he had taken in. Through the electronic scope on one of the world's most expensive personal weapons, which readouts gave him distance and wind velocity, of which he mostly ignored, he fired. The large round came free of the suppressor and the barrel recoiled without any kick as the cartridge was ejected.

The fifty-caliber round flew to its target over a mile away. The only thing visible was the puff of red spray as the personnel carrier came to a sliding stop.

"Nice bleedin' shot, mate," came the voice from behind him. "I believe you took that bugger's head clean off."

Tram moved his head as he turned to see who it was, when his world became a confused jumble of stars and explosions in his head. His face fell into the sand just as other Russian made personnel carriers passed the stalled one and advanced even faster than before.

Birnbaum had the canvas satchel full of heavy magazines for the Barrett still swinging in his hands after striking Tram in the side of his head. He stared down at the unconscious body of the small Vietnamese sergeant. He slowly brought out a nine-millimeter pistol and aimed at his head. He stopped, fearing the sound of the shot would be heard inside the 'Slick Willy'. He had business to conduct before any announcement of his true identity was learned by the unsuspecting fools.

RYAN, LEE, AND PIERCE HAD THE UPPER HALF OF THE BOMB FREED OF sand. Pierce expertly cut the heavy-gauge wires that allowed the 'Thin Man' to be suspended above the bomb-bay doors. They all jumped when the heavy bomb dropped three inches to rest on its belly.

"It's always a good sign when the atomic bomb you're playing around with doesn't explode," Ryan joked, as he wiped sweat from his face, allowing his knees to sink further into the sand. "Pretty good, Major, for a man that lost the instruction booklet almost eighty years ago."

"Yes, he is an amazing man."

The sudden report of the gunshot made Lee and Ryan jump as Major Pierce fell to the ground with a bullet in the back of his right shoulder. They both looked up into the semi-darkness as a large figure advanced on them with a smoking nine-millimeter still in his right hand. Lee went to his knees and checked on the moaning Major Pierce. He turned to face Professor Birnbaum.

"You are an honor-less pig!"

"Yes, I have no doubt you believe just that. But it is your honor that leaves much to be desired, Professor, keeping the Dragon Mineral all to yourselves for four thousand years. Perhaps you can discuss honor with your ancestors when you arrive."

"What did you do with Sergeant Tram?" Ryan asked, looking for even the slightest opportunity to spring on the traitorous man before him.

"He will meet the same fate as yourselves." He moved the pistol over to who he assumed was the greatest threat, and it wasn't Ryan, it was Lee. "Please do not raise your hands. Professor, I've seen what it is you can do when you put your mind to it."

"You can knock off the phony accent now, Comrade," Ryan said, growing as angry as he had ever been. He looked from Birnbaum to a barely moving Major Pierce. His anger grew.

"Yes, it was a disgusting way to perform." He aimed again and then started to put pressure on the trigger.

Ryan charged. He knew if they lost Lee they had no other way to get the bomb inside the mountain before the Russians or the Chinese arrived with enough force to take Shangri-La.

The aim of the pistol shifted faster than Jason thought it could. The man they thought as Birnbaum, fired. An explosion unlike any pistol Ryan had ever heard slammed into his eardrums like a Mac truck.

Jason hit the sandy deck as the bullet miraculously missed his head by mere inches, as he even felt the air pressure of the passing bullet. When he looked up, he saw that Birnbaum had no forehead. The trough that ran through the middle of his head was still smoking as a flap of skin covered the man's stunned expression. He followed his line of sight and saw a hole the size of a jar lid in the main bulkhead of the 'Slick Willy'. The hole was also still smoking. He turned back just as the large torso of Birnbaum fell forward, dead. His eyes widened when he saw their salvation. Ryan lowered his head and tried to still the heart that was threatening to burst from his chest.

In the growing darkness, he saw Henri Farbeaux step closer as he lowered the large Barrett. Behind him was Master Chief Jenks, who was holding up a still groggy Sergeant Tram.

"For once I am glad to see you both," was all Ryan could say, as he went to his ass and tried to still his nerves. "I would have appreciated maybe a little better timing."

Henri Farbeaux smiled.

"You know I like dramatic entrances, Mister Ryan."

THE EXTREME EASTERN ENTRANCE TO THE MOUNTAIN WAS A JUMBLE OF men, women, and young teens. They awaited the word from their new commander to take to the field. Jack and Carl were talking in soft voices with one of the elders of the group. They needed cover. From their location, the battle raged more than five miles away, but even so, a line of people would be noticed from the air almost immediately and attacked. They needed to get the populace to the preselected locations Jack and Carl had memorized from the terrain map created by Master Li Zheng. The old man they were speaking to spoke to them of an old plan once used against a man and his army that Kublai Khan had chased out of China centuries before. This group of desperate soldiers had come close to discovering by accident the hide-away of the people. Master Li Zheng had used a heavy line of thunderheads that dissuaded the army from going further in their retreat into eastern Mongolia.

"Sounds like the only thing we can do to get the people to their positions."

Jack agreed with Carl. He looked up at the now dark skies and saw no clouds there. "Can you generate enough moisture in the air to create the conditions you seek?"

The old man smiled. "Colonel Collins, the air is always full of water, you just have to know how to harvest it."

Collins looked outside and, from their position, they could discern that the Russian offensive was taking a toll on the Chinese air force. Although there were as many as a hundred tanks burning in the desert night, the Russians had expertly reinforced the attacking division with fresh men and equipment. As of that moment, it looked as if the Russians would arrive first to the mountain.

"It looks like we're it," Jack said. "Are your people ready?"

"Colonel, we have been preparing our minds for this fight since the day two thousand years ago when Master Li and General Chang brought us here. Yes, we are most assuredly ready. Our Master told me to express his gratitude for your assistance, gentlemen. However, he requests that once we have achieved our strategic goal of location, you are free to leave the battle."

Carl and Jack exchanged looks and then smiled.

"Sir, those are Russians out there. If we ran out on you and your people, how could we ever face ourselves in a mirror again?" Carl asked with all seriousness. "No offense to Master Li, but we'll stick it out if you don't mind."

Jack hefted two M-4s and tossed one to Carl before winking at the six air force commandos in his group. They understood perfectly what Everett had just said and were with them for the duration. The young boys didn't appreciate the welcome they received from the

Russian fighters who shot them down. They slammed magazines into receivers and awaited Jack's command.

"Okay, start the show, sir."

The elder smiled and then half-bowed to Jack and Carl, before walking out into the moonless night to prepare the battlefield for their occupation.

THE SMALL ELDER VANISHED BEHIND SOME ROLLING DUNES AS JACK tried his best to follow with his eyes, but could not see anything other than the evening stars that made their first appearance.

"Now that's something you don't see every day," Carl said, stepping out of the lee of the mountain.

Jack joined him, as did a young teen who was dressed in the blue and gold armor and blue helmet with yellow plume of the clan of Shangri-La. The boy looked up at the larger Americans and nodded.

"Grandfather used to surprise us in the mornings when we overslept by creating a rain squall over our beds. We were soaked more times than not on many days."

"He is your grandfather?" Jack asked.

"Yes, he was one of the original followers of the Master who fled across the Great Wall before its completion."

The amazing thing was that Jack and Carl had seen so many incredible things in their careers with the Event Group, that the amazing statement didn't give them a moment's hesitation of doubt.

They watched as bright specks of light illuminated the skies around for miles. They would swirl one way and then the other. Some would circle, and some would shoot straight into the sky. Suddenly, they coalesced into a million swirling balls of brilliant light, and then as one body shot into the night sky as if God himself had fired a mighty flare high into the heavens. The trail was long and phosphorous looking. It was if a meteor had reversed course and, instead of hitting the earth, it had rebounded. Then like a firework sent from hell, it exploded, creating giant shadows at the base of the mountain.

"Well, that certainly won't attract any attention," Carl said, as he charged the handle of his M-4.

Before Jack could say anything about Everett's comment, the skies darkened, blotting out the early evening stars. Then the rain came.

In the distance, two platoons of tanks, eight in all, turned toward the position they were now occupying. Jack cursed their luck and was about to rethink their strategy when the teen at his side bade him patience.

"You will know when, Colonel."

Suddenly the skies exploded with electrical activity. Lightning strikes against the earth exploded burning sand into the air. Strike after strike hit and shook the world around them. The elder reappeared and hugged his young grandson. He winked just as the people lining the interior of the eastern cave came charging out. Armor gleamed in the flashes of lightning, and swords caught the blaze of reflected fire as they ran to the positions that Jack had assigned them.

Another five platoons of Russian heavy armor peeled away from the main assault. They were coming on fast and strong, just behind the first. Then the rest made a sharp turn to the east. They had indeed attracted the attention of the Russian commander.

"This is about to get exciting real fast, Jack," Carl said, as he smiled and then joined the flight into the plain of Shangri-La.

"Crazy bastard!" Collins shouted and then joined fifteen teenagers as they came running by, screaming the name of their Master.

Thanks to the immense electrical storm, the T-90 and T-80 tanks could not get accurate information from their fire control computers. This did not stop them. They started to fire indiscriminately into the mass of humanity charging the field.

Strike after lightning strike made the drivers of the massive tanks swerve and lose valuable time in aiming their large bore weaponry on the people.

After getting to their designated area of the field, Jack dove for cover. He was amazed when the teens didn't. They hurriedly went forward and grabbed every piece of wood or dead brush that they could. As he looked around, others were doing the same. If viewed from the air, it would have looked like bands of ants scouring the floor of the valley for food. Soon, over two hundred small bonfires were burning brightly in the falling rain as the Russians started to get their bearings. The attack choppers started to brave the dying electrical storm as they began attack runs on the heat signatures they were picking up on the floor of the valley. Each signature was that of a Shangri-La soldier.

Missile after missile from the *Havoc* attack ships were fired at figures moving three miles ahead. Anti-personnel shells, HE rounds, started to decimate some of the positions. Jack winced when he saw a position, held by thirteen young people, explode in a cloud of destruction only three hundred yards from his position.

The teen who was huddling next to Jack stood and, before Collins could pull him back to the wet earth, he ran toward the bonfire to join fifteen others. As he looked around, he could see all across the defensive line that every isolated group was doing the same.

"Is someone going to tell me the damn plan?" Jack shouted after them.

As the teens and elders around other fires mimicked the same action, Jack was amazed to see them all dip their hands straight into the flames. Instead of pulling back in pain, they came up with hands full of brightly burning embers. They were closing their eyes. Then bright balls of fire shot out of their outstretched hands and flew with blinding speed into the sky.

An explosion overhead made Jack flinch as a fireball struck the leading Mil *Havoc*. The ball of fire smashed into the tail boom and tore it free from the engine housing just forward, and it exploded in midair, sending the five-bladed rotor veering off into the night.

Soon, many more were being struck and just as many fell from the clearing skies. But the tanks, however, were being struck with much less effectiveness. Behind the power of many inches of steel and reactive armor plate, the tanks were near impervious to fire. As the lightning storm dwindled to nothing, they started getting target data from their computers and began firing into the defenders with pinpoint accuracy.

Jack was aghast at the deadly accuracy of the Russian gunnery. Bodies were being torn asunder, being blasted into mist by the HE rounds landing among them. Still, the people fought with all they had. Large and small sand tornadoes confronted the armor as they bored into the eastern end of the valley. Position after position was soon knocked out of the fight, with the dead and dying strewn across the battlefield. Soon, he was horrified to see tracers fired from the citizens as they arched toward the tanks. Then even more so when he saw a group of teens and other young ones actually charge the closest tanks, waving their ceremonial swords and thrusting lances of the ancient ones. They were sliced to pieces by fifty caliber machine gun fire from thirty armored personnel carriers, which had joined the Russian onslaught.

"God, what have I done?" Jack asked himself as Carl came sliding into his position, out of breath and bleeding again from his recent wounds.

"We've lost half our strength, Jack. They're murdering those poor people!"

An HE round went off, deafening the rest of Everett's report and knocking both men from their feet. Still the fireballs burst out from the dunes to the amazement of the Russian troops.

"They've switched the focus of their main attack and swerved this way. The sacrifice of these people may have just given Ryan and Lee time to get that damn weapon into the mountain. Shall we see if we can help those kids and elders?" Jack said with determination.

"I didn't get all dolled up for nothing, let's go!" Carl said, as they both burst from cover, firing their M-4s and charging the first of the personnel carriers.

That was when the first Russian ground-attack jet fighters made their battlefield appearance.

HENRI AND JENKS HAD SOMEHOW GOTTEN ONE OF THE FIELD TEAMS'

stolen Range Rovers. They hurriedly made a makeshift sled out of the ribs of the 'Slick Willy' and Lee had used his magic to lift the heavy Thin Man from its sleeping place. They were just strapping it down to the sled when the focus of the battle seemed to have shifted away from their immediate front.

Ryan went to the back of the Range Rover and saw Major Pierce lying on a blanket. Tram was trying to stem the flow of blood coming from the Major's shoulder wound. Tram looked up and, in the light of a flashlight, gently nodded his head, indicating he thought the Major would make it.

"How you doin', old boy?" Jason asked when Pierce looked up with a moan.

"How am I doing?" He looked at Tram who was smiling down on him. "I've been shot, you stupid navy puke," he growled, taking another sly, suspicious look at Tram. "And it sure looks like I've been captured. How in the hell do you think I'm doing?"

Ryan smiled and then moved off just as he heard Pierce say loudly to Tram in the very unpolitic way of his; "Pierce, Major, U.S. Army Air Corps, and that's all you're getting outta' me, Tojo!"

He saw Henri looking to the east. "It seems Colonel Collins has found the fight he was seeking."

In the eastern skies, the bright flashes of light told Ryan the same. Jack and his people were taking a pounding. Jason looked at the final straps being placed around Thin Man by Jenks and Lee. They couldn't hurry fast enough for him. He was torn about delivering the bomb into the interior of the city or running off to die with Jack and Carl. Henri saw his dilemma.

"Don't be in such a hurry to die, Commander Ryan. Your chance will come soon enough when you light the fuse on that thing," he said, nodding toward Thin Man lying in its cradle.

"Its easy for you, isn't it? They're not your friends."

Henri spit out a mouth of dust but didn't say anything.

"That's it. Let's load up and get this thing off this field. All we need is a stray artillery round to hit that damn thing," Jenks said, as he joined the two men. "It's only seventy-five freakin' years old." He plopped a cigar into his mouth. He saw the silence between Ryan and Farbeaux.

"After all, you can just wait it out, right? I mean, Sarah would be waiting if Jack cashes in. Just wait it out, is that your plan?" Ryan said with all the distaste he could muster.

Farbeaux didn't respond nor even react to the comment.

"Hey, I don't much care for the cheese eatin' bastard either, but he did just save your ass, Mister," Jenks said. "He could have run like a normal man, but instead he stayed." Jenks spit out some tobacco from his chewed cigar and then saw Lee running their way.

"Gentlemen, we have company," Lee said running up to the trio of men. "I don't think I have the mental strength to stop them after lifting that thing out of the fuselage."

About three hundred yards ahead, they saw the Russian paratroops. Hearts deflated when a hurried count was made. Ryan stopped at two hundred. They were in firing range even before they were seen.

Henri moved to the bag he had near. He bent over and unzipped it. "In answer to your question, Mister Ryan, I have no desire to see your Colonel Collins dead. This would guarantee Sarah would forever mourn. I do not need to compete with a ghost. It would be a losing cause." He straightened after pulling something from his bag. He broke an object open in the dark that the others couldn't see, and then they heard a hollow 'clunk' sound as he inserted something. "I prefer for a woman to come to me of her own accord. Not because of need, but of want."

They all watched as Henri stepped past them, just as small arms fire started reaching their position. Henri raised the very pistol to the sky and a bright red flare was sent skyward.

"I fully intend on staying alive until such a day, Mister Ryan."

Henri tossed the pistol into the sand and then picked up his M-4. Then they all laid down and took up firing positions, all with the exception of Master Chief Jenks.

"I'm too old to go throwing myself into the dirt on account of some cowardly Russians!"

Bullets started to hit the rise on which they hid behind.

Before anyone realized what was happening, several screams of rage came from the surrounding dunes. They saw men on horseback, men in small pickups, and men on foot streaming from the many dunes behind the Russian paratrooper assault. Russian troopers turned in shock as the local tribesmen hit them where they least expected—from the rear. It was a slaughter. Russian soldiers were hit by bullets, rocks, arrows, and grenades.

Henri Farbeaux looked to his left at Ryan. "I fully intend for the game to continue between Sarah, Colonel Collins, and myself, Mister Ryan. I will win out in the end, but as a gentleman, not as a thief in the night."

Ryan heard the laugh as Jenks watched Russians being knocked down like bowling pins.

"That's where the sneaky bastard disappeared to, Ryan. Frenchy even has the local tribesmen in debt to him." Jenks smiled. "Seems a few years back Froggy was their main supplier of weapons."

"Jesus, Farbeaux!" Jason said, although he felt immense relief.

"Like Toad says, the cheese eatin', wine tasting thief can be one irritating son of a bitch, right, Commander shit-head?" Jenks lit his ever-present cigar. "Now, shall we see if this little firecracker is still operational before Colonel ground-pounder and Toad join *their* ancestors?"

CHAPTER FOURTEEN

Event Group Complex,
Nellis Air Force Base, Nevada

Several managers were hit and were writhing on the floor as the Russian assassin, Demi Blintnikov, slammed another clip into the nine-millimeter and then started to make his way toward his prime targets, Doctor Niles Compton, Virginia Pollock, and Alice Hamilton. All were struggling to remove a motionless Xavier Morales from atop them.

The man's eyes were those of a shark. They were black as doll eyes as his life's work was coming to fruition. His reward, to be honored by the very men who had sent him to his death. Not the rich fools in Siberia, but Doctor Vassick and his own group. His only regret was that he wouldn't live to see the glory that would be forced upon Siberia when Vassick was proven right about his choice of targets. He knows the value of assassination. The field team in Mongolia was never worth the trouble, in his and Vassick's view. He pulled back the slide on the Glock and chambered the round that would set the Event Group back at least ten years, as he stood over Niles Compton. He easily dodged a kick by a prone Alice Hamilton, and he let out a humorous laugh at her misbegotten bravery. Again, he sighted on his main target.

Everyone saw the look of shattered dreams on the Russian's face when six bullets slammed into his back. The seventh caught him in the back of the head. He started shaking as he turned to see Will Mendenhall standing in the broken doorway of the conference room, the smoking nine-millimeter still aimed in his direction. He started to move his jaws like he wanted to say something, but his brain was refusing all commands. Mendenhall fired one last time. The bullet hit the Russian right between his eyes and he immediately went down.

There were shouts of anger and pain as Will moved slowly into the room. He eased into the hologram depicting the battle in Mongolia and came through the other side still training his weapon on the downed spy. He reached around and tore his dress shirt open and then peeled the ballistic vest from his torso. He let it slide through his fingers to fall onto the floor.

"Should have waited until I took that shower, asshole!" he said, as he finally saw that there was no need to keep the Russian covered.

More shouts and screams erupted when ten security men and women came running in.

Will felt the pain in his chest where the bullets that were meant to kill him had struck the Kevlar material. Still, he moved quickly and with purpose. He first made sure the director was safe. Alice was the first up and was limping toward a chair after her infamous karate kick that missed. She was finally realizing that the days of the Amazing Mrs. Hamilton may be closer to the end than the beginning. Niles was up and assisting Virginia to her unsteady feet as Will made it to Xavier Morales. He feared the worst when he pulled the wheelchair off the kid. He shook his head, just knowing that the kid was dead. Then Xavier moaned. Will went to his knees as Niles came sliding in to see if he could help. Mendenhall turned Xavier over and checked his back as the computer genius cursed out that he was alive. There was a small line of blood where a bullet had seared through the chair and then hit a back brace he wore to stay upright while in the wheelchair. Xavier hissed in pain, not from the wound, but from the gash on his forehead he had received when he knocked Niles from his chair. He was also sore because when Alice had kicked out at their assassin she had missed, and her heel came down onto Morales' nose. It was definitely broken.

"You okay, Doctor?" Niles asked, as the paramedics came streaming into the conference room.

"I...I...don't think I'll...ever walk again, sir."

Niles looked from Xavier to Mendenhall.

"You couldn't walk anyway, smartass!" Niles said, cursing for possibly the first time Will had ever heard. "Welcome to the business end of the Event Group," Niles said, placing a hand on Xavier's chest and smiling his thanks to the man who had saved his life.

"Believe me, Xavier old son, it doesn't get any easier," Will said. He looked around the room. Several of the department heads had been hit, but none looked too serious. The man they thought had been Jack had one minor flaw in his training and his research on Collins, and it was this flaw that Carl had seen in Laos that had confused him to no end. The man could never duplicate the Colonel's proficiency with a handgun. There was only one man in the Group that was better, and it was Will himself.

"By the way, you're late for the staff meeting." Niles smiled, and then good-naturedly slapped Will on the shoulder, which caused him to nearly pass out from the blow because of the bruises from the nine-millimeter bullets he took to his chest.

Major William Mendenhall felt his head growing fuzzy as the men and women on the managerial team of Department 5656 slowly overcame the shock of the assault. Will cursed and then collapsed into the first available chair, and then he slowly placed the Glock on the table.

"I'm hungry and my chest hurts."

Tai Yin Valley (Valley of the Lion)
Southern Mongolia

THE CHINESE ARMORED COLUMN FINALLY REACHED THE PASS THAT would lead into the valley of Shangri-La. General Wei Li Cheng halted the first regiment of tanks as his brand-new state of the art attack choppers, the Z-19E, what the western democracies code named; 'Black Whirlwind', scouted ahead. He knew he was being over-cautious because of the news coming in from Mongolia. It was his understanding of the confused situation that the People's Air Force had sustained heavy casualties.

Amidst the loud idling of the tanks, they heard the sound of a helicopter as it swooped low over the lead regiment. Without being informed, the general knew who was landing. He pulled off his head-phones angrily and tossed them to the colonel. He climbed the ladder and exited the armored personnel carrier. He took a kerchief and wiped down his face, ridding it of the diesel and fuel and dirt he had been ingesting for the past eighteen hours. As the French-built Dauphin lazily settled to the ground, the general braced himself for another embarrassing dressing down by the woman he thought of as a necromancer, Ms. Chow.

As the 'Whirlwind' attack choppers shot overhead, the passenger compartment door of the Dauphin opened, and again he saw the shapely legs of the strange woman. She stepped out, and then, to the General's surprise, she stood rigid and held the door open for another. He saw the small man exit. He buttoned his coat and then looked around at the idling tanks. The visitor was the the same man who had confronted him on Ms. Chow's last visit. His suit was expen-sively tailored, and his jet-black hair pulled back into a long-braided ponytail. He noticed how Ms. Chow followed as if she were a concu-bine from days past. The man with the gleaming black beard saw the general but didn't move in his direction. Cheng understood the play. He walked up to the man amongst the diesel fuel and stench of a moving armored column. He faced the man with the dark eyes and came to attention.

"How may this humble plebe of the people serve you?" he said, as he snapped his polished heels together and then half-bowed.

The man continued looking at the line of tanks stalled at the opening of the pass. He glanced at Ms. Chow who stood silently at his side.

"The man asks how he may serve me," he said as his gaze fell on everything except the General. "How may you serve me?" he said with each word becoming louder than the one before it. The man took a breath and forcibly calmed himself. He twisted his neck and, after the pops of his vertebra were heard, he smiled and then placed his arm around the general who didn't know how to react. "You may serve me by rolling these armored monstrosities through the pass. We have lost over thirty-two fighters in just the past three hours due to your incompetence. They were there to cover an operation you were supposed to be leading. But here you are, responsible for a sacrifice of men and aircraft we cannot spare."

"Sir, if I have displeased high-command, I will immediately resign my post as commander of this division."

"General, don't act the fool. If by resign you mean forfeit your life, I understand and will accommodate your request. However, right now I need a man with experience, but also one with the drive needed to take the greatest prize in world history. I assume that man is you. Get me to the other side of the mountain, General, and you will reap such glory as you have never imagined."

"We are just waiting on a Recon report from our forward elements, sir."

"General, allow me to explain something to you. I am well versed in the art of warfare. I have led men into battle and survived many years to tell the tale. My exploits are well documented if you know how to look for them" He squeezed the general's shoulder to the point of pain. The small man was a lot stronger than it had first appeared. "I need this column moving. I want to be on the far side in less than two hours. I have a long-awaited appointment with a relative that is overdue. Is that clear enough, General?" The darkened eyes bore in on Cheng until all he could do was nod his head.

Ms. Chow came forward and handed the small man a large suitcase. She bowed her head and then returned to the helicopter.

"Well, I have all I need, shall we, General?"

General Cheng watched the man move off toward his personnel carrier with his suitcase in hand. On the life of his children, he failed to understand the horrid feeling he had when looking upon the strange little man.

A feeling of disaster pulsed even more heavily through his body than the long night in Beijing when he saw an entire army wiped out by something he could never understand or fathom. The forthcoming battle reminded him of what possibilities were to come.

The general moved off to follow the man, knowing he was walking to his own death.

THE RUNNER CAUGHT UP WITH GENERAL CHANG AND MASTER LI Zheng, who stood atop the highest knoll looking down on the advancing army of Emperor Qin Shi Huang. The boy, an experienced runner who had trained in track and field at Brisbane University, handed the General a note. Chang leaned over into the rising light of the moon and read. He nodded at the boy.

"Join the line of evacuees, young one. Escape the valley."

"I will return to the fight," the boy said hesitantly but with pride, half-bowing. "Besides, the children never made it to the middle pass. No one has heard or seen them since they left the city."

Master Li Zheng closed his eyes as the possibility of his sending the children to their deaths weighed heavily on him.

"May I return to the battle, General?"

"Do you know what this message says?" Chang asked the young teen.

"Yes, General."

"And you still wish to return to the battle, even though Colonel Collins said their defense will soon fail?"

"Of course, sir."

Chang looked from the eager boy to his Master. Li Zheng, without looking, sadly nodded his head.

"Very well. May the luck of your ancestors return with you."

The boy with the blue leather armor and the plume feather in his helmet bowed and then, without hesitation, turned and ran back to die with the rest of his friends.

"It is all right to shed a tear for the boy this day, General. I have shed many. The news about the children was not expected. I pray that I have not sent them all to their deaths."

"These Americans they travel with," General Chang started to say, "I have a deep faith in them. There is something about them that defies words. It's almost as if they were meant to be here, for this battle, the final one of our people. No, I believe the children are safe."

Li Zheng placed a hand on the shoulder armor of General Chang. He nodded to the first line of tanks cresting the pass. He lowered his hand and then closed his eyes.

"He has come, old friend."

Chang looked down into the pass and saw the muted lights of the armored column. He felt what his Master was feeling. Qin Shi Huang was among the attackers.

"You were right, Master Li. I thought him too much a coward to travel with his army. Yet, he has come."

Li laughed. "My half brother has been many things, General, but the word coward is not a word he is familiar with. He will wish to finish this himself. Even he fails to realize that the Dragon Asteroid isn't even his real goal. He has convinced himself it is, but his real quest is right here." He lightly touched an open palm into his robes.

"You?"

"Yes, this is why he has joined the battle. He wants to see the man and the people that he failed to bring under his heel. It has driven him mad since the time of the first battle for his empire over two thousand years ago." Master Li turned and smiled at General Chang. "I think I will accommodate him." He turned and took the General by both shoulders. "Tease him, General. Entice him. Show him the way to our home where I may meet him man to man, brother to brother, and Air Bender to Air Bender. The elements will be our only weapons. There, we will embrace and travel the road of our ancestors together. He will burn with a fire not of the Dragon Mineral's making, but the white-hot fire of mankind's proclivity for destruction."

"I will do as commanded, my Master."

"No, not Master today. We part as friends and meet again in a far better place as brothers."

Chang went to one knee and bowed his head to the ground at Li's sandaled feet. "For the past two thousand years, I have yet declined to carry out an order. But today, I am tempted to disobey your wishes. Please allow this uneducated soldier to come with you."

Li Zheng eased Chang back to his feet. He hugged the larger man. "To this I must say no. Goodbye, my real brother."

Master Li Zheng turned and walked into the last hour of his long life.

THE BLACK PAINTED HELICOPTER, WITH NO DISTINGUISHING registration numbers, flew high over the battlefield. Professor Vassick smiled as he was close to seeing his plan come to full fruition. He checked his watch and saw that it was early morning in the western United States, meaning only one thing to him—Doctor Niles Compton and a good portion of the upper echelon of the Event Group management were dead. He smiled as his gaze went to the burning plain below that was strewn with destroyed tanks, but even more dead bodies of the backward inhabitants of this godforsaken region. When the Siberian Council heard that he not only eliminated a powerful enemy of the new Russian regime, but also oversaw the taking of the ore deposits of this valley, a task that was preceded by his orders to eliminate the crew of the *Simbirsk* the previous month, there would be no denying his value and his place on the Council. He eased the headphones onto his head and spoke with his pilot.

"I have seen enough. Take me to the capital for my flight. Leave instructions that, after the mountain is taken, have the field engineers and geological report forwarded to me before the Council is informed. Is this clear?"

The pilot held up a thumb and Vassick pulled the headphones off and then leaned back as the heavy line of Russian tanks made their final run on the inept defenders of Shangri-La.

JACK AND CARL HUDDLED WITH THE LAST REMAINING GROUP COMPRISED of twenty-two teens and about thirteen surviving adults and elders. Their defense had been brilliant and brave. It was a confused jumble of a people who did not know how to fight but determined to do battle with a power that few of them understood.

"Damn, but they fought well, Jack," Carl said, as he popped up and stitched a line of tracers toward the lead tanks in range. The bullets 'pinged' harmlessly off their armor and they kept coming. A few fireballs and weakened sand tornadoes reached out for the enemy, but the defense was growing weaker by the moment.

Jack remained silent as he saw the wounded teens and elders being tended to. He then looked down at the open ejection port on his M-4. He removed the empty magazine and then tossed the weapon away.

"Fought well, they did." Jack once more saw the tragedy of death around him coming from a people who never knew want nor greed. They hadn't fought for land or riches or to enslave another race. They had fought for each other. "I think its time for us to try and save some lives here."

"Surrender?" Carl asked, as he fired the last rounds he had.

"There has to be a professional soldier out there that will refuse to kill children and old people for the sake of his masters in Siberia. I think that's the only hope we have of getting the last of these people the hell out of here. Either Ryan has the bomb inside the mountain or he doesn't, either way we need to get the rest out. Our lives be damned, that okay with you?"

"Ah, Anya's super pissed at me anyway, I think I would rather face the damn Russians."

"Sarah will still be hot, even if—"

The HE round went off fifty yards in front of their position, drowning out Jack's attempt at humor as they were both covered in dirt and debris.

Collins stood up, Carl followed suit. They raised their hands into the air and just hoped they lived to feel the humiliation of surrendering to the very murderers they had been chasing. The first line of fifteen T-90s came to a stop as the two Americans became visible in the smoke of the battlefield.

"Well, this is a first," Everett said, just as he saw a Russian tank commander open his turret's hatch. He looked over the positions in front of him and then he leaned back into his tank as suddenly a twenty-millimeter gun opened up on the surrendering Americans. Jack and Carl dove back to cover.

"Well, that was short and sweet," Jack hissed, as large tracer rounds flew past their heads.

"Yeah, you have to hand it to the Russians, they do know how to parlay."

Tank crewmen and soldiers started spilling from their armored vehicles. They would finish off the defenders up-close and personal, thereby saving what heavy munitions they had left for mopping up the Chinese forces that were reportedly on their way.

Jack cursed. Everett was angry, and the elders and teens resigned.

Suddenly they heard a sound that was out of a dream. There was a whistling noise as if an aerial bomb was being sent to finish them off. Then a tremendous explosion rocked the survivors. They heard shouts in Russian as men were scrambling back to their tanks and vehicles. Collins sat up and chanced a look as the elders and teens started to cheer wildly. What Jack saw stunned him. A giant boulder had fallen directly onto the turret of the very tank which had opened fire on the survivors. Flames were licking out of vents and the turret and its massive barrel was lying like a crushed beer can.

As they watched in amazement, more giant boulders fell from the skies over their heads. Tank after tank, personnel carrier after carrier, were struck by ten-ton missiles made of granite and sandstone. Tanks started moving, but the barrage was so heavy that the field was soon inundated with burning armor. Still, the cheers of the remaining survivors filled the night air as a meteor shower of pure power fell from the starlit sky. Stones the size of Volkswagens flew past the rising moon in a surreal display of might.

"Damn, Jack, it's the mountain, the boulders are coming from the side of the mountain!" Everett said as he scrambled for his binoculars. Collins stood up and viewed what magical power had come to their salvation.

Boulders the size of large sedans flew and whistled through the air. Some hit the earth and rolled, smashing into and knocking over the tracked vehicles, while others came straight down and squashed the T-80s and 90s like bugs. Men and tanks were everywhere trying to dodge death from above. Even as attack helicopters raced to the scene, small stones and rocks flew through the skies like anti-aircraft fire. Men and machines were falling out of the sky.

"I'll be damned, I'm going to kill that woman!" Everett shouted, and then smiled over at Jack as he tossed him the set of binoculars.

Jack focused on the area indicated by Carl. His heart almost burst from his chest with surprise and pride when he saw the small form of Sarah as she pointed out targets for the children of Shangri-La to aim at. He adjusted his sights and saw that Anya was doing the same. Then he saw the children as they lifted rocks and boulders with their Air Bending skills, and then as one would act as if shoving them into the sky. The movements of the boulders were shaky and unstable, but joined together as a group, the children controlled the heavy material with surprising ease. Rock after rock, boulder after boulder, came flying from the halfway point of the mountain. He even saw Charlie Ellenshaw jumping up and down every time a large rock smashed a Russian vehicle, turning to high-five children no older than five or six.

Jack heard Carl cheering with the rest and he turned to see the last of the Russian armor fleeing the strangest battlefield they had ever seen. There were at least a hundred burning and smashed tanks and personnel carriers strewn across the plain.

The battle for the plain of Shangri-La was over. The battle for the mountain would soon begin.

CHAPTER FIFTEEN

The Range Rover was overheating after dragging 'Thin Man' to its new and final resting place. Ryan and Farbeaux ordered everyone, with the exception of Lee who was driving, and the wounded Major Pierce, to exit the Rover. They had entered the mountain and followed a differing trail than the one they had taken the first time they had viewed the green and silverish asteroid the day before.

Henri slammed his palm on the hood of the Range Rover and Professor Lee brought it, and the sled carrying 'Thin Man', to a stop.

"Listen," Henri said.

"What?" Jenks asked. "I don't hear nothin', Frenchy."

"That's the point, Master Chief, there are no more explosions from above."

Ryan kicked out at the bomb in its cradle. He knew what that meant. The defense of Shangri-La had collapsed. He silently cursed the fact that he had not died with his friends.

"We must continue on with the plan. Professor, how far to the lowest level?" Farbeaux asked.

"About a mile."

Henri waved the group forward. Ryan was tempted to abandon

the mission and find out what happened outside, but the training Jack and Carl had given him made him realize the folly of the move. He cursed and then looked at Tram, who knew just what the navy man was thinking. They both followed the slow-moving bomb to its final destination.

JACK AND CARL STOOD IN FRONT OF SARAH, ANYA, AND CHARLIE Ellenshaw an hour later as they in turn stood in front of their small army, as the few teens and elders left alive embraced their salvation with hugs and tears.

"You know my last act as your commanding officer is that I plan to court-martial your little ass, Captain."

"I respectfully decline the kind offer, Colonel." Sarah looked at her wristwatch. "As of forty-five minutes ago, I am no longer an officer in the United States Army. So, Jack, you can kiss my ever-lovin' civilian ass, with all due respect of course."

Collins couldn't help it, he couldn't hold the angry glare any longer. He smiled and nodded his head. "Whatever you say, Mrs. Collins."

"Well, now what do we do?" Carl asked, as he and Anya were assisting the smaller children in their naturally frightened state.

Jack looked to the star filled sky. "Let's just hope that Europa and *Boris* and *Natasha* have been watching. If not, we better get these kids marching out of here fast. This place is about to get real hot."

At that moment, they heard a familiar sound coming from the skies. It was the sound of propeller blades cutting through the air at tremendous revolutions. The whine of the turbines were unmistakable.

"The Russians are coming back!" a young teen cried, as the frightened children clung to the remaining adults.

Jack held up a hand as he listened. "Angels on our shoulders," was all he said, and Carl was the only one to understand the relief in the comment.

The group of survivors watched as the smoke-filled skies were suddenly a mix of swirling vortexes as the first of five U.S. Marine Corps Bell-Boeing V-22 *Osprey* tilt-rotor aircraft started settling to the ground. The loudness of the *Ospreys* was frightening and, at first, the children, teens and elders didn't understand it was their salvation landing in front of them. As the first rotors of the lead *Osprey* wound down, a Marine Corps Crew Chief stepped out of his aircraft.

"Is there a Colonel Collins or Captain Everett here?" the man shouted.

Jack and Carl, with Anya and Sarah close behind, approached, as the other four *Ospreys* settled to the earth. Jack nodded his head at the young crew chief. "I'm Collins."

"Wow, that was some wait we had. We've been hiding these ugly things on the other side of the divide awaiting orders."

"Orders?" Carl asked.

"Yes, sir. We just received the Go-signal from National Command Authority to enter Mongolian airspace. I don't know exactly who you people are, Colonel, but the President of the United States said to give you his regards, and that it's time to come home."

Jack turned his head up and faced the high sky. He nodded his head, knowing that *Boris* and *Natasha* were relaying their satellite images to Nevada and Europa. He then turned to face Sarah and Anya, just as Charlie hissed under his breath, because he knew exactly what was coming.

"Don't even think about it, Jack," Sarah said.

"Doc, get these kids and elders the hell out of here. Sarah and Anya will remain here with us."

Sarah smiled and then nodded her head at Jack's easy surrender. Jack saw the map sticking out of the green flight suit of the Marine crew chief. He pulled it free and then opened it.

"What, Jack?" Carl asked.

"Master Li Zheng said the southern exit is right here," he jabbed the map at the southern portion of Mongolia. He looked at the crew chief. "Once the children and elders are in a safe zone, meet us here at the Great Wall. If we're not there in two hours, we won't be coming."

"What are you doing, Colonel?" the young Marine asked.

"I've still got people on the ground. I'm not leaving them."

The crew chief nodded his head in understanding. "The President will be pissed, sir."

Jack smiled as did Carl, Sarah, Anya, and even Charles Hindershot Ellenshaw III, after hearing the naïve marine's concern.

"That, young Marine, is the natural state of affairs with this group."

THE LEAD PERSONNEL CARRIER STOPPED SUDDENLY. THE ENTIRE COLUMN came to a grinding halt.

"Why have we stopped, General?"

Cheng turned and looked at the ridiculously dressed man in the co-driver's seat of the vehicle. The red feather at the apex of his ancient helmet and the bright red and black armor told the general in no uncertain terms that he was dealing with either a mad man, or a ghost from his nation's past. He chose to believe in the former and not the latter assessment.

"Our lead element is reporting that the pass is being blocked."

"What force is blocking it?" Qin Shi Huang asked angrily, expecting bad news about Russian aggression.

The general listened through his headphones. "Is that all? Why have you stopped for a single man?"

Emperor Qin Shi Huang felt his heart race when he heard the general's complaint. Instead of anger, he smiled as he stood from his seat. He held out a hand and the colonel handed him his sheathed sword.

"I will attend to this myself, General. Tell your men not to interfere with the man."

General Cheng lowered the microphone on his headset and watched as the strange man exited the vehicle. He only hoped that the man he faced would have the strength and the power to end this foolishness. He hoped deep in his heart never to see the man in ancient armor again.

Qin Shi Huang walked commandingly forward until he passed the first tank in line. Instead of ordering the tank crew to obliterate the man standing at the moonlit top of the pass, he smiled when he recognized the armor of the man confronting the column.

"General Chang." Qin Shi Huang half-bowed to a man he had grown up with and one that was a brother to his own deceased General Kang, lost these many years on the banks of the river that claimed his life.

"Little Ying Zheng, you have failed to grow much since I last saw you."

Anger flared in Qin Shi Huang. His hand went to his sword but held firm at the hilt, as he calmed. He did not want to prematurely destroy the pleasure that was now at hand in eliminating an irritant of much of his life.

"I beg your forgiveness, it is now Emperor Qin Shi Huang, is it not?" General Chang asked with a smirk. "I was always willing to proclaim you as such, just so you did not carry the same name as Master Li."

"For many years I was denied the opportunity to remove your head with my own sword. Now that time has come." Qin Shi Huang drew the long, sharp weapon and held it at his side. General Chang followed suit.

"Do you wish steel, or air, earth, fire, and water?"

"You are not worth a demonstration of my ever-growing power, General. Steel will suffice, as I wish to feel my sword cutting through bone and sinew as I remove your head from your shoulders."

"As my new American friends would say, come and get some!"

Qin Shi Huang charged with his sword raised high in the old ways of warfare. The steel gleamed in the moonlight as General Chang took up a position of defense with his own weapon raised high over his head.

The two men met at the highest point of the pass only a quarter mile from the entrance to Charlie Ellenshaw's mythical city of

Shangri-La. In the moonlit night, the two swords came together with a loud clang.

Crewmen from the lead tanks watched in amazement as the old world fought in front of the new. Two men in ancient armor met to do battle and it was as frightening as it was fascinating. They watched on as the larger of the two men fended off blow after blow from the smaller.

"You remember your lessons very well, little one," Chang said, as he stepped back to catch his breath.

"Over two thousand years of training, General, that is what I faced while looking for the cowards who ran from my embrace. Now, where is my one-time brother?" He swung his sword as an accent to his question. The blade clanged off the blue armored chest plate of the General and he staggered back a step, a deep cut in the thickened and hardened leather.

"Master Li Zheng awaits that embrace, my Emperor, but alas, you have to get through me first." He pointed the sword to the north. "The entrance you seek is right there. All you have to do is kill me to gain entrance, and the Master will greet you with love, understanding and," he swung the sword, barely missing the throat of the Emperor, "vengeance!"

The General went on a furious attack, hoping to save the confrontation that he knew would end his Master's life. Either way, he had fulfilled his last orders from Master Li.

The attack was so furious that Qin Shi Huang tripped as he fell back. He hit the earth and tried in vain to get his sword up in time before General Chang hit him with the killing blow. The blade of the General came flashing down from above like a God seeking death and vengeance.

The bullets struck him in the chest and face, throwing General Chang back three feet as his sword flew high in the air. The general hit the ground dead.

Qin Shi Huang was furious as he fought to gain his feet. He turned and saw the machine gun on the forward-most tank still smoking as the gunner had seen him in trouble and ended the

General's assault. Just as the Emperor gained his footing, he saw General Cheng advance with his pistol drawn.

Qin Shi Huang, with sword in hand, angrily used both of his hands, blade flashing brightly in the moonlight as he gathered the dirt and stones around him into a swirling ball of power before his own face, and then mentally pushed the rotating mass through the air, thrusting his hands forward until the small storm of earth hit the general and sent him flying backward. Then he turned and faced the tank that had cost him the life of General Chang. With a mighty intake of breath, Qin Shi Huang closed his eyes and then threw his sword at the frightened men watching from the armored protection of the tank. The sword moved so fast it was if the weapon had been fired from a cannon. The blade penetrated the turret with a clang and held firm just as the emperor raised his hands up and then, with a powerful blast of wind, sent the tank and its crew flipping over and over until the heavily armored machine fell to pieces.

The pass was silent as General Cheng got to his feet. He was filthy, and his face had a series of cuts and bruises from the small man's fury. He was stunned at the magical power that had been placed on display. His memories of the old myths and legends flooded his mind as Emperor Qin Shi Huang approached him. As amazing and unbelievable as it was, he knew immediately just who it was he was dealing with. He went to his knees and bowed at the small man's feet.

"My Emperor."

Qin Shi Huang looked from the man's bowed head to the forces now under his command. He reached down and placed a gloved hand on the general's head.

"Telling you who I was would have had no effect on your beliefs, General. Demonstration has always been my way. You will order your armor forward to stop any Russian incursion that could reach the mountain. We will take the remaining infantry and we will enter the mountain from here. Is this clear, General?

"My Emperor's will."

"Come, let us end this, so I may finally take my divine place as the rightful ruler of the Empire of the Dragon."

THE WINDING TUNNELS HAD SLOWED THEM DOWN FAR MORE THAN JACK had counted on. It had been an hour since the hostilities had ceased above ground, but that did not stop the feeling of impending doom that coursed through the minds of everyone.

The tunnel system was a maze of twisting turns and dead ends. Sarah had said that it looked as if water had been the cause of the tunnels' formation. She surmised that the asteroid had struck an ancient sea that used to cover most of Mongolia millions of years ago.

Suddenly they broke out into a large open space and they were forced to stop and admire the natural beauty of the giant cave.

"My God," Sarah said as she looked out over the amazing sight. "This is where they get all of their food from."

The expanse of green was amazing to behold There were berry bushes, apple trees, corn, rice crops in paddies waiting to be reaped. Deer, wild boar and even tigers roamed the expanse. From their high vantage point, they could just make out pockets of the Dragon Asteroid as it was exposed in some areas, while in others it was completely covered. Overhead they could see the glowing material as if large chunks of the asteroid had come apart upon impact. The mineral gave off brightly patterned light that shone down on one of the asteroid's greatest gifts—fertilizer from the stars.

"Can you imagine a universe that could have produced such a mineral. How far is it? How can we get there?" Anya asked no one in particular. "An element such as this could bring about world peace and end famine."

"Yeah, it has done nothing but make the world happy thus far," Everett said with mock excitement.

"Quit being so shallow and fatalistic," Anya said, jabbing Carl in the ribs once more with her elbow. "If we could only save this material."

"We need to move," Jack said.

THE LAND ROVER HAD COME TO A STOP FIFTY FEET BEFORE REACHING the bottom portion of the giant cave system that housed the Dragon Asteroid. Professor Lee assumed the engine block had cracked open from excessive heat. It seemed they were stuck only a few hundred yards away their goal.

"Can you get this thing down there?" Ryan asked Professor Lee.

Lee looked down and saw the expanse of asteroid. It was like a half-buried ball. The upper mound was clear of stone and natural growth. It was if they were looking at a small planet that resembled an alien world.

"I have nothing to reinforce the air to lift it. There is no loose debris. No, I cannot."

"Gentlemen, we have little time. We may have to set it off from here," Henri said as he shouldered the M-4.

"I think Frenchy is right. Will the megatonnage be enough to knock this thing to hell?" Jenks asked.

"It should be, yes," Lee said. He placed a hand on the hot hood of the Range Rover and thought. He was just about to speak again when he was suddenly just gone.

Ryan, Jenks, Tram, and Farbeaux were shocked when they heard Lee scream from high above them. Tram was the first to react as he fired two shots from the Winchester at the flapping wings of the giant bat as it carried Lee away. Henri and Ryan added more fire, but it was too late. Lee was gone.

Then another event happened that shook the world under the earth. A long hairy and hooked leg reached up from the grave of the Dragon Asteroid and took hold of the Range Rover. It tilted precariously. The giant spider climbed the last few feet and perched itself on the top of the four-wheeled vehicle. Seeing the men only feet away, it hissed at them. Large mandibles spread, and the legs started to move. The drumming on the steel top was near unbearable. Again, the men opened fire, hitting the spider over and over as it hissed and spat at them in pain and confusion. It turned to leap as Tram finally placed a bullet in its small brain. The spider collapsed on top of the Rover and then lay still.

"Well, isn't this a Disneyland of fun and thrills," Jenks said, as he was overcome with the shivers. He was deathly afraid of spiders.

Tram reached out and stopped Ryan from climbing up the stone wall in the direction of the giant bat. Tram stilled him with just a shake of his head.

"He is gone, Commander," Henri said. "We will lose you also if you persist in chasing down dead men."

Jason became angry. "How can you just stand there and be so cold? Lee was a good man."

"If we don't move, Commander, we'll lose more than just one good man."

Before Jason could advance on the Frenchman, another bat swooped out of the green tinted air and tried to grab the dead spider on the top of the Rover. It missed. It flapped its wings and hissed as it tried again. This time the large claws grabbed the luggage rack instead of the spider, and the Rover tipped once more, this time balancing on two wheels. Tram fired, the round striking the bat in the throat, and then it went down, screaming into the abyss below. Just as they thought they were safe, that was when they saw the Range Rover, with Major Pierce inside, and with 'Thin Man' behind, sliding off the edge.

It was the engineer Jenks who did the most childish thing of all of them. He placed his hands over his ears waiting for the atomic detonation of 'Thin Man'.

"Relax, Master Chief," Henri said, as he chanced a look over the side. He saw the Rover, and also 'Thin Man'. Both were on their side, right on top of the asteroid. "Well, that's one way of getting it down."

Ryan was gone before the others realized he had moved. He was over the side as he attempted to get Major Pierce out of that hell hole. Farbeaux shook his head.

"Sergeant, cover us the best you can." Henri, without hesitation, went over the side of the ledge following Ryan.

"Does everyone in this little party have a death wish or what?" Jenks said.

JASON JUMPED AS HE REACHED THE RANGE ROVER AS HENRI COUGHED after the exertion of climbing down the sixty feet of rock.

"Damn, I thought you were one of those spiders," he said. Then he raised a brow at Farbeaux. "But its only a giant rat."

"Your humor is beyond measure, Commander."

"If it isn't too much trouble, could you point out the son of a bitch that threw me off a cliff?" Major Pierce said from his position on the rear glass side-window. He was holding his aching shoulder and staring up at the two men. "I bet it was that Japanese fella, wasn't it?"

Ryan used his nine-millimeter and raising it up, thinking it could be Henri's head, shattered the glass, showering the old pilot with shards of glass. "He's Vietnamese, Major." He reached in and took Pierce's free and uninjured arm and pulled him up and out of the damaged Range Rover.

Henri was about to assist when a bullet hit him in the side. He went to the ground as did Major Pierce and Ryan when they realized they were under attack. This time not from the wildlife in the caves, but from above. They heard Tram and Jenks returning fire, but the cacophony of explosions told them this wouldn't be much of a fight. Jason chanced a look up and his heart froze at the sight of at least a hundred Chinese soldiers firing down on them, and then reaching out to Tram and Jenks. He shook his head and made sure Pierce had plenty of cover near the Rover, and then crawled over to Henri. He had taken a serious hit to his right side just below his ribcage. The wound was bleeding heavily as Ryan ripped off his shirt and placed pressure on the gushing wound. Ryan jumped at the sound of close fire support. He turned and saw a wounded Major Pierce as he popped off round after round of Ryan's nine-millimeter. He stopped only when the slide locked open.

"Hey, this thing is nice!"

Jason hurriedly tossed the B-29 pilot his last clip. Just as Pierce inserted the new gift, he aimed. As he pulled the trigger, a volume of fire erupted above them. On the far side of the immense cave system, Jack, Carl, Sarah, and Anya, along with the four remaining Air Force

Commandos, were laying down a withering covering fire, trying to give Ryan and Farbeaux a chance at getting away.

"Come on, Henri, we gotta get!" he said as he started to lift the heavy Frenchman. Henri said for him to stop.

"Time for the good guys to exit the building, Commander," Henri struggled to say.

"No, no, no. That's not the game we were taught to play, Henri. We all go or we all stay."

He watched as Farbeaux closed his eyes.

"Henri, Henri? Come on, you asshole, not on my watch!"

He hurriedly laid Farbeaux down and started to do chest compressions as bullets struck the rocks to his right and to his left. Henri wasn't responding. Ryan was growing angry and frustrated.

"Your friend is dying, young man," said a voice above him.

Ryan looked up and saw Master Li Zheng standing over them with barely a notice as to the firepower being brought onto their position. "He's not my friend. But he's not going to die here either." Ryan started his chest compressions once more, this time harder.

"I would say that you do not know the difference between friend or foe, young man. Your fear and your sympathy are easy things to read."

Ryan wiped sweat from his face and continued.

"Step aside."

Ryan ignored Li Zheng as he continued to try and bring life back into the body of the Frenchman.

An exasperated Li shook his head and then, with a gentle swipe of his right hand, he simply swatted Ryan aside. The air hit him so hard he thought he had been sucker-punched. Li Zheng leaned down and then with a gentle touch, felt Farbeaux's face. He smiled as he reached into his small leather pouch and brought out the green and silver mineral. He gently rubbed some of the dusty powder under Henri's nose before removing Ryan's shirt and placing a large amount into the wound. Henri's eyes opened suddenly, sending a frightened Ryan back far enough that he stumbled. The Frenchman fought to bring breath back into his lungs. Finally, he managed to catch the breath that death had robbed him of.

"That stuff smells nasty," was the first thing he said. "And why does my chest hurt so bad?" he asked as he was finally able to sit up.

"You can blame your young friend here. I believe he was attempting to punch you to death in an attempt to save your life."

Ryan sneered at Henri just as Farbeaux realized Ryan had tried to save his life. He could only shake his head at the confusing nature of Colonel Collins and his men.

"Now, may I suggest you join your friends and escape the mountain? It seems some very inhospitable men have come to seize it."

With bullets pinging all around them, Henri got to his feet with the help of Jason. He placed Henri's arm around his shoulders as he still had little strength after his near-death experience.

"Major Pierce, this way," Ryan said, trying to get the pilot's attention.

Pierce finally turned as Li Zheng placed a hand on his shoulder.

"Goodbye, old friend. It is now time for you to go home."

Pierce stopped shooting and faced the master. His eyes teared up. "But I thought I would stay and wait for 'Goodnight Ladies' to play. You know, finish the dance so to speak."

"That will not be necessary, my friend. You have done your duty to your country. It is time to finally go home."

Pierce looked from Master Li to a waiting Ryan and Farbeaux. Ryan just nodded his head indicating Li Zheng was right.

"I have nothing to go home to. Please, sir, may I stay to protect my home?"

RYAN FINALLY MANAGED TO GET HENRI UP THE STEEP SLOPE. HE WAS helped the final few feet by Tram and Jenks.

"What were you two taking your sweet time about down there?" Jenks asked. Then he saw that they were alone. "Where's Major Bugs Bunny?"

"He's staying home," Ryan said, nearly choking up.

"The hell you say?" Jenks said as he ran to the ledge and looked down, but was pulled back by Tram as several hundred bullets ricocheted off the rocks. "Sorry. I was growing kind of fond of that senile old bastard."

As they retreated into the interior of the tunnel that led them there, they were soon met by Jack and the others.

Jack saw the few that remained. His heart felt shattered.

"Lee?"

Silence from Tram, Jenks, Henri, and Ryan.

"Where's the Major?" Sarah asked, looking around, hoping they had just overlooked him.

"Major Pierce and Master Li are preparing a little welcoming basket for Zheng's half-brother," Ryan said as he eased Henri into the softer arms of Sarah. Henri smiled.

"Don't get any of your ideas, Henri," Sarah said.

"Why, I'm as innocent as the day is long, little Sarah."

"Alright, Casanova, we can take this up in Hong Kong later, for now, let's get as far away from 'Thin Man' as we can get."

The remains of the Event Group field team fell into step behind Jack as they made their way toward the Great Wall of China.

QIN SHI HUANG STEPPED INTO THE HOME OF THE DRAGON. HE LIFTED his face to the heavens and thanked his ancestors for finally guiding him to the home of magic in the world. General Cheng holstered his sidearm and ordered his men to cease fire on the Americans. They were no longer a threat to the Emperor.

"Qin Shi Huang, Emperor of all China!"

The emperor smiled when the echo finally died down. He looked around and traced the voice. When his eyes fell on the Dragon Asteroid, he knew who it was that called to him over the thousands of years. The General pulled his pistol once more, but Qin Shi Huang stayed his hand.

"Perhaps it is time for mortals to step aside, General. You need not get in between two of the last Gods ever to walk this earth."

The general stepped back.

"It is time we embrace as brothers once more!"

Qin Shi Huang stepped to the ledge and with a single movement of his legs, stepped over the edge and came down softly on the object of his obsession for over two thousand years. He went to a knee and rubbed the Dragon Asteroid with a loving hand.

"Finally, it is mine. You will deliver me the world."

"Will that satisfy you, brother?"

The emperor looked up and then stood quickly as he faced Li Zheng for the first time in two thousand years of searching. He was dressed in the simple orange and white robes of a monk.

"Nice armor, brother," Li Zheng said.

"Not that I will need it to serve you justice, brother Li." He stepped forward, feeling the power of the dragon beneath his feet. "Shall I show you the lessons I have learned? Thanks to your foolish wife, I have come a long way. She thought that I was only interested in you, dear brother. When I removed her and your son's heads, she realized too late my real intention was to capture the real power of the Dragon." He stomped his booted foot down on the asteroid. "With this there is no limit to what my empire can and will achieve."

"Your problem has always been that you refuse to hear when the world speaks to you. Father knew this flaw, and that is why you were never given the secrets of the Dragon."

"And you, my brother? How have you enriched the world with all the power you had at hand? I see suffering in every corner of the world. I see murderers and confidence men taking high office, and I see nature that runs amok because these fools think our planet has inexhaustible resources. So, where was the power of the Dragon? Hiding in caves inside Mongolia?" He laughed. "Noble brother Li."

"Everything you say is true. I have failed the Dragon. I have failed my people. But most of all, I have failed you, brother. If I would have met you those many years ago on the field of battle, this crime against the world may not have occurred. It was my arrogance in thinking I was the only one who could control the Dragon, when it was highly capable of being controlled by mere children as so ably demonstrated this night."

"My own father forsook his only son when he brought the bastard son of his bitch concubine into my lands. He loved her, and you, far more than his own first born."

Li Zheng was shocked that he had been wrong for the past two thousand years. It wasn't the power of the Dragon that set Qin Shi Huang on his path of murder and war. It was the pain of being over-looked by a father who refused to see a son with ambition. He had been as big a fool as his brother.

Li was taken off guard by his own inner thoughts. Qin Shi Huang had raised his sword to the high ceiling of the cave system and threw it with every ounce of power the dragon could provide him. He used that power to advance the speed in which the sword travelled. In the moment before the sword struck, he saw his younger brother smile. The sword penetrated Li Zheng, and the Master of Shangri-La went down to his knees as his brother approached. Li Zheng watched Qin Shi Huang come slowly forward. There was no joy in his dark eyes, only remorse that the long chase had finally come to a conclusion. He knelt before the dying Li Zheng and then pulled his scaled glove from his right hand. A single tear flowed down the cheek of the emperor of all mankind, as he saw death slowly overtaking his brother. He saw Li Zheng smile sadly as blood eased from the corner of his mouth.

"Finally, I see my real brother, Ying Zheng. Remember playing in the bamboo forest of our youth?"

The emperor removed his helmet and leaned into the chest of Li Zheng as the memory of youth flooded in.

"You were always faster than I." He looked up into the grey eyes of his only brother. "You cheated quite often as I recall."

"I had...to...you were always...too smart."

"Forgive me, brother, for what I did to your family. I will someday await their justice."

"Help me to my feet," Li Zheng said.

Qin Shi Huang did as he was asked, careful to avoid striking the sword he had murdered his brother with.

"There is a long journey ahead for both of us," Li Zheng said, taking his brother in his arms and then hugging him tightly, and in doing so ramming the sword further into his own chest and heart. He slumped in his brother's arms. "It is I who seek your forgiveness, brother."

Qin Shi Huang felt the life leave Li Zheng. He held him and cried, and then slowly laid him on the moss-covered surface of the Dragon Asteroid. He stood and replaced his helmet and then gently pulled the sword from his brother's body.

"Noooo!" came a shout from beside the asteroid bed.

Qin Shi Huang turned and saw a crazed man in gray colored overalls and an old flyer's hat on his head. He was holding a small hammer. He was standing near what looked like a long cylindrical tube and a large access panel was open. The emperor's eyes widened in terror as he turned to look up. He saw the general and his men on the ledge above.

"Kill that man!"

As shots slowly started to ring out, Major Pierce became absolutely clearheaded for the first time in half a century. Even as five bullets entered his chest and arms. He had a mission to complete. He went to one knee over 'Thin Man' and then smiled up at the man who called himself emperor.

"Okay, time to get onboard the Chattanooga choo, choo, track twenty-nine, I hope you make it on time, you Jap sons of bitches!"

The small ballpeen hammer came down on the glass tube of mercury that once connected 'Thin Man' to the altimeter trigger.

Qin Shi Huang saw heaven in the blink of an eye.

The world went white.

THE ENTIRE MOUNTAIN ROSE THREE FEET FROM ITS BASE AS THE TRAPPED energy of 'Thin Man' was released. Then the entire world came crashing back to earth with a rumble that would be felt all the way to Australia.

The Chinese armored column, which had just breached the pass, was caught in the wrath of the American atomic bomb. The entire mountain top came down and buried the entire brigade.

But 'Thin Man' wasn't done with its work just yet. When the pressure wave of heat met the unyielding strata of solid rock, before dissolving the stone, it gave way and released its power to the subterranean waters that had been captured by the Dragon Asteroid's original impact. The deep waters of the underworld spewed forth, inundating the eastern edge of the Gobi Desert, creating the largest fresh water lake in the world.

The waves crashed against the Great Wall of China, and then rebounded back into the bowl that had been the Gobi.

"JESUS CHRIST!" THE MARINE PILOT SHOUTED, AS THE CREW CHIEF looked out his window as they hovered above the Great Wall.

Giant jets of water moving at the speed of sound shot out of thousands of tunnels that had been the biproduct of the asteroid's initial strike millions of years before. From on high, the crew of the V-22 *Osprey* saw the mountain range crumble on the far side of the border to nothing. The air roiled and the *Osprey* barely maintained its altitude. The pilot fought for control as the giant wave struck the Great Wall, sending a wall of water up and over the ancient construction.

"There isn't anyone coming out of there," the pilot said, turning the Marine Corps bird around to head south.

"Wait, look!" the crew chief said as he shook his head in utter amazement.

As the pilot changed course, he saw eight people as they were hanging on for dear life at the top of the Great Wall. There was a man atop the wall trying desperately to flag then down.

The *Osprey* lowered to the top of the wall and set down as the waves receded. He smiled when he saw several men and women running their way.

"Well, take a good look, those are the luckiest sons of bitches in all of China right there!"

EPILOGUE

THE MEMORIES OF DRAGONS

The dragon looms before him with waiting wanting jaws and with its talon-ed fingertips it grasps him in its claws.

~Sarah Spang
The Dragon

Paris, France

Professor Vassick sat at the table and slowly sipped at his glass of Russian vodka. He received the news about the failure in Mongolia and was content to live with the fact that it was the Siberian Council's failure and not his own. As for the failure in Nevada, he had the out of blaming the rogue agent, Demi Blintnikov, for disobeying his orders.

As he awaited his flight crew to make ready his private jet to Moscow, Vassick started forming a new plan to bring the American group in Nevada to heel.

A waiter approached and placed another drink on the table. Vassick looked up.

"From the gentleman at the bar, Monsieur."

Vassick looked over and his heart froze. It was Number One. Known for never leaving the borders of Russia, it was quite a shock to see him in Paris. The professor stood up as the tall man approached. He was followed by four men in black clothing. His personal security. The professor buttoned his coat and then bowed his head.

"Professor, nice to see you. May I sit?"

Vassick eyed the four men as they dispersed to somewhat more benign areas of the five-star restaurant, he gestured to Number One to take a chair. "Please."

"A very busy day for the Council, wouldn't you say?" Number One said as he refused the waiter's visit. He placed his left leg over his right and smiled.

"Unfortunate, I would say. Obviously, we had inept leadership in Mongolia."

Number One's blue eyes failed to give Vassick an indication of where this was heading. He remained silent for a long time.

"Evidently our forces ran into an anomaly of determined resistance." He smiled. "I believe from reports by the Mongolian President that this force consisted of the very American field team you had designs on eliminating."

"Yes, this was unexpected. My agent went rogue on me and superseded his direct orders. His attempt on this American agency was clumsy and unforgivable."

"The man in Laos you reported as," he paused, his blue eyes drilling into Vassick, "what did you say, oh yes, on his way to the motherland. What became of him, Professor?"

"I have not received an update. Perhaps—"

"Perhaps he was in Mongolia?"

"Impossible."

"Nonetheless," was the simple reply that Vassick knew didn't require an answer to. "We have some serious problems, Professor. This foul up has placed that fool at the head of our government scrambling for lies to tell. Very messy indeed."

"I will set things right when I return home."

"Yes, I suspect you will." One of the bodyguards approached and handed Number One a note. He read it and then stood. "Anyway, enjoy your flight home, I have business to conduct here in Paris." He looked around at the excellently dressed men and women sitting in the restaurant. "The City of Light. I can never get enough." He looked down at Vassick and nodded his head once in farewell.

Vassick watched him go with chills running down his spine. He removed his cell phone and called his flight crew.

"There has been a change. File a flight plan for Barcelona." He put the phone down as the chills at seeing Number One finally faded to a bad memory.

THREE HOURS LATER VASSICK'S PRIVATE LEARJET WAS BANKING TO COME at Barcelona from the Sea of Sardinia to line up with the correct runway at El Prat airport. Vassick was near drunk as he fled the wrath of the Council and the memory of the coldest blue eyes he had ever seen when Number One bid him farewell. He finished off his fifth vodka as the pilot announced that they were on final approach to Barcelona.

As the expensive jet leveled off, they failed to detect the MiG 29 as it approached from its radar's blind spot. The fighter had been tracking the Learjet since it left Paris.

The R-27 radar guided missile came off the left rail of the MiG, which immediately turned away after launch. The R-27 locked on the gleaming fuselage of the Learjet and closed at over a thousand miles per hour. It slammed into the right wing and severed it, sending the Lear rapidly into the sea fifteen miles short of Barcelona.

Professor Vassick had been terminated from the highly secretive Council in Siberia.

Las Vegas, Nevada

THE BALLROOM AT THE GRAND HYATT IN LAS VEGAS WAS LOUD AND festive as the members of Department 5656 celebrated the union of

Jack Collins and Sarah McIntire. Sarah, now a civilian Professor in charge of the Group's geology Department, was dancing with Charlie Ellenshaw. The Professor thrilled the gathered members by twirling Sarah and then lightly setting her down. Jack and Carl laughed at the sight. Almost as funny was the sight of Anya dancing with a very sore Xavier Morales as she sat in his lap as he spun the wheelchair in a dizzying circle.

Will Mendenhall and Jason Ryan were sitting together arguing over which duty was more dangerous, field work or sitting in the office at the Complex. They could see that Will had won the argument when he raised the front of his shirt and exposed the four eighteen-inch purple and black bruises he had received when the assassin's bullets struck him. Ryan winced at the sight and then called the waiter over to order drinks.

As for Alice Hamilton, she was walking around the room in a cast and on crutches. She had broken her leg trying to impersonate Bruce Lee during the attack and had paid dearly for it. She was helped by Virginia Pollock, and a grumbling Master Chief Jenks, who was complaining about old broads that can't walk on their own.

Jack and Carl were approached by Niles Compton who looked spiffy in the same suit he had worn for the past fifteen years for the special occasion.

"Gentlemen," he said as he leaned against the bar with drink in hand.

"Mr. Director," they both said at the same moment.

"The President sends along his congratulations, Jack. He said he would have sent a gift, but it seems he had to pay for a flight of *Ospreys* in China. Said he's a little short this month. Imagine that."

They exchanged looks and smiled.

"By the way, the department of defense tracked down the two children of Major Pierce. They were given each one of his dog-tags. They seemed happy to know what became of their father. I imagine it didn't hurt getting old Dad's seventy-three years of back pay."

"I wish we could have brought the old man home," Jack said with regret.

Niles placed a reassuring hand on both men's shoulders. "You brought enough home, gentlemen."

"Henri?" Carl asked.

"Well, our friend is still down in the dumps. But he did send you and Sarah this," Niles held out a small box but refused to let Jack take it. He unwrapped it himself. "For your wedding."

"Wow!" Carl said when he saw the diamond earrings and the man's bracelet studded with the same.

Jack had to laugh. "Don't tell me, they're stolen from some collection, right?"

"Not some collection, Jack. They're from our own vaults. They are from Marie Antoinette's personal jewelry box."

"Easy come, easy go. Don't tell Sarah, she'll want to keep them." He paused a moment and then asked, "Where is old Henri?" he asked.

"I don't know, but I imagine he will turn up soon enough."

"Niles, what about the descendants of Shangri-La?" Carl asked.

"Ah, yes," he said, draining his whiskey. "After our medical team got a chance to examine them, it was their conclusion, sad to say, that their abilities of Air Bending will slowly fade over time. Being separated from the Dragon Asteroid will eventually drain that phenomenal ability. Then all we have left are just kids. Just kids."

A sergeant in Will's security department entered and looked around and then finally found Niles. He came forward and held out a manila envelope.

"Sir, this was delivered to Gate Two an hour ago."

Niles took it and then nodded his thanks.

"You mean someone off the street walked right into the pawn shop and delivered it?" Jack asked, suspicious as hell.

"Yes sir. Its been checked for radiological and explosive materials. No bacteria other than normal bugs."

"Thank you," Niles repeated.

"Sir, there is also a deputy sheriff outside that says he needs to see you."

Niles nodded his head and ripped open the envelope. He pulled out a newspaper clipping. He looked it over and then held it out to Jack and Carl. "You may find this of interest."

They both saw the headline from a Barcelona daily newspaper.

Private aircraft vanishes off the coast of Barcelona. No survivors. The plane was reportedly owned by Russian oligarch, Professor Demetri Vassick. No cause of the crash has yet been determined.

Niles pulled out a note and read it and then handed it to Jack.

Please accept this small token of regret over the unpleasantness of the past week. Certain aspects of our failure have been corrected. Here's hoping for a better and more peaceful tomorrow—

"The son of a bitch finally crossed the line," Carl said.

"One life for over two hundred innocent sailors is not enough." Jack said, wadding up the handwritten note. He smiled, "but it's a start."

Evidently the sheriff's deputy couldn't wait any longer. He came into the ballroom and found Compton. Jack recognized the young officer because he was on the Event Group list of friendlies in Las Vegas. Curious, Jack and Carl followed.

"Sir, I hate to bother you here," he paused as Jack and Carl approached. "Congratulations, Colonel," he said, shaking Jack's hand. "Anyway, the property you own up on North Flamingo Road, the one on the hill?"

Niles grew suspicious. "Yes," he said.

"We had some vandals cause quite a stir up there, sir. I told my Captain that I would inform the owner."

"Vandals?" Niles asked.

"Yes, sir, I suggest you go and see for yourself before some reporters start snooping around."

"Thank you, deputy," Niles said as the man tipped his hat and left.

"North Flamingo Road? Isn't that where—" Carl started to say.

"Jack, I hate to break in on your party, but we had better get up there."

The three men left the ballroom without a word to anyone.

THE THREE MEN FOUND THEMSELVES AT THE DESERT ROSE CEMETERY. The private lot was owned by the Group and was where all department members who had no family were buried upon their deaths.

They entered with flashlights and saw the crime scene tape long before getting to it. They saw the grave of Garrison Lee. The marker for Pete Golding, whose body was claimed by his brother after he was killed, and then the grave of Doctor Denise Gilliam. Next to that the scene made all three men almost double over. There was the grave of Gus Tilly, and next to that the burial mound of Matchstick Tilly.

It was empty.

"Oh, my God," was all Niles could say.

Jack felt stunned as he looked into the open pit. But it was Carl who stepped up to the black hole, and then went to a knee. He reached down and picked up some dried earth. He rubbed it together in his fingers. He stood up.

"This grave wasn't broken *into*, it was broken *out of*."

As they shined the lights on the scene, they all realized that Carl was right. The dirt was pushed up out of the grave. Jack shined his flashlight on the ground and his heart froze. There were small four toed footprints leading away into the desert.

The three men of the Event Group grew cold as they stared out into the night.

CPSIA information can be obtained
at www.ICGtesting.com
Printed in the USA
LVHW041158141118
596829LV00008B/136/P